Disney's
Princess
Treasury

DISNEY'S
Princess
Treasury

Disney
PRESS

NEW YORK

Disney's
Princess
Treasury

C·O·N·T·E·N·T·S

Walt Disney's

Snow White
and the Seven Dwarfs

Adapted from the film by Jim Razzi

CHAPTER ONE

In a little kingdom graced with rolling hills, sparkling rivers, and bountiful forests, there once lived a lovely young princess named Snow White. Snow White was not only kind but beautiful as well. Her hair was the deepest ebony, her complexion the purest ivory.

Snow White's father, the king, was dead, and so she lived in the palace with her stepmother, the queen. And although the queen was also very beautiful, her beauty was only skin deep. Inside she was cold and heartless and as evil as an ugly old witch.

The queen was very jealous of Snow White's beauty. So much so that she forced the little princess to dress in tattered rags and made her work long hours as a scullery maid.

The queen thought that, disguised in this way, Snow White's beauty could never rival her own. Still, that wasn't enough to satisfy her vanity.

In a dark and foreboding part of the castle, the queen kept a magic mirror. And every day she would stand before the ornate mirror and chant, "Magic mirror on the wall, who is the fairest of them all?"

And every day, the surface of the mirror would swirl like a dark whirlpool, and a grim face would appear, as if rising from the depths.

"*You* are the fairest one of all," the face would answer.

The queen would smile and nod and be content.

As time went on, however, Snow White's beauty became more and more apparent in spite of the queen's efforts to hide it. So it was that on one bright and sunny day, when the queen asked the mirror her usual question, it replied in its deep, somber voice:

> *Famed is thy beauty, Majesty,*
> *but hold—a lovely maid I see—*
> *rags cannot hide her gentle grace.*
> *Alas, she is more fair than thee.*

The queen stiffened in shocked surprise. Then she lowered her eyebrows and said, "Alas for *her*. Reveal her name."

And the face in the mirror answered:

> *Lips red as a rose, hair black as ebony,*
> *skin white as snow . . .*

"Snow White!" the queen hissed.

At the very moment the queen was consulting her magic mirror, Snow White was busy scrubbing the stone steps of the courtyard below. The work was hard, but Snow White performed the task in good spirits. And now she sang prettily as a flock of white doves fluttered around her, cooing and bobbing.

When she turned to draw water from a nearby well, Snow White peered down at her reflection and was quite startled to see another face next to hers.

"Oh!" she cried. Looking up, she saw a handsome man in the fine dress of a prince standing right beside her.

"Oh!" she cried again, backing away.

"Did I frighten you? I didn't mean to," the prince said with concern. "It's just that I heard such a lovely song as I was riding by."

Snow White was so flustered she couldn't speak. Finally, she bolted toward the castle door, scattering the doves in her wake.

"Wait! Please don't go," cried the prince. "I'd like to talk to you some more." But Snow White was already running up the castle's winding stone steps to a small balcony that overlooked the courtyard. When she reached the balcony, she peeked past the heavy curtains and looked down.

The prince was still there, gazing up at the castle. He looked so handsome and seemed so kind that Snow White felt drawn to him.

Timidly at first and then more boldly, she stepped closer to the balcony's edge.

When the prince saw her, he couldn't help but smile. She was the most beautiful girl he had ever seen.

"Please come back," he urged. "I must get to know you."

Snow White smiled, too, but still did not move from the balcony.

As the prince continued to entreat her to return, a dove flew up onto Snow White's hand. On impulse, she kissed the

dove and bade it fly down to the young man below. The dove gently fluttered down to the prince and kissed him in return. The prince blushed and cried, "I shall never forget you!"

And with that, Snow White withdrew into the dark castle.

Unknown to either Snow White or the prince, the queen had been watching this tender scene, which filled her with even more anger and jealousy.

Now the ruler nodded as if she had made up her mind to carry out an evil plan. And in fact, she had. She called her chief huntsman to her throne.

When the huntsman arrived, the queen commanded him in a firm voice, "Take Snow White far into the forest. Find some secluded glade where she can pick wildflowers."

"Yes, Your Majesty," answered the huntsman.

"And there, my faithful huntsman, you will *kill* her!"

Although the huntsman was a hardened man, he gasped and stared up at his queen.

"But Your Majesty," he cried, "the little princess!"

"Silence!" snapped the queen. "You know the penalty if you fail."

The huntsman bowed his head.

"Yes, Your Majesty," he said solemnly.

Then the queen paused and held out an ornate red box. Its clasp was formed by a jeweled dagger piercing a golden heart.

"But to make doubly sure you do not fail," the queen continued, "bring back her *heart* in this."

The huntsman took the box and slowly nodded his head.

CHAPTER TWO

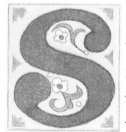now White was soon wandering cheerfully through a lush green meadow, with the huntsman following close behind. She had been told that the queen wanted some wildflowers for her table, and she was glad of the chance to go out into the surrounding countryside.

She was reaching to pick from a cluster of bright daisies when she spied a baby bird on the ground beside a large rock. "Why, hello there," Snow White said.

The tiny creature shook its blue speckled wings and chirped a hello in response. Snow White bent down to pick up the bird and suddenly noticed a large, dark shadow creeping up the rock. She whirled around in fright and then cringed in terror as she saw the huntsman looming over her, a sharp knife in his hand. She pressed herself against the rock and put her hands up to shield her face.

The huntsman came at her grimly, his knife poised to strike. But at the last moment, his hand shook and his face fell in dismay.

"I can't do it," he cried as he dropped to his knees. "Forgive me. I beg of Your Highness, forgive me."

"Why . . . why . . . I don't understand," stammered the frightened princess.

"She's mad, jealous of you," the huntsman said. "She'll stop at nothing."

Snow White stared at the huntsman for a moment in shock and confusion. "But who?" she gasped.

"The queen!" answered the huntsman.

"The queen?" echoed Snow White, her face growing pale.

"Yes," said the huntsman. "Now quick, child. Run. Run away and hide!"

"But . . . where shall I go?" asked Snow White in a trembling voice.

"Into the woods—anywhere," said the huntsman, gesturing wildly at the thick forest just beyond the meadow. "Now go! Run and don't come back."

Without another word, Snow White whirled and fled into the dark forest. She could hear the huntsman urging her on as she stumbled blindly through dense trees and brush. And as she ran, the things in the forest took on shapes and forms she had never before imagined. The branches of trees sprang to life around her, their clawlike hands reaching out to grab her. Rocks became hunched wild animals ready to rear up at a moment's notice.

Snow White ran across a hilly bog, and all at once the spongy ground gave way underneath her and she fell into a dark pool full of half-rotted logs. As she frantically struggled to free herself from the murky waters, the floating logs were

transformed into terrifying crocodiles, snapping at her with wide jaws.

She finally stumbled out of the pool and ran again, deeper and deeper into the forest until she saw her path blocked by an enormous black tree. Its gnarled trunk showed a grotesque and frightening face, and its thick branches reached out as if to grab and crush her. Snow White screamed and stumbled into a nearby clearing. There she fell to the mossy earth, sobbing in terror until she was so exhausted that she fell fast asleep where she lay.

CHAPTER THREE

he next morning, as the rays of the rising sun streamed down into the woods, curious eyes peeked out from the surrounding trees and bushes and stared at the sleeping girl.

Three fawns bobbed their heads and then cautiously picked their way forward. They were joined by a group of chattering chipmunks and bushy-tailed squirrels zigzagging their way across the clearing. A rabbit family hopped out of its hiding place behind an old tree, followed by two black-eyed raccoons and a small flock of quail.

As a half dozen bluebirds fluttered down from the trees to join the other animals, one frisky little rabbit, bolder than the rest, hopped right up to Snow White. With a twitching pink nose it sniffed her hair. The princess stirred and raised her head. "Oh!" she cried.

The rabbit seemed as startled as Snow White, and it bounded away while the other creatures also scurried for cover.

Snow White looked around and said, "Please don't run away. I won't hurt you."

As if they understood her, the forest animals reappeared. Snow White smiled at them.

"I'm awfully sorry," she continued. "I didn't mean to frighten you all. But you don't know what I've been through!"

The gentle creatures now came out and surrounded her. A baby bluebird perched on Snow White's hand, and she was heartened by its trust.

"I really feel quite happy now," she said. "I'm sure I'll get along somehow."

The animals all nodded in agreement.

"But I do need a place to sleep," Snow White said. "Maybe you know where I can stay?" she asked the animals kindly.

A group of bluebirds chirped and twittered in response.

"You do?" Snow White cried as she rose to her feet. "Will you take me there?"

In answer, the birds took Snow White's cape with their small beaks and urged her to follow them. Soon a small parade of animals was following Snow White and the birds as they made their way through the tangled woods.

The birds led Snow White to a snug little house nestled deep in the forest.

As soon as she saw the cottage, Snow White's spirits rose. It was a tiny house with white walls and a brown thatched roof. A small wooden bench stood outside as if to welcome a weary traveler.

"Oh, it's adorable," Snow White murmured. "Just like a dollhouse. I like it here already," she said as she inspected the house from close up.

Snow White went to a window and wiped a clear circle in the grimy glass. "It's so dark inside," she said. "I don't think there's anyone home."

Nevertheless, she went back to the doorway, which was framed by leafy vines on either side, and politely knocked on the thick wooden door. No one answered.

She turned to the animals. "I guess there's no one home," she said.

She knocked again and waited, but there was no answer.

Then she noticed that the door had opened a crack. With brisk steps she entered the tiny house and called, "Hello! May I come in?"

No one answered.

Snow White ventured further into the house. And when she did, she stared around in wonder. Everything was so *small*!

"What a cute little chair!" she exclaimed.

Then she saw there were *seven* little chairs.

"Why, there must be seven little children living here," Snow White said to her animal friends.

And as she looked around, she also realized that the whole cottage was full of dust and dirt. The sink was filled with unwashed dishes, there were dirty clothes everywhere, and the fireplace looked as if it hadn't been swept out in years!

"Why, they've never swept this room," Snow White said. "You'd think their mother would . . ."

Then she paused as a thought occurred to her.

"Maybe they have no mother," she said.

The animals nodded their heads in sad agreement.

"Then they're orphans," Snow White said. "That's too bad."

She gazed around at the untidy little house for a long moment, then suddenly announced, "I know what we'll do!"

The animals all waited expectantly for Snow White to continue.

"We'll clean up and surprise them!" Snow White clapped her hands in satisfaction.

"Then when they see how helpful I can be, maybe they'll let me stay," she said.

Again the animals nodded as if they understood Snow White's intentions.

"Well, let's not just all stand here," she said with a good-natured laugh. "Let's get busy!"

And in no time at all they did.

The squirrels scurried cheerfully around the cottage, sweeping the floor and dusting off the furniture with their bushy tails.

The raccoons helped Snow White wash the clothes by rubbing the garments together between their paws to get them sparkling clean.

The birds eagerly flew up to every nook and cranny in the ceiling, pulling down cobwebs and balls of dust with their strong beaks.

The deer and the rabbits pushed and pulled tables and chairs into their proper places.

Even the tiny chipmunks gladly helped, carrying dirty

cups, dishes, and silverware in their paws and mouths and depositing them in a wooden sink to be washed.

With everyone doing their share, the work went smoothly throughout the afternoon as the sun slowly lowered to the west.

While all this was going on, the people who lived in the cottage were in the hills not far away, digging for jewels in a deep, dark mine. There were seven men in all, and they were dwarfs. And in spite of their different personalities, the dwarfs got along quite well together and worked side by side in perfect harmony. As they swung their picks and shovels, they sang a work song that echoed back to them throughout the caverns and tunnels of the mine.

Just as they started to sing another chorus, a clock in the mine struck five. One of the dwarfs looked up and cried, "Heigh-ho!" The others quickly collected their tools and marched out of the mine in single file. They traveled along a well-worn path that wound through woods and over rocky hills and small ravines. And all the while, they whistled and sang, content to be heading home after a good day's work.

Back at the cottage, Snow White and the animals looked around with pride at the sparkling-clean room. "Now let's see what's upstairs," she said.

Snow White led the way up the small wooden steps as the animals followed behind. She saw that there was a bedroom with seven little beds in it. On each wooden bed board, a name

was carved. Snow White looked at each one in turn.

"What funny names for children," she said. "Doc, Happy, Sneezy, Dopey . . ."

Snow White laughed as she continued reading, "Grumpy, Bashful, Sleepy . . ."

Just then she yawned.

"I'm a little sleepy myself," she murmured.

Snow White lay across three of the little beds and sighed. The animals gently pulled a sheet up to cover her and then, one by one, found cozy spots of their own. Snow White's eyes closed, and soon she and the forest creatures were fast asleep.

CHAPTER FOUR

s Snow White and her friends slept in the little cottage, the low sound of singing echoed through the forest. It woke the animals instantly. With tails twitching and noses quivering, they listened as the singing grew louder. It was the dwarfs making their way home from work!

With startled leaps and bounds, the deer, squirrels, rabbits, and chipmunks scampered out of the house and back into the woods, leaving Snow White still sleeping peacefully on the tiny beds.

As the dwarfs approached the house, Doc pointed and said, "Look! Our house—the lit's light—I mean, the light's lit!"

The dwarfs immediately took cover behind a grove of thick pines.

"Jiminy crickets!" they all cried at once.

"Door's open, chimney's smoking," said Doc. "Something's in there!"

"It . . . it may be a ghost," stammered Happy.

"Or a goblin," whispered Bashful.

"It might be a—*a-achoo*—dragon," said Sneezy, his nose tickled by the scent of the pines.

The other dwarfs glared at him and motioned him to be quiet.

Grumpy scowled and said, "Mark my words, there's trouble a-brewing. Felt it coming all day. My corns hurt."

The dwarfs all looked at each other in concern.

"What'll we do?" asked Sleepy. "I'm too sleepy to think."

"Let's sneak up on it," Happy exclaimed.

"Yes! Huh?" Doc answered, suddenly aware of what Happy was proposing. Then he stood up straighter and addressed the others. "We'll squeak up—uh, I mean, sneak up on it. Come on, hen—uh, men. Follow me!"

The dwarfs slowly and cautiously crept up to the house, one behind the other. When they got to the door, they filed in, quiet as mice, with Dopey in the rear. They were so close to each other they looked glued together. Suddenly Dopey slammed the door shut.

The dwarfs screamed and huddled against each other, expecting the worst. When they realized it was just Dopey, they put their fingers to their lips and said, *"Shhhh!"*

Dopey nodded. Then he turned to the door, put his finger to his lips, and repeated, *"Shhhh."*

As the dwarfs crept through the house, they noticed that things didn't seem quite the same as they had left them that morning.

"Look. The floor's been swept," said Doc.

Grumpy rubbed a finger along the top of a chair.

"Huh. Chair's been dusted," he said in disgust.

"And our window's been washed," cried Happy as he looked out at the forest beyond.

"Why, the whole place is clean," Doc finally announced.

"There's dirty work afoot!" growled Grumpy.

Just then Happy spied their big black kettle bubbling in the fireplace and sniffed.

"Something's cookin'," he said. "And it smells good!"

Happy grabbed a spoon and was about to dip it into the kettle when Grumpy snatched it away and yelled, "Don't touch it, ya fool, it might be poison!"

Glancing nervously around the room, the dwarfs felt sure that some sort of unknown and terrible creature had invaded their home.

CHAPTER FIVE

hile the dwarfs were creeping about below, some birds were hiding in the rafters above. Nodding and winking at each other, they knew who the unexpected visitor was. Suddenly they tapped their beaks against the rafters, and the dwarfs huddled together fearfully.

"Hear that?" whispered Grumpy. "Whatever it is, it's in this room, right now!"

The birds couldn't help twittering to themselves in mischievous delight. Suddenly they let out a high-pitched shriek, and the dwarfs tumbled all over themselves in panic and fright.

When they finally settled down once more, Doc pointed upstairs.

"It's . . . it's up there," he said in a low voice.

"Yeah, in the bedroom," agreed Bashful.

Doc nodded solemnly.

"One of us has got to go down and chase it up—uh, I mean, go up and chase it down," he said.

The dwarfs all nodded in agreement. Dopey nodded eagerly—even after everyone else had stopped. Finally, he noticed that the other dwarfs were all staring in his direction. He turned

to look behind him, but there was no one there. They were staring at *him*. They wanted him to lead the way!

Dopey tried to run, but the dwarfs grabbed him. Doc handed him a candle.

"H-here, take it," said Doc, shaking. "D-don't be nervous."

The dwarfs pushed Dopey ahead of them, up the stairs.

"Don't be afraid," said Doc. "We're right behind you."

"Yeah, right behind you," echoed the others from a good distance.

Dopey took a deep gulp, climbed the darkened stairs to the bedroom, and slowly opened the door. A long, low moan emanated from the darkness, and in the flickering light of the candle, Dopey saw something moving underneath the sheets across three of the beds.

Suddenly the candle went out, and with a yelp, Dopey burst out of the bedroom and started to pound down the dark stairs.

"It's the creature!" the other dwarfs cried as they proceeded to fall all over each other, trying to get out of the way. They yelled and screamed and ran out of the cottage, slamming the door behind them. Once outside the house, they hid behind the pine trees and waited.

Meanwhile, Dopey thought the creature was right behind *him*, and in his frantic haste to escape he crashed into a cupboard, causing pots and pans to come tumbling out. One large soup pot fell over his head, and as he blindly stumbled about, he jammed one foot into another, smaller pot. Dizzily turning

this way and that, he finally groped his way out of the cottage and headed toward the other dwarfs.

"Here it comes!" yelled Happy as he saw the strange figure with the metal head clanking and clumping toward them.

"Now's our only chance, men!" said Doc. "We mustn't be spared—er, I mean, scared."

The dwarfs bravely jumped on the creature as it passed by them.

"Tie it up!" yelled Grumpy.

"Yeah, don't let it get away!" cried Doc.

As the dwarfs struggled to hold the creature, its metal head fell off and hit the ground with a thump, and in its place was a head they recognized immediately—it was Dopey!

"Aw, fuss and fiddlesticks," grumbled Grumpy. "All that trouble fer nothin'!"

When the dwarfs finally calmed down and helped Dopey to his feet, they showered him with questions. "Did you see the creature? How big was it? Was it a dragon? Was it breathing fire? What *was* it doing?"

Dopey quickly gestured that the creature was *sleeping!*

"He says it's a monster!" Doc cried. "A-asleep in our beds!"

"Let's attack!" growled Grumpy. "While it's still sleeping!"

Doc agreed. "Hurry, men," he shouted. "It's now or never!"

So the dwarfs marched bravely back into the house, this time determined to face whatever danger there was. They crept

quietly into the bedroom and right up to the beds where Snow White lay sleeping peacefully under the sheets.

They surrounded the beds, holding up picks and clubs as weapons. Doc slowly and shakily pulled back the covers.

The dwarfs were just about to strike when they saw Snow White. As one, they lowered their weapons and stood motionless.

Doc was the first to recover.

"Well . . . ah . . . ah," he stammered.

"What is it?" asked Happy, gazing at the sleeping princess.

"Why, I, it—it's," stuttered Doc, "it's a girl!"

Sneezy and Bashful both smiled.

"She's mighty purty," said Sneezy.

"She's *beautiful*," said Bashful, blushing. "Just like an angel."

All the dwarfs were captivated by Snow White. All but Grumpy, that is. "Angel, huh!" he said sourly. "She's a female. And all females is poison. They're fulla wicked wiles."

"What're wicked wiles?" asked Bashful.

"I dunno," answered Grumpy. "But I'm against them!"

Doc told Grumpy not to speak so loudly or the lovely young girl might wake up.

"Aw, let her wake up," replied Grumpy. "She don't belong here nohow."

At that, Snow White's eyelids fluttered.

"She's waking up!" whispered Happy.

The dwarfs quickly hid at the foot of the beds.

Snow White yawned and opened her eyes. She sat up and looked around, remembering where she was.

"Oh dear," she said to herself. "I wonder if the children are—"

Just then she saw the dwarfs peeking over the edge of the bed boards.

"Oh!" cried Snow White as she pulled the covers up around her. But then she sat up straighter and stared in surprise.

"Why, you're not children at all," she said. "You're little men!"

Snow White smiled prettily and said, "How do you do."

"How do you do what?" answered Grumpy with a frown.

But Snow White was not ruffled by Grumpy's rudeness, and she just continued gaily, "Oh, you can talk. I'm so glad."

Snow White looked from one dwarf to the other and smiled. "Let me try to guess your names," she said, pointing first at Doc.

"You must be Doc."

"Yes," answered Doc politely.

Then she pointed at Sleepy, who was busy yawning.

"I *know* you're Sleepy," Snow White said.

Sleepy answered with a bob of his head.

Snow White looked at Dopey, who was gazing at her with large blue eyes.

"You must be Dopey," she said.

Dopey nodded excitedly.

She cocked her head and looked at Happy, who was smiling from ear to ear.

"And you've got to be Happy," Snow White said.

Happy chuckled in glee. "Why, that's right!" he cried.
"How did you guess?"

Then she leaned forward to look at Bashful, who was
trying to hide behind the others.

"You're Bashful," she said.

"Uh, yup. I mean—*gulp!*" Bashful answered, his face
turning a bright pink.

Just then Sneezy piped up. "Can you guess—*a-a-
chooo!*—who I am?"

Snow White giggled. "I would say you were Sneezy!" she
answered.

Sneezy held a finger under his nose and said in a muffled
voice, "Tha-tha-that's right. *A-choooo!*"

When Snow White finally came to Grumpy, she looked
at his folded arms and stern expression and took the same pose.

"And you must be Grumpy," she said in a deep voice.

But Grumpy just turned to Doc and said, "*We* know who
we are. Ask her who *she* is and what she's doing in our house!"

And so the dwarfs asked. Snow White told them who she
was and all about her terrible flight through the forest.

When the dwarfs learned that she was the princess Snow
White, they were honored to have her as a guest in their tiny
forest home. All except Grumpy. He insisted that she should
be made to leave.

Snow White looked at the dwarfs entreatingly.

"Please don't send me away," she pleaded. "If you do, she'll kill me!"

"Who?" they asked.

And so Snow White told the dwarfs all about her evil stepmother, the queen.

When she was finished, the dwarfs all clucked their tongues in sympathy.

"She's wicked," said Bashful.

"She's bad," said Happy.

"She's an old *witch*!" said Grumpy. "And I'm warning ya, if the queen finds Snow White here, she'll sweep down and wreak her vengeance on all of us!"

"But she doesn't know where I am," said Snow White.

"She doesn't? Heh!" answered Grumpy. "She knows everything!

"She's full of black magic," he continued. "She can make herself invisible. Why, she might even be in this room right now."

The other dwarfs looked around the room uneasily. But Snow White sat up straighter.

"Oh, she'll never find me here," she said brightly. "And if you let me stay, I can help with the chores. I'm a good cook, too."

"A good cook!" cried the dwarfs, suddenly remembering their own hunger and the aroma coming from the kettle.

"She stays!" shouted the dwarfs in spite of Grumpy's glowering face.

CHAPTER SIX

now White went downstairs, followed by seven hungry dwarfs. She went over to the kettle, dipped a spoon in, and tasted the contents. The dwarfs sniffed the air.

"It's soup—hooray!" they cried as they made a rush for the dining table.

Snow White put up her hand.

"Just a minute," she said. "Supper's not quite ready. You'll just have time to wash."

"Wash!" cried Doc.

"Wash?" said Bashful.

"Wash!" yelped Happy.

Grumpy threw down the spoon he had just picked up.

"Heh, I know'd there be a catch to it!" he said.

"Why wash?" said Bashful. "We ain't going nowhere."

"Yeah," Doc chimed in. "And 'tain't New Year's or anything."

Snow White put her hands on her hips and raised her eyebrows. She looked at the dwarfs.

"Oh, perhaps you have washed already," she said with a knowing smile. "Recently?"

Doc nodded and said, "Yes, that's right. Perhaps we, er, yes, perhaps we have."

"When?" asked Snow White.

"Er, like you said, er, recently," answered Doc.

The other dwarfs murmured happily in agreement.

"Ohhhh," said Snow White with a suspicious look. "*Recently*. Then let me see your hands," she said in a firm voice.

The dwarfs lined up and, one by one, hesitantly showed Snow White their hands. Each pair was dirtier than the last.

"Oh, how shocking!" said Snow White. "Worse than I thought."

She shook her head slowly from side to side.

"I don't think that will do," she said to the shamefaced men.

Then she pointed at the door.

"March straight outside and wash, or you'll not get a bite to eat," she said with conviction.

The dwarfs turned and slowly walked out of the house, moaning and groaning to themselves. All except Grumpy. He stood with his arms folded and a sour expression on his face.

"Well, what about you?" asked Snow White. "Aren't you going to wash?"

Instead of answering, Grumpy just sulked.

"What's the matter?" said Snow White teasingly. "Cat got your tongue?"

At that, Grumpy stuck out his tongue and headed out of the house in a huff.

The other dwarfs were gathered around the big wooden tub in the yard.

"Courage, men, courage," Doc urged.

"But the water's wet!" moaned Happy.

"Cold, too!" complained Sneezy. "We ain't gonna *really* do it, are we?"

"Well, er," said Doc, struggling for a good reason. "It'll please the princess."

Happy beamed at that.

"Okay, then," he said, looking at the water doubtfully. "I'll take a chance for her."

"Me, too," agreed the rest all together.

Grumpy sat on a barrel close by, listening to the others.

"You see?" he said. "Her wiles are beginnin' to work."

Then he pointed at the dwarfs and lectured.

"I'm a-warning ya. Ya give 'em an inch and they'll walk all over ya!"

Doc looked sternly at Grumpy and told the other dwarfs not to listen to him. And with that, the men bravely started to scrub their faces, wash their hands, brush their teeth, and comb their hair.

When they were through, they looked at each other in awe. They hardly recognized themselves.

"Hah," cried Grumpy, still sitting on the barrel. "Bunch of old nanny goats. Ya make me sick! Next thing ya know, she'll be tyin' your beards up in pink ribbons and smellin' ya up with that stuff called, er, perfumy. Hah! What a fine bunch of water lilies!"

The dwarfs looked at Grumpy and then at each other. Then they all nodded.

"Get 'im!" Doc suddenly cried.

The dwarfs pounced on Grumpy and carried him over to the tub.

"Hey, lemme loose, ya fools!" Grumpy yelled as he squirmed to free himself.

But the dwarfs paid no attention. Instead they dumped Grumpy right into the tub of soapy water and started to scrub him good.

"Now scrub hard, men!" Doc urged. "It can't be denied, he'll look mighty cute as soon as he's dried."

Grumpy fumed and fussed.

"You'll pay for this!" he cried as he continued to struggle to get out of the tub. Suddenly they heard a loud clang as Snow White banged a spoon on the kettle.

"Supper!" she called out.

"Supper!" the men shouted.

They all let go of Grumpy at once, and he dropped back into the tub, sputtering and blowing bubbles as he gulped a mouthful of soapsuds.

Muttering and complaining, Grumpy finally got out of the tub and headed for the house. With a "Hmph!" he joined the other dwarfs now seated at the table, eagerly awaiting their supper.

CHAPTER SEVEN

ack at the castle, the queen was once again consulting her magic mirror. But as she waited calmly for the expected reply, it said instead,

Over the seven jeweled hills,
Beyond the seventh fall,
In the cottage of the seven dwarfs
Dwells Snow White,
Fairest one of all.

Shocked and outraged, the evil queen realized that she had been tricked. Snow White was still alive! The huntsman had not brought back Snow White's heart in the box but that of a forest animal!

The queen immediately began to plot a way to put an end to Snow White on her own.

"I'll go to the dwarfs' cottage myself," she muttered, "in a disguise so complete, no one will ever suspect it's me."

She swept down a flight of stone steps into her deep, dark dungeon. As the queen made her way across the dingy chamber, scurrying rats squealed and ran for cover. Spiders, beetles, and a host of other crawling things crept away at the sight of the

evil queen. The only creature that didn't move was the queen's pet raven, who watched her approach with unblinking eyes and an evil expression to match her own.

But the queen took no notice of these things. She went straight to her book of black magic and flipped through its pages until she found what she wanted.

"Ah," she murmured. "A peddler's disguise. Perfect!"

She went over to a table cluttered with vials and beakers filled with all sorts of bubbling, smoking liquids. She selected one beaker and poured a steaming green liquid into a large goblet.

"First, some mummy dust to make me old," she said as she sprinkled a fine gray powder into the glass. "To shroud my clothes, the black of night." She added a drop of black liquid. "To age my voice, a drop of crow's blood." Then a ruby red drop was added to the brew.

The queen continued mixing her potion until she was satisfied that she had done everything exactly right. When she was finished, she held the goblet before her. The brew bubbled and hissed and spilled over the rim of the glass. She smiled grimly, and then with one quick motion she swallowed the foul liquid.

As soon as she had done so, the queen clutched her throat as if she were choking. The dungeon seemed to spin crazily around her, and a powerful wind sprang up, rustling her robes and hair as if she were in the midst of a hurricane.

The queen moaned as she shook violently and then crum-

pled over as if a powerful hand were squeezing the youth from her body.

And as she quivered in the grips of the magic potion, her lustrous black hair began turning a dingy white, and her smooth face started to fold into hideous wrinkles. Her long beautiful fingers twisted into clawlike talons, and her elegant robe changed color and shape until it was no more than a faded black rag.

Suddenly a flash of brilliant green light filled the dungeon, and when it was gone, a haggard old witch stood in place of the once-beautiful queen! She shrieked in both triumph and agony as the awful transformation reached its final stage.

The witch glanced in a mirror and cackled.

"Yes, a perfect disguise," she croaked, and hobbled over to her book of spells once more.

"And now," she hissed, "I must plan a special sort of death for one so fair. What shall it be?"

The queen flipped through the pages until she stopped and cried, "Ah, yes! Perfect. A poisoned apple!"

She read the spell aloud as her gnarled fingers traced the words.

"One taste of the poisoned apple and the victim's eyes will close forever in the sleeping death."

The old hag threw back her head and laughed long and loud, the sound echoing throughout the deep, dark dungeon like the shrieks of a hundred black crows.

CHAPTER EIGHT

s darkness settled over the forest, music rang out from inside the dwarfs' cottage while they entertained their new guest. Doc played the bass; Happy, Dopey, and Sneezy yodeled and danced; Sleepy played the horn, lazily keeping time with his foot; and Bashful played the accordion and sang. Even Grumpy grudgingly joined in. He played the organ and yodeled in a low, growling voice. Snow White danced and sang along with them all.

When the song was over, Snow White sank into a chair and sighed contentedly.

"That was fun!" she said, her face flushed with color. "You were all so marvelous."

"Now you do somethin'," said Happy.

"Well, what shall I do?" asked Snow White.

"Tell us a story," piped up Sleepy.

All the dwarfs nodded in agreement.

"Yes, tell us a story," they cried.

"A *true* story," added Happy.

"A looove story," said Bashful with a blush.

Snow White looked at their eager faces and gathered them around her.

"Well," she began. "Once there was a princess—"

"Was the princess you?" Doc interrupted.

Snow White nodded gently as she continued.

"And she fell in love with a prince," she said.

"Was it—*a-chooo!*—hard to do?" asked Sneezy.

Snow White shook her head and laughed.

"It wasn't hard at all. It was very easy. Anyone could see that the prince was as good as he was charming."

Then Snow White looked away for a moment and sighed. "I knew he was the only one for me."

The dwarfs showered her with questions.

"Was he big and tall?"

"Did he say he loved ya?"

"Did he steal a kiss?"

"No, but he *was* romantic," answered Snow White. "I couldn't help being drawn to him. I had always known that someday I would meet someone I could love, and I did."

Then Snow White smiled and started to sing in a soft, pleasant voice. And through the song, she poured out all the secret longings of her young heart.

Just as the song was ending, the clock struck the hour.

"Oh my goodness," cried Snow White. "It's past bedtime. Go right upstairs, all of you," Snow White said, playfully shooing the dwarfs out of the room.

"Hold on there, men," Doc cried. "The princess will sleep upstairs in our beds."

"But where will you sleep?" asked Snow White.

"Why, er," answered Doc, "we'll be as bug as a snug in a rug—I mean, as snug as a bug in a rug down here."

"In a pig's eye," snapped Grumpy.

"Yep, in a pigsty—I mean, a pig's eye," echoed Doc. Then he realized he had agreed with Grumpy's sour remark, and he shook his head in dismay.

"We'll be comfortable, won't we, men?" he said to the dwarfs, looking especially at Grumpy.

"Oh yes," they answered, not sure whether they meant it or not.

Doc turned back to Snow White and said, "Go right up now, uh, my dear."

"Well, if you insist," answered Snow White.

Then she smiled sweetly at them and said good night.

Snow White knelt beside the beds and murmured low, "Bless the seven little men who have been so kind to me, and . . . and may my dreams come true."

She started to rise, but quickly knelt down again.

"Oh yes," she added. "And please make Grumpy like me."

And with that, she crept into the beds and pulled up the covers.

CHAPTER NINE

oon the whole house was still, with only the snoring of the seven dwarfs downstairs to break the silence. Outside, the forest, too, was quiet, its creatures having settled down for the night.

But there was someone who was wide awake and busily concocting a deadly present—the evil queen!

The old hag held a large apple on a string over a steaming cauldron.

"Dip the apple in the brew," the queen-witch intoned. "Let the sleeping death seep through."

The apple disappeared into the bubbling liquid, and when the witch pulled it out again a few seconds later, the brew dripped down the apple's sides, leaving the shape of a skull on its skin.

"Ah," sighed the witch. "On the skin, the symbol of what lies within. Now turn red," she commanded, "to tempt Snow White, to make her hunger for a bite."

At that, the apple turned a beautiful ruby red.

The witch held the apple in her hand and thrust it at her pet raven.

"Have a bite?" she murmured wickedly.

The bird shuddered and backed away from the poisoned treat.

The witch laughed in mischievous glee.

"It's not for you, anyway," she cried in a raspy voice. "It's for Snow White! When she breaks the tender peel to taste the apple in my hand," the hag went on, "her breath will still, her blood congeal. Then I'll be fairest in the land!"

Then the witch paused and frowned.

"Wait," she said to the raven. "There may be an antidote. Nothing must be overlooked."

She scurried over to her book of spells and flipped through it once again. Suddenly her bony fingers stopped at one of the pages.

"Ah, I was right. Here it is," she said.

The witch started to read.

"The victim of the sleeping death can be revived only by love's first kiss.

"Love's first kiss!" she hissed. "Bah, no fear of *that*. The dwarfs will think she's dead, and they'll bury her *alive*!

"Buried alive!" she screeched over and over as she grabbed a basketful of other apples and gently placed the poisoned one among them.

With the basket of apples under one arm, the witch left the dungeon and descended the stone steps leading to the river that streamed beneath the castle. She got into a small boat and started to row away into the night. A pale moon hung overhead, and shadows fell over her craggy features, making her face look like a ghastly white skull.

CHAPTER TEN

he next morning, Snow White rose to see a bright yellow sun and blue sky peeking through the branches of the trees overhead.

She had just enough time to give the men a hearty breakfast before they went off to work in the mine.

As the dwarfs were leaving, Doc said, "Now, don't forgit, my dear. The old queen's a fly—er, I mean, a sly one."

He wagged a finger at the princess.

"She's fulla witchcraft," he continued. "So beware of strangers."

"Don't worry," answered Snow White. "I'll be all right."

One by one she kissed the dwarfs on the forehead and said good-bye. And one by one they warned her to be alert. Grumpy was the last to leave, and just before he joined the others, he cleared his throat and said, "Now, I'm warnin' ya. Don't let nobody or nothin' in the house."

Snow White looked down at him and smiled.

"Oh, Grumpy, you *do* like me after all!" she cried.

And with that, she bent down and planted a kiss on his forehead.

"Hey, stop that mushy stuff," scowled Grumpy as he broke away from Snow White's hug and stomped off. But after a few steps, he turned around and gazed at Snow White with an adoring expression. Snow White blew him a kiss. Grumpy held his smile for a few seconds more until he suddenly realized what he was doing. He immediately scowled again and hurried off to join the others.

Not far from the cottage, the wicked witch was making her way through the forest.

"The little men will be off," she cackled to herself. "And she'll be alone. Alone, with a harmless old peddler woman!" She laughed long and loud, and two vultures in a nearby tree flapped away in alarm. But she quickly grew silent as she saw the cottage of the seven dwarfs come into view.

CHAPTER ELEVEN

A s soon as the dwarfs had left, Snow White busied herself preparing food for that evening. She felt it was the least she could do to repay the dwarfs for their kindness.

After cutting up some carrots and potatoes, Snow White decided to bake some gooseberry pies for dessert. She was near the window and just putting the finishing touches on one of them when a dark shadow passed over her cutting board.

Snow White looked up in surprise and saw an old woman peering into the house from the window.

"All alone, my pet?" asked the old woman.

"Why . . . why, yes, I am, but . . . ," answered Snow White, a little frightened of the strange woman.

"The little men are not here?" cut in the old woman.

"No, they're not," said Snow White.

The old woman smiled.

"Hmmm," she said. "Makin' pies?"

"Yes, gooseberry pies," answered Snow White, more at ease. After all, this was only a harmless peddler woman.

The old woman smiled toothlessly.

"It's apple pies that make menfolk's mouths water," she said.

Then she took the deep red apple from her basket and held it up. "Pies made from apples like these," said the old woman.

"Oh, they do look delicious," said Snow White.

"Yes," murmured the old peddler, "but wait until you taste one, dearie."

Then she held the poisoned apple out to Snow White.

"Like to try one, hmmm?" the old woman asked.

Snow White stepped back from the window a bit, not sure of what to do. Her animal friends fretted and paced anxiously in the woods nearby. The birds had twittered in alarm at the sight of the old peddler, and now they flapped their wings in helpless frustration as they watched Snow White about to take the tempting treat.

But just as Snow White reached for the apple, the birds swooped down and knocked it from the old woman's hand. Then they fluttered around her, pecking at her head and body.

The witch waved her feeble arms around and cried, "Oh, go away! Leave me alone!"

Snow White ran out of the house and shooed the birds away.

"Stop it. Stop it right now," Snow White cried.

The birds flew off back into the trees, where they perched restlessly.

"Shame on you," Snow White scolded. "Frightening a poor old lady."

The birds hung their heads, not knowing what to do.

Snow White went to the old woman, who by now was on her hands and knees recovering the apple.

The princess helped the woman to her feet, then said, "I'm sorry, I don't know what has gotten into those birds. They are usually so gentle and kind."

The old woman nodded absently, then grasped her chest and cried convincingly, "Oh, my poor heart."

Snow White held the woman up by the arm and looked at her with concern.

"Please take me into the house," the woman said. "Let me rest a while. Perhaps I may have a glass of water?"

Snow White nodded and took the old peddler into the house.

The birds and other animals rushed to the window to peek inside. They watched as Snow White helped the peddler into a chair and then gave her a cup of water. When Snow White turned away a moment, the old woman leered at them. The animals backed away and, one by one, scampered off to find the seven dwarfs.

CHAPTER TWELVE

he animals crashed through thicket and brush as if a fire were chasing them. Finally, they reached the mine and started to push and prod the dwarfs in the direction of the cottage. The men thought the animals had gone mad.

"What ails these crazy critters?" cried Doc.

"They've gone plumb daffy!" yelled Bashful.

"Go on, git!" cried Doc as a deer bumped him from behind.

Then he turned to the other dwarfs.

"These pesky critters won't stop," he said.

" 'Tain't natural," cried Happy, flapping his arms to shoo away the birds.

"There's somethin'—*a-choo!*—wrong," cried Sneezy.

Even Grumpy agreed. "They ain't actin' this way for nothin'," he grumbled.

Sleepy looked at everyone with half-closed eyes.

"Maybe the old queen's got Snow White," he said as he stifled a yawn.

"*The queen!*" cried Doc.

"*Snow White!*" cried the others.

Grumpy pounded his fist into his hand.

"The queen'll kill her! We've gotta save her!" he cried.

Then he hopped onto the back of a deer and said, "Giddyap!"

One by one the dwarfs leapt onto deer and galloped back toward their cottage.

The strange parade of running creatures hurtled through the forest, leaping over rocks and streams.

"Faster!" Doc urged the others. "We haven't got a moment to lose!"

Meanwhile, back at the cottage, the witch had pretended to recover her strength and was now carrying on a warm conversation with Snow White.

She held up the poisoned apple once more.

"Because you've been so good to old granny," she said, "I'll share a secret with you."

Snow White leaned forward in interest.

"This is no ordinary apple," the old woman said as she got to her feet. "It's a magic *wishing* apple!"

"A wishing apple?" said Snow White.

"Yes," answered the witch. "One bite and all your dreams will come true."

"Really?" said Snow White.

"Yes, girlie," murmured the peddler. "Now make a wish and take a bite."

With a crooked smile, she held out the poisoned apple to Snow White.

CHAPTER THIRTEEN

The dwarfs raced on through the forest, hoping to reach home and find Snow White safe. But time was running out.

"There must be something your little heart desires," murmured the woman, still holding the apple in her hand. "Perhaps there is someone you love?"

"Well, there is someone," answered Snow White slowly.

"I thought so," answered the woman slyly. "Ha, ha, old granny knows a young girl's heart."

The old woman handed the apple to Snow White and patted her hand. "Now take the apple, dearie, and make a wish," she said.

Snow White gazed at the apple and said, "I wish . . ."

"That's it. Go on, go on," the witch urged.

". . . that I will meet my prince again, and together we will travel to his kingdom," Snow White said more boldly.

"Fine," smiled the old woman. "Now take a bite—hurry! Don't let the wish grow cold."

Snow White held the ruby red apple up and took a bite. As soon as she had done so, she tottered on her feet.

"Oh, I feel so strange!" she cried.

The old woman rubbed her hands in satisfaction as she intoned, "Her breath will still."

"Oh," cried Snow White as she put her hand to her forehead.

"Her blood congeal," hissed the old woman.

"Oh," moaned Snow White one final time before she sank to the ground and lay as still as death. The apple fell out of her hand and rolled away.

The old woman dropped all pretense now and threw back her head and howled.

"It is done!" she cried. "Now I'll be fairest in the land!"

The witch turned and hurried out of the cottage and into the woods. A sudden crack of lightning ripped across the sky, followed by a torrent of rain. It was as if the heavens themselves were angry at the witch for her wicked deed. But the old hag wasn't afraid. She had finally gotten rid of Snow White and could feel only joy at her achievement.

She cackled low in her throat as she hobbled through the woods, anxious to return to her castle and her former self. She started to climb toward a small cliff when she saw the seven dwarfs coming straight at her.

"There she goes!" cried Grumpy. "After her!"

The dwarfs chased the witch as she scrambled up the rocky hill.

The old woman cried out in frustration as she saw the dwarfs in close pursuit. Now frightened and desperate, she climbed farther out onto a long slab of rock overhanging a deep ravine. The wind and rain lashed at her face and clothing.

The witch looked wildly around her as she realized she was cornered.

"I'm trapped," she cried. "What will I do? The meddling little fools."

Then she picked up a broken tree limb from the ground, and using it as a lever, she started to pry loose a huge boulder that was perched on the slab. Her magic now gave her the strength of ten men, and the boulder started to teeter back and forth.

"I'll fix you! I'll fix you!" she cried out to the dwarfs. "I'll crush your bones!"

"Look out!" cried Grumpy. "She's going to roll that boulder right over us!"

The witch laughed triumphantly as the boulder started to come loose. But just as it was about to roll down onto the dwarfs, a bolt of lightning struck the outcropping rock. In an instant, it shattered and fell away, carrying the witch and the boulder with it.

The witch gave out a long, horrifying shriek as she fell all the way to the jagged rocks below.

One by one the dwarfs approached the edge of the broken slab and looked down. They couldn't see the witch, but when they saw two vultures swoop down with greedy eyes, they knew she was gone forever.

When they finally reached their cottage, they found Snow White laying motionless on the floor.

"She . . . she's dead," cried Sleepy.

The others nodded sadly. The queen had won after all.

CHAPTER FOURTEEN

he dwarfs could not bear to bury the princess, so they fashioned a coffin of gold and glass and placed Snow White in it. Then they carried the coffin to a peaceful glen in the woods. Every day, the dwarfs kept vigil at the coffin and placed flowers around it.

One day the following spring, the dwarfs were keeping their usual vigil. They had opened the glass top and placed a bouquet of flowers in Snow White's hands. Then they knelt before the coffin and bowed their heads.

They were surprised to see a handsome prince ride into the clearing on a white horse. He was the very same young man who had first met Snow White at the well. He had heard of the beautiful maiden who slept in the glass coffin and was curious to see if it was the same princess he had once met.

As he approached the coffin, the prince realized that it *was* the same girl. Sadly, he knelt by the coffin and bowed his head. Then he bent over the still form and gave Snow White one farewell kiss. And when he did, he saw to his surprise and joy that Snow White's eyes fluttered open.

She was alive!

Snow White slowly sat up and smiled. It was as if she had just woken up from a good night's sleep. When she saw the prince, her eyes lit up in surprise, and she held out her arms to him. The prince quickly took her in his arms and lifted her up.

For a moment the dwarfs stood silent and unbelieving. But they soon threw their hats in the air and yelled and cheered in delight.

When they had finally calmed down again, Snow White went over and looked at each one of them fondly.

"You have been good, kind friends," she said in a soft voice. "And I shall never forget you."

One by one the dwarfs stood by while Snow White kissed each of them on the forehead.

"Good-bye, Princess," they called as the prince lifted Snow White onto his horse.

"Good-bye," she called back.

Then the prince took the reins of his steed and slowly led it away.

"Good-bye!" Snow White called out once more as she and the prince slowly disappeared from view.

When Snow White and the prince had gone, the dwarfs looked at each other and smiled. Even though they would miss her, they knew Snow White's wish had finally come true. She had found her true love, and she would live happily ever after. And that made them happy, too. Even Grumpy.

Walt Disney's
Sleeping Beauty

Adapted from the film by A.L. Singer

CHAPTER ONE

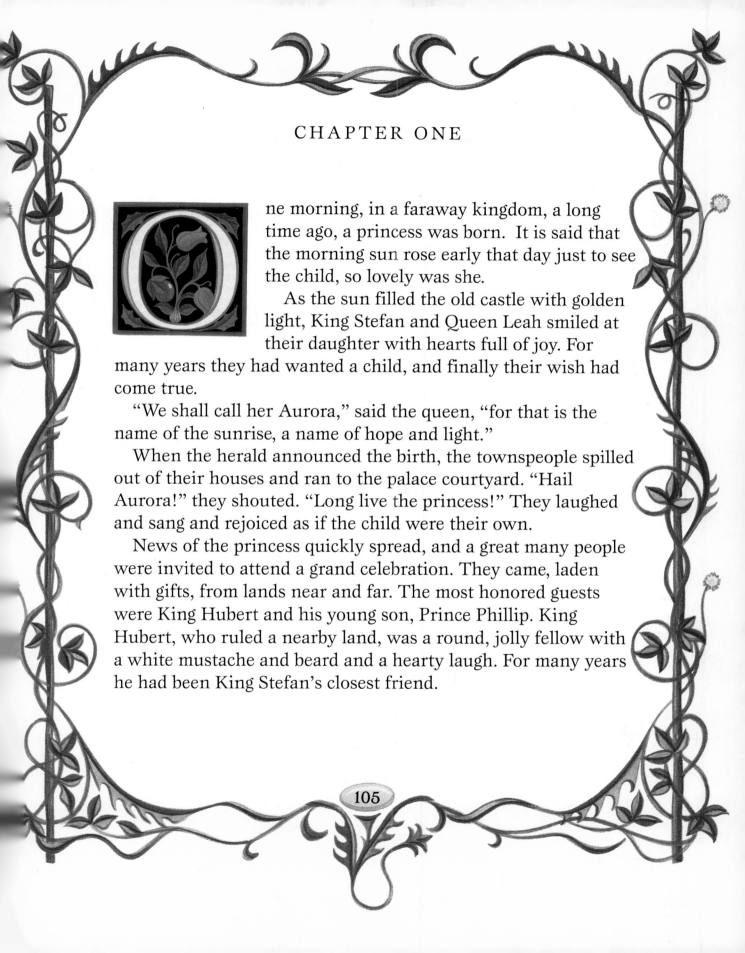

One morning, in a faraway kingdom, a long time ago, a princess was born. It is said that the morning sun rose early that day just to see the child, so lovely was she.

As the sun filled the old castle with golden light, King Stefan and Queen Leah smiled at their daughter with hearts full of joy. For many years they had wanted a child, and finally their wish had come true.

"We shall call her Aurora," said the queen, "for that is the name of the sunrise, a name of hope and light."

When the herald announced the birth, the townspeople spilled out of their houses and ran to the palace courtyard. "Hail Aurora!" they shouted. "Long live the princess!" They laughed and sang and rejoiced as if the child were their own.

News of the princess quickly spread, and a great many people were invited to attend a grand celebration. They came, laden with gifts, from lands near and far. The most honored guests were King Hubert and his young son, Prince Phillip. King Hubert, who ruled a nearby land, was a round, jolly fellow with a white mustache and beard and a hearty laugh. For many years he had been King Stefan's closest friend.

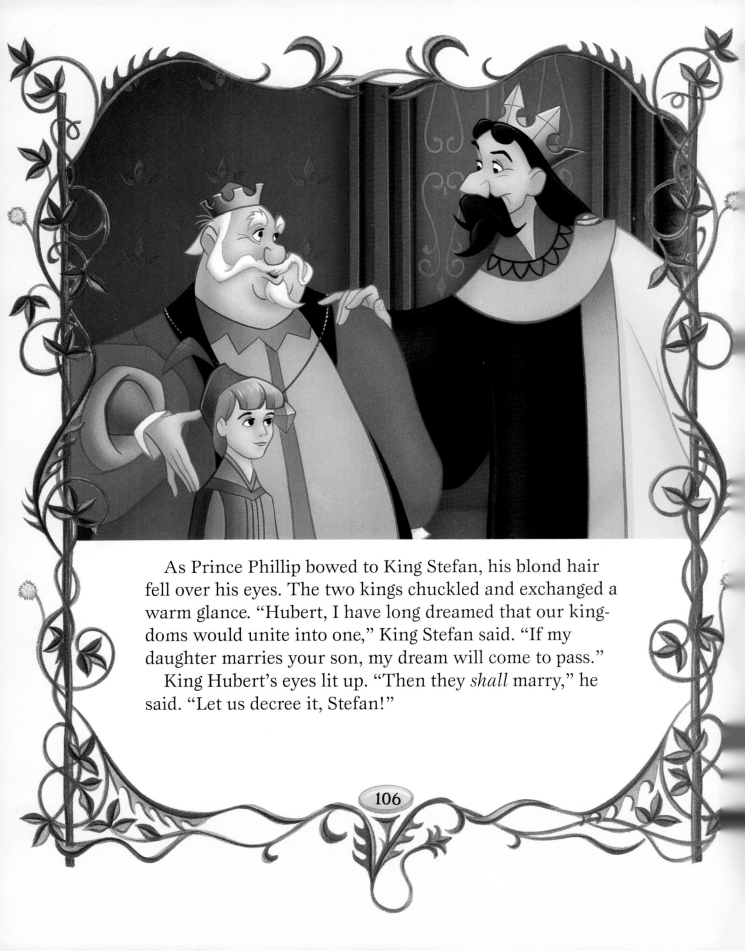

As Prince Phillip bowed to King Stefan, his blond hair fell over his eyes. The two kings chuckled and exchanged a warm glance. "Hubert, I have long dreamed that our king-doms would unite into one," King Stefan said. "If my daughter marries your son, my dream will come to pass."

King Hubert's eyes lit up. "Then they *shall* marry," he said. "Let us decree it, Stefan!"

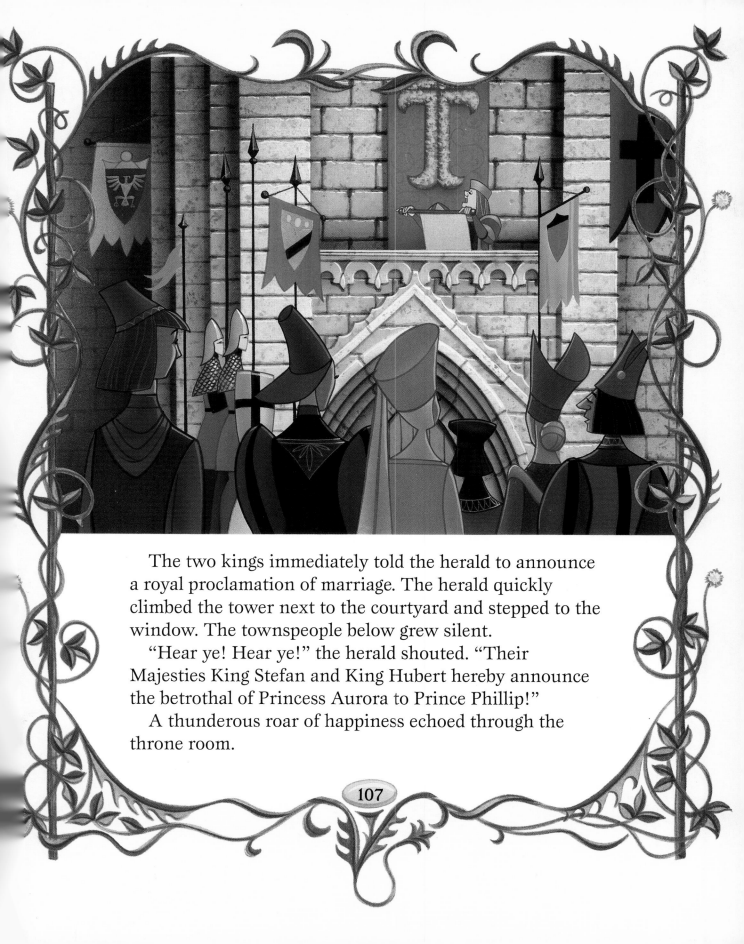

The two kings immediately told the herald to announce a royal proclamation of marriage. The herald quickly climbed the tower next to the courtyard and stepped to the window. The townspeople below grew silent.

"Hear ye! Hear ye!" the herald shouted. "Their Majesties King Stefan and King Hubert hereby announce the betrothal of Princess Aurora to Prince Phillip!"

A thunderous roar of happiness echoed through the throne room.

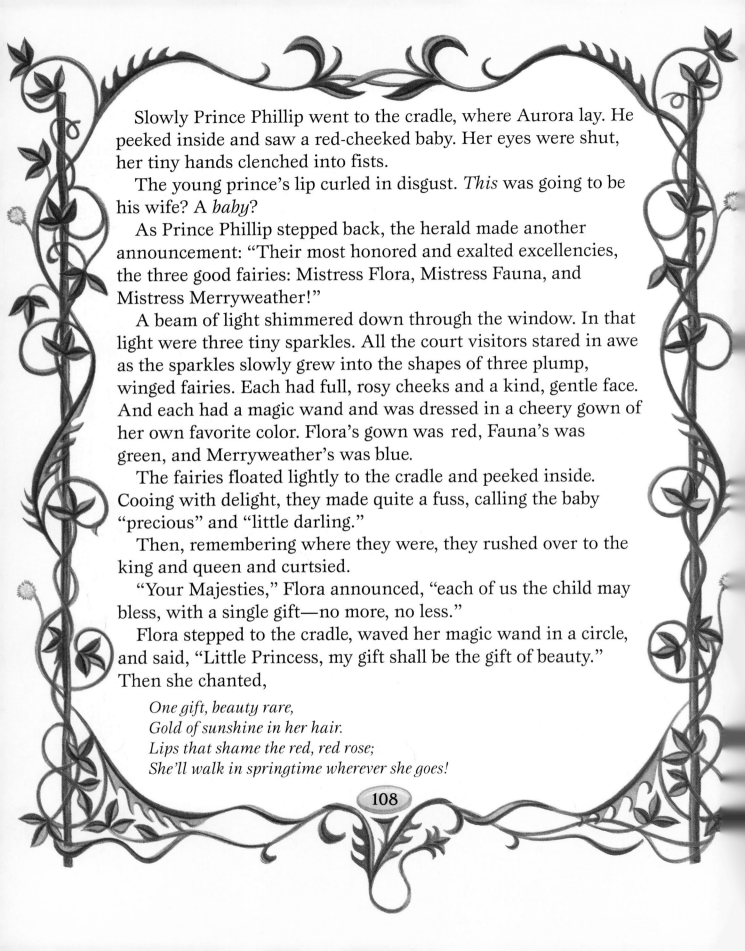

Slowly Prince Phillip went to the cradle, where Aurora lay. He peeked inside and saw a red-cheeked baby. Her eyes were shut, her tiny hands clenched into fists.

The young prince's lip curled in disgust. *This* was going to be his wife? A *baby*?

As Prince Phillip stepped back, the herald made another announcement: "Their most honored and exalted excellencies, the three good fairies: Mistress Flora, Mistress Fauna, and Mistress Merryweather!"

A beam of light shimmered down through the window. In that light were three tiny sparkles. All the court visitors stared in awe as the sparkles slowly grew into the shapes of three plump, winged fairies. Each had full, rosy cheeks and a kind, gentle face. And each had a magic wand and was dressed in a cheery gown of her own favorite color. Flora's gown was red, Fauna's was green, and Merryweather's was blue.

The fairies floated lightly to the cradle and peeked inside. Cooing with delight, they made quite a fuss, calling the baby "precious" and "little darling."

Then, remembering where they were, they rushed over to the king and queen and curtsied.

"Your Majesties," Flora announced, "each of us the child may bless, with a single gift—no more, no less."

Flora stepped to the cradle, waved her magic wand in a circle, and said, "Little Princess, my gift shall be the gift of beauty." Then she chanted,

One gift, beauty rare,
Gold of sunshine in her hair.
Lips that shame the red, red rose;
She'll walk in springtime wherever she goes!

108

Suddenly brightly colored sparkles swirled together high above the cradle. Spinning round and round, they transformed into beautiful flowers and fell gently around the baby princess.

Then Fauna stepped forward, waved her magic wand, and said,

Tiny Princess,
My gift shall be the gift of song;
Melody your whole life long!

A bright whirl of colors appeared again. Inside it, a magical image of a girl and a castle appeared. On the girl's finger was a nightingale, singing sweetly.

At last it was Merryweather's turn. She went to the cradle with her wand and said, "Sweet Princess, my gift shall be the—"
BOOOOOM!

A huge crash echoed through the throne room as the castle doors blew open with the fury of a tornado. Merryweather ran to the other fairies in fright. The king and queen stood up, their robes whipping around them. Banners snapped in the wind, and hats and helmets blew off of heads. With a sudden *crack* of thunder, the room grew dark.

Then a bolt of lightning struck the center of the room. Hissing green flames shot upward from the floor. Terrified, the townspeople backed away, gasping. A dark figure appeared in the flames—the figure of a tall, narrow woman shrouded in black. She held a long, thin staff with a glowing knob on top. An ugly black raven perched on the knob.

Her hard face was calm, but her eyes burned with fury. She stared around the court, finally fixing her gaze on the king.

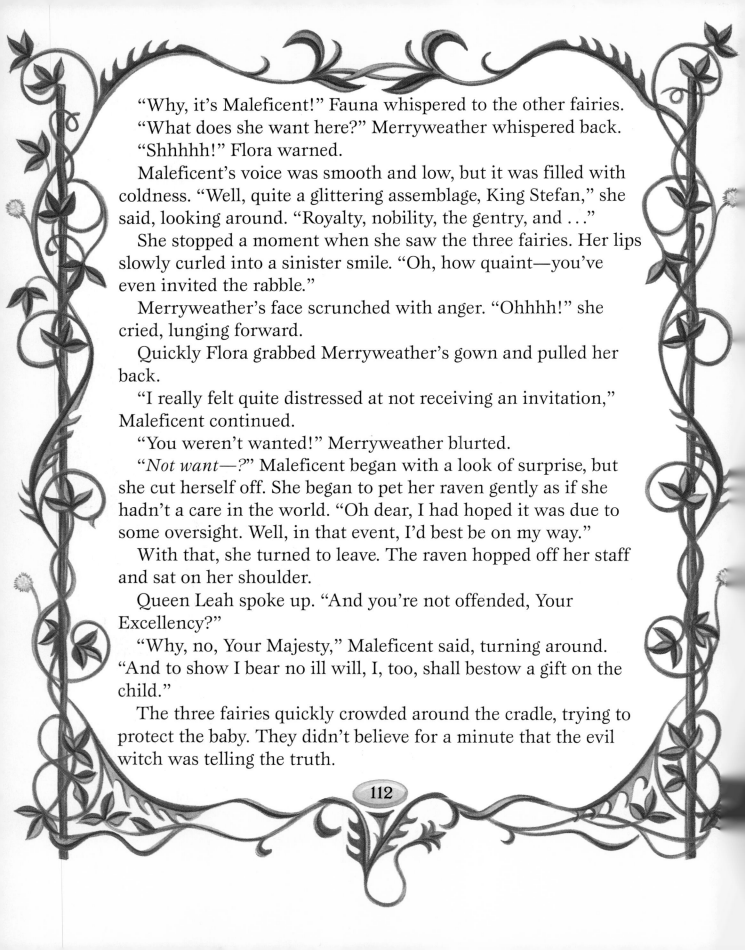

"Why, it's Maleficent!" Fauna whispered to the other fairies. "What does she want here?" Merryweather whispered back. "Shhhhh!" Flora warned.

Maleficent's voice was smooth and low, but it was filled with coldness. "Well, quite a glittering assemblage, King Stefan," she said, looking around. "Royalty, nobility, the gentry, and . . ."

She stopped a moment when she saw the three fairies. Her lips slowly curled into a sinister smile. "Oh, how quaint—you've even invited the rabble."

Merryweather's face scrunched with anger. "Ohhhh!" she cried, lunging forward.

Quickly Flora grabbed Merryweather's gown and pulled her back.

"I really felt quite distressed at not receiving an invitation," Maleficent continued.

"You weren't wanted!" Merryweather blurted.

"*Not want—?*" Maleficent began with a look of surprise, but she cut herself off. She began to pet her raven gently as if she hadn't a care in the world. "Oh dear, I had hoped it was due to some oversight. Well, in that event, I'd best be on my way."

With that, she turned to leave. The raven hopped off her staff and sat on her shoulder.

Queen Leah spoke up. "And you're not offended, Your Excellency?"

"Why, no, Your Majesty," Maleficent said, turning around. "And to show I bear no ill will, I, too, shall bestow a gift on the child."

The three fairies quickly crowded around the cradle, trying to protect the baby. They didn't believe for a minute that the evil witch was telling the truth.

Maleficent's face grew dark with hate. She brought her staff to the ground with a crash. "Listen well, all of you!" she bellowed. "The princess shall indeed grow in grace and beauty, beloved by all who know her. But before the sun sets on her sixteenth birthday, she shall prick her finger on the spindle of a spinning wheel and *die*!"

As she spoke, the small knob on top of her staff pulsed with light. It grew into a crystal ball, aglow with the image of a spinning wheel, its sharp spindle glistening. Bats flew around it, squealing and shrieking.

113

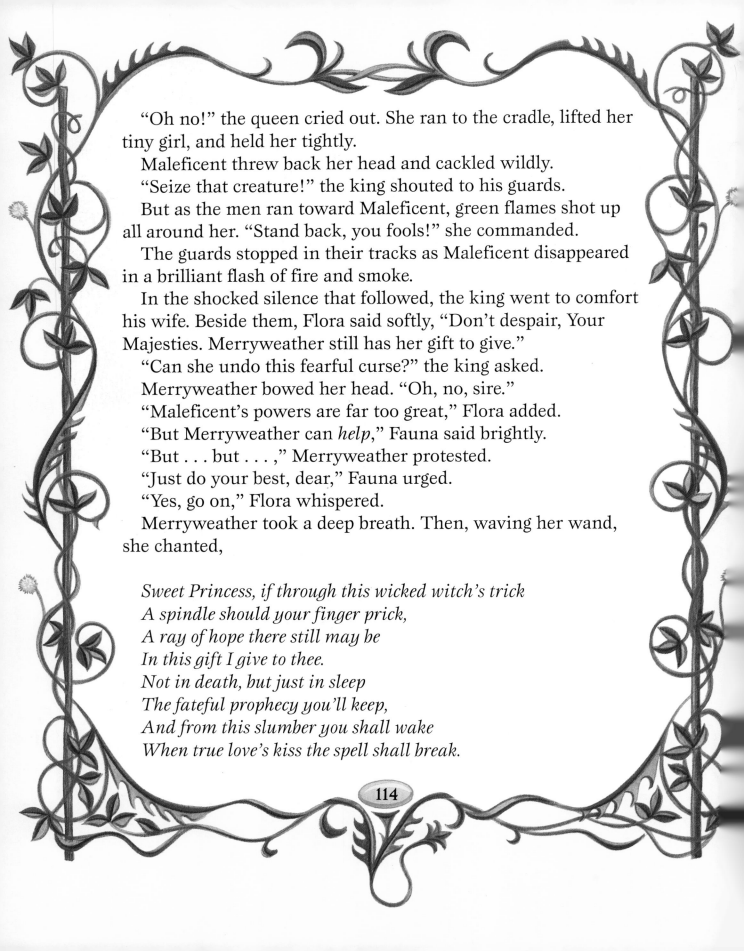

"Oh no!" the queen cried out. She ran to the cradle, lifted her tiny girl, and held her tightly.

Maleficent threw back her head and cackled wildly.

"Seize that creature!" the king shouted to his guards.

But as the men ran toward Maleficent, green flames shot up all around her. "Stand back, you fools!" she commanded.

The guards stopped in their tracks as Maleficent disappeared in a brilliant flash of fire and smoke.

In the shocked silence that followed, the king went to comfort his wife. Beside them, Flora said softly, "Don't despair, Your Majesties. Merryweather still has her gift to give."

"Can she undo this fearful curse?" the king asked.

Merryweather bowed her head. "Oh, no, sire."

"Maleficent's powers are far too great," Flora added.

"But Merryweather can *help*," Fauna said brightly.

"But . . . but . . . ," Merryweather protested.

"Just do your best, dear," Fauna urged.

"Yes, go on," Flora whispered.

Merryweather took a deep breath. Then, waving her wand, she chanted,

Sweet Princess, if through this wicked witch's trick
A spindle should your finger prick,
A ray of hope there still may be
In this gift I give to thee.
Not in death, but just in sleep
The fateful prophecy you'll keep,
And from this slumber you shall wake
When true love's kiss the spell shall break.

114

Would Merryweather's spell truly protect Aurora from death? King Stefan did not want to find out. He immediately gave an order for all the spinning wheels in the kingdom to be burned.

A fire soon blazed in the royal courtyard, fueled by spinning wheels new and old. But the king was still not satisfied. He had seen Maleficent's power. Perhaps she would simply create a spinning wheel by magic.

Something else had to be done to protect Aurora—but what?

CHAPTER TWO

The three fairies pondered this question for hours. They talked and talked, and talked some more. And after every last person had left the throne room, they were still talking.

Finally Flora heaved a great sigh and said, "Ohhhh, silly fiddle-faddle!"

Fauna sat down and waved her wand. Instantly a teapot appeared. Flora and Merryweather flopped down next to her. Halfheartedly they waved their wands and—*pop!* Three teacups were floating in the air.

"Well," Merryweather said between sips, "a bonfire won't stop Maleficent."

"Perhaps we can reason with her," Fauna said. "She can't be *all* bad."

Flora rolled her eyes. "Oh yes she can!"

"Ohhhh!" Merryweather said with frustration. "I'd like to turn her into a fat old hoptoad!"

"Now, dear, that isn't a very nice thing to say," Fauna said. "Besides, our magic can only do good—to bring joy and happiness."

Merryweather made a cookie appear and bit into it. "Well, turning her into a hoptoad would make *me* happy!" she grumbled.

"But there must be some way . . . ," Flora said. Suddenly her face lit up. "There is!"

"What is it, Flora?" Fauna asked.

"Shhh!" Fauna replied. "Even the walls have ears. Follow me!"

Zzzing! With a sweep of her wand, she made herself shrink to the size of a butterfly.

Zzzing! Zzzing! Flora and Merryweather did the same. They flew across the throne room, trailing sparkles like three tiny shooting stars.

On a table near the throne, there was a small decorative box. It was a gift for the baby princess, with a silver cup and spoon inside.

Flora, Fauna, and Merryweather flew inside and closed the box. Now no one would hear them. "I'll turn the princess into a flower!" Flora said, practically bursting with excitement. "A flower can't prick its finger, because it hasn't any! She'll be perfectly safe."

"Until Maleficent sends a frost," Merryweather remarked.

Flora's face sank. "Oh dear, you're right. And she'll be expecting us to do something like that."

"What *won't* she expect?" Merryweather said bitterly. "She knows everything."

"Oh, but she doesn't, dear," Fauna said. "Maleficent doesn't know anything about love or kindness or the joy of helping others."

Flora jumped up. "That's it! It's the only thing she can't understand, and she won't expect it!" She began pacing around, deep in thought. "Now, we'll have to plan. . . . Let's see, the abandoned woodcutter's cottage. . . . Of course, the king and queen will object, but when we explain it's the only way—"

"Explain what?" Merryweather interrupted.

"About the three peasant women raising a foundling child deep in the forest," Flora explained.

"Oh, that's very nice of them," Fauna said.

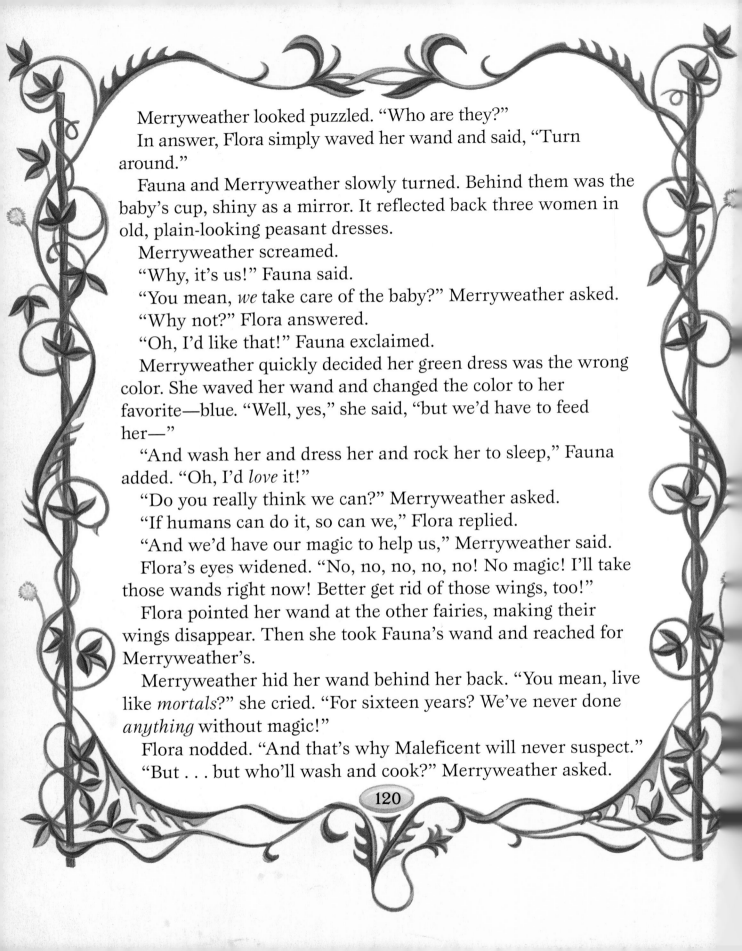

Merryweather looked puzzled. "Who are they?"

In answer, Flora simply waved her wand and said, "Turn around."

Fauna and Merryweather slowly turned. Behind them was the baby's cup, shiny as a mirror. It reflected back three women in old, plain-looking peasant dresses.

Merryweather screamed.

"Why, it's us!" Fauna said.

"You mean, *we* take care of the baby?" Merryweather asked.

"Why not?" Flora answered.

"Oh, I'd like that!" Fauna exclaimed.

Merryweather quickly decided her green dress was the wrong color. She waved her wand and changed the color to her favorite—blue. "Well, yes," she said, "but we'd have to feed her—"

"And wash her and dress her and rock her to sleep," Fauna added. "Oh, I'd *love* it!"

"Do you really think we can?" Merryweather asked.

"If humans can do it, so can we," Flora replied.

"And we'd have our magic to help us," Merryweather said.

Flora's eyes widened. "No, no, no, no, no! No magic! I'll take those wands right now! Better get rid of those wings, too!"

Flora pointed her wand at the other fairies, making their wings disappear. Then she took Fauna's wand and reached for Merryweather's.

Merryweather hid her wand behind her back. "You mean, live like *mortals*?" she cried. "For sixteen years? We've never done *anything* without magic!"

Flora nodded. "And that's why Maleficent will never suspect."

"But . . . but who'll wash and cook?" Merryweather asked.

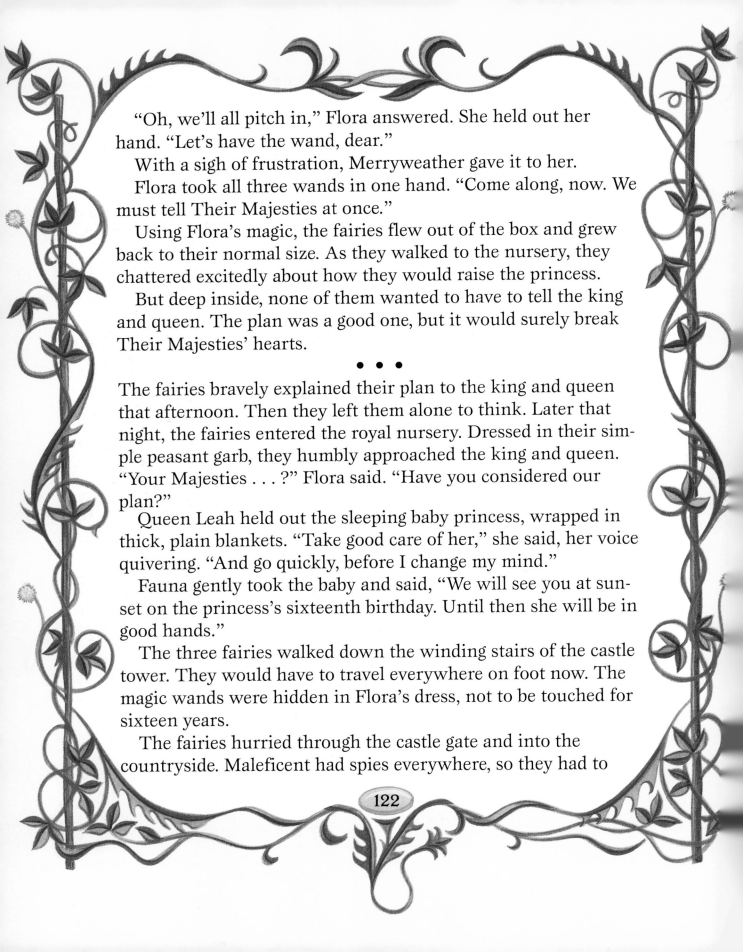

"Oh, we'll all pitch in," Flora answered. She held out her hand. "Let's have the wand, dear."

With a sigh of frustration, Merryweather gave it to her.

Flora took all three wands in one hand. "Come along, now. We must tell Their Majesties at once."

Using Flora's magic, the fairies flew out of the box and grew back to their normal size. As they walked to the nursery, they chattered excitedly about how they would raise the princess.

But deep inside, none of them wanted to have to tell the king and queen. The plan was a good one, but it would surely break Their Majesties' hearts.

• • •

The fairies bravely explained their plan to the king and queen that afternoon. Then they left them alone to think. Later that night, the fairies entered the royal nursery. Dressed in their simple peasant garb, they humbly approached the king and queen. "Your Majesties . . . ?" Flora said. "Have you considered our plan?"

Queen Leah held out the sleeping baby princess, wrapped in thick, plain blankets. "Take good care of her," she said, her voice quivering. "And go quickly, before I change my mind."

Fauna gently took the baby and said, "We will see you at sunset on the princess's sixteenth birthday. Until then she will be in good hands."

The three fairies walked down the winding stairs of the castle tower. They would have to travel everywhere on foot now. The magic wands were hidden in Flora's dress, not to be touched for sixteen years.

The fairies hurried through the castle gate and into the countryside. Maleficent had spies everywhere, so they had to

travel quickly and quietly. Above them, the king and queen watched from a parapet. But the fairies made sure not to look back.

And it was a good thing, too, because the grief on Their Majesties' faces would have been enough to melt a heart of stone.

CHAPTER THREE

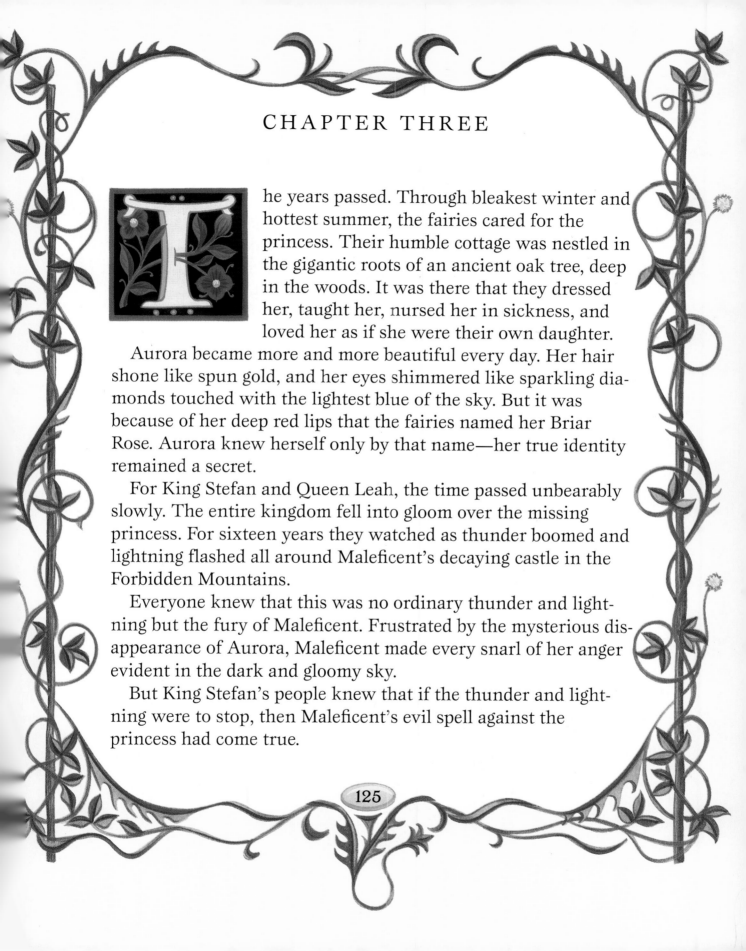

The years passed. Through bleakest winter and hottest summer, the fairies cared for the princess. Their humble cottage was nestled in the gigantic roots of an ancient oak tree, deep in the woods. It was there that they dressed her, taught her, nursed her in sickness, and loved her as if she were their own daughter.

Aurora became more and more beautiful every day. Her hair shone like spun gold, and her eyes shimmered like sparkling diamonds touched with the lightest blue of the sky. But it was because of her deep red lips that the fairies named her Briar Rose. Aurora knew herself only by that name—her true identity remained a secret.

For King Stefan and Queen Leah, the time passed unbearably slowly. The entire kingdom fell into gloom over the missing princess. For sixteen years they watched as thunder boomed and lightning flashed all around Maleficent's decaying castle in the Forbidden Mountains.

Everyone knew that this was no ordinary thunder and lightning but the fury of Maleficent. Frustrated by the mysterious disappearance of Aurora, Maleficent made every snarl of her anger evident in the dark and gloomy sky.

But King Stefan's people knew that if the thunder and lightning were to stop, then Maleficent's evil spell against the princess had come true.

On the eve of the princess's sixteenth birthday, the noisy storm was louder than ever. Finally the mood of the kingdom began to lift. Soon the princess's birthday would pass, and she would be home, safe.

• • •

Soon the princess's sixteenth birthday would pass. It was all Maleficent could think about, too. And it made her blood boil.

Her raven sat on her shoulders as she paced the crumbling floor of her throne room. She scowled angrily at a group of her warriors—all of them hideous, snout-faced monsters with sharp teeth and small brains. "It's incredible," she hissed. "Sixteen years and not a trace of her! Are you sure you searched everywhere?"

The warriors looked at each other dumbly. Finally the leader among them spoke up. "Uh . . . uh . . . yep, we looked everywhere! The town, uh, the mountains . . . uh, uh, the houses, and uh, let me see . . . uh, all the cradles!"

Maleficent stared at him. "Cradles?" she said, her eyes ablaze. "All these years you've been looking for a *baby*?"

She threw her head back and shrieked with laughter. One by one her warriors began to laugh, too.

"Idiots!" Maleficent shrieked. "Imbeciles!"

The warriors fell silent. Maleficent thrust her arm forward. With a deafening *zzzzzapp*, lightning bolts shot out from the tip of her staff.

"*Ooooo! Ooch! Ouch!* " Yelping with pain, the creatures jumped away from the lightning. They fell over each other trying to rush out the door.

Maleficent stormed over to her throne. Its cold stone seat was damp and cracked, its arms curving forward into sharp claws. "They're a disgrace to the forces of evil," she said to her raven.

"You are my last chance."

She lifted the raven in her hand and brought it to an open window. "Circle far and wide," she commanded. "Search for a maid of sixteen with hair of sunshine gold and lips red as the rose. Go, and do not fail me!"

With that, she released her beloved black-feathered pet. There wasn't much time; the girl's sixteenth birthday was the following day. But as Maleficent watched the raven fly into the thick clouds, she felt an evil glimmer of hope.

127

CHAPTER FOUR

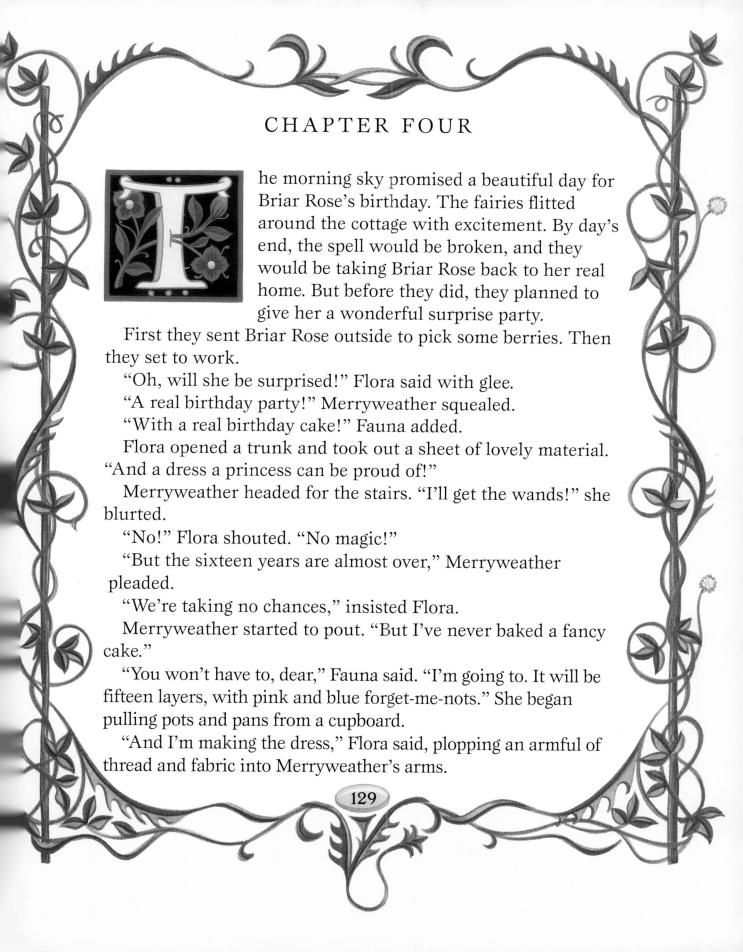

he morning sky promised a beautiful day for Briar Rose's birthday. The fairies flitted around the cottage with excitement. By day's end, the spell would be broken, and they would be taking Briar Rose back to her real home. But before they did, they planned to give her a wonderful surprise party.

First they sent Briar Rose outside to pick some berries. Then they set to work.

"Oh, will she be surprised!" Flora said with glee.

"A real birthday party!" Merryweather squealed.

"With a real birthday cake!" Fauna added.

Flora opened a trunk and took out a sheet of lovely material. "And a dress a princess can be proud of!"

Merryweather headed for the stairs. "I'll get the wands!" she blurted.

"No!" Flora shouted. "No magic!"

"But the sixteen years are almost over," Merryweather pleaded.

"We're taking no chances," insisted Flora.

Merryweather started to pout. "But I've never baked a fancy cake."

"You won't have to, dear," Fauna said. "I'm going to. It will be fifteen layers, with pink and blue forget-me-nots." She began pulling pots and pans from a cupboard.

"And I'm making the dress," Flora said, plopping an armful of thread and fabric into Merryweather's arms.

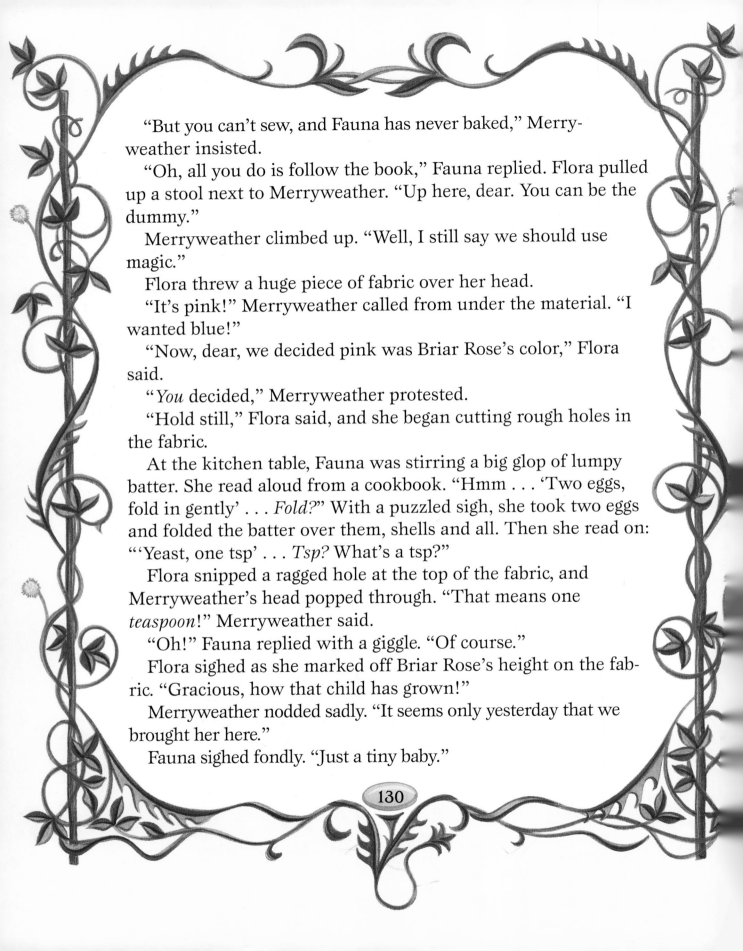

"But you can't sew, and Fauna has never baked," Merryweather insisted.

"Oh, all you do is follow the book," Fauna replied. Flora pulled up a stool next to Merryweather. "Up here, dear. You can be the dummy."

Merryweather climbed up. "Well, I still say we should use magic."

Flora threw a huge piece of fabric over her head.

"It's pink!" Merryweather called from under the material. "I wanted blue!"

"Now, dear, we decided pink was Briar Rose's color," Flora said.

"*You* decided," Merryweather protested.

"Hold still," Flora said, and she began cutting rough holes in the fabric.

At the kitchen table, Fauna was stirring a big glop of lumpy batter. She read aloud from a cookbook. "Hmm . . . 'Two eggs, fold in gently' . . . *Fold?*" With a puzzled sigh, she took two eggs and folded the batter over them, shells and all. Then she read on: "'Yeast, one tsp' . . . *Tsp?* What's a tsp?"

Flora snipped a ragged hole at the top of the fabric, and Merryweather's head popped through. "That means one *teaspoon*!" Merryweather said.

"Oh!" Fauna replied with a giggle. "Of course."

Flora sighed as she marked off Briar Rose's height on the fabric. "Gracious, how that child has grown!"

Merryweather nodded sadly. "It seems only yesterday that we brought her here."

Fauna sighed fondly. "Just a tiny baby."

"After today she'll be a princess," Merryweather sniffled, "and we won't have any Briar Rose."

Fauna's happy expression melted. "Oh, Flora!" she cried.

Flora fought back tears. "Now, now, now, we . . . we . . . we all knew this day had to come. . . ."

"But why did it have to come so soon?" Fauna asked tearfully.

Now all three of them were on the verge of weeping. Finally Flora cleared her throat and said, "Ah, good gracious, we're acting like ninnies! Come on, she'll be back before we get started!" Quietly the three fairies went back to work.

Not far away, Briar Rose stepped lightly through the woods, an empty wicker basket on her arm bouncing along with each step. The sunlight gently warmed her face, and the smell of spring blossoms was tart and sweet. Through the trees came the happy twittering and piping of birds. Spinning around, Briar Rose began to sing along in a high, clear voice.

In every burrow and every hollow log, the animals of the forest listened. So lovely was Briar Rose's voice that even the birds stopped to hear her. Before long she had her own private audience: a squirrel, a bluebird, a cardinal, two rabbits, even an old owl.

Clear across the forest, someone else was enchanted by her voice, too—someone kind and handsome—a young man dressed in the finest silk clothing. As he dashed along on his great white horse, Briar Rose's song reached his ears.

"Whoa, Samson!" he called to his horse. "Do you hear that? How beautiful! What is it? Let's find out."

But Samson had a mind of his own. He wouldn't budge.

"Aw, come on," the young man said with a smile. "For an extra bucket of oats and a few carrots?"

Samson took off like a shot. The young man whooped with joy as Samson leapt high over one log, then another, then . . .

BONK!

Samson stopped short. Above him was a large tree branch— and there was no one in the saddle anymore. He turned around to look for his master.

The young man was sitting in a pond, looking like an over-grown frog. Samson hung his head in embarrassment.

With a shake of his soggy head, the young man said simply, "No carrots!"

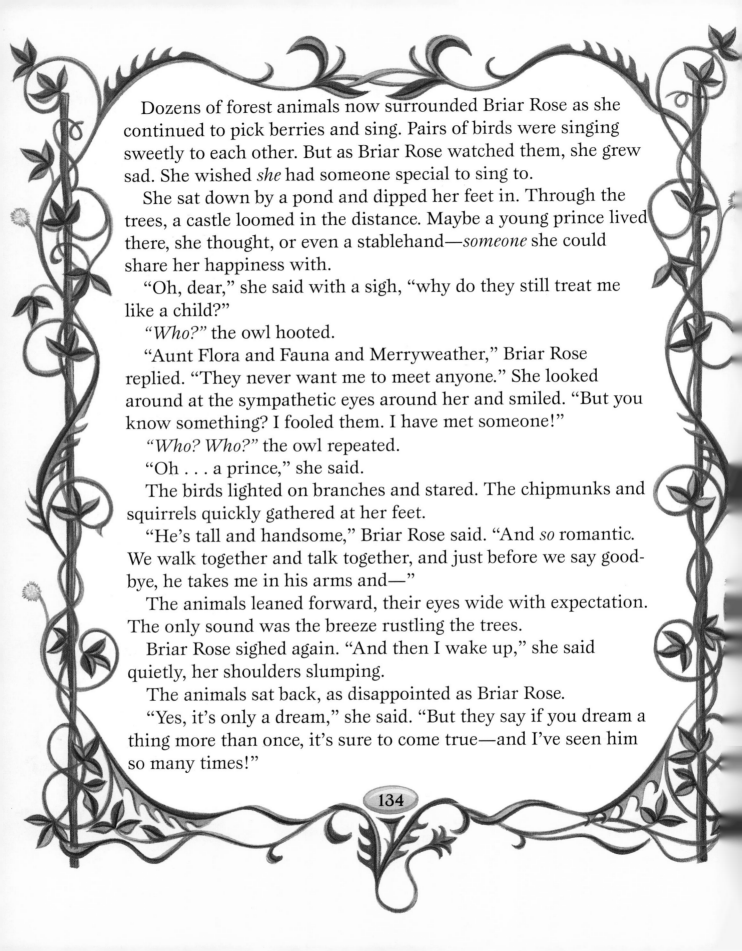

Dozens of forest animals now surrounded Briar Rose as she continued to pick berries and sing. Pairs of birds were singing sweetly to each other. But as Briar Rose watched them, she grew sad. She wished *she* had someone special to sing to.

She sat down by a pond and dipped her feet in. Through the trees, a castle loomed in the distance. Maybe a young prince lived there, she thought, or even a stablehand—*someone* she could share her happiness with.

"Oh, dear," she said with a sigh, "why do they still treat me like a child?"

"*Who?*" the owl hooted.

"Aunt Flora and Fauna and Merryweather," Briar Rose replied. "They never want me to meet anyone." She looked around at the sympathetic eyes around her and smiled. "But you know something? I fooled them. I have met someone!"

"*Who? Who?*" the owl repeated.

"Oh . . . a prince," she said.

The birds lighted on branches and stared. The chipmunks and squirrels quickly gathered at her feet.

"He's tall and handsome," Briar Rose said. "And *so* romantic. We walk together and talk together, and just before we say good-bye, he takes me in his arms and—"

The animals leaned forward, their eyes wide with expectation. The only sound was the breeze rustling the trees.

Briar Rose sighed again. "And then I wake up," she said quietly, her shoulders slumping.

The animals sat back, as disappointed as Briar Rose.

"Yes, it's only a dream," she said. "But they say if you dream a thing more than once, it's sure to come true—and I've seen him so many times!"

Briar Rose was so lost in her thoughts that she didn't notice a squirrel scurry along a tree branch and then return a few minutes later.

One by one the little squirrel got the attention of the cardinal, the bluebird, the two rabbits, and the owl. Quietly they slipped away to another part of the woods.

There they found another small pond and a young man drying his clothes on a branch.

"You know, Samson," the young man said, "that voice was too beautiful to be real. Maybe it was a mysterious being. . . ."

He had his back to the animals. His cap and cape were on the branch, his two boots on the ground. Quickly the squirrel ducked under the cap and carried it away. The birds and the owl flew off with the cape, and each rabbit hopped away with one boot.

Behind them, they could hear the man shouting, "Hey! Stop!"

They raced through the woods, and as they got closer to Briar Rose, they arranged themselves in a special way. The owl wore the cape, the ends of which were carried by the two birds. On the owl's head was the cap, with the squirrel squinched inside it, its tail sticking out the back like a brown plume. Then the birds, the owl, and the squirrel positioned themselves right over the rabbits in the boots.

Together the animals had created the form of a tall man—more or less.

When Briar Rose saw them, she laughed, "Why, it's my dream prince!" Then she said with playful shyness, "You know, I'm really not supposed to speak to strangers, but we've met before . . . once upon a dream!"

The birds carried the cape closer to Briar Rose. She curtsied and said, "Your Highness, I'd be delighted!" She held out her arms and began to dance. The rabbits hopped along nimbly in the boots.

They glided over the mossy ground and over soft beds of pine needles. Briar Rose threw her head back and imagined that the floating clothes had a real person inside. A real, handsome prince who would take her to live in a glorious castle—just like in her dream.

For a few moments she closed her eyes. And when she opened them, she was looking at the face of her dream prince. Yes, he had that loving smile that warmed her from head to toe. Even the strong, gentle grip of his hands was the same—

Suddenly she froze. The grip was warm and firm. The face was real. *He* was real. He was dressed like a prince, but with no cap, cape, or boots.

And he was the very first person Briar Rose had ever seen besides her aunts.

"Oh!" she cried out, backing away.

"I'm awfully sorry," the young man said. "I didn't mean to frighten you."

"It wasn't that," she replied. "It's just that you're a . . . a . . . stranger."

The young man smiled. "But don't you remember? We've met before."

"We . . . we have?"

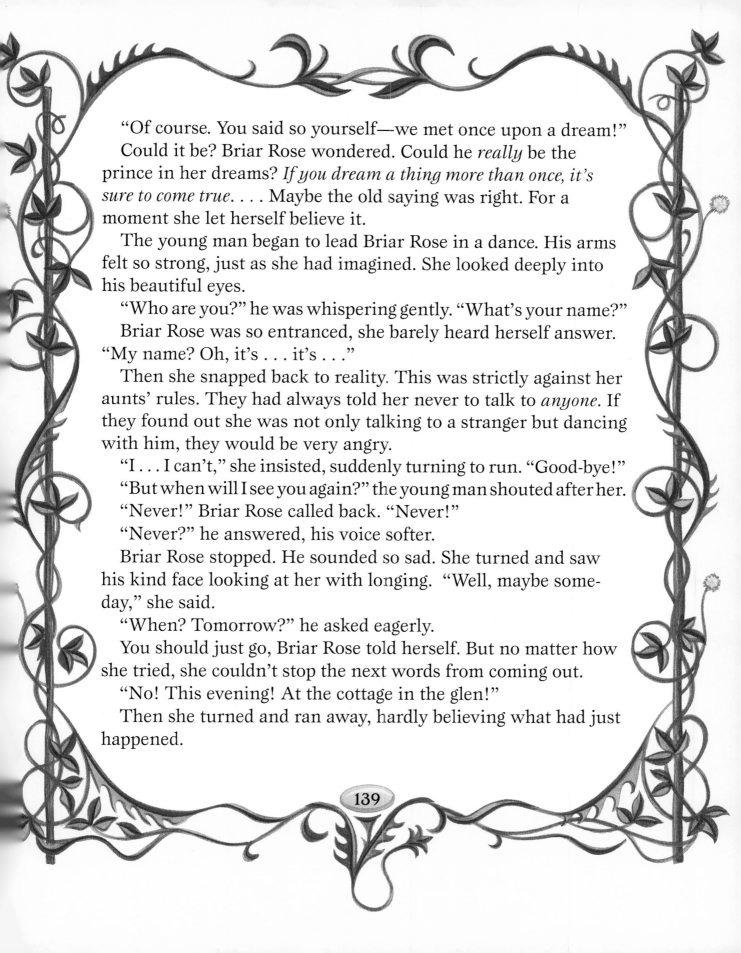

"Of course. You said so yourself—we met once upon a dream!"

Could it be? Briar Rose wondered. Could he *really* be the prince in her dreams? *If you dream a thing more than once, it's sure to come true. . . .* Maybe the old saying was right. For a moment she let herself believe it.

The young man began to lead Briar Rose in a dance. His arms felt so strong, just as she had imagined. She looked deeply into his beautiful eyes.

"Who are you?" he was whispering gently. "What's your name?"

Briar Rose was so entranced, she barely heard herself answer. "My name? Oh, it's . . . it's . . ."

Then she snapped back to reality. This was strictly against her aunts' rules. They had always told her never to talk to *anyone*. If they found out she was not only talking to a stranger but dancing with him, they would be very angry.

"I . . . I can't," she insisted, suddenly turning to run. "Good-bye!"

"But when will I see you again?" the young man shouted after her.

"Never!" Briar Rose called back. "Never!"

"Never?" he answered, his voice softer.

Briar Rose stopped. He sounded so sad. She turned and saw his kind face looking at her with longing. "Well, maybe someday," she said.

"When? Tomorrow?" he asked eagerly.

You should just go, Briar Rose told herself. But no matter how she tried, she couldn't stop the next words from coming out.

"No! This evening! At the cottage in the glen!"

Then she turned and ran away, hardly believing what had just happened.

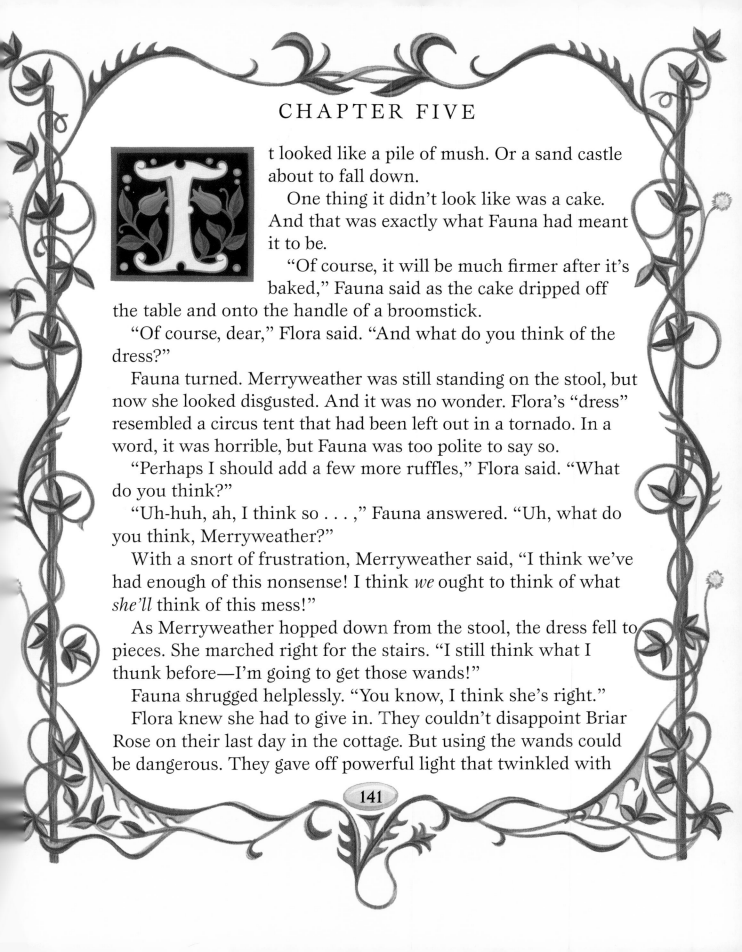

t looked like a pile of mush. Or a sand castle about to fall down.

One thing it didn't look like was a cake. And that was exactly what Fauna had meant it to be.

"Of course, it will be much firmer after it's baked," Fauna said as the cake dripped off the table and onto the handle of a broomstick.

"Of course, dear," Flora said. "And what do you think of the dress?"

Fauna turned. Merryweather was still standing on the stool, but now she looked disgusted. And it was no wonder. Flora's "dress" resembled a circus tent that had been left out in a tornado. In a word, it was horrible, but Fauna was too polite to say so.

"Perhaps I should add a few more ruffles," Flora said. "What do you think?"

"Uh-huh, ah, I think so . . . ," Fauna answered. "Uh, what do you think, Merryweather?"

With a snort of frustration, Merryweather said, "I think we've had enough of this nonsense! I think *we* ought to think of what *she'll* think of this mess!"

As Merryweather hopped down from the stool, the dress fell to pieces. She marched right for the stairs. "I still think what I thunk before—I'm going to get those wands!"

Fauna shrugged helplessly. "You know, I think she's right."

Flora knew she had to give in. They couldn't disappoint Briar Rose on their last day in the cottage. But using the wands could be dangerous. They gave off powerful light that twinkled with

magic dust. If any of that light were to escape the cottage, maybe, just maybe, someone outside would spot it. Surely Maleficent's spies were still searching for the princess.

"All right," Flora said. "But we can't take any chances. Lock the doors! Close the windows! Plug up every cranny!"

Merryweather ran back downstairs with the wands. In a flurry the fairies raced around, following Flora's instructions. They made sure even the tiniest knothole in the cottage wall was plugged with a rag.

Then they each took hold of the tiny magic sticks that were once so familiar to them. With a grand wave, they really began to prepare for the party.

Zzzing! Merryweather made the bucket, mop, and broom burst to life. They bustled about, cleaning the cottage.

Zzzing! Fauna created a magnificent cake out of the ingredients on the table.

Zzzing! Flora made the material come together to form a stunning pink gown.

Merryweather took one look at the gown and cried out, "Oh no, not pink! Make it blue!" With a wave of her wand, the gown's color instantly changed to blue.

"Merryweather!" Flora scolded. "Make it pink!" *Zzzing!* She waved her wand and changed it back to pink.

Zzzing! Merryweather made it blue again.

Zzzing! Flora made it pink.

Zzzing! Blue!

Zzzing! Pink!

Blue and pink magic dust shot through the cottage, bouncing

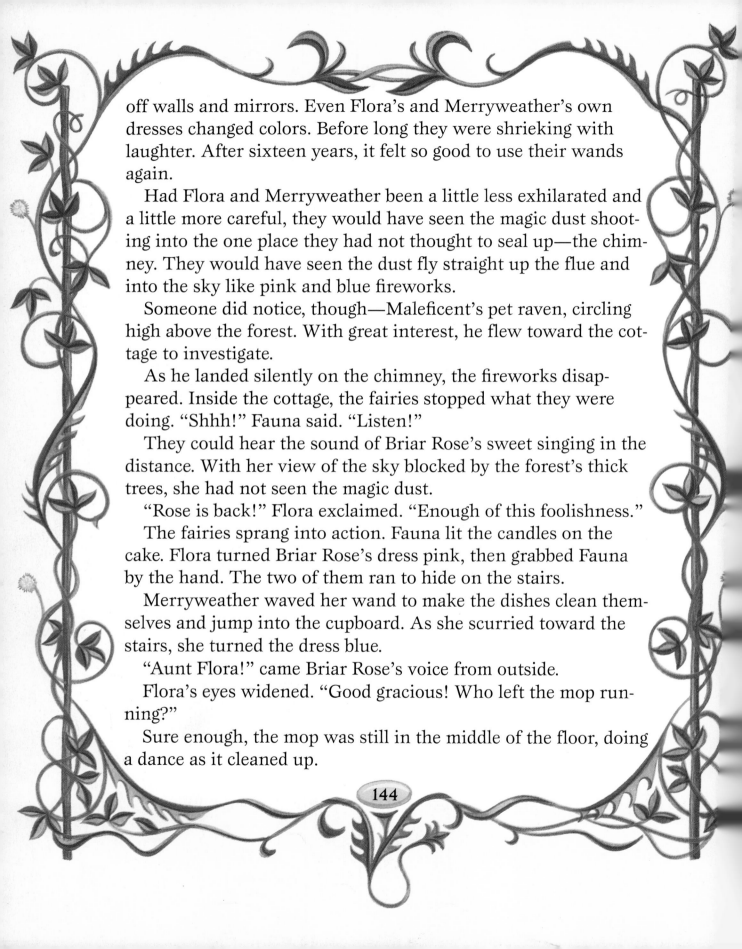

off walls and mirrors. Even Flora's and Merryweather's own dresses changed colors. Before long they were shrieking with laughter. After sixteen years, it felt so good to use their wands again.

Had Flora and Merryweather been a little less exhilarated and a little more careful, they would have seen the magic dust shooting into the one place they had not thought to seal up—the chimney. They would have seen the dust fly straight up the flue and into the sky like pink and blue fireworks.

Someone did notice, though—Maleficent's pet raven, circling high above the forest. With great interest, he flew toward the cottage to investigate.

As he landed silently on the chimney, the fireworks disappeared. Inside the cottage, the fairies stopped what they were doing. "Shhh!" Fauna said. "Listen!"

They could hear the sound of Briar Rose's sweet singing in the distance. With her view of the sky blocked by the forest's thick trees, she had not seen the magic dust.

"Rose is back!" Flora exclaimed. "Enough of this foolishness."

The fairies sprang into action. Fauna lit the candles on the cake. Flora turned Briar Rose's dress pink, then grabbed Fauna by the hand. The two of them ran to hide on the stairs.

Merryweather waved her wand to make the dishes clean themselves and jump into the cupboard. As she scurried toward the stairs, she turned the dress blue.

"Aunt Flora!" came Briar Rose's voice from outside.

Flora's eyes widened. "Good gracious! Who left the mop running?"

Sure enough, the mop was still in the middle of the floor, doing a dance as it cleaned up.

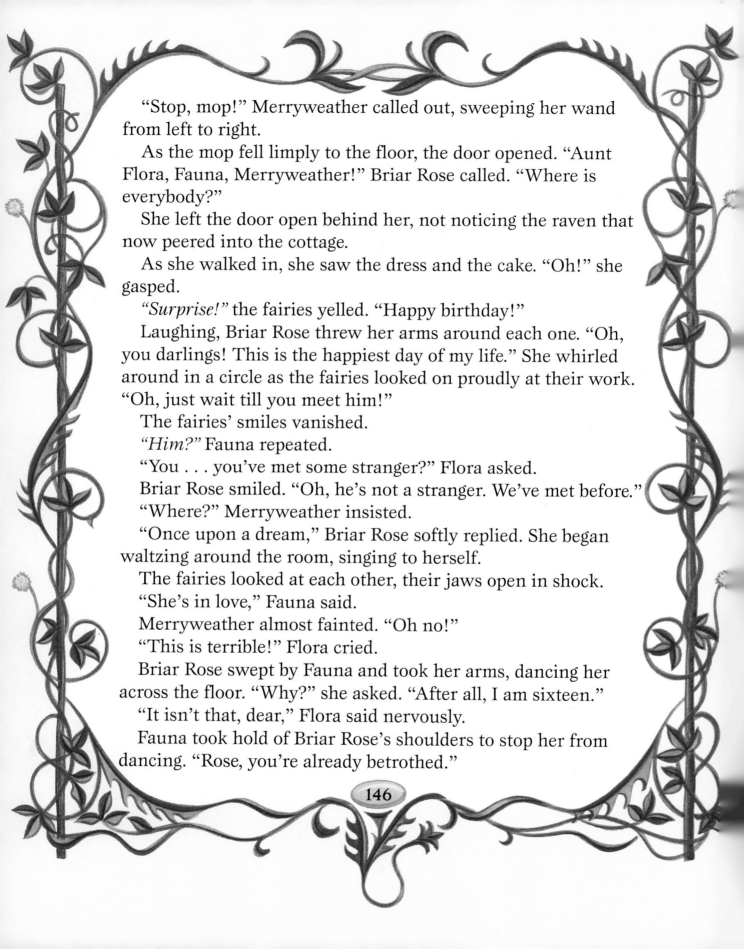

"Stop, mop!" Merryweather called out, sweeping her wand from left to right.

As the mop fell limply to the floor, the door opened. "Aunt Flora, Fauna, Merryweather!" Briar Rose called. "Where is everybody?"

She left the door open behind her, not noticing the raven that now peered into the cottage.

As she walked in, she saw the dress and the cake. "Oh!" she gasped.

"*Surprise!*" the fairies yelled. "Happy birthday!"

Laughing, Briar Rose threw her arms around each one. "Oh, you darlings! This is the happiest day of my life." She whirled around in a circle as the fairies looked on proudly at their work. "Oh, just wait till you meet him!"

The fairies' smiles vanished.

"*Him?*" Fauna repeated.

"You . . . you've met some stranger?" Flora asked.

Briar Rose smiled. "Oh, he's not a stranger. We've met before."

"Where?" Merryweather insisted.

"Once upon a dream," Briar Rose softly replied. She began waltzing around the room, singing to herself.

The fairies looked at each other, their jaws open in shock.

"She's in love," Fauna said.

Merryweather almost fainted. "Oh no!"

"This is terrible!" Flora cried.

Briar Rose swept by Fauna and took her arms, dancing her across the floor. "Why?" she asked. "After all, I am sixteen."

"It isn't that, dear," Flora said nervously.

Fauna took hold of Briar Rose's shoulders to stop her from dancing. "Rose, you're already betrothed."

Briar Rose looked blankly at her. "Betrothed? You mean . . . engaged?"

"Since the day you were born," Merryweather said.

"To Prince Phillip, dear," Fauna added.

"But that's impossible," Briar Rose said. "How could I marry a prince? I'd have to be . . ."

Her voice trailed off. She realized there was a reason she'd been here all these years, a reason why she wasn't supposed to see anyone else.

Merryweather finished her sentence. "A princess," she said, curtsying deeply.

"And you *are* a princess, dear," Fauna said.

Carefully, clearly, Flora told the secret they'd been keeping all

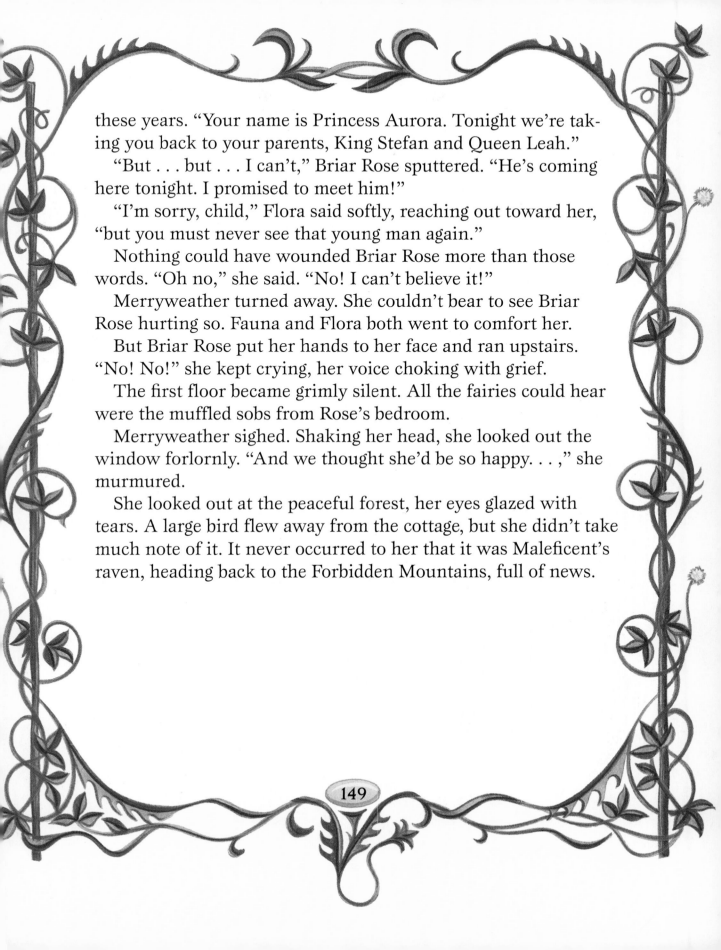

these years. "Your name is Princess Aurora. Tonight we're taking you back to your parents, King Stefan and Queen Leah."

"But . . . but . . . I can't," Briar Rose sputtered. "He's coming here tonight. I promised to meet him!"

"I'm sorry, child," Flora said softly, reaching out toward her, "but you must never see that young man again."

Nothing could have wounded Briar Rose more than those words. "Oh no," she said. "No! I can't believe it!"

Merryweather turned away. She couldn't bear to see Briar Rose hurting so. Fauna and Flora both went to comfort her.

But Briar Rose put her hands to her face and ran upstairs. "No! No!" she kept crying, her voice choking with grief.

The first floor became grimly silent. All the fairies could hear were the muffled sobs from Rose's bedroom.

Merryweather sighed. Shaking her head, she looked out the window forlornly. "And we thought she'd be so happy. . . ," she murmured.

She looked out at the peaceful forest, her eyes glazed with tears. A large bird flew away from the cottage, but she didn't take much note of it. It never occurred to her that it was Maleficent's raven, heading back to the Forbidden Mountains, full of news.

CHAPTER SIX

ing Hubert gobbled down another piece of cake. Laid out before him was a feast fit for a king—two kings, to be exact. The royal table was overflowing, in celebration of Princess Aurora's return. But for all King Hubert's appetite, King Stefan had not eaten a thing.

He paced the floor anxiously, looking out the window for the hundredth time.

Outside, it was gloomier than ever. Maleficent's thunder practically shook the ground, which was a good sign. It was getting late, and soon Aurora's birthday would be over.

"No sign of her yet, Hubert," King Stefan said.

" 'Course not," King Hubert said in midchew. "There's a good half hour till sunset. Come, man, buck up! The battle's over. The girl's as good as here!"

King Stefan exhaled deeply. "I'm sorry, Hubert, but after sixteen years of worrying, never knowing . . . "

"All in the past!" King Hubert reassured him. Grabbing a bottle of wine, he poured two glasses. "Tonight we toast the future!"

They raised their glasses and clinked them together. "To the future, Hubert," King Stefan said, a smile growing across his face. "To the marriage of our children and the uniting of our kingdoms!"

"And to the new home, eh?" King Hubert said.

"New home?" King Stefan asked.

King Hubert snapped his fingers, and an attendant quickly ran over with a thick roll of parchment. As King Hubert unfurled

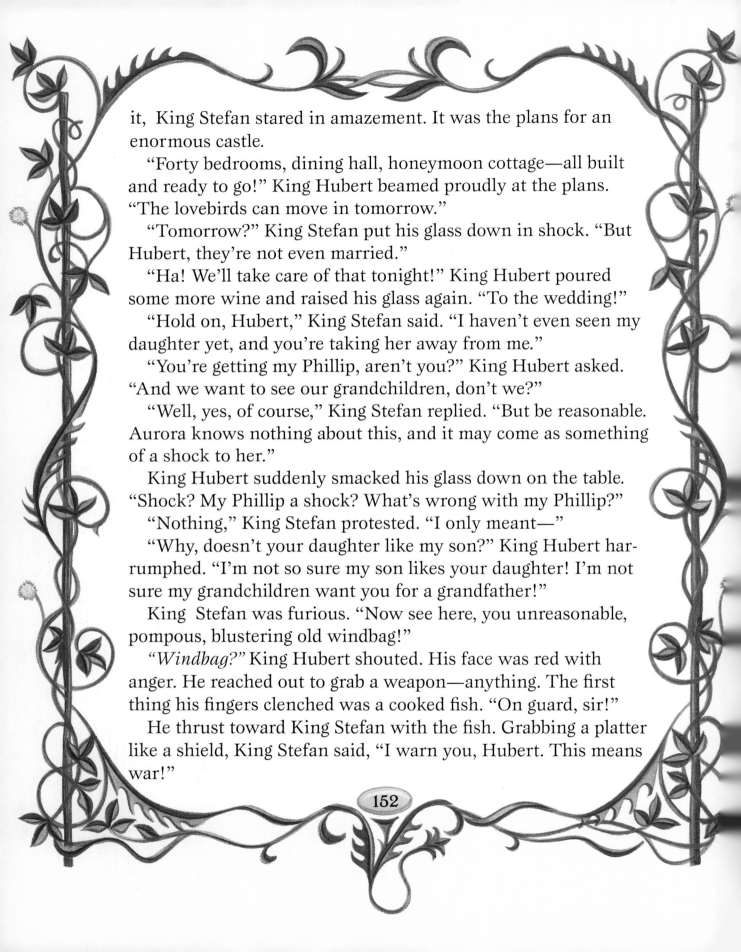

it, King Stefan stared in amazement. It was the plans for an enormous castle.

"Forty bedrooms, dining hall, honeymoon cottage—all built and ready to go!" King Hubert beamed proudly at the plans. "The lovebirds can move in tomorrow."

"Tomorrow?" King Stefan put his glass down in shock. "But Hubert, they're not even married."

"Ha! We'll take care of that tonight!" King Hubert poured some more wine and raised his glass again. "To the wedding!"

"Hold on, Hubert," King Stefan said. "I haven't even seen my daughter yet, and you're taking her away from me."

"You're getting my Phillip, aren't you?" King Hubert asked. "And we want to see our grandchildren, don't we?"

"Well, yes, of course," King Stefan replied. "But be reasonable. Aurora knows nothing about this, and it may come as something of a shock to her."

King Hubert suddenly smacked his glass down on the table. "Shock? My Phillip a shock? What's wrong with my Phillip?"

"Nothing," King Stefan protested. "I only meant—"

"Why, doesn't your daughter like my son?" King Hubert harrumphed. "I'm not so sure my son likes your daughter! I'm not sure my grandchildren want you for a grandfather!"

King Stefan was furious. "Now see here, you unreasonable, pompous, blustering old windbag!"

"*Windbag?*" King Hubert shouted. His face was red with anger. He reached out to grab a weapon—anything. The first thing his fingers clenched was a cooked fish. "On guard, sir!"

He thrust toward King Stefan with the fish. Grabbing a platter like a shield, King Stefan said, "I warn you, Hubert. This means war!"

"Forward!" King Hubert screamed. He raised the fish high and brought it down over King Stefan's head. "For honor, for country, for . . . "

Splaaaaatt! The fish squashed against King Stefan's platter.

The two kings stopped. They both looked at the limp fish in King Hubert's hand. King Stefan tried as hard as he could to hold back a laugh.

But it was too late. King Hubert exploded with a "Haaah!" and in an instant both kings were shaking with laughter.

"What's this all about, anyway?" King Hubert said. "Our children are bound to fall in love with each other, eh?"

"Precisely!" King Stefan agreed.

As they picked up their glasses again for another toast, a herald's voice sounded from the courtyard. "His Royal Highness, Prince Phillip!" he cried.

"Excuse me, Stefan," King Hubert said. He bolted out of the dining room and ran into the courtyard.

There atop a great white horse was a handsome young man in damp clothes. Villagers and servants looked at him in admiration, and many a young woman tried to catch his attention. But Prince Phillip had only one person in mind—the lovely girl who had danced with him in the forest. The girl whose name he did not even know.

"Steady, Samson," he said as he dismounted.

"Phillip!" King Hubert shouted as he approached his son. "Hurry, boy! Change into something suitable. Can't meet your bride looking like that!"

"But I have met her, Father!" Prince Phillip said with a huge grin.

"You . . . you have? Where?" King Hubert asked.

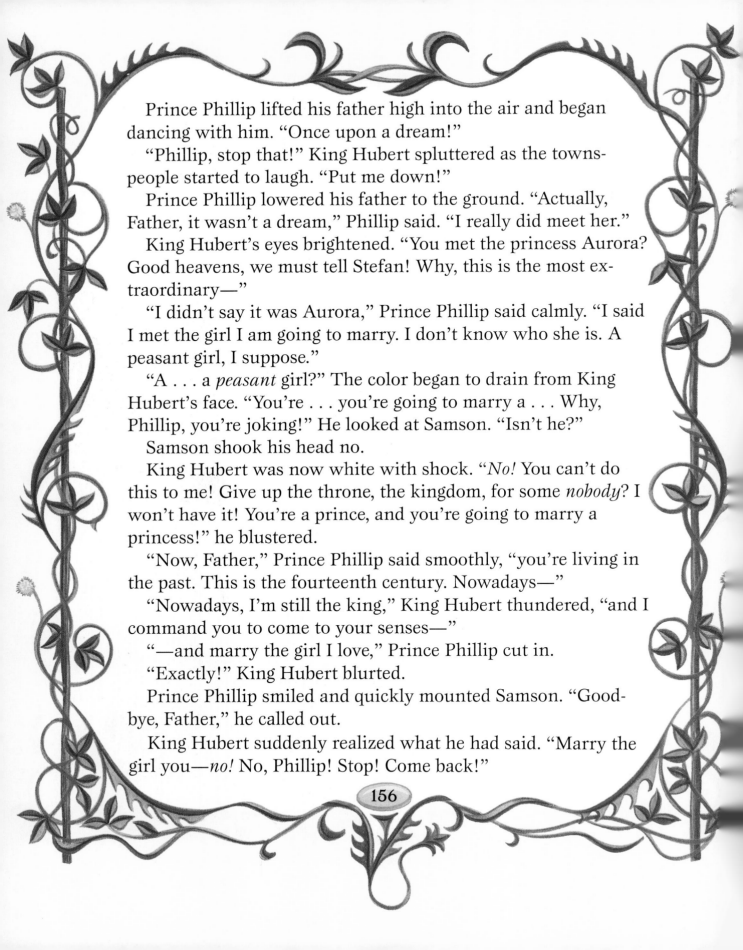

Prince Phillip lifted his father high into the air and began dancing with him. "Once upon a dream!"

"Phillip, stop that!" King Hubert spluttered as the towns-people started to laugh. "Put me down!"

Prince Phillip lowered his father to the ground. "Actually, Father, it wasn't a dream," Phillip said. "I really did meet her."

King Hubert's eyes brightened. "You met the princess Aurora? Good heavens, we must tell Stefan! Why, this is the most ex-traordinary—"

"I didn't say it was Aurora," Prince Phillip said calmly. "I said I met the girl I am going to marry. I don't know who she is. A peasant girl, I suppose."

"A . . . a *peasant* girl?" The color began to drain from King Hubert's face. "You're . . . you're going to marry a . . . Why, Phillip, you're joking!" He looked at Samson. "Isn't he?"

Samson shook his head no.

King Hubert was now white with shock. "*No!* You can't do this to me! Give up the throne, the kingdom, for some *nobody*? I won't have it! You're a prince, and you're going to marry a princess!" he blustered.

"Now, Father," Prince Phillip said smoothly, "you're living in the past. This is the fourteenth century. Nowadays—"

"Nowadays, I'm still the king," King Hubert thundered, "and I command you to come to your senses—"

"—and marry the girl I love," Prince Phillip cut in.

"Exactly!" King Hubert blurted.

Prince Phillip smiled and quickly mounted Samson. "Good-bye, Father," he called out.

King Hubert suddenly realized what he had said. "Marry the girl you—*no!* No, Phillip! Stop! Come back!"

But Prince Phillip was already on his way. He wasn't going to have his marriage arranged for him. Sixteen years ago, Princess Aurora had been a little baby. He had no idea what she was like now, but he knew she couldn't be lovelier and sweeter than the girl he'd met today.

This evening, at the cottage in the glen was what the girl had said. And Phillip intended to be there.

CHAPTER SEVEN

urora shivered as she crossed the bridge to the castle. The hood she was wearing didn't seem to keep out the chilly air. Around her, the three fairies walked on tiptoes. They wanted no one to see or hear them.

Princess Aurora. She repeated her new name in her mind, but it was hard to think of herself as anything but Briar Rose. How different everything would be now.

As they approached the castle, Briar Rose was astounded by its grandeur. It was breathtaking. It rose up against the light of the low orange sun and seemed to touch the clouds. After so many years in the modest little cottage, Aurora could scarcely believe that this was her real home.

But still, she couldn't help thinking about the young man she'd left in the forest. Right about now, he'd be arriving at the cottage to meet her. She imagined the look on his face when he found her gone. Would he be hurt? Angry?

It didn't matter, she told herself. She would never see him again. She was engaged to be married to someone she knew nothing about.

They crossed the empty courtyard and came to a heavy wooden door at the base of the castle. Flora pulled it open and waved the others inside. "Come along now," she urged.

They walked up a winding set of stairs that took them to a small, dark room. "Bolt the door, Merryweather," Flora whispered. "Fauna, pull the drapes."

As the two fairies scurried about, Flora gently led Aurora to a seat before a large mirror. Waving her magic wand, she chanted,

This one last gift, dear child, for thee,
The symbol of thy royalty:
A crown to wear in grace and beauty,
As is thy right and royal duty!

160

In a whirl of magic sparkles, a gold crown appeared on Aurora's head. It was light and delicate, yet it glittered with many fine jewels. The fairies sighed happily as Aurora turned to face the mirror.

The girl in the reflection was a stranger to Aurora—she was a princess now, not Briar Rose. She knew she should feel thrilled. From now on, life would be full of fine clothes and wonderful feasts. But what good was all of that if she couldn't share it with her true love?

A tear formed in the corner of Aurora's eye. She saw it in the mirror, and suddenly she couldn't hold her sadness in any longer. With an anguished sob, she buried her face in her arms and wept.

"Come," Flora said sadly to the other fairies. "Let her have a few moments alone."

Quietly they left the room. "It's that boy she met," Merryweather whispered.

"Whatever are we going to do?" Fauna asked.

They sat on a bench against the wall outside Aurora's room. "Oh, I don't see why she has to marry any old prince," Merryweather said.

"Now, that's not for us to decide," Fauna replied.

As the three fairies talked outside, the fireplace inside Aurora's room suddenly grew dark. Aurora lifted her head and saw a small green ball of glowing light where the fire had been. The moment she looked at it, she couldn't take her eyes away.

The light glowed brighter in the fireplace. Aurora rose from her seat as if pulled by an invisible force. Sorrow and grief left her face. Her expression became blank. Slowly, mechanically, she walked into the fireplace.

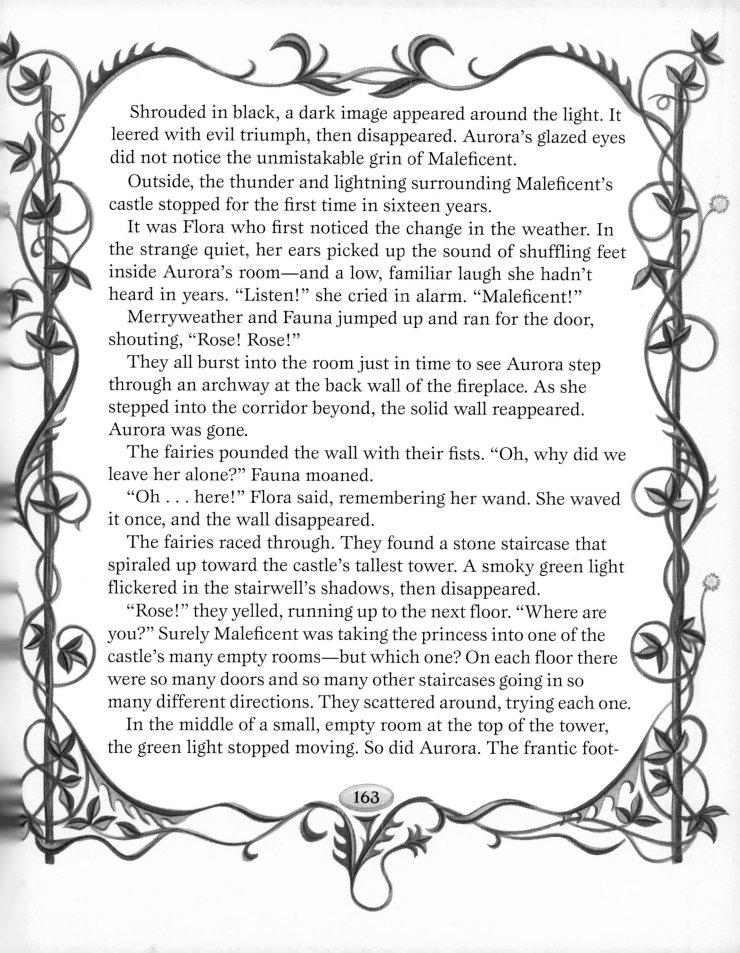

Shrouded in black, a dark image appeared around the light. It leered with evil triumph, then disappeared. Aurora's glazed eyes did not notice the unmistakable grin of Maleficent.

Outside, the thunder and lightning surrounding Maleficent's castle stopped for the first time in sixteen years.

It was Flora who first noticed the change in the weather. In the strange quiet, her ears picked up the sound of shuffling feet inside Aurora's room—and a low, familiar laugh she hadn't heard in years. "Listen!" she cried in alarm. "Maleficent!"

Merryweather and Fauna jumped up and ran for the door, shouting, "Rose! Rose!"

They all burst into the room just in time to see Aurora step through an archway at the back wall of the fireplace. As she stepped into the corridor beyond, the solid wall reappeared. Aurora was gone.

The fairies pounded the wall with their fists. "Oh, why did we leave her alone?" Fauna moaned.

"Oh . . . here!" Flora said, remembering her wand. She waved it once, and the wall disappeared.

The fairies raced through. They found a stone staircase that spiraled up toward the castle's tallest tower. A smoky green light flickered in the stairwell's shadows, then disappeared.

"Rose!" they yelled, running up to the next floor. "Where are you?" Surely Maleficent was taking the princess into one of the castle's many empty rooms—but which one? On each floor there were so many doors and so many other staircases going in so many different directions. They scattered around, trying each one.

In the middle of a small, empty room at the top of the tower, the green light stopped moving. So did Aurora. The frantic foot-

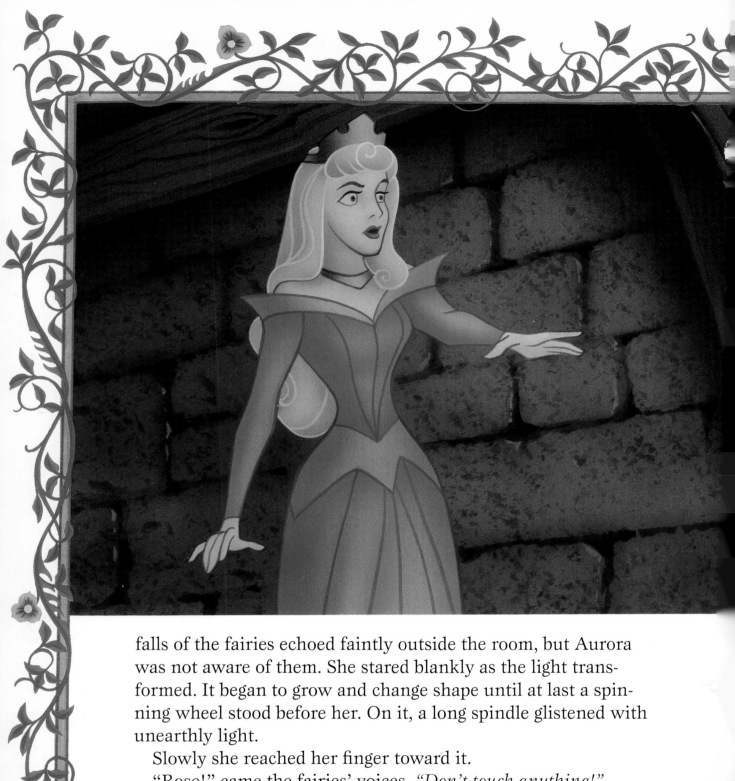

falls of the fairies echoed faintly outside the room, but Aurora was not aware of them. She stared blankly as the light transformed. It began to grow and change shape until at last a spinning wheel stood before her. On it, a long spindle glistened with unearthly light.

Slowly she reached her finger toward it.

"Rose!" came the fairies' voices. *"Don't touch anything!"*

The words were loud and strong. They broke through the

witch's spell ever so slightly. Aurora drew back her hand.

"Touch the spindle!" Maleficent hissed, invisible in the darkened room. *"Touch it, I say!"*

Aurora's eyes glazed over. Once again, she reached toward the blinding white pinpoint.

Out in the hallway, Merryweather heard the witch's horrible voice. "In here!" Merryweather cried, pointing to the room.

Together the fairies barged in.

As the door crashed open, they gasped. There in a cloud of smoke stood Maleficent. Her cape billowed around her, covering most of the room in folds of deep, lifeless black. "You poor, simple fools," she snarled, "thinking you could defeat me—*me*, the mistress of all evil!"

Neither Flora, Fauna, nor Merryweather could find the words to answer. Their eyes searched the room for Aurora, but they could see nothing behind the cape.

With one strong sweep that sent a blast of frigid air through the room, Maleficent pulled her cape aside. Her voice was a vicious rasp. "Well, here's your precious princess!"

In the smoky swirl, Aurora lay motionless on the floor, her eyes closed.

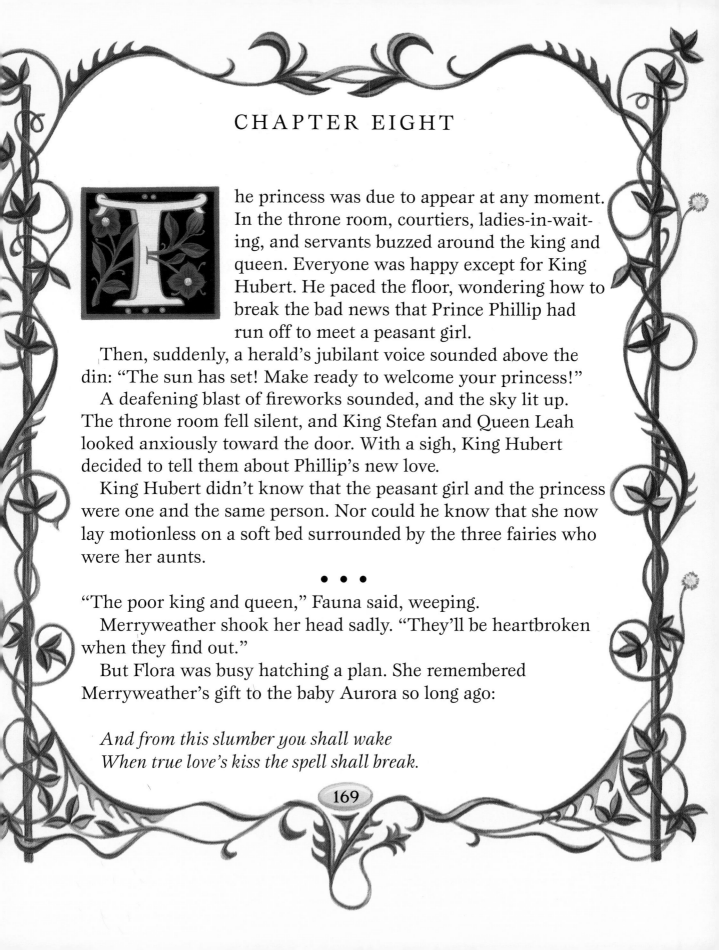

CHAPTER EIGHT

The princess was due to appear at any moment. In the throne room, courtiers, ladies-in-waiting, and servants buzzed around the king and queen. Everyone was happy except for King Hubert. He paced the floor, wondering how to break the bad news that Prince Phillip had run off to meet a peasant girl.

Then, suddenly, a herald's jubilant voice sounded above the din: "The sun has set! Make ready to welcome your princess!"

A deafening blast of fireworks sounded, and the sky lit up. The throne room fell silent, and King Stefan and Queen Leah looked anxiously toward the door. With a sigh, King Hubert decided to tell them about Phillip's new love.

King Hubert didn't know that the peasant girl and the princess were one and the same person. Nor could he know that she now lay motionless on a soft bed surrounded by the three fairies who were her aunts.

• • •

"The poor king and queen," Fauna said, weeping.

Merryweather shook her head sadly. "They'll be heartbroken when they find out."

But Flora was busy hatching a plan. She remembered Merryweather's gift to the baby Aurora so long ago:

And from this slumber you shall wake
When true love's kiss the spell shall break.

If they could only find the young man Aurora had met, perhaps his kiss would bring her back to life. In the meantime, there was a way to keep the king and queen from heartbreak. "We'll put them all to sleep until Rose awakens!" Flora said.

The others agreed. At once, they transformed themselves into tiny specks of light. They flew out the window, sprinkling magic dust over the entire courtyard.

The dust glittered and fell, looking like a part of the fireworks display. It settled over the townspeople and the court guards. Each of them fell asleep instantly. In seconds, the courtyard was filled with slumbering bodies.

Flora reached the throne room first. As she blanketed the room with magic dust, she heard King Hubert say, "You see, Stefan, I've just been talking to Phillip. Seems he's fallen in love with some peasant girl." With a yawn, he put his heavy head on the arm of King Stefan's throne.

Flora couldn't believe what she was hearing. She dove down next to him. Flying close to his ear, she whispered, "Peasant girl? Who is she? Where did he meet her?"

"Oh . . . ," he said, yawning again, "just some peasant girl he met . . . once upon a dream."

"Once upon a dream?" Flora repeated. Those were the same words Aurora had used after she met the young man in the woods! Could it be? Could he have been Prince Phillip?

Flora remembered that Aurora had invited him to the cottage that night. If the prince's love for Aurora was as true as her love for him, perhaps his kiss *would* break the dreadful spell.

Flora darted up to the chandelier, where Fauna and Merryweather hovered. "Come on!" Flora urged. "We've got to get back to the cottage!"

Like three tiny shooting stars, the fairies sped over the still courtyard.

● ● ●

Deep in the woods, Prince Phillip approached the cottage door. Feeling nervous for the first time in his life, he adjusted his cap, then readjusted it. Taking a deep breath, he knocked on the door.

"Come in!" called a soft female voice.

Prince Phillip opened the door and stepped in.

At first he didn't see anyone. Suddenly the door closed behind him.

"Yeeeeeaaaahhh!" With bloodcurdling shrieks, a team of small, vicious creatures pounced on him. He fell to the ground, his cap flying off. Prince Phillip fought fiercely, but he was outnumbered. The creatures skittered around him, tying him up with strong twine.

As he struggled and kicked, the tall figure of Maleficent materialized before him. Above her, the raven perched on a rafter. "Well, this is a pleasant surprise," Maleficent said in her low, cruel voice. "I set my trap for a peasant—and lo, I catch a prince!"

As she cackled with glee, Prince Phillip felt an icy chill run through his veins.

"Away with him," Maleficent commanded her creatures. "But gently, my pets, gently. I have plans for our royal guest!"

Howling with laughter, the ghoulish creatures pushed the helpless prince out the door.

CHAPTER NINE

By the time the fairies got to the cottage, all that was left of Prince Phillip was his cap.

"Maleficent!" they all said at the same time.

"She's got Prince Phillip!" Merryweather cried.

"At the Forbidden Mountains!" Flora added.

Fauna's eyes widened in horror. "But we can't go there!"

In spite of their magic powers, the fairies had never dared venture into Maleficent's domain.

"We *can*," Flora said firmly, "and we *must*!"

Without another word, the fairies were off. They raced out of the cottage and into the darkness of the Forbidden Mountains. The jagged spires of Maleficent's decaying castle loomed closer.

The fairies quickly flew past the crumbling stone bridges and the horrid winged gargoyles. A chilly wind pitched them right and left as they flew in and out of broken remnants of the castle walls.

The fairies could hear loud screeches coming from one wing of the castle. They flew toward the noise at once. Hiding on a deep window ledge, their tiny faces flickered with red and orange as they watched a crackling bonfire in the room below. Maleficent's creatures danced wildly around the fire, screaming so loudly that the fairies had to cover their ears.

Watching the bonfire coolly from her throne, Maleficent smiled. "What a pity Prince Phillip can't be here to enjoy the cel-

ebration," she said. She turned to her raven, who sat contentedly
on her shoulder. "Come. We must go to the dungeon and cheer
him up."

She rose from the throne and walked out of the room, carrying
her staff. The fairies fluttered silently behind, following her and
the raven through a long cavernous hallway and down a steep,
drafty stairwell. At the bottom, Maleficent pushed open a heavy
wooden door.

Inside was the slumped figure of Prince Phillip. He sat on a bench across the room, his wrists and ankles shackled to the wall with chains.

"Oh, come now, Prince Phillip," Maleficent said as a wicked smile crossed her lips. "Why so melancholy? A wondrous future lies before you."

She tipped her staff toward him. Its crystal ball began to glow with an image of Aurora, motionless on her bed. "Behold King Stefan's castle!" Maleficent said. "And in yonder topmost tower, dreaming of her true love, is the princess Aurora!"

Prince Phillip gasped.

"Surprised?" Maleficent taunted. "Yes, it is the same peasant maid who won the heart of our noble prince just yesterday. But have no fear. I shall let you go . . . someday. The gates of the dungeon shall part, and you will ride valiantly away to awaken your love with true love's kiss."

The image changed. Now the crystal ball showed the prince as a stooped, white-haired old man, entering the castle grounds on a limping horse.

Prince Phillip gritted his teeth. He pulled at his chains violently, but they held fast.

Maleficent only laughed. "Come, my pet," she said to her raven. "Let us leave our noble prince with these happy thoughts."

The fairies flew into a crack in the wall as Maleficent walked out the door. "A most gratifying day," the witch purred, slamming the dungeon door behind her. "For the first time in sixteen years, I shall sleep well."

When Maleficent was gone, the fairies flew out of the crack. Waving their wands, they returned to normal size.

Prince Phillip looked up with a start. "Who—"

"Shhh!" Flora insisted. "No time to explain!" With a stroke of their magic wands, she and Fauna destroyed his chains, and Merryweather did the same to the lock on the door.

Finally free, Prince Phillip hopped to his feet. His eyes burned with vengeance as he bolted for the door.

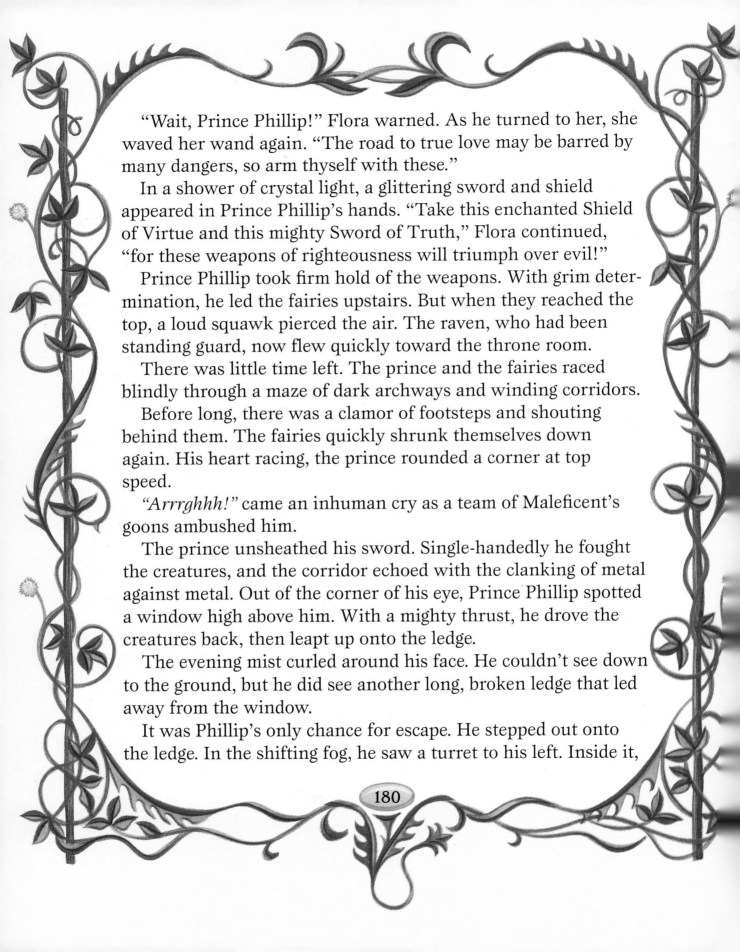

"Wait, Prince Phillip!" Flora warned. As he turned to her, she waved her wand again. "The road to true love may be barred by many dangers, so arm thyself with these."

In a shower of crystal light, a glittering sword and shield appeared in Prince Phillip's hands. "Take this enchanted Shield of Virtue and this mighty Sword of Truth," Flora continued, "for these weapons of righteousness will triumph over evil!"

Prince Phillip took firm hold of the weapons. With grim determination, he led the fairies upstairs. But when they reached the top, a loud squawk pierced the air. The raven, who had been standing guard, now flew quickly toward the throne room.

There was little time left. The prince and the fairies raced blindly through a maze of dark archways and winding corridors.

Before long, there was a clamor of footsteps and shouting behind them. The fairies quickly shrunk themselves down again. His heart racing, the prince rounded a corner at top speed.

"Arrrghhh!" came an inhuman cry as a team of Maleficent's goons ambushed him.

The prince unsheathed his sword. Single-handedly he fought the creatures, and the corridor echoed with the clanking of metal against metal. Out of the corner of his eye, Prince Phillip spotted a window high above him. With a mighty thrust, he drove the creatures back, then leapt up onto the ledge.

The evening mist curled around his face. He couldn't see down to the ground, but he did see another long, broken ledge that led away from the window.

It was Phillip's only chance for escape. He stepped out onto the ledge. In the shifting fog, he saw a turret to his left. Inside it,

he could see Maleficent's guards frantically aiming their bows and arrows at him.

Below him, he heard Samson whinny. There was no time to think. He jumped.

The prince landed on a mound of earth. He slid down to the bottom and found himself in a courtyard of broken stone. Samson stood shackled to the wall a few feet away.

"Phillip, watch out!" came Flora's voice.

Prince Phillip's eyes shot upward. Maleficent's warriors lined the castle walls. With a rumble that shook the ground, heavy black boulders were being hurled toward him. Even his shield wouldn't protect him from those.

Flora waved her magic wand, sending fairy dust toward the rocks. *Zzzing!* They instantly changed into delicate bubbles that floated harmlessly away.

Merryweather shot fairy dust at Samson's shackles, breaking them to pieces. Prince Phillip hopped on his saddle, and Samson sped across the courtyard.

The creatures were screaming with anger. From the turret they now shot a barrage of arrows at the prince, and from directly overhead they poured out a vat of boiling oil.

But the fairies were ready. *Zzzing! Zzzing!* The arrows became lovely flowers, and the oil changed into an arched rainbow. Phillip galloped right underneath it at full speed.

A small shadow streaked over Merryweather's head. She looked up to see the raven. "You . . . ," she muttered angrily. Clutching her wand, she began to chase him.

The raven dodged in and out of the castle's spires and gargoyles. Merryweather shot fairy dust at the bird again and again but missed each time. Finally, as he flew behind a tower, she sim-

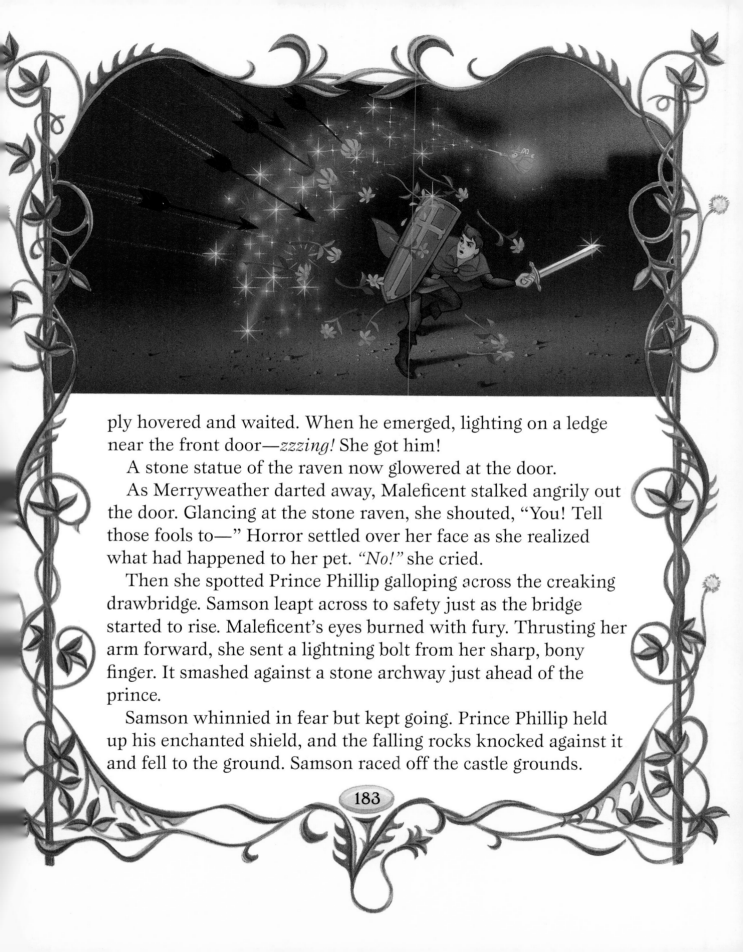

ply hovered and waited. When he emerged, lighting on a ledge near the front door—*zzzing!* She got him!

A stone statue of the raven now glowered at the door.

As Merryweather darted away, Maleficent stalked angrily out the door. Glancing at the stone raven, she shouted, "You! Tell those fools to—" Horror settled over her face as she realized what had happened to her pet. *"No!"* she cried.

Then she spotted Prince Phillip galloping across the creaking drawbridge. Samson leapt across to safety just as the bridge started to rise. Maleficent's eyes burned with fury. Thrusting her arm forward, she sent a lightning bolt from her sharp, bony finger. It smashed against a stone archway just ahead of the prince.

Samson whinnied in fear but kept going. Prince Phillip held up his enchanted shield, and the falling rocks knocked against it and fell to the ground. Samson raced off the castle grounds.

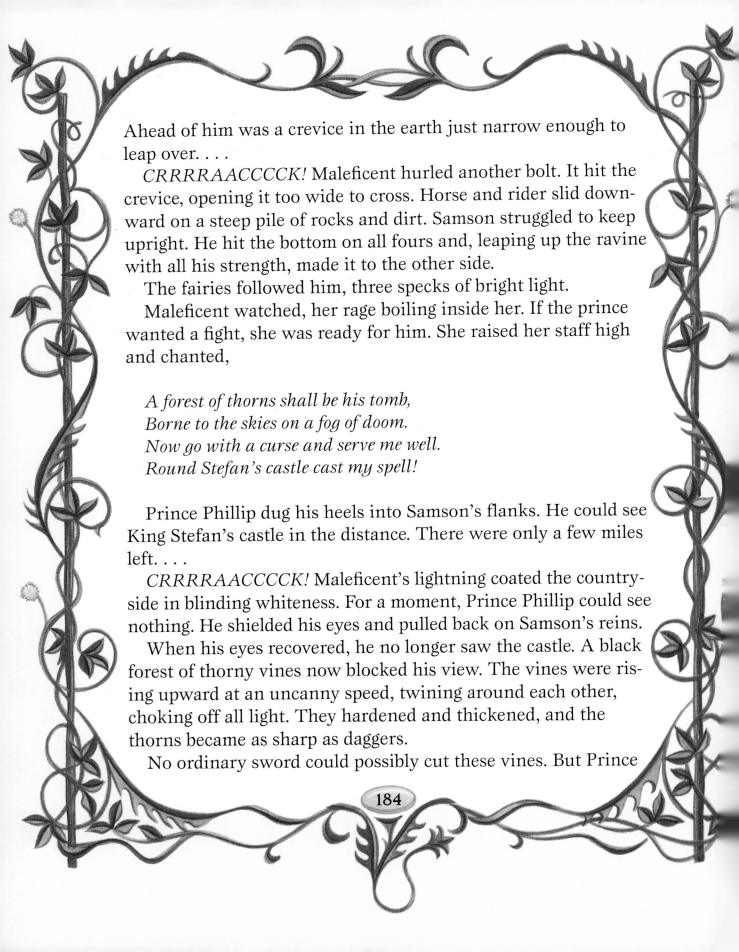

Ahead of him was a crevice in the earth just narrow enough to leap over. . . .

CRRRRAACCCCK! Maleficent hurled another bolt. It hit the crevice, opening it too wide to cross. Horse and rider slid downward on a steep pile of rocks and dirt. Samson struggled to keep upright. He hit the bottom on all fours and, leaping up the ravine with all his strength, made it to the other side.

The fairies followed him, three specks of bright light.

Maleficent watched, her rage boiling inside her. If the prince wanted a fight, she was ready for him. She raised her staff high and chanted,

A forest of thorns shall be his tomb,
Borne to the skies on a fog of doom.
Now go with a curse and serve me well.
Round Stefan's castle cast my spell!

Prince Phillip dug his heels into Samson's flanks. He could see King Stefan's castle in the distance. There were only a few miles left. . . .

CRRRRAACCCCK! Maleficent's lightning coated the countryside in blinding whiteness. For a moment, Prince Phillip could see nothing. He shielded his eyes and pulled back on Samson's reins.

When his eyes recovered, he no longer saw the castle. A black forest of thorny vines now blocked his view. The vines were rising upward at an uncanny speed, twining around each other, choking off all light. They hardened and thickened, and the thorns became as sharp as daggers.

No ordinary sword could possibly cut these vines. But Prince

Phillip's blade glowed with the magic of the fairies. He rode forward at full speed, swinging with all his might.

Whack! His sword sliced cleanly through a vine. It fell to the ground with a heavy thump.

Whack! Whack! Whack! Vine after vine tumbled away. With each thrust, the prince fought his way ever closer to the castle.

Far behind him, Maleficent stared in disbelief. "It cannot be!" she said.

In a fiery whirl, the witch rose into the air. She hurtled herself across the countryside, landing in front of Prince Phillip in a blazing ball of fire.

Samson reared up at the flames. The prince struggled to keep him steady.

"Now you shall deal with me, O Prince," Maleficent thundered, "and all the powers of *evil*!"

She disappeared into the ball of fire, which began to swell. The prince drew back his sword. The fairies looked on, terrified at whatever might happen next.

BOOOOMMMM! An explosion shook the ground, and the ball of fire seemed to swallow everything around it, as if Maleficent had suddenly brought the sun to the earth.

Then, in the midst of the jumping flames, Maleficent's figure shot upward and transformed into a huge dragon. Its head loomed higher than the highest tree, and its eyes were a fiery orange. Its deep violet scales glinted like armor. Each time it breathed, its mouth spewed a roaring column of fire. The heat of its breath knocked Prince Phillip off Samson, who galloped away in terror.

HHHHHAAAAAA! A fiery blast shot toward the prince. He scrambled behind a thicket of vines.

By the silence that followed, he could tell the dragon had lost sight of him. He waited, watching the shadow of the dragon's head coming closer . . . closer . . .

At the last moment the prince jumped out of hiding. With a solid *whack*, he struck the dragon over the head.

The sword bounced off. Bellowing with anger and pain, the dragon blew fire over the entire forest. Flames rose from the ground, surrounding Prince Phillip on all sides.

"Up!" came Flora's voice from above. "Up this way!"

Phillip looked around to see his only path of escape—up a smooth cliff untouched by the flames. Digging in with his fingers, he scrambled to the top.

The prince barely had time to get to his feet before the dragon materialized before him. Now it, too, stood on the cliff.

Prince Phillip was trapped. If he moved backward, he would fall over the cliff into a bed of flames.

The dragon lunged toward him. It opened its mouth to draw a breath. Prince Phillip raised his magic shield.

HHHHHAAAAA! The flame hit the shield like the volley of a cannon. The shield flew out of the prince's hands and over the cliff.

He held up his sword, but it was of little use. The heat was now too great for him to get close to the dragon. In desperation, he drew back his arm and took aim at the dragon's head.

Above him, the fairies hovered anxiously. Together they sent a flurry of magic dust toward his sword.

Flora quickly chanted, "Sword of Truth fly swift and sure, that Evil die and Good endure!"

Phillip threw the sword, and it sliced through the air, its point gleaming with the good magic of the fairies. For a moment, it seemed to disappear into the flames.

But the anguished screech of the dragon left no doubt where the sword had landed. Staggering forward, the dragon opened its huge mouth. The sword was buried deep in its heart. It bared its teeth and lurched toward the prince, ready to swallow him whole.

Prince Phillip ducked away. The giant jaws snapped shut inches from his face. The dragon, weakened with pain, could not stop itself from falling forward.

With a bellow that seemed to blot out all other sounds on earth, the dragon plunged over the cliff to its fiery death.

The prince looked over the edge. He could see the shank of his sword among the smoldering flames. Impaled on the sword was a black cape. It was all that remained of Maleficent.

CHAPTER TEN

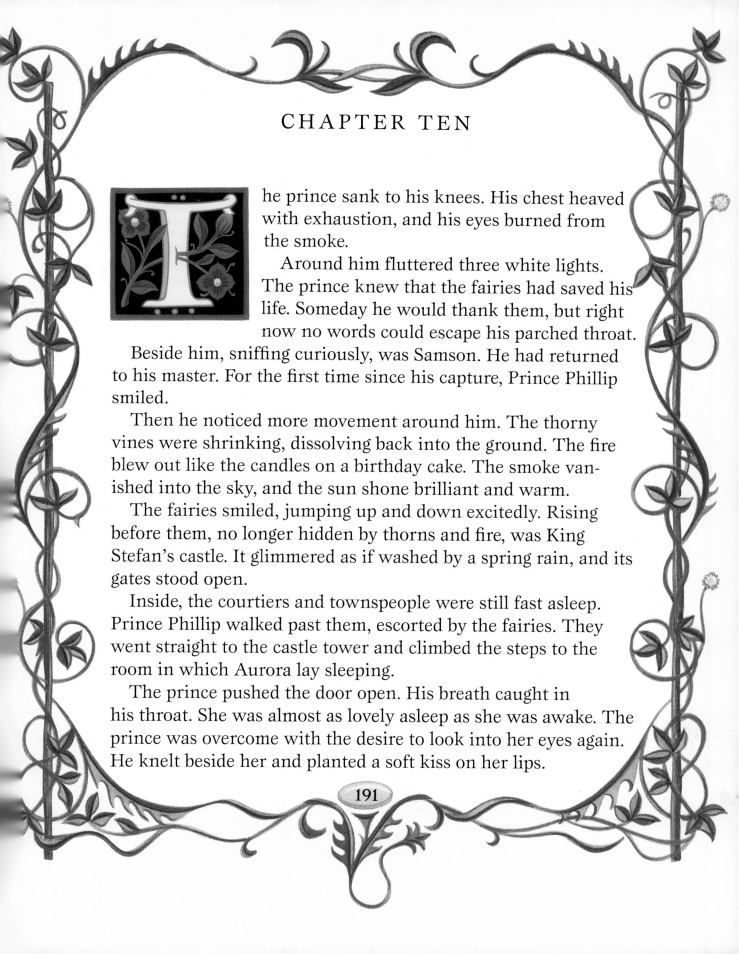

he prince sank to his knees. His chest heaved with exhaustion, and his eyes burned from the smoke.

Around him fluttered three white lights. The prince knew that the fairies had saved his life. Someday he would thank them, but right now no words could escape his parched throat.

Beside him, sniffing curiously, was Samson. He had returned to his master. For the first time since his capture, Prince Phillip smiled.

Then he noticed more movement around him. The thorny vines were shrinking, dissolving back into the ground. The fire blew out like the candles on a birthday cake. The smoke vanished into the sky, and the sun shone brilliant and warm.

The fairies smiled, jumping up and down excitedly. Rising before them, no longer hidden by thorns and fire, was King Stefan's castle. It glimmered as if washed by a spring rain, and its gates stood open.

Inside, the courtiers and townspeople were still fast asleep. Prince Phillip walked past them, escorted by the fairies. They went straight to the castle tower and climbed the steps to the room in which Aurora lay sleeping.

The prince pushed the door open. His breath caught in his throat. She was almost as lovely asleep as she was awake. The prince was overcome with the desire to look into her eyes again. He knelt beside her and planted a soft kiss on her lips.

The fairies held their breath.

Slowly Aurora's eyes flickered once, then twice. When they caught sight of Prince Phillip, they opened fully. Then a warm smile brought the princess's face back to life.

Bursting with happiness, the fairies squealed and hugged each other. "Come, you two!" Flora said happily to the couple. "To the royal court!"

All over the castle, people began to stir. Arms stretched, and mouths yawned.

In the throne room, a groggy King Stefan picked up his head. "Oh . . . forgive me," he said to King Hubert, who was yawning beside him. "You were saying . . . something about Phillip?"

"Huh?" King Hubert mumbled. "Oh, yes! Well, to come to the point, my son Phillip says he's going to marry a—"

The blare of a trumpet fanfare cut him off. All eyes focused on the top of the grand stairway. Prince Phillip and Princess Aurora appeared arm in arm, beaming with a joy that lit up the room.

King Stefan rose to his feet. His heart filled with happiness. His daughter was alive and well—and more beautiful than he could have imagined. "It's Aurora!" he cried.

King Hubert rubbed his eyes. "And . . . and . . . *Phillip?*"

The young couple approached the throne. Queen Leah's eyes brimmed with tears of relief. The years of worry seemed to rise from deep within her and fly away.

When Aurora got close to the queen, she could restrain herself no longer. She ran into Leah's arms. And she received an embrace that poured sixteen years of a mother's love into her heart.

Around them, the courtiers and townspeople burst into applause. It was the happiest day any of them had ever known.

The couple hugged and kissed King Stefan, then King Hubert.

"What . . . what does this mean, boy?" King Hubert asked his son, still confused.

But the court musicians had struck up a dance, and Prince Phillip whisked the princess away to the dance floor.

"I don't understand," King Hubert muttered. Then, with a sigh, he shrugged his shoulders and swayed to the music.

From a balcony high above, the fairies watched the prince and the princess dance. Fauna sobbed uncontrollably.

"Why, what's the matter, dear?" Flora asked.

Fauna sniffed. "Oh, I just love happy endings."

"Yes, I do, too," Flora said. She turned contentedly to see Aurora swirling gracefully, her dress a whirl of sky blue. *"Blue?"* she blurted, her contentment disappearing.

Zzzing! She waved her wand and turned it pink.

Now Merryweather's smile disappeared. *"Blue!"* she demanded. *Zzzing!* went her wand.

On the dance floor, Aurora looked lovingly into the eyes of her prince. Her dress flashed pink and blue in a swirl of motion. But to her and everyone around her, it was just another magical part of this most magical dream come true.

Cinderella

Adapted from the film
by Zoë Lewis

Prologue

Once upon a time in a faraway land there was a tiny kingdom that was peaceful, prosperous, and rich in romance and tradition. There, in a stately château, lived a widowed gentleman with his little daughter, Cinderella. A kind and devoted father, he gave his beloved child every luxury and comfort. Still, he felt she needed a mother's care, and so he married again. For his second wife he chose a woman of good family with two daughters just Cinderella's age: by name, Anastasia and Drizella.

It was upon the untimely death of this good man, however, that the stepmother's true nature was revealed—cold, cruel, and bitterly jealous of Cinderella's charm and beauty. She was grimly determined to forward the interests of her own two awkward daughters.

As time went by, the château fell into disrepair. The family fortunes were squandered upon the vain and selfish stepsisters while Cinderella was forced to become a servant in her own home.

Yet through it all, Cinderella remained ever gentle and kind. With each and every dawn she found new hope that someday her dreams of happiness would come true. . . .

Chapter One

A beam of golden sunshine fell across Cinderella's bed as two bluebirds flew in through her open window.

"Cinderella," one bluebird chirped.

Cinderella sighed and rolled over, pulling a pillow over her head as she burrowed deeper under the covers.

"Cinderella," the other bird sang softly in her ear.

"Wake up!" chirped the first bird, poking its head under the pillow.

Cinderella reached out from under the covers and flicked the bluebird's tail. "Well, serves you right," she said to the startled bird. "Spoiling people's best dreams!" She laughed as the birds chirped and flew to the windowsill. "I know it's a lovely morning, but it was a lovely dream, too."

The birds whistled loudly.

Cinderella sat up and began to unbraid her shoulder-length blond hair. "What kind of a dream, you ask? It's a secret. Just like a wish, if you tell your dreams, they won't come true."

Cinderella sometimes thought her dreams were all that kept her from

sinking into despair. Ever since the death of her beloved father, Cinderella had been treated like a slave by her jealous stepmother— Lady Tremaine—and her nasty stepsisters, Anastasia and Drizella. They ordered her around, dressed her in rags, and forced her to do all their household chores. To forget her troubles, Cinderella often escaped into dreams of a happier life. She dreamed of falling in love . . . of being loved in return . . . of someday leaving her horrible home behind forever. And because her dreams were all she had, Cinderella never stopped believing in them.

Cinderella yawned and stretched. She smiled at the birds and mice

who had come into the room—they were the only real friends she had. Then she sighed as she heard the loud ringing of the palace clock tower. She got out of bed, went to the window, and glared at the majestic clock. "I hear you! 'Come on, get up,' you say! Even that clock orders me around," she said to the birds and mice. "Well, there's one thing no one can order me to do. They can't order me to stop dreaming."

The birds chirped in agreement.

"And perhaps someday," Cinderella said wistfully, "my wish will come true."

*   *   *

With the help of her animal friends, Cinderella quickly straightened her little room, which was located at the top of a steep, winding staircase in the château's highest tower. She made her bed and put on an old brown dress. Then she tied back her thick golden hair, put on her apron, and was ready to face another day of washing and scrubbing and listening to the demands of her stepfamily.

She was about to leave her bedroom when two mice darted under her door. Chattering excitedly, they scampered up to the top of the bureau, waving their arms frantically to attract Cinderella's attention.

"Wait a minute. One at a time, please," Cinderella told the mice patiently. She turned to one of them, a skinny mouse dressed in red. "Now, Jaq, what's all the fuss about?"

"There's a new mouse in the house," Jaq squeaked. "A visitor."

Cinderella smiled. "How nice," she said. She opened the drawer where she kept extra clothing for the mice. "He'll need a jacket . . . and shoes . . ."

The other mouse, who was dressed in blue, squeaked loudly.

"What's the matter, Luke?" Cinderella asked, concerned.

"We gotta get him out of the trap," Jaq blurted out before Luke could answer.

"He's in the trap? Well, why didn't you say so?" Cinderella exclaimed. She rushed out of the room with the mice at her heels and headed straight for the rusty old mousetrap at the bottom of the stairs. Inside the trap, a plump brown mouse cowered in a corner.

"The poor little thing is scared to death," Cinderella said.

She opened the door, and Jaq entered cautiously. "Take it easy," Jaq reassured the newcomer, who was trying to back even farther away. "There's nothing to worry about. Cinderella is our friend. She likes you. We all like you."

• 204 •

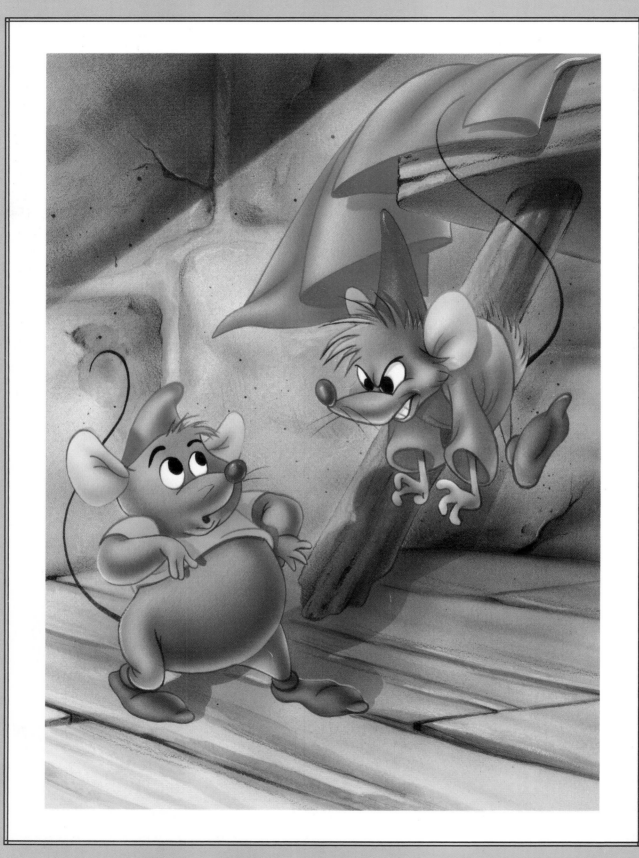

Cinderella flashed the frightened mouse a bright smile, and he finally smiled back and relaxed a little. "That's better," Cinderella said as Jaq led the new mouse out of the trap. "We have to give you a name. How about Octavius? Gus for short!"

By the smile on the new mouse's face, Cinderella knew she had made a good choice—and a new friend.

"Now I've got to get to work. See that Gus keeps out of trouble, Jaq," Cinderella said as she turned to leave. "And don't forget to warn him about the cat!"

"Have you ever seen a cat?" Jaq asked after Cinderella had gone.

Gus looked confused. "A cat?" he repeated.

"Lucifer, that's him," Jaq explained. "He's mean and sneaky." Jaq curled his fingers to imitate a cat's claws. "He'll jump at you and bite you! He's big—big as a house!"

"Lucifer," Gus said thoughtfully. He planned on staying far, far away from him.

Chapter Two

The second-floor hallway was dark and desolate until Cinderella walked to the window and opened the heavy drapes, letting in a flood of morning sunlight. She stepped up to the first of three closed doors, hesitated for a moment, took a deep breath, and opened it. In the darkness of her stepmother's bedroom Cinderella could hardly see the elaborate round cat bed where a fat black cat was sleeping.

"Here, kitty, kitty," Cinderella called softly from the doorway.

The cat slowly climbed to his feet, yawned, stretched, and gave Cinderella a disdainful look before turning his back and lying down again.

"Lucifer, come here!" Cinderella hissed impatiently.

Only then did the cat slowly and reluctantly get up from his bed and saunter across the floor.

"I'm sorry if Your Highness objects to an early breakfast," Cinderella said sarcastically. "It's certainly not my idea to feed you first. I'm just following orders. Now, come on." She started down the stairs with Lucifer close behind her.

When Cinderella entered the kitchen, the room was dark. She opened the door to let in the sunlight, then knelt beside the big brown dog stretched out on the floor. "Bruno, it's time to wake up," she urged him quietly. He awoke with a start from his dreams of chasing Lucifer.

Cinderella went back to the kitchen door and stepped out into the beautiful bright day. Every morning she looked forward to feeding her animal friends their breakfast. Now they rushed toward her from every direction as she tossed handfuls of corn into the yard. "Breakfast time!" she called. "Everybody up!"

Jaq, Luke, Gus, and the other mice gathered up bits of corn to carry back to their homes. Gus was so intent on carrying his breakfast that he didn't notice a huge dark shadow looming over him as he reentered the house. The other mice scattered in fear while Gus continued across the floor, balancing a precarious pile of corn in his arms.

When Lucifer sprang into action, Gus saw him coming just in the nick of time. The plump little mouse dropped his corn and scampered up onto the kitchen table. He leaned against a teacup to catch his breath, thinking he was safe.

But Lucifer was reaching up stealthily behind him. The cat suddenly grabbed the cup and slammed it down over the startled mouse. Lucifer's mouth stretched into an evil grin. Now Gus was right where Lucifer wanted him.

Claws at the ready, the cat carefully began to lift the cup to uncover his victim. But suddenly Lucifer let the cup drop again, startled by the shrill ringing of a row of bells high on the kitchen wall. "Cinderella!" an even shriller voice called out.

"All right, all right. I'm coming," Cinderella called, rushing back into the kitchen from the barnyard.

"Cinderella!" another voice shrieked, followed by more of the piercing bells.

"Cinderella!" a third voice shouted.

"Coming!" Cinderella cried. It was the same thing every morning. Her stepmother and stepsisters wanted their breakfast. Cinderella hurried over to the table and grabbed the three tea trays she had prepared, including the one on which Gus was trapped. Lucifer followed her out of the kitchen, eyeing the teacup Gus was under.

Cinderella climbed to the second floor and entered the first doorway in the hall. "Good morning, Drizella," Cinderella greeted her stepsister cheerfully. Cinderella always made an effort to be nice—even though her stepsisters rarely made the same effort in return. "Sleep well?"

Her thin, homely stepsister sat up in bed. Drizella's dark hair stood on end, and her pointed features were pinched into a frown. "Hmmph!" Drizella grumbled. "As if you cared." She snatched one of the trays from Cinderella's hands, then dumped a basket of wrinkled clothing at her feet. "Take that ironing and have it back in an hour," she commanded. "One hour, do you hear me?"

"Yes, Drizella," Cinderella replied. Balancing the basket on one hip,

she left the room and moved down the hall to the next bedroom.

"Good morning, Anastasia," Cinderella said as she entered.

"Well, it's about time," Anastasia muttered. Like Drizella, Anastasia was thin and homely. Her wiry red hair was a mess, and her sickly pale skin was whiter than her bed linens. She shoved another basket into Cinderella's arms. "Don't forget the mending. And don't be all day getting it done, either!"

"Yes, Anastasia," Cinderella said.

She hurried down the hall to the third room. She opened the door and greeted her stepmother. Beyond the light of the doorway, the room was dark and forbidding.

Lady Tremaine's cold voice cut through the blackness. "Don't just

stand there, child. Put that down. Then pick up the laundry and get on with your duties."

"Yes, Stepmother," Cinderella answered. She left the room and shut the door behind her. Carrying the heavy piles of ironing, mending, and laundry, she walked back down the hall. She was almost at the stairs when a terrible scream rang out from the second room.

Lucifer turned and raced down the hall to Anastasia's closed door, smiling in anticipation. As Anastasia continued to shriek, Gus ran out from under the door—right into Lucifer's waiting paws.

Cinderella rushed to Anastasia's room to see what the trouble was. "*You* did it!" Anastasia screeched, throwing open the door and pointing an accusing finger at Cinderella. "You did it on purpose!"

Chapter Three

"other!" Anastasia howled. She ran into Lady Tremaine's room and closed the door.

Drizella emerged from her room and gave Cinderella a withering glance. "*Now* what did you do?" she snapped. Then she hurried after her sister into her mother's room.

"She put it there!" Cinderella could hear Anastasia shouting, even through the closed door. "A big, fat, ugly mouse! Under my teacup!"

Cinderella turned to stare suspiciously at Lucifer, who was curled up nearby with an innocent look on his face. "All right, Lucifer. What did you do with Gus?" Cinderella asked.

Lucifer opened his empty paws and smiled slyly.

"Oh, you're not fooling anybody," Cinderella said, picking up the big cat and shaking him out like a dusty mop. And there, under his hind foot, quivering and shivering, was Gus.

"Poor Gus," Cinderella said as the little creature scooted between her feet and disappeared into a hole in the wall. She sighed and turned back to the cat. "Oh, Lucifer. Won't you ever learn? Sometimes I wonder what I—"

"Cinderella!" Lady Tremaine's cross voice interrupted.

"Coming," Cinderella answered. She walked toward her step-mother's bedroom. Both her stepsisters had come out and were hovering in the hallway. Lucifer slipped into the room through the open door.

"Hmmph!" Drizella grumbled.

"Are you going to get it!" Anastasia added nastily as Cinderella entered the dim, eerie room.

"Close the door, Cinderella," Lady Tremaine said evenly from her

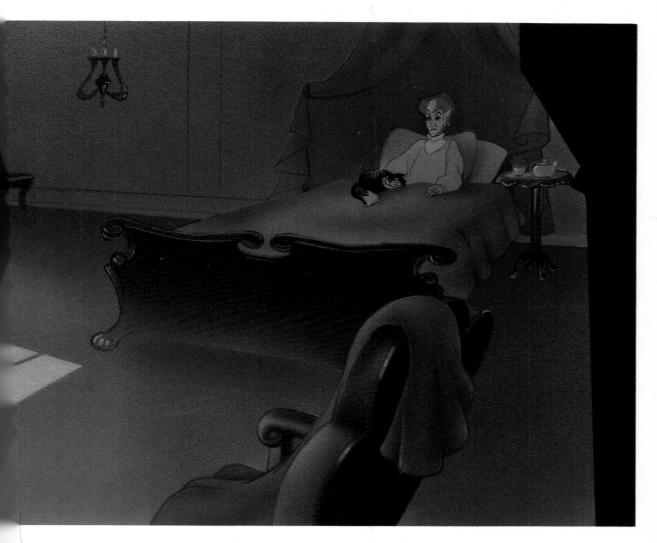

bed. She was stroking Lucifer, who had settled on her lap. Her expression was cold and malevolent.

"Oh, please," Cinderella began. "Surely you don't think that I—"

"Hold your tongue," her stepmother ordered sharply. Cinderella could see Lucifer's golden-green eyes glittering in the dimness.

Lady Tremaine picked up her teacup. "It seems we have time on our hands, Cinderella. Time for vicious practical jokes," she said. "Perhaps we can put that time to better use."

Cinderella could barely see her stepmother's cruel smile in the

shadowy darkness. She didn't know what was coming, but she was sure she wouldn't like it.

"Now, let me see," Lady Tremaine said. "There's the large carpet in the main hall—clean it! And the windows, upstairs and down—wash them! Oh, yes, the tapestries and draperies, too."

"But I just finished—," Cinderella began.

"Do them again!" her stepmother interrupted, glaring at her. "And don't forget to weed the garden, scrub the terrace, sweep the halls and the stairs, and clean the chimneys. And of course there's still the

mending, ironing, and laundry to be done." She paused for a breath and took a sip of tea. "Oh, yes, one more thing . . ."

Lucifer looked up at his mistress, eager to hear what other chores she had in mind for Cinderella. "See that Lucifer gets his bath," Lady Tremaine finished. Lucifer frowned in annoyance.

Cinderella walked out of her stepmother's room, her shoulders slumped in dejection. She had never felt so frustrated and angry. Despite all her wishes, hopes, and dreams, it seemed as if her life just kept getting worse.

Chapter Four

Meanwhile, inside the sparkling white castle that Cinderella could see through her bedroom window—if she had the time to look!—the portly, white-haired king was slumped on his throne.

"It's high time my son got married and settled down," he proclaimed to his closest adviser, the grand duke.

"Of course, Your Majesty," the grand duke answered. "But we must be patient."

"I am patient!" the king shouted impatiently. "But I'm not getting any younger, you know. I want to see my grandchildren before I go." The king calmed down, then continued sadly, "You don't know what it means to see your only child grow older and farther away from you. You don't know how lonely I am in this desolate old place." He wiped a tear from his eye. "I want to hear the pitter-patter of little feet again."

"Now, now," said the grand duke sympathetically. "Perhaps if we just let him alone . . ."

"Let him alone!" the king bellowed. "Him and his silly romantic ideas?"

"But sire," the grand duke protested timidly. "In matters of love—"

"Love!" The king cut him off. "Hah! What is love? Just a boy meeting a girl under the right conditions. So, we must simply arrange the conditions."

"But—but Your Majesty," the grand duke stammered. "How? And if the prince should even suspect, I'm sure he wouldn't—"

"Bah!" the king said in disgust. "The boy is coming home today, isn't he? Well, what could be more natural than a ball to celebrate his return?" He smiled. "And if all the eligible maidens in my kingdom just

happened to be there, he'd be bound to show interest in one of them. Wouldn't he?"

"Yes, sire," the grand duke agreed halfheartedly. In truth, he wasn't convinced at all that the king's plan would work, but he didn't want him to start shouting again. He hated it when the king got angry.

The king giggled happily, imagining the scene. "We'll have soft lights, romantic music, all the trimmings! It can't possibly fail."

"Very well, sire. I shall arrange the ball," the grand duke said.

"Make it tonight!" the king commanded. "And see that *every* eligible maiden is there!"

Chapter Five

Cinderella hummed softly to herself as she scrubbed the floor in the foyer of the château. As she worked, she dreamed of happier days long ago with her father, and she fantasized about someday being as free as the soap bubbles that wafted into the air as she scrubbed. Her reverie was interrupted by a loud knocking at the door.

"Open in the name of the king," a voice boomed. Cinderella opened the door, and a messenger handed her a large white envelope. "An urgent message from His Majesty." The messenger spun on his heel and left.

As Cinderella turned from the door, gazing curiously at the letter, Jaq and Gus poked their heads out of a mousehole. "What's it say?" they squeaked in unison.

"I don't know," Cinderella replied, examining the king's seal. "But he said it's urgent. I'd better take it up right away."

Cinderella walked up the stairs to the music room, where her step-sisters were having their lessons. She stepped cautiously into the room.

"Cinderella! I've warned you never to interrupt us," her stepmother scolded her harshly.

"But this just arrived—from the palace," Cinderella explained, holding out the white envelope.

"From the palace!" Anastasia gasped. Both sisters rushed over to Cinderella.

"Give it here!" Drizella demanded, grabbing the letter.

"No, let me have it!" Anastasia plucked it out of her sister's hands.

"No! It's mine!" Drizella shrieked. "You give that back!"

"*I'll* take it," their mother said, putting an end to the argument. She tore open the letter and read it. "Well," she said, "it seems there's to be a ball."

"A ball!" Anastasia and Drizella shrieked in unison.

Their mother nodded. "In honor of His Highness, the prince. And by royal command, every eligible maiden is to attend."

"Why, that's us," Drizella said eagerly.

"And I'm *so* eligible," Anastasia added with a sigh.

For a moment Cinderella said nothing. She was too stunned to

speak. It seemed that this day would turn out to be special after all. " 'Every eligible maiden' . . . why, that means that I can go, too," she said at last.

"Ha!" Drizella laughed, and poked her sister in the side. "Could you imagine *her* dancing with the prince? Ha!"

"I'd be honored, Your Highness," Anastasia said mockingly. "Would you mind holding my broom?" The sisters collapsed into a fit of giggles at the thought.

"Well, why not?" Cinderella said defensively. She couldn't believe that even her stepsisters were mean enough to want to rob her of a single night of happiness. "After all, I am a member of the family. And it does say 'by royal command, every eligible maiden is to attend.' "

"Yes, so it does," Lady Tremaine said slowly. "Well, I see no reason why you can't go—"

"Mother!" Drizella and Anastasia cried out in shock.

"—if," their mother went on, with a crafty look in her eye, "*if* you get all of your work done . . ."

"Oh, I will," Cinderella promised happily. The news of the ball was the most wonderful thing to happen in Cinderella's life since before her father had died. Nothing was going to make her miss this night.

". . . *and* if you can find something suitable to wear," her stepmother finished.

"I'm sure I can come up with something!" Cinderella said joyfully as she hurried out of the room. "Thank you!"

"Mother! Do you realize what you just said?" Drizella complained after Cinderella had left the room.

"Of course," her mother replied coolly. "I said 'if'!"

"Oh, *if*," Drizella said slyly as she and her sister realized what their mother had in mind.

Chapter Six

A few minutes later Cinderella rummaged through the trunk at the foot of her bed and pulled out a cloud of bright pink silk. As she held it up against her shoulders, the fabric unfurled into a long, full gown. Still holding the dress in front of her, she whirled around the room, imagining what it would be like to dance the night away at the ball. Perhaps she would sip some champagne while strolling through the palace garden under the stars. Perhaps she would meet the gentle, loving young man of her dreams. Cinderella could hardly contain her excitement.

"Isn't it lovely?" Cinderella said aloud as she held up the dress once more. "It was my mother's," she said wistfully to the crowd of mice and birds who had gathered to see what she was doing.

The animals looked on in awe. "Beautiful," one of the mice said. "But it looks kind of old."

"Well, maybe it is a bit old-fashioned," Cinderella admitted. "But I can fix that." She took a pattern book out of her sewing basket.

"There ought to be lots of good ideas in here," she said as she thumbed through the pages. "Like this one!"

She held out the book for her friends to see. There, on the opened page, was a picture of a stylish ball gown.

"Oh, that's a nice one," one of the mice said.

"Of course, I'll have to shorten the sleeves," Cinderella said thoughtfully. "And I'll need a sash, and a ruffle, and something for the collar, and—"

"Cinderella!" a voice suddenly shrieked from below.

Cinderella sighed and put down the pattern book. "Oh, now what do they want?" she asked woefully.

"Cinderella! Cinderella!" the angry voice persisted.

"All right, all right. I'm coming," Cinderella answered impatiently. "I guess my dress will have to wait," she said sadly, stroking the pink silk one last time.

"Poor Cinderella!" Jaq said as Cinderella left the room. "She won't be able to go to the ball. That's their plan. They'll make her work, work, work. Cinderella will never get her dress done in time!"

"Poor Cinderella," Gus agreed sadly.

All the birds and mice were silent for a moment, wondering what to do. A mouse named Blossom scampered over to study the pattern book Cinderella had left behind.

Suddenly Blossom smiled. "*We* can do it!" she piped up. "*We* can help Cinderella fix her dress! There's nothing to it, really. We can do it! Our Cinderella will look so beautiful!"

All the other animals jumped up and surrounded the small mouse as she began assigning them jobs. "Hurry, hurry! You can do the measuring, and we can do the sewing." She turned to Jaq and Gus. "And you two can go out and gather the trimmings."

• 235 •

Jaq nodded and turned to Gus. "Follow me," he said. "I know where to go!" The two mice sped off to accomplish their mission. Their first stop was Anastasia's room.

As the two mice peeked into the room from a hole in the wall, they saw Anastasia, Drizella, and Lady Tremaine giving Cinderella more chores.

Anastasia was tossing clothes on top of a heap Cinderella was balancing in her arms. "And these, too, Cinderella, and don't forget to—"

"Cinderella, take my dress," Drizella interrupted, adding another garment to the pile.

"Mend the buttonholes! Press my skirt! Mind the ruffles—you're always tearing them!" As Anastasia and Drizella kept shrieking orders to their stepsister, Jaq and Gus couldn't tell which sister was saying what anymore.

Then Cinderella's stepmother came forward. "And Cinderella," she said with a sneer. "When you're through with all that—and before

you begin your regular chores—I have a few more little things for you to do."

With her face barely visible above the towering pile of clothes, Cinderella could manage only a weak "Very well." She walked out of the room with her shoulders slumped. Jaq and Gus could see that there were tears shining in her blue eyes. Cinderella truly looked as though her heart was breaking.

Jaq and Gus remained where they were as Anastasia started to complain loudly. "Mother, I don't see why everybody else has such nice things to wear and I always end up in these old rags. Just look at this!" She held up a lovely pink sash. "Why, I wouldn't be seen dead in it," she cried, throwing it down on the floor and stalking out of the room.

"She should talk," Drizella whined. "Look at these beads!" She tossed a sparkling necklace on top of the sash. "Trash! I'm sick of them." She, too, marched out of the room, with her mother right behind her.

As soon as the door closed behind them, the two mice hopped out of their hiding place and ran over to the discarded sash and necklace.

"We can use these!" Jaq exclaimed in delight.

Gus nodded eagerly.

Just then the two mice noticed a black ball of fur curled on top of a footstool just inches away. At that same moment Lucifer woke up, spotted them, and pounced. Jaq and Gus grabbed the sash and scurried back to the mousehole, popping through it just in time to escape Lucifer's claws.

Jaq and Gus looked at each other. They had the sash—now what about the beads? They peered out of the hole and saw that Lucifer was perched right on top of the shiny necklace, a smug look on his face.

Jaq acted quickly. He dashed out and started to pull the buttons off one of Anastasia's dresses. Lucifer hesitated, glancing over at Gus waiting in the mousehole, but the temptation was too great for the cat to resist. While Lucifer leaped after Jaq, Gus rushed out and grabbed the beads. A moment later both mice were once again safely back in the mousehole, along with Drizella's discarded beads.

Jaq and Gus gathered up the sash and the beads and scrambled back to Cinderella's room, where they found a gang of mice and birds busily working on the dress. They were measuring, marking, and cutting while others sewed, snipped, or studied the pattern book. Jaq and Gus proudly draped the pink silk sash around the waist of the dress, and two birds tied it in a big beautiful bow. Then more birds laid the gleaming strand of beads at the collar.

Slowly but surely the beautiful dress was coming to life. It was hard work, but they all knew it would be worth it. They were making it possible for their friend Cinderella to attend the ball—and maybe make some of her dreams come true.

Chapter Seven

As evening fell, every maiden in the kingdom was bustling with excitement. Every maiden except one, that is.

Cinderella stood in the upstairs hall gazing forlornly out the window. She had finally managed to finish her chores. There had been no time for her to fix her dress, and the carriage was due to arrive at any moment to take Lady Tremaine and her daughters to the ball.

Cinderella sighed. It just didn't seem fair. She worked so hard and asked so little. . . . But there was no sense in spending any more time wishing for something that wasn't to be.

She was about to turn away from the window when she heard the clip-clop of horse's hooves approaching. As the sound grew louder, a gleaming black carriage being pulled by a proud white horse came into view and stopped in front of the château. Cinderella sighed, left the window, and headed down the hall.

"The carriage is here," she announced, knocking softly on her step-mother's door.

"Why, Cinderella," Lady Tremaine said as she opened the door. She looked her stepdaughter up and down, pretending to be surprised. "You aren't dressed for the ball."

"I'm not going," Cinderella nearly whispered. "I didn't have time to fix my dress."

"Oh, what a shame!" her stepmother said. She turned and smiled triumphantly at Drizella and Anastasia, who were primping by the mirror. They smirked back. "But of course there will be other times," Lady Tremaine added, turning back to face Cinderella.

"Yes," Cinderella said, fighting back tears. "Good night."

Cinderella hurried upstairs to her room. She couldn't bear to stay downstairs and watch her stepsisters and stepmother leave for the ball—the wonderful, magical ball that Cinderella herself was going to miss. Without turning on the light, she walked straight to the window and stared out at the palace on the horizon.

"Oh well, what's a royal ball?" she said aloud into the darkness. "After all, I suppose it would be frightfully dull . . . and bor-

ing . . . and completely . . . completely *wonderful*," she admitted sadly.

Suddenly the room lit up behind her. As Cinderella spun around in surprise, two bluebirds circled the room. Then they pushed back a screen to reveal the most beautiful dress Cinderella had ever seen. "Oh my goodness," she said, stunned. "Why, it's my—"

"Surprise!" the mice squeaked, popping out of their hiding places.

"Surprise!" the birds chirped.

Cinderella was speechless. Could it be? Might she really be able to go to the ball after all? "Why, I never dreamed," she finally cried out. "This is such a wonderful surprise!" Holding the dress in front of her, she smiled at her friends and murmured, "How can I ever thank you?"

Moments later Cinderella was dressed in her beautiful new gown. She glanced out the window. The coach was still there—she wasn't too late. "Wait!" she cried, hurrying down the stairs. "Please! Wait for me!"

Lady Tremaine and her daughters were nearly out the door when Cinderella caught up to them. "Isn't it lovely?" Cinderella exclaimed,

twirling before them so that the skirt of her gown swirled out around her. "Do you like it? Do you think it will do?"

Anastasia and Drizella glared at Cinderella. "Mother!" both girls cried.

"She can't—," Anastasia howled.

"She wouldn't—," Drizella shrieked.

"Girls! Please!" Lady Tremaine shouted. "After all," she said more calmly, "we did make a bargain." She took a step toward Cinderella and stared straight into her eyes. "Didn't we?"

Cinderella smiled uncertainly.

"And I never go back on my word," her stepmother muttered thoughtfully, looking long and hard at Cinderella's dress. "How very clever, these beads. They give it just the right touch. Don't you think so?" she said sharply, turning to Drizella.

"No, I don't," Drizella said grumpily. "I think she's—" Suddenly Drizella's jaw dropped as she recognized the beads she'd thrown away. "Why, you little thief!" she screeched at Cinderella. "They're my beads! Give them here!" Drizella reached out and ripped the beads right off Cinderella's neck.

"And that's my sash! She's wearing my sash!" Anastasia shouted, tearing the sash from Cinderella's waist.

Cinderella stood between the sisters, dazed. "Oh, no, please, don't—"

But her two stepsisters continued to tear her dress apart.

Drizella grabbed a handful of the skirt. "You horrible sneak!" she screamed.

Anastasia yanked at a seam. "Ungrateful wretch!" she shrieked.

They pawed and pulled, they tugged and wrenched, they clawed and scratched . . . until Cinderella stood wearing only pink tatters and shreds.

Chapter Eight

Blinded by tears, Cinderella ran out of the house and across the yard, past the horse, past Bruno the dog, past Gus and Jaq and all her friends. When she finally reached the garden, she threw herself down on a bench in the shadows under a willow and buried her face in her arms. She had never felt so hopeless. She vowed then and there not to believe in dreams anymore, or in happiness or hope, either. Instead she resigned herself to living a miserable life of drudgery and pain.

"It's just no use," she sobbed. "No use at all! There's nothing left to believe in . . . nothing!"

"Nothing, my dear?" a melodious voice asked. "Oh, now, you don't really mean that."

"Oh, but I do!" Cinderella insisted. She lifted her head and caught her breath. A moment ago the garden had been dark and deserted. But now a smiling white-haired woman was seated on the bench, surrounded by a circle of sparkling light.

The woman helped Cinderella to her feet. Wiping a tear from Cinderella's face, she said, "Nonsense, child. If you had lost all of your

faith, I couldn't be here. But, as you can see, here I am! Now, dry those tears. You can't go to the ball looking like that."

"The ball?" Cinderella repeated, tears welling up in her eyes again. "I'm not going to the ball."

"Of course you are," the woman assured her cheerfully. "But we'll have to hurry. Even miracles take a little time, you know."

Cinderella shook her head in confusion. "Miracles?" she asked.

"Just watch," the woman said brightly. She paused, and a puzzled look crossed her face. "Now, what in the world did I do with my magic wand?"

"Magic wand," Cinderella repeated in amazement. "Why, then you must be—"

"Your fairy godmother, of course!" the woman finished for her. Then, with a wave of her hand, she magically produced a wand from

thin air. "Now, let's see," she went on. "I'd say the first thing you need is . . ."—her eyes scanned the garden—". . . a pumpkin!"

"A pumpkin?" Cinderella repeated doubtfully. She had been expecting the woman to say something about her ruined gown.

"Now for the magic words," the fairy godmother said. "Um, uh . . ." She turned toward a big round pumpkin at the edge of the garden and waved her wand. "Oh, yes, I remember: Salaga-doola, menchicka-boola, bibbidi-bobbidi-boo!"

Cinderella could hardly believe what happened next. As the fairy godmother waved her wand and sang out the magic words, the pumpkin shivered . . . and jumped . . . and expanded—and suddenly, with a jolt, the ordinary pumpkin was transformed into a magnificent, gleaming, extraordinary coach.

Cinderella gasped, and she heard smaller gasps all around her. She

saw that all her animal friends had gathered from the house and barn-yard. They looked as amazed as she was at what they had just seen.

But the fairy godmother wasn't finished yet. "Now," she continued. "To draw an elegant coach like that, of course, we'll simply have to have"—and letting her gaze roam over and then past the family's eager-looking horse, she concluded—"mice!"

With another wave of her wand and some more magic words she turned Gus, Jaq, and two other mice into sleek horses.

"Now, where were we? Oh goodness, yes. You can't go to the ball without a coachman." With that, she turned the horse into a well-dressed coachman. Then she turned to Bruno. "As for you, you'll be a footman tonight," she said. And the big brown dog was changed into just that.

The fairy godmother turned to Cinderella. "Well, well, hop in, my dear. We mustn't waste time."

Cinderella hesitated and looked down at her torn dress. "But, uh . . ."

"Now, don't try to thank me," the fairy godmother said.

"Oh, I wasn't," Cinderella began, still astonished at the magic she had just witnessed. "I mean, I do," she added quickly. "But don't you think my dress . . ."

The fairy godmother finally took a good look at Cinderella's tattered gown and let out a shriek of dismay. "Good heavens, child," she exclaimed. "You can't go in that!"

Cinderella smiled and shook her head.

One last time the fairy godmother fluttered her magic wand and sang out the magic words. Suddenly Cinderella felt the force of the fairy godmother's magic surrounding her. She looked down and saw that the tattered remains of her pink dress had been transformed into a stunning, shimmering, silvery gown that gleamed in the moonlight.

With matching long gloves, a black velvet choker, and a sparkling diamond tiara, Cinderella looked like a princess. On her feet were a pair of dainty glass slippers. She rushed over to admire her reflection in a nearby fountain. Cinderella had never felt so beautiful.

She felt her heart fill up once again with hope and faith and delight. "Why, it's like a dream—a wonderful dream come true!"

"Yes, my child," the fairy godmother said tenderly. "But like all dreams, I'm afraid this one can't last forever. You'll have only until midnight, and then—"

"Midnight!" Cinderella cried gratefully. "Oh, thank you!"

"You must understand, my dear," the fairy godmother continued seriously. "On the twelfth stroke of midnight, the spell will be broken, and everything will be as it was before."

"I understand," Cinderella said happily. "But it's so much more than I ever hoped for."

"Bless you, my child." The fairy godmother smiled and waved Cinderella into the coach.

Chapter Nine

The grand ballroom of the palace was crowded with dozens of excited young maidens from all over the kingdom. As each young lady entered the hall, the royal chamberlain announced her and introduced her to the handsome young prince, who stood on a dais at one end of the room.

As maiden after maiden came in and curtsied, the prince found himself stifling yawn after yawn. He couldn't understand why his father was making such a fuss over him by hosting this ball—or why the king was so eager to introduce him to all these young ladies. The prince didn't have any trouble meeting young ladies on his own; he just had trouble meeting anyone he felt he could care about.

He raised a hand to cover yet another yawn. The chamberlain cleared his throat as the next two young ladies approached the dais. "The mademoiselles Drizella and Anastasia Tremaine, daughters of Lady Tremaine," he announced.

The prince bowed politely to the two homely girls, who were practically tripping over their own feet as they curtsied. As he straightened up again, his gaze wandered past them to another young lady

who had just entered at the far end of the hall and was looking around uncertainly.

He stared, transfixed. She was the most beautiful girl he had ever seen. She was wearing a shimmering gown and a sparkling tiara. Her golden hair was piled atop her head, framing her lovely face. The prince suddenly had the feeling that this night might not turn out to be hopelessly boring after all. He stepped down from the dais and pushed his way between the startled Anastasia and Drizella, his eyes never leaving the maiden in the silvery gown.

Cinderella was overwhelmed by the beauty and grandeur of the palace. She felt almost dizzy as she looked around. The sound of rapidly approaching footsteps brought her back to reality. She looked up and caught her breath as she found herself gazing into the deep brown eyes of a tall, broad-shouldered young gentleman. When he gave her a kind smile and politely asked her to dance, Cinderella was astonished. She could hardly believe she was already being asked to dance—especially by someone so handsome. She had been hoping to get a look at the prince, but she decided that that could wait. She was

sure that even the prince couldn't possibly be any more handsome than this charming young man.

She returned his smile and gave him her hand. As the gentleman kissed her hand and swept her off into a waltz, Cinderella felt as though she really were living a dream—no, it was even better than a dream. It was as if she and this handsome stranger had been dancing together forever. And she knew without his saying so that he felt the same way. Without even knowing each other's name, the two young people were quickly falling in love.

As the beautiful young couple swayed wordlessly to the music, the other guests looked on—some with pleasure, and some with envy.

"Who is she, Mother?" Anastasia asked peevishly.

Drizella was trying to get a good look at the prince's partner, but such a crowd had gathered that she could catch only brief glimpses of her. "Do we know her?" she added.

"I know I've seen her before," Anastasia said.

With narrowed eyes, Lady Tremaine watched the couple dance.

"There is something familiar about her," she said slowly. She left her daughters and moved through the crowd, trying to get a closer look. But a moment later the prince led his partner out of the room and toward the royal gardens. Lady Tremaine tried to follow but found her path blocked by the grand duke, who had been ordered by the king to see that the young couple had all the privacy they needed. Frustrated, Lady Tremaine returned to the ballroom, puzzling over her strange feeling that she'd seen the beautiful young lady somewhere before.

Meanwhile, Cinderella and the prince danced across the terrace and then walked hand in hand into the moonlit garden. They strolled across a romantic little bridge, pausing in the middle to watch the sparkling water drifting by below. Cinderella looked up at the handsome young man, her eyes filled with the same love she could see reflected in his own. A moment later their lips met in a long, tender kiss.

They were interrupted by the sound of a chime from the clock tower. Cinderella broke away from the prince's embrace and glanced up at the clock, startled. "Oh my goodness!" she exclaimed. "It's midnight!" She realized she had completely lost track of the time. At the twelfth stroke of the clock all the fairy godmother's magic would be undone.

"Yes, so it is," the prince replied. "But—"

"Good-bye," Cinderella whispered, tearing herself away from his embrace.

"No! Wait! You can't go now," the prince protested.

"But I must," Cinderella replied as the clock struck again. "Please, I must!"

"But why?" the prince asked, confused by her urgency.

Cinderella desperately searched her mind for an excuse. "Well, I, uh, I haven't met the prince yet," she stammered. She turned and rushed off through the garden toward the palace.

The prince stared after her. "The prince?" he repeated with a puzzled frown. "But didn't you know—" Could she really not have known that *he* was the prince? "Wait! Come back!" he called, rushing after her. "Oh, please come back! I don't even know your name—how will I find you?"

As the clock continued to strike, Cinderella reached the palace and

rushed through the ballroom past the grand duke, who had dozed off while guarding the door to the garden. He woke with a start. "Oh, I say! Young lady, wait!"

The grand duke joined the prince in his chase, but Cinderella was already hurrying down the wide front steps of the palace toward her waiting coach. She held up her skirt so she wouldn't trip, but as she ran, one foot suddenly came out of its glass slipper. Cinderella turned to retrieve the shoe, but just then she saw the grand duke burst through the door and run toward her.

"Oh, bless me," he gasped. "Young lady, just a moment!"

Cinderella turned and ran, leaving the slipper lying where it had fallen on the steps. As the grand duke shouted for the guards to follow her, she threw herself into her carriage and sped off into the night. Down the winding hill and over a rickety bridge the carriage clattered, wildly pursued by the king's guards. Cinderella could hear the palace clock as it continued its striking: nine . . . ten . . . eleven . . .

At the stroke of midnight, the spell was instantly broken. The coach turned back into a pumpkin and the horses into mice. Bruno and the horse returned to their usual forms as well. Hearing the guards approaching, Cinderella and her animal friends jumped into the brush beside the road, shaken but unharmed.

The pumpkin was not so lucky. The thundering hooves of the guards' horses smashed it into a thousand pieces as they sped by on the road. To Cinderella's relief, the guards didn't see her.

"I'm sorry," Cinderella told her friends after the guards had passed. "I guess I forgot about everything, even the time. But it was so wonderful! And he was so handsome! And when we danced . . ."

She sighed at the memory. "I'm sure the prince himself couldn't have been more charming." She sighed again, sadly. "And I don't even know his name. I'll probably never see him again."

She looked down at her tattered old dress and saw, peeking out from under the skirt, one bare foot . . . and one sparkling glass slipper. Cinderella gasped and reached down to remove the slipper. She cradled it gently in her hands, overjoyed to have a memento of the most marvelous evening of her life.

She looked up at the starry sky, thinking of the kind fairy godmother who had made it all possible. "Thank you!" she cried out joyously. "Thank you so very much . . . for everything!"

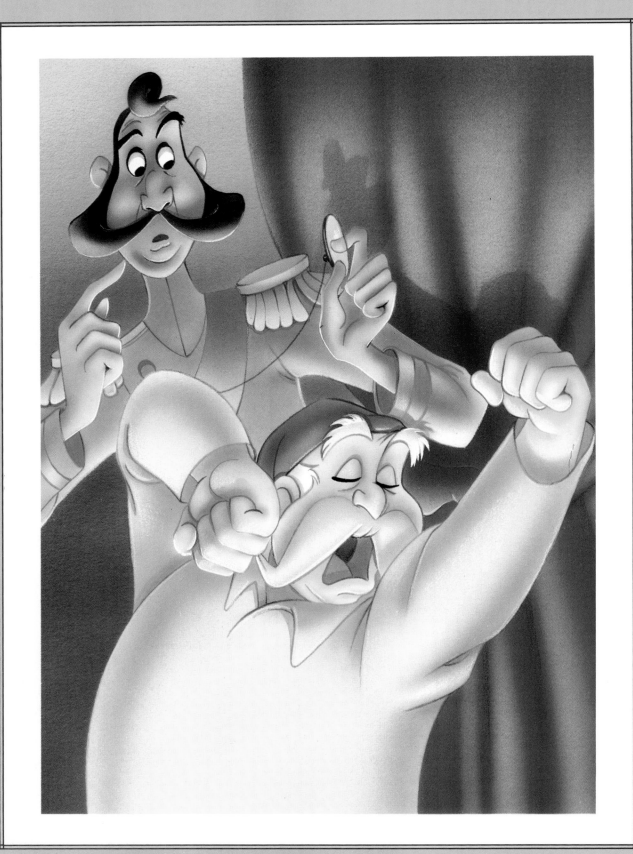

Chapter Ten

The next morning the grand duke stood nervously outside the king's bedroom. Summoning all his courage, he knocked gingerly on the door. The king had left the ball soon after the prince and Cinderella had started dancing, so he didn't yet know about the girl's hasty exit. The grand duke wished more than anything that he didn't have to be the one to give the king the news.

"Come in!" the king called.

The grand duke slowly opened the door and peeked inside.

The king sat up in bed and wiped the sleep from his eyes. When he saw the grand duke he jumped out of bed. "So! Has he proposed already?" he asked jubilantly. "Tell me all about it. Who is she? Where does she live?"

"W-well," the grand duke stammered, "I didn't get a chance to—"

"No matter. We have more important things to discuss—arrangements for the wedding, invitations, all those sorts of things."

The grand duke gulped. "But—"

"Here, have a cigar," the king said, shoving one into the grand duke's mouth. "To celebrate the marriage of my son, and your knighthood."

"Knighthood?" the grand duke repeated, tears welling in his eyes. He couldn't stand it any longer. He had to tell the king the truth. "Sire, she got away," he blurted out.

The king's face turned crimson as the meaning of the words sank in. "She what?" he bellowed.

"I tried to stop her," the grand duke cried. "But she vanished into thin air."

"A likely story," the king said, rushing across the room and grabbing his sword.

"But it's true, sire," the grand duke insisted, his hands trembling as he pulled out the slipper he had picked up from the steps. "All we could find was this glass slipper."

"The whole thing was a plot," the king shouted, swiping vigorously at the grand duke with his sword.

The grand duke ducked. "But your son loves her," he explained quickly. "He won't rest until he finds her. He's determined to marry her."

The king's expression softened. "He what?"

"The prince swears that he'll marry none but the girl who fits this." The grand duke held out the glass slipper in his shaking hand.

The king snatched the slipper and kissed it. He paused and scratched his chin thoughtfully. "Then," he said finally, "you will try this on every maiden in the land. And as soon as you find one this shoe fits, we will have the biggest wedding this kingdom has ever seen!"

It didn't take long for the news to spread. Lady Tremaine rushed to wake Anastasia and Drizella the moment she heard about the slipper.

Cinderella was preparing breakfast when she heard her step-mother shouting, "Get up, quick! This instant! Anastasia! Drizella! We haven't a moment to lose!" Cinderella hurried to finish her task, curious to discover what the fuss was about. There was such a commotion that even the mice peeked out from their holes in curiosity.

Anastasia groggily sat up in bed as her mother bustled about the room, opening the drapes and grabbing clothes from the closet. "Huh? What's going on?" she asked with a yawn.

"Everyone's talking about it," her mother said. "The whole kingdom. Hurry now. He'll be here any minute."

"Who?" Drizella asked. She was standing in the doorway, scratching herself sleepily.

"The grand duke. He's hunting for that girl, the one who lost her slipper at the ball last night," Lady Tremaine explained, just as Cinderella arrived at the door with the tea trays. "They say the prince is madly in love with her—"

Crash! The breakfast trays slipped from Cinderella's hands onto the floor. She gasped and brought her hand to her mouth. "He was the prince!" she whispered to herself.

"You clumsy little fool!" her stepmother cried. "Clean that up! And then help my daughters dress."

"What for?" Drizella said.

"That's right," Anastasia agreed grumpily. "If he's in love with that girl, what good does getting dressed up do us?"

Cinderella absentmindedly started to pick up the mess, still stunned at the news that her handsome stranger was the prince.

"Now you two listen to me," Lady Tremaine told her daughters sharply. "There's still a chance that one of you can get him. No one—not even the prince—knows who that girl is."

Gus and Jaq were watching and listening. "We know!" Gus squeaked excitedly. "It's Cinderella!" Jaq shushed him, anxious to hear every word.

"The glass slipper is their only clue," Lady Tremaine continued. "The grand duke has been ordered to try it on every girl in the kingdom. And if one can be found whom the slipper fits, then by the king's command that girl shall be the prince's bride."

"His bride!" the two sisters shrieked.

"His bride . . . ," Cinderella echoed softly in awe.

"Cinderella! You must get my things together right away," Drizella commanded.

"Never mind her, Cinderella," Anastasia said. She ran around the room wildly gathering up clothes. "Mend these now!"

"Not until she irons my dress," Drizella said.

Soon both girls began tossing heaps of clothing into Cinderella's arms.

Cinderella stood motionless, staring off into space with a dreamy expression on her face. Such wonderful thoughts were whirling around in her head that she could hardly take them all in. She had to be dreaming, she decided.

"What's the matter with her?" Anastasia said irritably, noticing Cinderella's distracted expression.

"Wake up, stupid. We've got to get dressed," Drizella snapped.

At the sound of her stepsisters' voices, Cinderella snapped out of her reverie. With a burst of happiness she realized that she wasn't

dreaming after all—it was all true! The gentle, handsome, charming prince really wanted to marry *her!* "Dressed," Cinderella said joyfully. "Oh, yes, we must get dressed!" Without another word Cinderella dropped the clothing and left the room, humming the tune of the waltz from the previous night.

"Mother, did you see what she did?" Drizella whined.

"Are you just going to let her walk out?" Anastasia demanded.

"Quiet!" their mother said, staring after Cinderella with narrowed eyes. She recognized that tune from the ball. Could it be? she thought. She left the room and headed down the hall toward the staircase Cinderella had just climbed.

In her room Cinderella was standing at her mirror, combing her hair, still humming. Finally, finally my dreams are to come true, she thought ecstatically. After all her years of suffering she would be happy at last. Cinderella flashed a glorious smile to the mice who had gathered around her.

Just then Cinderella looked up and caught her stepmother's reflection in the mirror. Her stepmother was standing at the bedroom door, her eyes dark, her mouth twisted in a snarl.

As Cinderella spun around, startled, she heard the sound of the door slamming and the clink of a key in the lock.

Cinderella raced across the room and pulled at the door, but it wouldn't budge. Her stepmother had locked her in.

"Please," Cinderella begged. "You can't do this! You just can't!" She threw herself against the door, crying, "Let me out! You must let me out!"

Chapter Eleven

Jaq and Gus watched with the other mice as Cinderella sobbed brokenheartedly. "We've got to get that key," Jaq said with determination. "We've just got to!" The two mice slipped under the door and quietly followed Lady Tremaine downstairs.

"Mother! He's here," Drizella cried excitedly.

"Oh, do I look all right?" Anastasia asked, primping at the mirror.

Drizella elbowed her sister aside. "What about me?"

"Girls!" their mother said. "Now remember. This is your last chance. Don't fail me." She hurried to open the door.

A royal footman stood at the threshold. "Announcing His Imperial Grace, the grand duke!" The footman waved the grand duke in with a flourish.

Lady Tremaine smiled and bowed. "May I present my daughters, Drizella and Anastasia."

The grand duke peered at the ugly stepsisters and shuddered. "Charmed, I'm sure," he said. But in reality he was already quite certain

that neither of these homely creatures could be the young lady with whom the prince had waltzed the night before.

"His Grace will read a royal proclamation," the footman announced. He pulled a scroll from his pocket, unrolled it, and held it up for the grand duke to read.

The grand duke cleared his throat. " 'All subjects of His Imperial Majesty,' " he began, taking the scroll from the footman's hands, " 'are hereby notified that in regard to a certain glass slipper . . .' "

As the grand duke continued to read, the footman held up a pillow covered by a cloth. He pulled back the cloth with a flourish, revealing the dainty glass slipper.

"Why, that's my slipper!" Drizella shrieked, rushing forward.

"What?" Anastasia cried. "Well, I like that! It's *my* slipper!"

"Girls! Girls!" their mother scolded. "Remember your manners. A thousand pardons, Your Grace," she said to the grand duke.

The grand duke cleared his throat again and read on. As Lady Tremaine listened intently, Gus and Jaq cautiously climbed up the table next to her and inched their way toward the pocket of her skirt, which contained the key to Cinderella's room. Jaq teetered on the edge of the table, and with Gus holding on to his tail, he lowered himself down into the pocket.

"Now, let us proceed with the fitting," the grand duke said at last.

"Of course," Lady Tremaine agreed. "Anastasia, dear," she called, motioning the girl to a chair.

Anastasia daintily pulled back the hem of her dress, and the footman slid the slipper right onto her bare foot.

"There!" Anastasia said triumphantly. "I knew it was my slipper. It's exactly my size. I always wear the same size. . . ."

Her voice trailed off as the footman lifted Anastasia's foot and more of the dress fell back, revealing the tiny slipper dangling off one of her huge toes.

"Oh well," said Anastasia, her face turning red. "It may be a trifle snug today. You know how it is . . . dancing all night. It's always fit perfectly before!"

But no matter how she pushed, she could not force her large, knobby foot into the dainty slipper.

"Are you sure you're trying it on the right foot?" her mother asked, bending over to help. As she did so, Jaq—and the key—came tumbling out of her pocket and onto the floor with a clank.

Luckily Anastasia and her mother were so busy struggling with the shoe that they didn't even notice. Staggering under the weight of the heavy key, Jaq and Gus headed for the stairs.

"I don't think you're half trying," Anastasia said to the footman.

"Next, please!" the duke commanded, pointing to Drizella.

By the time they reached the top of the long, steep stairway leading up to Cinderella's room, Jaq and Gus were more exhausted than they had ever been in their lives. But they knew they had to free their friend from her room before the grand duke left—her future and her happiness depended on it.

Cinderella heard a sound on the landing outside her room. She peeked through the keyhole and immediately stopped crying. For there, just outside the door, were two little mice and one big brass key.

Cinderella's face lit up in a smile when she saw Jaq squirm under her door. But the smile quickly faded when she heard a loud crash from outside. Peering out through the keyhole again, she saw Lucifer smiling smugly. He had Gus—and the key—trapped under a glass bowl.

"Lucifer! Let him go!" she pleaded. "Please, let him go!"

Jaq squeezed back under the door. He rolled up his sleeves and bravely faced his foe. "Let him out!" he squeaked, baring his teeth.

Before the cat could respond, Jaq grabbed his black furry tail and bit down hard. Lucifer shot up off the ground in surprise and pain, his paws clawing at the air. But before Jaq could free Gus, Lucifer fell back down and grabbed the bowl again.

Within seconds a whole army of Cinderella's friends came to the rescue. Mice hurled forks like spears at the sneaky cat. Birds flew

overhead, dropping dishes on his head. But despite their best efforts, Gus and the key remained trapped.

"Bruno! Get Bruno!" Cinderella cried through the keyhole.

Two bluebirds flew off to find the dog. Moments later Bruno came charging up the stairs. That did it—Lucifer took one look and ran for his life.

As soon as the coast was clear, three of the strongest mice lifted the glass bowl and freed Gus. Then Jaq and Gus picked up the key once more and dragged it under the door into Cinderella's room.

Chapter Twelve

O f all the stupid idiots," Drizella screamed as the footman struggled to fit the glass slipper onto her gigantic
foot. "I'll do it myself. I'll make it fit." She grabbed the
shoe out of the footman's hands.

After moaning and groaning, squeezing and squashing and bending,
Drizella finally managed to cram her foot into the slipper. "There!" she
exclaimed, triumphantly holding her foot out for inspection.

"It fits?" the grand duke said in surprise. But suddenly Drizella's tor-
tured toes uncoiled. The too-tight slipper shot off her foot and flew
straight up into the air.

The grand duke and the footman both lunged to catch the fragile
slipper. They bumped into each other and crashed to the floor just as
the glass shoe came plummeting down to earth. Spread out flat on the
floor, the grand duke reached out his hand . . . and caught the slipper
on the tip of one finger.

"Oh, Your Grace, I'm dreadfully sorry," Lady Tremaine said, gazing
down at the grand duke in horror. "It won't happen again."

"Precisely, madam," the grand duke replied from his awkward

position on the floor. He stood up and brushed himself off. "You are the only young ladies of the household, I hope—er, I mean, I presume," he said to Anastasia and Drizella.

"There's no one else, Your Grace," Lady Tremaine assured him.

"In that case, then, good day," the grand duke said. He was eager to leave this unpleasant household.

But just as he turned to go, a gentle voice called out from the top of the stairs. "Your Grace! Please wait!"

All eyes turned to Cinderella, who was hurrying down the stairs. "May I try it on?" she asked.

"Pay no attention to her," Lady Tremaine told the grand duke. "It's only Cinderella."

"Our scullery maid," Anastasia explained.

"From the kitchen," Drizella added.

But the grand duke was not listening to the stepfamily anymore. "Come, my child," he said to Cinderella kindly, taking her by the hand and leading her to a chair.

As soon as she was seated, the footman came running with the slipper. Suddenly an evil smile crossed Cinderella's stepmother's face. When the footman was only a few steps away from Cinderella, Lady Tremaine stuck out her cane and tripped him.

The footman and the slipper went flying. The footman fell to the floor with a thud; the slipper shattered into a million bits of broken glass on the floor at Cinderella's feet.

"Oh, no, no, no!" the grand duke cried out, falling to his knees and staring at the shards in disbelief. "This is terrible! What will the king say?"

Lady Tremaine smiled smugly. This time she was sure she had put Cinderella in her place for good.

"Perhaps," Cinderella spoke up softly, "if it would help—"

"No, no," the grand duke moaned. "Nothing can help now."

"But you see," Cinderella said, "I have the other slipper." She pulled the other glass slipper out of her pocket and handed it to the grand duke while Lady Tremaine and her daughters looked on in shock.

The grand duke grabbed the precious slipper and kissed it. He smiled at Cinderella and gently slid the dainty slipper onto her foot. It fit perfectly, of course, and both Cinderella and the grand duke laughed with delight.

Cinderella held up her foot, admiring the tiny, perfect slipper sparkling in the light. She didn't even notice her stepfamily's jealous scowls. The face of her gentle, handsome prince filled her mind, and her heart brimmed over with the knowledge that she would never be unhappy again.

Epilogue

The bells of the palace clock tower chimed merrily as Cinderella and the prince ran from the church. Two chirping bluebirds held up the train of Cinderella's beautiful white wedding gown as she smiled at the townspeople who had gathered to see the happy couple. The well-wishers showered the newlyweds with rice as they ducked into their honeymoon coach. The whole kingdom seemed to be aglow with love and goodwill.

Cinderella turned to her new husband, holding his hand tightly. As the coach carried them off to begin their new life together, Cinderella thought only of good things. She thought of the happy times she had shared with her father. She thought of her faithful animal friends at the château. She thought of the kind fairy godmother who had made her new life possible. She thought of her loving prince, with whom she would live in happiness and harmony all the days of their lives.

And finally, as the prince leaned over to kiss his new bride, Cinderella thought about how she had learned never, ever to give up on her dreams.

Disney's

THE LITTLE
MERMAID

*Adapted from the film
by A. L. Singer*

CHAPTER ONE

"Heave-ho!" The crew aboard the fine three-masted ship grunted as they pulled up a net filled with fish. It was all in a hard day's work at sea.

A young prince named Eric stood at the railing and lifted his face to the sea air. His faithful sheepdog, Max, stood by his side. The salty wind brushed back Eric's dark hair, and he smiled. The sea was his first love, and he could think of no better place to spend his birthday.

Eric gazed up into the thick clouds. "Isn't this great?" he said. "The salty sea air, the wind blowing in your face. A perfect day to be at sea!"

Near Eric, a gangly older man was bent over the railing. Slowly he raised himself. "Oh, yes," he said, his face green with seasickness. "Delightful." With a groan, he leaned over the side again.

Eric chuckled to himself. Old Grimsby had been his manservant for years, but he had never developed his sea legs.

"A fine strong wind and a following sea!" a sailor called out. "King Triton must be in a friendly mood."

"King Triton?" Eric asked, rushing over to help tie down a sail.

A crusty sailor named Sea Dog piped up, "Why, he's ruler of the merpeople, lad. Thought every good sailor knew about him."

"Hmph! Merpeople!" Grimsby said. "Eric, pay no attention to this nautical nonsense."

Sea Dog frowned. "But it ain't nonsense," he insisted, shaking a fish in Grimsby's face. "It's the truth! They're half fish and half human. I'm telling you, they live down in the depths of the ocean."

Eric had heard this argument many times before. Sea Dog and some of the other sailors were convinced that mer-people existed. Grimsby was absolutely certain they did

not. As for Eric, well, he simply didn't know what to think.

But if Eric could see to the bottom of the ocean, then he would know *exactly* what to think. For there, fathoms below Eric's ship, was the bustling kingdom of Atlantia. Merpeople and all the other creatures of the deep lived there—far away from human eyes—in a world all their own, a world presided over by the just and noble King Triton.

And on this very day, the entire kingdom had gathered to see the King's daughters sing in concert.

King Triton arrived at the concert hall in a golden chariot pulled by dolphins. His subjects cheered wildly. Soon after, a small crab appeared on a seashell pulled by goldfish. This was Sebastian, the royal court composer.

"I'm really looking forward to this performance, Sebastian," King Triton called out.

"Your Majesty," Sebastian replied, "this will be the finest concert I've ever conducted. Your daughters will be spectacular!"

"Yes," King Triton agreed. "And especially my little Ariel."

The King loved all his daughters. Each was a beauty and a great talent. But when it came to singing, Ariel out- shone them all. Fish, crabs, sharks, clams—all the living things in the sea would stop to listen. Even the coral was said to sigh with pleasure at the sound of Ariel's singing.

"Ah, Ariel has the most beautiful voice!" Sebastian agreed. But as he rode toward the podium, he grumbled to himself, "If only she'd show up for rehearsals once in a while."

Ariel always seemed to have something better to do than attend her music lessons. And when she did show up, she was late more often than not. But with a big apology, a winning smile, *and* her lovely voice, it was hard for Sebastian to stay angry at her. As for where she had been keeping herself, nobody knew.

Sebastian climbed the podium. When he raised his baton, an orchestra of fish musicians lifted their instruments. An octopus drummer became poised with his drumsticks.

Down came the baton, and the musicians began to play. A curtain of bubbles rose upward. Three huge clamshells appeared on the stage. They opened to reveal six mermaids, all daughters of King Triton—Aquata, Andrina, Arista, Attina, Adella, and Alana.

As they swam around, singing sweetly, another closed clamshell swirled onto the stage. Everyone knew that Ariel was inside—and they couldn't wait to hear her sing.

Slowly, with all eyes upon it, the shell opened, and there, in the middle, stood…no one. The shell was empty.

The sisters stopped singing. Sebastian dropped his baton. The audience gasped in shocked surprise.

King Triton rose from his seat, clenching his trident. His face turned red with fury as he let out a bellow that shook the seafloor.

"Ariel!"

CHAPTER TWO

Ariel glided through the water at top speed. With each tail stroke, her red hair swept back like a thick flame. In her right hand she clutched a sturdy, empty sack. In a few minutes the sack would be filled with fascinating things—things from the world above the water. She couldn't wait.

Ariel stopped swimming when she reached an old shipwreck. The ship's rotting hull was covered with seaweed and barnacles, and the mast was broken in two. Through the portholes Ariel could see a glimpse of the dark and eerie interior.

To Ariel this was the most beautiful sight in the sea. A shipwreck was mysterious, exotic. It was from that *other* world.

Merpeople were forbidden to go above the water. It was King Triton's strictest rule—and one that Ariel just could not obey. Whenever she could, Ariel would sneak up to the surface to look around. She'd even made friends with a sea gull named Scuttle.

Ariel was curious about everything above the surface, especially the land creatures called humans. She knew her father's rule was designed to keep his subjects—including his daughters—from interacting with humans. King Triton said that these land creatures were dangerous and could not be trusted. Ariel had never seen any humans up close before, but she didn't understand how, if they could make all the beautiful things she had collected from the ocean floor, they could be so evil.

"Isn't this ship fantastic?" Ariel called over her shoulder.

"Yeah, sure," answered a small roly-poly fish, huffing and puffing to keep up with her. His name was Flounder, and he was Ariel's best friend.

He was not only terribly out of breath, he was scared, too.

"Uh, let's get out of here, Ariel," Flounder said. "It looks damp in there. And I think I may be coming down with a cough."

"Well, I'm going inside," Ariel said. "You can just stay here and watch for sharks."

Ariel swam through a porthole. "Sharks?" Flounder squeaked. *"Ariel, wait!"*

Flipping his fins wildly, Flounder headed right into the porthole—and got stuck. "Ariel, help!" he called out, twisting himself right and left.

Inside the ship, at the top of a staircase, Ariel turned. "Oh, Flounder...." Laughing, she swam back toward him.

Flounder shook with fear. "Ariel," he whispered, "do you really think there might be sharks around here?"

"Flounder, don't be such a guppy," Ariel said.

"I'm not a guppy!"

Thoonk! With a strong yank, Ariel pulled her friend into the ship.

Flounder stayed close to Ariel. The darkness frightened him. In every corner he saw strange, shadowy shapes. And he had an uneasy feeling that he and Ariel were being watched.

Ariel and Flounder swam up, through a hole in the ceiling, to the next level of the ship. There, on a pile of broken boards, lay a shiny, dented fork. Ariel gasped with delight and quickly swam over to seize it.

"Flounder," she sighed, "have you ever seen anything so wonderful in your life?"

"Wow! Cool!" Flounder said. "But what is it?"

"I don't know," Ariel said. "But I bet Scuttle will!"

Rrrrrrommm! Flounder jumped at the sound. Something had sped by the ship, something very large.

"What was that noise?" Flounder asked.

But Ariel was busy examining a curved tobacco pipe. "Hmm, I wonder what *this* is...."

Flounder turned to look behind him. A pair of angry yellow eyes stared in at him through a large window.

Below the eyes was a mouth filled with razor-sharp teeth.

"A shark!" Flounder shrieked. "Ariel, swim!"

CRRRRRAAASSSSSH! With a mighty thrust, the shark burst through the window, his jaws gaping wide.

Flounder sped off. With a loud *wham*, the shark's jaws clamped shut. Flounder could feel the water ripple behind him.

Ariel quickly threw the pipe into her sack. She and Flounder darted up to the next floor. They raced away, over broken wooden planks that jutted up from below.

Suddenly Ariel felt herself being jerked backward. She looked down in horror.

Her bag was stuck on a plank. Quickly she grabbed it and, just inches ahead of the shark, swam for her life. She and Flounder swam out of the ship and went spiraling up around the mast of another.

Bonk! In his panic Flounder banged into the mast. The blow stunned him, and he sank slowly down toward the ocean floor.

Ariel sped to catch her friend before the shark did. She reached through the ring of an enormous anchor and snatched Flounder just inches from the ground.

With the shark advancing rapidly toward them, Ariel and Flounder popped back through the ring. Flounder had now recovered from his blow, and he and Ariel swam off as quickly as they could.

The speeding shark was concentrating so hard on his prey that he swam straight into the ring, where his neck became stuck tight. He wriggled angrily, but the ring held fast.

Flounder, sensing that the danger had now passed, turned back and stuck out his tongue. "You big bully!" The shark growled with fury, and Flounder recoiled in fear.

Ariel couldn't help chuckling. "Flounder, you really *are* a guppy," she said.

"I am not!" Flounder protested as the two friends made their way up to the surface.

CHAPTER THREE

When Ariel and Flounder burst through the surface of the water, they were greeted by a glorious sunny day. They blinked to adjust to the sunlight, and then Ariel spotted Scuttle lounging on a rock and singing a song out of tune.

The two friends swam quickly toward him, calling out, "Scuttle!"

Scuttle was a plump, jolly gull. He had a big heart, and he loved jokes. Although he wasn't the brightest of birds, he always *sounded* as if he knew what he was talking about.

"Scuttle, look what we found!" Ariel held out her sack.

"Human stuff, huh?" Scuttle said. He reached in and pulled out a fork. "Wow! This is special. This is very, very unusual!"

"What is it?" Ariel asked.

"It's a...a dinglehopper!" Scuttle replied. "Humans use these little babies to straighten their hair out." He demonstrated by combing his head feathers.

"Wow, a dinglehopper," Ariel said with admiration.

"What about *that* one?" Flounder asked as Scuttle took out the tobacco pipe.

"This I haven't seen in years!" Scuttle replied. "It's a banded, bulbous snarfblatt. It dates back to prehysterical times when humans used to sit around and stare at each other all day. It got very boring, so they invented this snarfblatt to make fine music. Allow me." He took a deep breath and blew into the pipe.

Seaweed and water gushed out the top. "It's stuck," Scuttle said with a groan.

Music. The word made Ariel remember the concert. "Oh my gosh!" she cried. "I'm late! My father's going to kill me. I've got to go—but thank you, Scuttle!"

Scuttle gave Ariel back the pipe. "Anytime, sweetie!"

He watched Ariel and Flounder dive beneath the surface and waved until they were out of sight.

Someone else was watching, too—someone not so friendly. In a dark corner of the sea lay the lair of Ursula the Sea Witch. Ursula had two arms and long black tentacles. She was enormous, she was ugly, and she was greedy. Worst of all, she was bent on destroying King Triton.

In a crystal ball that floated above Ursula's cauldron, an image of Ariel and Flounder shone brightly. Ursula stared at it intently. Flotsam and Jetsam, her two eel assistants, hovered nearby. They each had one yellow eye and one white eye that glowed with evil.

"Yes, hurry home, Princess," Ursula said in a mocking tone. "We wouldn't want to miss Daddy's celebration now, would we?"

Now, as always, all Ursula could think about were the good old days, the days when she had lived at the palace—before King Triton had thrown her out of the kingdom.

All Ursula could think about was revenge.

"Look at me!" she cried. "Banished and exiled while Triton and his flimsy fish folk celebrate! Well, I'll give them something to celebrate soon enough. Flotsam! Jetsam! Keep an extra-close watch on this pretty little daughter of his. She may be the key to Triton's undoing!"

CHAPTER FOUR

Ariel stood before her father in the throne room, her head bowed slightly while he scolded her for missing the concert. Flounder hid behind the throne room door.

"I just don't know what we're going to do with you, young lady," the King bellowed, the disappointment in his voice clear. "As a result of your careless behavior, the entire celebration was—"

Suddenly his flowing white beard parted. Sebastian peered out and said, "Ruined! It was ruined! Completely destroyed. This concert was to be the pinnacle of my entire career. Now, thanks to you, I am the laughingstock of the entire kingdom!"

Flounder hated to hear Ariel being yelled at. Before he could even think to stop himself, he swam toward the throne.

"It wasn't her fault!" he cried out, suddenly aware that he now had the full attention of both Sebastian and the King. He was instantly nervous. "Well, um, first this shark chased us, but we got away. Then there was this sea gull, and—"

"*Sea gull?*" King Triton bellowed.

Whoops. Flounder quickly hid behind Ariel.

"You went up to the surface again, didn't you?" King Triton said. "How many times must we go through this? You could have been seen by one of those barbarians, by one of those humans! Do you think I want my youngest daughter to be snared by some fish-eater's hook?"

"But Daddy, I'm sixteen years old," Ariel began in her defense. "I'm not a child anymore!"

"Don't you take that tone of voice with me, young lady," the King thundered. "As long as you live under *my* ocean, you'll observe *my* rules!"

"But if you would only listen—"

"Not another word! And you are *never* to go to the surface again. Is that clear?"

Ariel tried to stare at her father to show him that she wouldn't back down. But it was no use. She could feel her lip start to quiver and her eyes start to tear. She turned and swam out of the throne room, with Flounder following close behind.

King Triton sighed. It was not easy being tough on his daughters; he loved them so dearly.

"Do you think I was too hard on her?" he asked Sebastian.

"Definitely not!" Sebastian replied. "These teenagers, they think they know everything. You give them an inch, they swim all over you! Why, if Ariel were my daughter, I'd show her who was boss. None of this flitting to the surface and other such nonsense. No, sir, I'd keep her under tight control!"

King Triton sat back. Sebastian was giving him an idea. "You know, you're absolutely right, Sebastian," he said. "Ariel needs constant supervision."

"Constant!" Sebastian echoed.

"Someone to watch over her, to keep her out of trouble."

"All the time!"

"And you are just the crab to do it!"

Sebastian froze. That was not what he had in mind. Taking care of Ariel would be a full-time job. He was the royal court composer, not a baby-sitter. But he knew there would be no arguing with the King. When the King asked you to do something, you did it.

Sebastian sank into his shell. Muttering to himself, he swam away from the King's chamber and out into the ocean, where he caught sight of Ariel and Flounder. They were looking around suspiciously—as if they didn't want to be followed.

"Hmm," Sebastian said. "I wonder what that girl is up to now." He swam off behind Ariel and Flounder, hiding in the shadows.

The two friends came to a rock wall in front of which

a large boulder was lodged. With a grunt and some effort, Ariel pushed the boulder aside.

Sebastian gasped. Behind the huge rock was the opening to a dark grotto. Ariel and Flounder disappeared inside.

Thrusting his tiny legs forward as quickly as he could, Sebastian raced in after them. He hid in a corner and looked around in wonder.

The cave was enormous. It rose so high Sebastian couldn't see the ceiling. On the shelflike crags in the walls he could make out small objects: vases, plates, books, clocks, candle holders, eyeglasses, a harp. Sebastian had never seen such things, but he knew they must have come from the human world.

"Oh, Flounder," Ariel said, sitting gloomily on the cave floor. "If only I could make Father understand. I just don't see things the way he does. I don't see how a world that makes such wonderful things could be so bad." She swam upward, admiring all her treasures. "What I wouldn't give to see what the human world is like!"

Sebastian was listening so intently to Ariel that he backed right into a beer stein. With a *thunk*, the top swung shut and the stein fell over and rolled off the edge of a crag. It bumped down the wall and crashed onto the cave floor.

"Sebastian!" Ariel cried in shock.

Sebastian lay in a tangle of knickknacks. "Ariel, what is all this?" he said as he stood up quickly.

"It's just my collection," Ariel replied.

"If your father knew about this place, he'd—"

"You're not going to tell him, are you?" Flounder asked.

"Oh, please, Sebastian," Ariel pleaded. "He would never understand."

Sebastian took Ariel's hand and began pulling her toward the cavern's entrance. "You're under a lot of pressure down here, Princess," he said. "Come with me. I'll take you home and get you something warm to drink."

Ariel felt a shadow pass over them. She looked up at the small opening, way above them, at the top of the cave.

"Hmm, what do you suppose *that* is?" Ariel murmured. She slipped out of Sebastian's grip and swam upward.

"Ariel!" Sebastian screamed, and swam after her. He could hardly believe that after everything that had just happened, the little mermaid was heading for the surface again!

CHAPTER FIVE

Sebastian was furious. He certainly had no business being above the water. And there were Ariel and Flounder, just bobbing in the water, looking at something straight ahead of them.

"Ariel," Sebastian said, demanding an explanation. "What are you—"

KABOOOOM! An explosion cut Sebastian off. He turned around and gasped in shock. A large three-masted ship lay anchored in the water close by. Fireworks from the ship lit up the night sky in bright colors, their sparks floating gently down to the water.

The next thing Sebastian knew, Ariel was swimming toward the ship. She ignored his calls to return at once, as she was so intent on seeing what was happening on board.

Ariel peeked through an opening in the side of the ship, hidden by the darkness. She watched as a shipful of sailors in striped shirts and brown trousers laughed and sang and danced.

What fantastic things their legs were! she thought. The men used them to leap, skip, jump, and dance.

Barbarians? Was that what her father had called humans? They sure didn't look that way to Ariel.

There was a shaggy, furry creature on board that barked and jumped around on four legs. When it saw Ariel, it bounded over and licked her face.

"Max!" called a strong voice. "Here, boy!"

The dog leapt happily over to one of the young men.

The man laughed, and his cheeks dimpled. His dark hair fell across his forehead as he lifted a fife to his mouth.

Ariel had never stared at anyone this way. This man was so different from the rest. Her breath caught in her throat. He was *beautiful*.

Scuttle flapped his way next to Ariel and interrupted her thoughts. "Hey there, sweetie!" he called loudly. "Quite a show, huh?"

"Be quiet, they'll hear you!" Ariel said, grabbing Scuttle's beak. "I've never seen a human this close before. He's very handsome, isn't he?"

Scuttle looked at Max. "He looks kind of hairy and slobbery to me."

"Not that one," Ariel said with a laugh. "The one playing the snarfblatt!"

An older human began shouting, "Silence! Silence!" He stood by a large object covered with a canvas. As the music

fizzled out, the older man announced, "It is now my honor and privilege to present our esteemed Prince Eric with a very special, very expensive, very large birthday present."

"Hurrah!" shouted the men. Some of them clapped the handsome sailor on the back.

Ariel leaned forward to listen.

Prince Eric blushed and said, "Ah, Grimsby, you ol' beanpole, you shouldn't have!"

He's humble, too, Ariel thought. She liked that.

With a smile, Grimsby pulled off the canvas sheet. It fell to the deck, revealing a statue of Eric underneath.

All the sailors applauded. Grimsby looked proud of himself. But Eric thought that while the *face* on the statue looked like his, the pose certainly wasn't him. This figure looked the part of a conquering hero. His chest was puffed

out with pride, he gripped a sword in his hand, and he looked
about to scramble up a rock.

"Gee, Grim, it's...uh, it's really something," Eric managed
to say.

"Well, I had hoped it would be a wedding present, but..."

Eric chuckled. "Come on, Grim, don't start that again."

"Oh, Eric," Grimsby said with a sigh. "It isn't me alone. The
entire kingdom wants to see you happily settled down with the
right girl."

Eric walked to the railing and looked out to sea. Ariel followed him with her eyes, hypnotized. "Oh, she's out there somewhere. Believe me, Grim, when I find her, I'll know. It'll just hit
me, like lightning."

BOOOOOM! As if on cue, a thunderclap sounded, and lightning bathed the ship in harsh light. "Hurricane a-coming!" a sailor shouted. "Stand fast; secure the rigging!"

The crew leapt into action. They quickly tied down the sails and ropes. A huge wave rose over the ship, crashing over Ariel's head. A few yards behind her, Flounder and Sebastian disappeared under the water. Scuttle flapped his wings, but the wind forced him backward. "Ariel!" he shouted.

Ariel tried to hold on to the ship, but it was impossible. She plunged into the sea, head over tail. Struggling against the current, she fought her way upward.

She got back to the surface just in time to see a crack of lightning strike the ship. Instantly the mainsail went up in flames.

Ariel watched in horror as the flames spread. She saw Eric at the steering wheel, trying to guide the ship away from a sharp outcropping of rocks.

CRASH! With a sickening sound, the ship's hull bashed into the rocks. Sailors slid across the deck. Eric lost his balance. He hurtled into Grimsby. Flailing their arms, they both fell overboard.

They landed near a rowboat that the first mate had cut loose from the ship. "Grim, hang on!" Eric shouted. He hopped aboard the rowboat and pulled Grimsby in after him.

"Arf! Arf!"

Above the roaring tempest, Eric heard Max's bark. His eyes darted toward the ship. It was engulfed in fire—and Max was trapped.

Eric dove overboard and swam against the raging sea. Gasping for breath, he finally reached the burning ship and climbed aboard.

"Max!" Eric called, pulling himself up on deck.

CRRRAAACK! Above Eric, the mainmast broke. It tumbled downward, burning like a mammoth torch. Flames immediately began to spread right down to the lower deck, where the room holding the fireworks and gunpowder was.

Eric jumped away and looked up to see Max standing on the top of a staircase. He was shaking, afraid to jump.

"Come on, boy!" Eric held out his arms. "Jump!"

Max barked again and looked about fearfully. Finally, on unsteady legs, he jumped into Eric's arms.

Eric ran with Max to the railing, but his foot broke through the wooden deck and became firmly stuck there. The force of the sudden stop caused Eric to toss Max over-

board. The dog landed in the water with a splash and swam to the safety of the rowboat.

Before Eric could dislodge his foot, the fire reached the explosives room. And as Grimsby and the others watched helplessly from the rowboat—and Ariel looked on in horror from the water—the ship was blown sky-high in a smoky ball of flames.

CHAPTER SIX

Ariel felt as if her heart had stopped. Splinters of wood and pieces of twisted metal were raining down around her. She shielded herself, desperately looking for Eric amid the floating wreckage.

Finally she saw a slumped figure dressed in tattered clothing, clinging to a piece of driftwood. It was Eric. She watched as he slipped off the wood and sank slowly under the water. She swam to him as fast as she could, wrapped her arm around him, and lifted his head above the water. While fireworks exploded all around them, Ariel swam with the unconscious man toward the shore. The waves tossed them up and down. Rain whipped their faces. She wanted so much to swim under the sea, but she had heard that humans could drown. So she just gritted her teeth and kept on going until she reached land.

Scuttle joined Ariel, who sat watching the motionless Prince.

"Is he…dead?" Ariel asked.

Scuttle lifted Eric's bare foot and put it to his ear. "I can't make out a heartbeat."

"No, look, he's breathing," Ariel said. She smiled as Eric let out a small sigh. "He's so beautiful."

Ariel could feel something well up inside her. It was more than joy, more than happiness. A gentle love song formed in her heart, and she began to sing it softly.

Sebastian and Flounder arrived in time to see Eric open his eyes. Sebastian's jaw dropped in shock as Eric blinked and looked straight at Ariel. In his daze and in the glare of the sun he couldn't see her very clearly. But he could hear her song.

And then—"*Arf! Arf!*"—Max came bounding over a sand dune. Barking happily, he jumped on Eric and licked his face.

"Eric!" Grimsby shouted from nearby.

Ariel quickly jumped into the water and swam to a nearby rock, just out of Eric's sight. Sebastian and Flounder followed close behind.

"Eric!" Grimsby said, coming over the dune. "My boy, you do enjoy making me worry, don't you?"

Eric shook his head. He was still dizzy, still not quite conscious. "A girl rescued me...," he mumbled. "She...she was singing. She had the most beautiful voice!"

Grimsby hoisted Eric to his feet. "Ah, Eric, I think you've swallowed a bit too much seawater. Come on now, off we go!"

From her perch Ariel watched them walk over the hill.

"We are going to forget this whole thing ever happened!" Sebastian spoke nervously. "The Sea King will never know. *You* won't tell him. *I* won't tell him. And, I will stay in one piece!"

Ariel wasn't listening. Her mind was still on Eric. He was gone now—over the dune, into a world where she was not allowed. A world of air and trees, of sand and grass; a world of humans.

Someday, she vowed to herself, *someday I'll find a way to be part of that world.*

Deep in the ocean, Ursula the Sea Witch began to laugh. Her eyes were glued to the crystal ball. In it she could see Ariel. And she recognized the look on the girl's face.

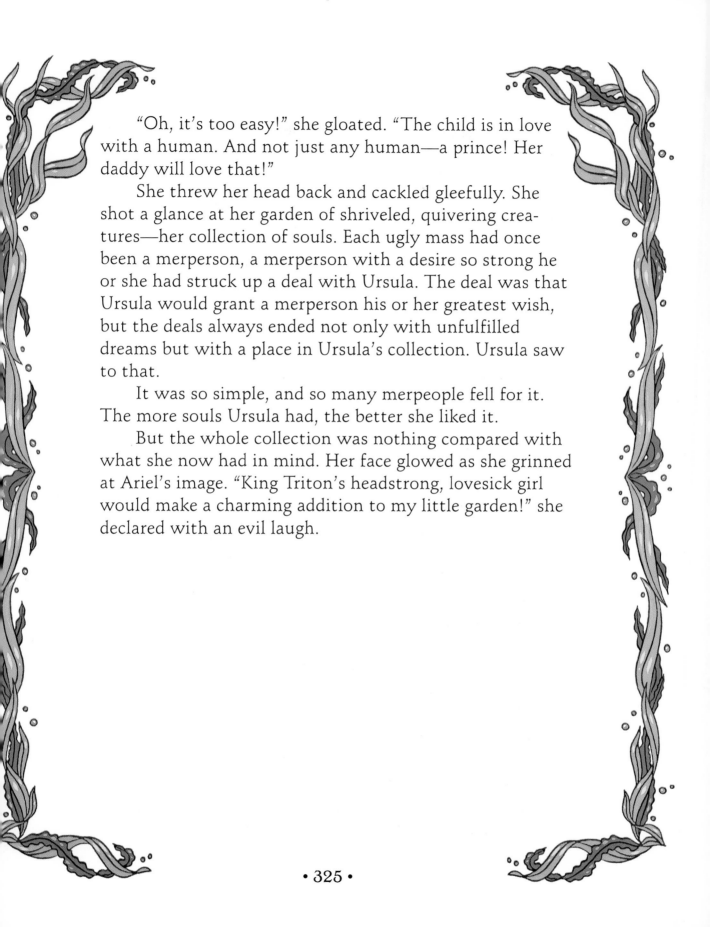

"Oh, it's too easy!" she gloated. "The child is in love with a human. And not just any human—a prince! Her daddy will love that!"

She threw her head back and cackled gleefully. She shot a glance at her garden of shriveled, quivering creatures—her collection of souls. Each ugly mass had once been a merperson, a merperson with a desire so strong he or she had struck up a deal with Ursula. The deal was that Ursula would grant a merperson his or her greatest wish, but the deals always ended not only with unfulfilled dreams but with a place in Ursula's collection. Ursula saw to that.

It was so simple, and so many merpeople fell for it. The more souls Ursula had, the better she liked it.

But the whole collection was nothing compared with what she now had in mind. Her face glowed as she grinned at Ariel's image. "King Triton's headstrong, lovesick girl would make a charming addition to my little garden!" she declared with an evil laugh.

CHAPTER SEVEN

Her sisters could tell that Ariel was in love. She had that faraway look in her eyes and day-dreamed more than ever. They all assumed she'd fallen for a merman. Only Sebastian and Flounder knew the whole truth.

Sebastian paced the ocean floor, worried sick. Ariel sat on a rock above him, plucking the petals of a yellow sea flower.

"He loves me, he loves me not…," she said.

"Okay. So far, so good," Sebastian said. "I don't think the King knows…but it will not be easy keeping something like this a secret for long!"

"He loves me! I knew it!" Ariel exclaimed as she pulled off the last petal.

"Ariel, stop talking crazy!" Sebastian said.

"I've got to see him again. Tonight! Scuttle knows where he lives. I'll swim up to his castle. Then Flounder will splash around and get his attention. Then we'll—"

"Ariel! Will you get your head out of the clouds and back in the water where it belongs? Down here is your home! The human world, it's a mess. Life under the sea is better than anything they've got up there! Safe and happy. Everything is beautiful. Humans like to put us in bowls, and when they get hungry—ha! Guess who is cooked for dinner?"

Sebastian went on and on, gesturing and pacing. When he looked up, Ariel was gone.

"Ohhh," he said with frustration, "somebody's got to nail that girl's fins to the floor!"

"Sebastian!" a voice called from behind.

Sebastian turned to see a sea horse racing toward him. "I've got an urgent message from the Sea King!" the sea horse announced. "He wants to see you right away. Something about Ariel!"

Sebastian gulped. The King had found out! Sebastian's career was over, he just knew it. He had failed to take care of Ariel. The King would surely banish him—if he were lucky.

Shaking, Sebastian swam toward the castle.

In the throne room King Triton chuckled to himself. Imagine! His youngest daughter in love—and that rascal Sebastian had kept it a secret. Who could the lucky merman be? he wondered.

When Sebastian entered, the King decided to tease him a bit. "Uh, Sebastian, I'm concerned about Ariel. Have you noticed she's been acting peculiar lately?"

"Peculiar?" Sebastian asked with a smile.

"You know," said Triton, "mooning about, daydreaming, singing to herself?"

"Oh, ooh, well, I—" Sebastian stammered.

King Triton raised an eyebrow. "Sebastian," he said, "I know you've been keeping something from me."

"K-k-keeping something?"

"About Ariel."

"Ariel?" Sebastian's legs were clattering now.

"Being in love?" King Triton picked up his trident and pointed it playfully at Sebastian. "Hmmm?"

Suddenly Sebastian fell to his knees. He grabbed the King's beard and began to whimper. "I tried to stop her, sir! She wouldn't listen! I told her to stay away from humans! They are bad! They are trouble. They—"

King Triton sat bolt upright. His eyes glowed with a fiery rage. "*Humans?*" he bellowed. "What about humans?"

His trident began to glow brightly. He lifted Sebastian to eye level.

Sebastian gulped. He had a lot of explaining to do.

"Come on!" Flounder called to Ariel as he led her into the grotto.

"Flounder, why can't you tell me what this is about?" Ariel pleaded.

"You'll see. It's a surprise!"

Ariel stopped short when she saw what was in the
center of the grotto. There, tilted to one side, was the
statue of Prince Eric.

"Oh, Flounder, you're the best!" Ariel exclaimed. "It
looks just like him. It even has his eyes!"

She floated around it. If only it really were him, she
thought. "Why, Eric, you want me to run away with you?"
she said with a giggle. "This is all so sudden!"

She twirled around with happiness. The room seemed
to spin. She saw the shelves, the hole in the ceiling, the
entrance, Sebastian, her father—

Her father!

"Daddy!" Ariel cried.

Flounder darted behind a large chest. Sebastian began biting his claw nervously.

King Triton stepped out of the entrance and into the grotto. In the uneven light his face was etched in shadows. "I consider myself a reasonable merman. I set certain rules, and I expect those rules to be obeyed," he said sternly. "Is it true you rescued a human from drowning?"

"Daddy, I had to!" Ariel protested.

"Contact between the human world and the merworld is strictly forbidden. Ariel, you know that. Everyone knows that!"

"He would have died!"

"One less human to worry about!" King Triton scowled angrily.

"You don't even know him," Ariel said heatedly.

"Know him?" Triton roared. "I don't have to know him. They're all the same—spineless savage harpooning fish-eaters! Incapable of any feeling or—"

"Daddy, I love him!"

Ariel gasped and put her hands to her mouth. She couldn't believe she admitted that to her father. But it was true, truer than anything she had ever said in her life.

The words hit King Triton like a fist. His jaw dropped in shock. "No! Have you lost your senses completely? He's a human, you're a mermaid!"

"I don't care!" she replied.

"So help me, Ariel, I am going to get through to you," the King said through clenched teeth. "And if this is the only way, so be it!"

His trident began to glow a bright, angry orange. He

lifted it high and pointed it at the shelves filled with objects from the human world.

WHAM! A beam of orange light shot from the trident and smashed a candelabra.

WHAM! A ceramic globe exploded into bits.

Ariel's face went pale with horror. "Daddy! No!" she screamed.

WHAM! WHAM! WHAM! One by one King Triton destroyed object after object. Ariel swam to her father's side. "Stop it! Stop it!" she pleaded.

But the King's eyes were focused on the statue now. That must be the human Ariel loved, he reasoned. That was the one who could threaten the lives of everyone in his kingdom. He pointed the trident directly at it.

"*Daaaddddy!*" Ariel screamed.

CCRRRRRRAAACCK! The trident's bolt of energy was enormous. The statue exploded into tiny pieces and fell into all the corners of the grotto.

And that was it. The King gave Ariel another stern glance. Then his trident stopped glowing.

Ariel looked over to where the statue had been. There was now only a flat rock with a few jagged pieces of stone. She put her head down and began to cry.

The King's face softened in sadness at his daughter's unhappiness, and he left the grotto with his head bowed. Slowly Flounder and Sebastian came out of their hiding places. They swam toward Ariel.

"Ariel," Sebastian said softly. "I—"

"Just go away," Ariel replied.

Sebastian nodded. He felt awful. He and Flounder gave each other a look. They knew Ariel needed to be alone so, quietly, with sad faces, they swam away.

Ariel didn't see them go. And she didn't see Flotsam and Jetsam approach, either.

"Poor, sweet child," Flotsam said.

"She has a very serious problem," said Jetsam.

"If only there was something we could do for her."

Flotsam and Jetsam stared at Ariel, trying to look concerned.

Ariel glanced up. She had never seen these two eels before. Their words were kind, but she didn't feel comfortable with them.

"Who are you?" she asked.

"Don't be scared," Flotsam said. "We represent someone who can make all your dreams come true."

"You and your prince," Jetsam added.

"Together forever," they chimed at the same time.

"I—I don't understand," Ariel said warily.

Flotsam grinned. "Ursula has great powers."

"The Sea Witch?" Ariel was filled with disgust. "Why, that's...I couldn't possibly. No! Get out of here! Leave me alone!"

"Suit yourself," Jetsam said, turning to swim away.

"It was only a suggestion." As Flotsam left, he swam over the rubble of Prince Eric's statue. The face was lying there, staring blankly upward. Flotsam flicked it with his tail, and it rolled toward Ariel.

Ariel gently picked up the broken sculpture. It was an amazing likeness.

Spineless. Savage. Incapable of feeling. King Triton's words came back to her. How could anyone call Eric those things? Her father was wrong, so wrong!

She looked around. Shattered pieces of her collection lay strewn about. Her beautiful grotto was now a junk pile. And why? Because of her father! Who was really the savage one? Who was the one incapable of feeling?

Ariel's eyes filled with tears. The grotto became blurry. Flotsam and Jetsam were now two distant shadows moving away. In a moment they would be gone.

"Together forever," they had said. But what if it was a trap? What if Ursula had some sinister plan?

Ariel sighed. She couldn't imagine how her life could be any worse than it was now....

"Wait!" The word flew out of Ariel's mouth before she could think. "I'm coming with you."

Flotsam and Jetsam both turned around. As they smiled, their eyes seemed to pulse with electricity. "Wonderful choice, my dear!" Jetsam said.

As the eels led Ariel out of the grotto, they passed by Flounder and Sebastian.

"Ariel!" Sebastian gasped. "Where are you going? What are you doing with this riffraff?"

"I'm going to see Ursula," Ariel retorted.

"Ariel, no!" Sebastian said. "She's a demon!"

Ariel didn't have much use for Sebastian now. After all, he was the one who had betrayed her. "Why don't you go tell my father?" she taunted. "You're good at that!"

Ariel turned and swam away. Sebastian and Flounder hurried after her as quickly as they could.

CHAPTER EIGHT

Ariel hesitated when she reached Ursula's lair. The entrance was the open jaw of an enormous fish skeleton shrouded in puffs of black smoke. The smoke curled around the jaw's pointed fangs.

"This way," Flotsam and Jetsam urged.

Ariel gulped but swam on.

Suddenly something cold and slimy grabbed Ariel's wrist and yanked her downward. She shuddered. It was a shivering, sad-eyed lump, one of many such creatures who moaned and quivered and looked at Ariel with terrified yellow eyes. Gasping with horror, Ariel pulled herself loose.

"Come in, come in, my child," Ursula called.

Ariel spun around. The Sea Witch was leering down at her.

Ariel backed away in fear. This trip didn't seem like such a good idea anymore.

Ursula slid across the seafloor and heaved her massive body toward a vanity table. She admired herself in the mirror and applied lotion to her hair.

"Now then," she began, "you're here because you have a thing for this human, this prince fellow. Not that I blame you. He is quite a catch, isn't he? Well, angelfish, the solution to your problem is simple."

Ursula painted her lips a bright red and gave a twisted smile. "The only way to get what you want is to become a human yourself."

"Can you change me into one?" Ariel asked.

"My dear sweet child, that's what I do. It's what I live for. To help poor, unfortunate merfolk like yourself. Poor souls with no one else to turn to. Many have come to me for my help…and for a price, I grant their wishes." Ursula glanced at the souls huddled by the entrance. "Of course, some can't pay the price, but you needn't worry about that."

Ariel's mouth opened in disbelief. Those horrible-looking creatures were once ordinary merfolk! But because they couldn't pay Ursula's "price," they were lost forever.

"Now here is the deal," Ursula said, pulling Ariel close. As she led Ariel away from the souls, Sebastian and Flounder swam to the entrance. In shock, they stopped and watched.

"I will make you a potion that will turn you into a human for three days," Ursula continued. "You must get dear old Princie to fall in love with you. If he gives you the kiss of true love before the sun sets on the third day, you'll remain human permanently. But if he doesn't, you turn back into a mermaid—and you belong to me!"

"No, Ari—" Sebastian started to scream, but Flotsam quickly wrapped himself around Sebastian's mouth while Jetsam grabbed Flounder.

"Have we got a deal?" Ursula asked before Ariel could notice Sebastian and Flounder.

"If I become human," Ariel said, thinking out loud, "I'll never be with my father or sisters again."

"That's right, but you'll have your man," Ursula replied with a broad smile. "Oh, and there is one more thing. We haven't discussed the subject of payment."

"But I don't have anything!" Ariel said.

"I'm not asking much. Just a token, really. A trifle. You'll never even miss it." Ursula smiled reassuringly. She gave Ariel a gentle touch under the chin. "What I want from you is your voice."

"My...voice?" Ariel couldn't believe her ears.

"That's right; you've got it. No more talking, singing, zip!"

"But without my voice, how can I—"

"You'll have your looks and your pretty face. And you can use body language! Men aren't impressed by conversation. They like women who are demure and quiet."

Ursula proceeded to grab flask after flask of liquid off a shelf and toss them into a cauldron. Ariel watched in fright as pinkish

smoke began to rise. It mushroomed and puffed and swirled around. In the midst of its billows Ariel could see Eric's face form.

"So, have we got a deal?" Ursula asked. She flicked her wrist, and a large golden scroll appeared.

Although Ariel was still very much afraid of Ursula, she leaned forward to read the inscription on the scroll: I Hereby Grant unto Ursula the Witch of the Sea One Voice, for All Eternity. Signed, _____.

In a flash of light, a pen materialized above Ariel's head. "Go ahead," Ursula said. "Make your choice, dear."

Everything was happening so fast. Ariel didn't feel quite right about making a deal with Ursula. But it all did seem rather

simple. So, mustering up all her courage, Ariel grabbed the pen and signed her name.

Ursula's eyes glowed with victory. A horrible, wicked smile came across her face. She waved her arms over the cauldron, chanting a magic spell. The smoke swirled like a tornado, and from the cauldron rose two green, smoky hands.

"Now sing!" Ursula commanded.

Ariel obeyed, and as she sang, a bright light began to glow within her throat.

The long green hands reached toward Ariel and plucked the light from her throat.

Ariel's hands instinctively went to her neck. She was no longer making any sounds, but her *voice* was still singing. Her voice was inside the light!

Ursula began to laugh. She held up a seashell locket that hung around her neck and watched in satisfaction as the hands placed the light inside.

Cackling with glee, Ursula waved her hand over the cauldron again. Enormous blasts of smoke shot upward, and a huge orange bubble encircled Ariel.

Ariel flailed desperately. She flipped her tail, trying to swim away. Then, in two flashes of light, her tail was gone. So was the bubble.

She looked down. Where her tail had been, there were now two legs.

Ariel couldn't breathe. She tried to swim, but she was not used to her legs. She felt strangely weighted down. Was *this* what it was like to be human? Was this…drowning?

Sebastian and Flounder broke loose from Ursula's eels. They grabbed Ariel and raced with her toward the surface.

CHAPTER NINE

Prince Eric sighed. Since his rescue, he hadn't been the same. All he could think about was that girl on the beach.

According to Grimsby, she was just a figment of Eric's imagination.

It was true that Eric hadn't seen her very clearly. He had been too groggy. But there was one thing about her that Eric could never have dreamed up—one thing so beautiful it *had* to be real.

Her voice.

He wanted so badly to hear that girl sing once more. No sound on earth had ever seemed so lovely to him.

Eric picked up his fife and began to play. A sad tune floated across the beach and echoed off the stone wall of his castle.

As the last notes of his song faded away, Eric began walking down the shore. Soon Max was panting along beside him.

Eric tousled the dog's hair and smiled. "Max, I can't get that voice out of my head," he said. "I've looked everywhere for her. Where could she be?"

He paced silently on the sand, hoping against hope he might find her.

Ariel, Sebastian, and Flounder lay exhausted from their swim, on a pile of rocks near where Prince Eric was walking. Ariel slowly lifted her head and blinked in the brightness of the sun. Not too far away, she saw an old shipwreck rotting on the sand. Where was she?

She looked down in the water, just below her feet.
Feet?

Ariel lifted one of her legs. She wiggled her toes. What
a feeling! She giggled silently.

"Well, look at what the catfish dragged in!" Scuttle
landed gently on Ariel's leg and laughed. "Look at you!
Look at you! There's something different. Don't tell me.
It's your hairdo! You've been using the dinglehopper,
right?"

Ariel shook her head.

Scuttle rested a wing on Ariel's toes. "Hmm, I got to
admit, I can't put my foot on it right now, but—"

"She's got legs, you idiot!" Sebastian cried out. "She
traded her voice to the Sea Witch and got legs!"

"Ariel's been turned into a human!" Flounder chimed

in. "She has three days to make the Prince fall in love with her, and he's got to kiss her."

Ariel couldn't say a word now, but she still felt wonderful. Carefully she tried to stand on her new legs. Boy, did they feel shaky! She didn't know how humans could possibly—

SPLASH! She toppled over and landed in the water.

"Just look at her!" Sebastian said. "Oh, this is a catastrophe. Her father is going to kill me! I'm going to march myself straight home now and tell him—"

Ariel lifted him up and shook her head, silently begging Sebastian to change his mind.

"Well, maybe there's still time," Sebastian said, trying to convince Ariel that this was the right thing to do. "If we could get that witch to give you back your voice, you could go home with all the normal fish and just be—" The expression on Ariel's face made him stop. He'd never seen her so sad. With a sigh, he finished his sentence. "Just be miserable for the rest of your life. All right, all right, I'll try to help you find that prince."

Ariel gave Sebastian a kiss. As she lowered him to the rock, he muttered, "Boy, what a soft shell I'm turning out to be."

"Now, let's put some clothing on you," Scuttle said, flying toward the nearby shipwreck. "I'm telling you, if you want to be human, the first thing you have to do is dress like one."

Scuttle pulled a white sail and some rope off the shipwreck and brought them to Ariel, who had waded to shore. She draped the sail around her and tied it in place with the rope.

"You look sensational, kid!" Scuttle said.

Ariel looked at Sebastian and Flounder. Before they could react, a loud sound came over a nearby dune.

"Arf! Arf!"

Flounder screamed and dove underwater. Scuttle flew off. Sebastian leapt into a fold of Ariel's costume.

Max came bounding over the dune. He ran to Ariel and began licking her.

"Max! Hey, Max, what's gotten into you, fella?"

It was Eric's voice. Ariel looked toward the dune. And then, in an instant, there he was, looking at Ariel. Max tore himself away and ran toward his master.

"Are you okay, miss?" Eric asked. "I'm sorry if Max scared you. He's really harmless."

Ariel smiled. Eric was so handsome, so gentle. She wished she could say something to him. Instead she blushed and smiled.

"You seem familiar to me," Eric said. "Have we met?"

Max got behind Eric and pushed him closer to Ariel. "We have met!" he said, taking Ariel's hands. "You're the one I've been looking for! What's your name?"

Looking into his eyes, Ariel knew she was in love. Quickly she opened her mouth to say "Ariel," but no sound came out.

"What is it?" Eric asked. "You can't speak?"

Sadly Ariel shook her head.

"Oh, then you can't be who I thought," Eric said, disappointed.

But Ariel was determined not to give up. She began pantomiming what had happened. She pointed to her throat, made swimming motions with her hands, and pretended to pass out. Then she slipped from her rock and fell right into Eric's arms.

"Whoa, careful!" Eric clutched her tightly. "Gee, you must have really been through something. Don't worry, I'll help you. Come on."

Ariel felt unsure on her new legs, but Eric patiently helped her walk. Behind them, Flounder and Scuttle smiled and waved and wished her good luck.

CHAPTER TEN

At the castle Ariel was turned over to Eric's housekeeper, Carlotta. Carlotta drew a hot bubble bath for Ariel and sent her sailcloth dress to the washroom. Then she found a lovely pink ball gown for Ariel to wear to dinner.

Sebastian, however, had a very different experience. Hidden in Ariel's sailcloth dress, he traveled to the washroom, where he was dumped into the wash basin. The soapy water made him cough and sputter. He grabbed on to a shirt in the wash, and when one of the housemaids hung the shirt out to dry, Sebastian went with it.

He lifted his head and peered out the shirt pocket. The clothesline was next to an open window in the castle. Sebastian jumped inside, and with a small thump, he landed on a wooden table. He sighed with relief.

Then he saw the knife—a huge knife stuck in the table between two cut-up halves of a fish. Sebastian looked away in horror—and saw two stuffed crabs on a plate.

Stuffed crabs!

Sebastian gasped in horror. All around him were creatures from the sea—stuffed, fried, baked, and broiled. And every one of them was very, very dead.

"What is this? I have missed one!"

Sebastian spun around to see the chef. His white apron was stained with blood, and he held a sharp cleaver in his hand.

"Eeek!" Sebastian screamed.

"You are alive?" Holding the cleaver high, the chef came after Sebastian.

With a yelp, Sebastian ran as fast as his claws could carry him.

In the royal dining room Eric stood silently by the window. He watched the sun slowly setting over the water. The table was set, but Ariel had not yet arrived.

Sitting at the table, Grimsby filled his pipe with tobacco. "Eric," he said, "nice young ladies just don't swim around rescuing people in the middle of the ocean."

"I'm telling you, she was real," Eric insisted. "I'm going to find that girl—and I'm going to marry her!"

Carlotta's voice drifted into the room from the hallway. "Come on, honey," she said. "Don't be shy."

Eric turned to see Ariel, looking magnificent in a beautiful gown. Eric was speechless.

Ariel smiled shyly as she walked in.

"Eric, isn't she a vision?" Grimsby said, showing Ariel to her place at the table.

"Uh, you look wonderful" was all Eric could say.

"Comfy, my dear?" Grimsby said. "It's not often we have such a lovely dinner guest, eh, Eric?"

Ariel spotted a fork beside her plate. A dinglehopper, she thought. She grabbed it and began combing her hair.

Eric and Grimsby stared silently. Whoops, Ariel said to herself. Maybe it was bad manners to use a dinglehopper at the table. She quickly put it down.

Grimsby lit his pipe and began to smoke. Ariel stared at the snarfblatt and smiled.

"Uh, do you like it?" Grimsby asked, holding the pipe out with admiration.

Ariel took the pipe and blew into it. A cloud of black soot flew into Grimsby's face.

"Pkacchh!" Grimsby cried.

Ariel was horrified. Eric and Carlotta burst into laughter.

"Very amusing," Grimsby muttered as he wiped the soot from his face. "Carlotta, what's for dinner?"

"Oh, you're going to love it! Chef Louis has been fixing stuffed crabs!" Carlotta said as she headed for the kitchen.

Ariel felt sick to her stomach. Imagine eating crabs!

Carlotta returned with three plates, each covered with a sterling silver lid. Ariel tried not to look when Grimsby uncovered his plate, but she couldn't believe her eyes when she saw what was on it.

Sebastian!

It was a good thing Ariel had no voice or she would have screamed. She quickly lifted the lid off her plate and gestured for Sebastian to hide there.

"You know, Eric," Grimsby was saying, "perhaps our young guest would like a tour of the kingdom."

Quickly Sebastian skittered across the table and onto Ariel's plate. She slammed the lid closed.

"Well, what do you say?" Eric asked.

Ariel leaned on the lid and nodded with delight.

"Wonderful!" Grimsby said. "Now, let's eat before this crab wanders off my plate...." His voice trailed off. There was only a pile of bread crumbs where his crab should have been.

Ariel breathed a sigh of relief.

So did Sebastian.

That night, Ariel was shown to a splendid guest room. From there she could hear Eric and Max playing in the courtyard. Smiling, she sank into the soft satin sheets of her bed.

On her dresser Sebastian was still picking bits of lettuce and spices from his shell. "This has got to be, without a doubt, the single most humiliating day of my life!" he said. "I hope you appreciate what I go through for you, young lady. Now then, we've got to make a plan to get that boy to kiss you. Tomorrow you've got to look your best. You've got to bat your eyes and pucker up your lips—"

He turned to look at Ariel, but her eyes were already closed. With a shake of his head, Sebastian said tenderly, "You are hopeless, child, you know that?"

Yawning, he walked to the candle and blew it out. Then he curled up next to Ariel on the bed and drifted into a deep sleep.

CHAPTER ELEVEN

"Oh, what have I done?" King Triton moaned to himself.

All night long his subjects had been searching for Ariel. Now it was morning, and no one had seen her. They had searched every corner of the seafloor.

None of them suspected the truth. None of them would have thought to look on the land, where Ariel and Prince Eric had just set out for a carriage ride. As they sped over a country bridge, Flounder leapt out of the water below. He spotted Sebastian hiding on the side of the carriage.

"Has he kissed her yet?" Flounder called up.

"Not yet," Sebastian answered.

The tour lasted all day. Ariel fell more in love with Eric every minute. They admired the sights, stopped at a country fair, had a picnic, and danced to an outdoor orchestra. Eric bought her a bouquet of flowers and a beautiful new hat. He even offered her the reins of the carriage. In her enthusiasm Ariel made the horses go so fast that the carriage bounced across a cliff.

That evening, Eric took her on a rowboat across a lagoon. The sunset streaked the clouds with spectacular colors. Sitting in that boat, watching Eric row, Ariel could not imagine a greater happiness.

Nearby, Scuttle sat on a rock and watched. Flounder floated in the water below him. "Nothing is happening! Only one day left, and that boy ain't puckered up once,"

Scuttle said. "This calls for a little vocal romantic stimulation."

Scuttle flew up to the branches of a tree, pushing aside some bluebirds. Clearing his throat, he began to sing: "BRRAAAWK! CAAAAAW! SKRAAACCKK! EEEEK!"

Ariel knew who it was right away. She cringed.

"Ow, that's horrible," Eric said. "Somebody should find that poor animal and put it out of its misery."

Hiding at the edge of the rowboat, Sebastian rolled his eyes. "I'm surrounded by amateurs," he said to himself. "If you want something done, you've got to do it yourself!"

He dove into the water and broke off the tip of a long reed. Using it as a baton, he summoned the lagoon animals to attention. "First we've got to create the mood!

"Percussion!" Ducks began tapping a soft drumbeat on turtles' shells.

"Strings!" Grasshoppers rubbed their hind legs together to sound like violins.

"Wind instruments!" Reeds vibrated in the gentle breeze. Together they all played a soft love song.

Sebastian sang in a caressing voice. His words urged Eric to kiss Ariel.

"Do you hear something?" Eric asked.

Ariel could only smile and shrug.

"You know," Eric said, "I feel really bad, not knowing your name. Maybe I could guess. Is it…Mildred?"

Ariel made a face and shook her head.

Eric laughed. "Okay, how about Diana? Rachel?"

As the music continued, Sebastian leapt onto the edge of the boat. He whispered up to Eric, "Her name is Ariel!"

"Ariel?" Eric asked.

Ariel nodded.

"Hmm, that's kind of pretty," Eric said. With a broad smile, he took her hand. "Okay, Ariel."

They floated along, hand in hand, to Sebastian's song. Soon a full moon began to rise over the lagoon. It cast its amber light over the still water. Ariel felt her heart quicken. Eric leaned closer. His smiling face drew nearer. He puckered his lips.

Sebastian grinned. Scuttle wanted to cheer. Flounder flipped his tail with excitement. This was it!

Ariel closed her eyes. She puckered her lips as Eric leaned closer…and closer…and closer…

SPLASHHHHHH!

The rowboat flipped over, and Ariel and Eric fell into the water. "Don't worry!" shouted Eric. "I've got you!"

All at once, the music stopped. Ducks flew away; turtles ducked underwater. Sebastian groaned. Scuttle and Flounder stared in shock. The romantic mood was broken. The kiss would have to wait for the next day.

Just beneath the rowboat, two shadowy figures laughed. They clasped their tails together, congratulating each other for tipping the boat.

Then, under cover of darkness, as Ursula watched in her crystal ball, Flotsam and Jetsam began to swim home.

"That was a close one," Ursula said to herself. "Too close. At this rate he'll be kissing her by sunset tomorrow, for sure. It's time to take matters into my own tentacles!" From her shelves she pulled a bubbling potion and a glass ball containing a small, delicate butterfly.

She threw the potion and the ball into her cauldron, creating a loud explosion and a big burst of flames.

"Triton's daughter will be mine!" Ursula gloated. "And then I'll make him wriggle like a worm on a hook!"

Ursula cackled. White smoke encircled her. The seashell necklace around her neck began to glow. Over Ursula's laughter, it sang out loud and clear in Ariel's voice.

Then, slowly, Ursula changed. Her enormous body turned slender. Her tentacles became two legs, and her hideous face was transformed into that of a beautiful dark-haired woman.

With a loud thunderclap, Ursula transported herself instantly to the shore near Prince Eric's castle. She waded out of the ocean, singing. To Eric, who was staring out to sea, deep in thought, she appeared at first as a vision. And then, when the glow from Ursula's necklace was reflected in his eyes, she changed into the girl who had saved his life—the one he had been searching for.

The next morning, Ariel awoke to a shout.

"Ariel!"

Her eyes fluttered open. Sebastian was fast asleep on the pillow beside her. The morning sun was coming in through the window—and so was Scuttle.

"Ariel, I just heard the news." Scuttle landed with a thud on her bed. "Congratulations, kiddo, we did it!"

Sebastian turned around and yawned. "What is this idiot babbling about?"

Scuttle grinned. "As if you two didn't know. The whole town's buzzing about the Prince getting married this afternoon!" He jumped onto the headboard and patted Ariel's cheek. "I just wanted to wish you luck. Catch you later! I wouldn't miss it for anything!"

As Scuttle flew out the window, Ariel and Sebastian gasped. *The Prince was getting married?*

Ariel jumped out of bed. She wanted to scream with joy. She picked up Sebastian and twirled around.

Why hadn't Eric said anything? He must have wanted to surprise her. She was dying to see him, so she put Sebastian down and ran out of her room and down the hall. She practically flew down the staircase; she could barely feel her feet touch the ground.

Then, suddenly, she stopped. The blood rushed from her face. Eric was at the foot of the stairs, arm in arm with a gorgeous dark-haired young woman.

Grimsby stood next to the couple. "Well, now, Eric," he said, "it appears that this mystery maiden of yours does in fact exist. And she is lovely." He took the young woman's hand. "Congratulations, my dear."

"Vanessa and I wish to be married today!" Eric announced. "The wedding ship departs at sunset."

CHAPTER TWELVE

How could he?

Ariel kept asking herself that question over and over. Eric had seemed so open, so honest, so kind. And he had been in love with her. She just *knew* it.

She slumped against a pillar on the royal dock. The entire day had passed, and Eric hadn't looked at her even once. It was as if she'd never existed.

Now, under a glorious sunset, Eric's wedding ship was sailing out to sea. Hundreds of people were aboard, laughing and singing. And Ariel had not even been invited.

She buried her head in her arms and began to weep. Alongside her, Sebastian looked on helplessly. From the water below them, Flounder's little sobs floated upward.

At that same moment, Scuttle swooped down over the ship, humming a wedding tune. It would be so exciting to see Ariel get married. He especially wanted to see the bride kiss the groom.

Through a porthole Scuttle could see Ariel fixing her hair and singing. But wait! That dark-haired girl *sounded* like Ariel, but she sure didn't look or act like her.

Scuttle flew closer, and when the girl looked in the mirror, Ursula's reflection looked back out! He heard her say, "Hah! I'll have that little mermaid soon. And when I do, the entire ocean will be mine!"

"The Sea Witch!" Scuttle said to himself.

There was no time to waste. He immediately flew to the dock. "Ariel!" he cried, flustered and out of breath. "I

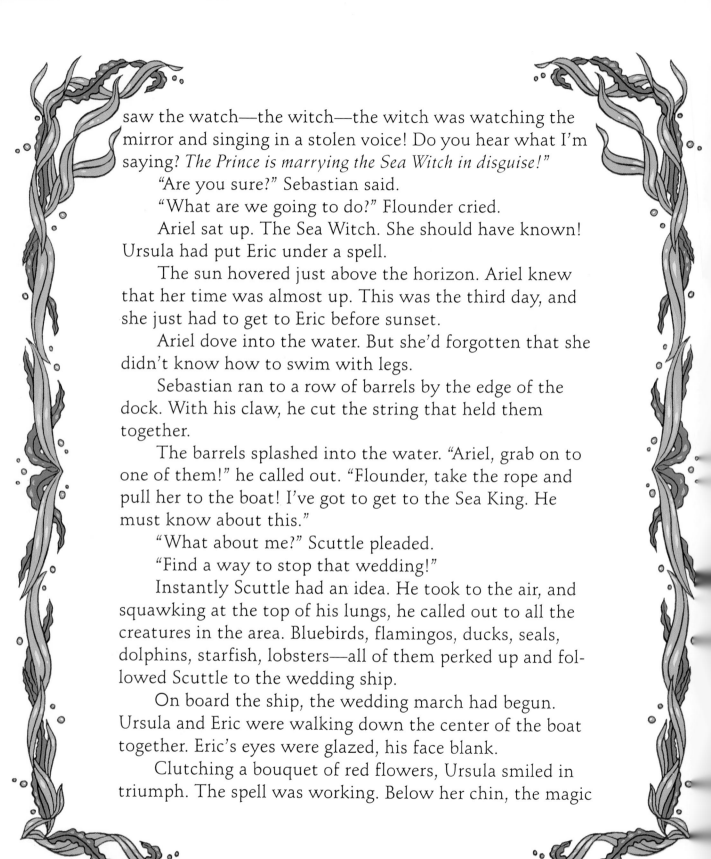

saw the watch—the witch—the witch was watching the mirror and singing in a stolen voice! Do you hear what I'm saying? *The Prince is marrying the Sea Witch in disguise!*"

"Are you sure?" Sebastian said.

"What are we going to do?" Flounder cried.

Ariel sat up. The Sea Witch. She should have known! Ursula had put Eric under a spell.

The sun hovered just above the horizon. Ariel knew that her time was almost up. This was the third day, and she just had to get to Eric before sunset.

Ariel dove into the water. But she'd forgotten that she didn't know how to swim with legs.

Sebastian ran to a row of barrels by the edge of the dock. With his claw, he cut the string that held them together.

The barrels splashed into the water. "Ariel, grab on to one of them!" he called out. "Flounder, take the rope and pull her to the boat! I've got to get to the Sea King. He must know about this."

"What about me?" Scuttle pleaded.

"Find a way to stop that wedding!"

Instantly Scuttle had an idea. He took to the air, and squawking at the top of his lungs, he called out to all the creatures in the area. Bluebirds, flamingos, ducks, seals, dolphins, starfish, lobsters—all of them perked up and followed Scuttle to the wedding ship.

On board the ship, the wedding march had begun. Ursula and Eric were walking down the center of the boat together. Eric's eyes were glazed, his face blank.

Clutching a bouquet of red flowers, Ursula smiled in triumph. The spell was working. Below her chin, the magic

seashell locket glowed brightly. She stole a glance at the
sunset. Yes, she thought. I've done it!

"*Grrrrrr...,*" Max growled angrily as she passed him.

Whump! She kicked him with the back of her
foot.

Eric and Ursula stopped in front of the minister.
Slowly he began the ceremony. Ursula ground her teeth
impatiently. The bottom of the sun was now just touching
the horizon.

Finally he came to the vows. "Do you, Eric, take
Vanessa to be your lawfully wedded wife for as long as you
both shall live?"

Eric stared forward in a trance. "I do," he said.

"And do you, Vanessa—"

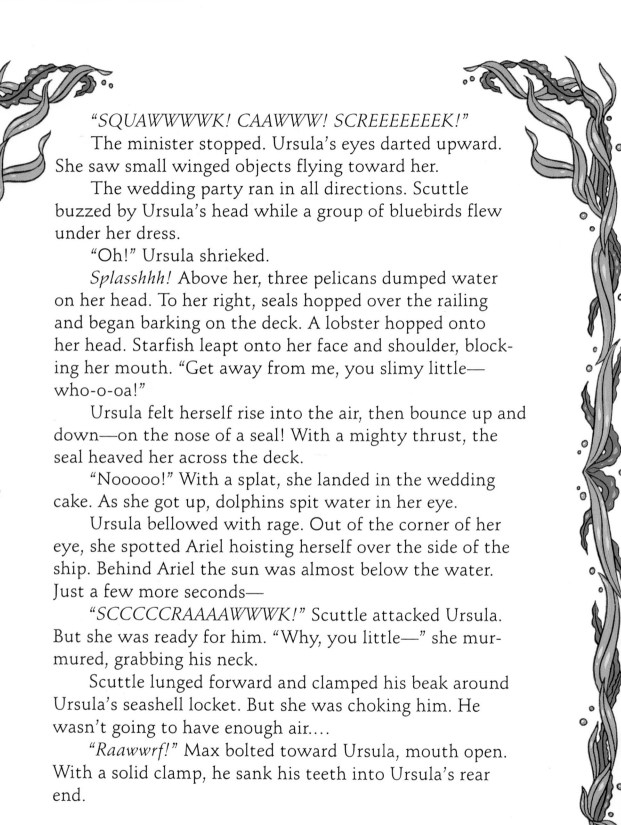

"*SQUAWWWWK! CAAWWW! SCREEEEEEEK!*"

The minister stopped. Ursula's eyes darted upward. She saw small winged objects flying toward her.

The wedding party ran in all directions. Scuttle buzzed by Ursula's head while a group of bluebirds flew under her dress.

"Oh!" Ursula shrieked.

Splasshhh! Above her, three pelicans dumped water on her head. To her right, seals hopped over the railing and began barking on the deck. A lobster hopped onto her head. Starfish leapt onto her face and shoulder, blocking her mouth. "Get away from me, you slimy little—who-o-oa!"

Ursula felt herself rise into the air, then bounce up and down—on the nose of a seal! With a mighty thrust, the seal heaved her across the deck.

"Nooooo!" With a splat, she landed in the wedding cake. As she got up, dolphins spit water in her eye.

Ursula bellowed with rage. Out of the corner of her eye, she spotted Ariel hoisting herself over the side of the ship. Behind Ariel the sun was almost below the water. Just a few more seconds—

"*SCCCCCRAAAAWWWK!*" Scuttle attacked Ursula. But she was ready for him. "Why, you little—" she murmured, grabbing his neck.

Scuttle lunged forward and clamped his beak around Ursula's seashell locket. But she was choking him. He wasn't going to have enough air....

"*Raawwrf!*" Max bolted toward Ursula, mouth open. With a solid clamp, he sank his teeth into Ursula's rear end.

"Yeeeaaaaaaaaaagghhhhhh!" Ursula shrieked. She let go of Scuttle. He fell to the deck. The seashell locket hurtled through the air.

Then, with a small clatter, the shell crashed against the deck and broke.

Ariel's voice began to sing. In a golden mist her voice lifted into the air, ringing out over the din, swirling... swirling...

Right into Ariel's throat.

Ariel stood tall and opened her mouth. It was *her* voice again. She let it grow. She gave it all the sweetness and strength she could.

All other sounds stopped. The birds alighted, and the seals and dolphins slipped happily back into the water.

And Eric snapped out of his trance. He shook his head—and when he looked at Ariel, his eyes were alive again. Alive and filled with amazement. But there was something beyond amazement, too, something that could only be love.

"Ariel?" he said, his voice a hoarse whisper.

Ariel felt like bursting with happiness. She cleared her throat. Then she said her first word as a human—the word she had been wanting to say for three days.

"Eric."

"*Arf! Arf!*" Max jumped beside them, barking happily.

"You can talk!" Eric said. "You *are* the one!"

Ursula looked desperately at the sea. The sun had not quite disappeared. "Eric, get away from her!" she shouted.

But her own voice had returned, harsh and scratchy. She put her hand to her mouth in shock.

"It was you all the time!" Eric said to Ariel, taking her hands.

Ariel drew herself closer to him. "Oh, Eric, I wanted to tell you—" She didn't finish. She didn't need to. Eric was leaning down to her. His lips were a breath away from hers. The setting sun gave its final wink of light on the horizon.

"Eric, no!" Ursula cried.

Eric paused for a split second. The sun slipped below the water.

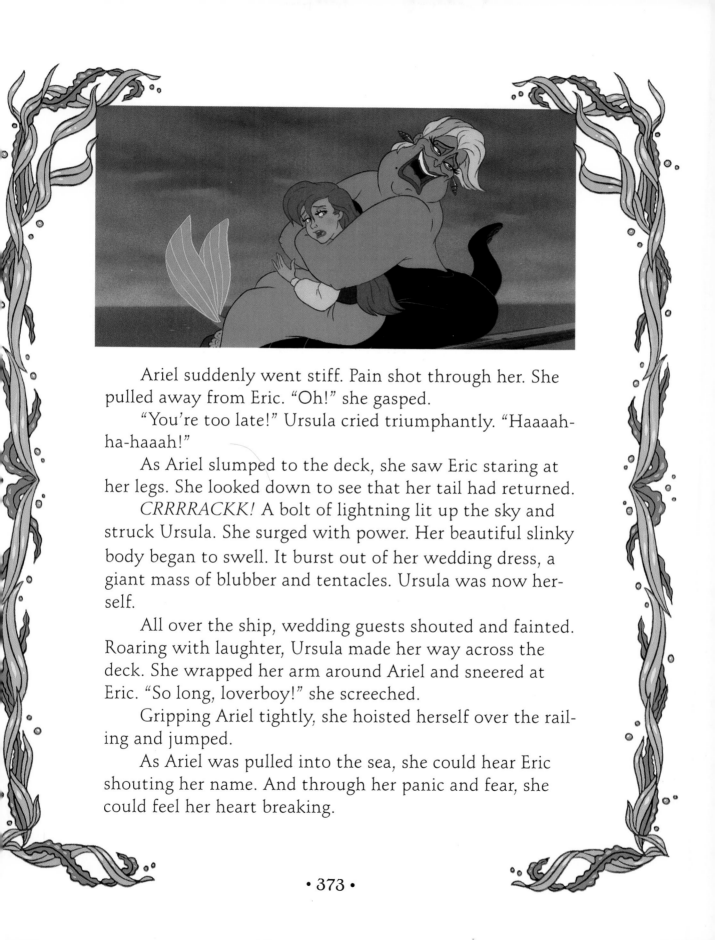

Ariel suddenly went stiff. Pain shot through her. She pulled away from Eric. "Oh!" she gasped.

"You're too late!" Ursula cried triumphantly. "Haaaah-ha-haaah!"

As Ariel slumped to the deck, she saw Eric staring at her legs. She looked down to see that her tail had returned.

CRRRRACKK! A bolt of lightning lit up the sky and struck Ursula. She surged with power. Her beautiful slinky body began to swell. It burst out of her wedding dress, a giant mass of blubber and tentacles. Ursula was now herself.

All over the ship, wedding guests shouted and fainted. Roaring with laughter, Ursula made her way across the deck. She wrapped her arm around Ariel and sneered at Eric. "So long, loverboy!" she screeched.

Gripping Ariel tightly, she hoisted herself over the railing and jumped.

As Ariel was pulled into the sea, she could hear Eric shouting her name. And through her panic and fear, she could feel her heart breaking.

CHAPTER THIRTEEN

Ursula pulled Ariel downward, toward her underwater lair. Behind them swam Flotsam and Jetsam.

Ariel felt the dark currents rush by her. She longed for the air. She longed for the feeling of legs, the warmth of Eric's glance. All of that was gone now.

"Poor little Princess!" Ursula gloated. "It's not you I'm after. I've got bigger fish to—"

"URSULA! STOP!"

Ursula pulled up short. In front of her, holding his glowing trident, was King Triton.

Sebastian sat on a nearby rock. He was glad he'd summoned the King in time. "Hmmph," he said, puffing out his chest.

"King Triton, how are you?" Ursula said, grinning.

"Let her go!" King Triton commanded.

Ursula reached forward and gave the King a shove. "Not a chance. She's mine now!" With a blast of magic, Ursula made the scroll appear. "You see, we made a deal!"

Flotsam and Jetsam wrapped their tails around Ariel, holding her prisoner. "Daddy, I'm sorry," Ariel cried. "I didn't mean to! I didn't know!"

King Triton leaned forward and read: I Hereby Grant unto Ursula the Witch of the Sea One Voice, for All Eternity. Signed, Ariel.

With a blast from his trident, King Triton tried to destroy the contract. But the trident had no effect.

"You see," said Ursula, "the contract is legal, binding and completely unbreakable." She shrugged and threw the scroll over her shoulder. It dissolved into a golden swirl and circled around Ariel.

Quickly Ariel began to shrink. She cried out in agony. Her body was shriveling. She was becoming one of the poor souls in Ursula's collection.

King Triton's eyes were wide with horror. But before he could react, Ursula gave him a sly smile. "Of course, I always was a girl with an eye for a bargain. The daughter of the great Sea King is a precious thing to have. But I might be willing to make an exchange—for someone even better!"

Ariel froze. Her father was staring at her. Sorrow lined his face.

The golden swirl lifted from Ariel and hovered in the water. Within it, the scroll materialized again. "Now, do we have a deal?" Ursula asked.

King Triton pointed his trident toward the scroll. It sent out a blast of gold light. Suddenly Ariel's signature disappeared.

Now, at the bottom of the scroll, it said King Triton.

Ursula threw back her head with laughter. "It's done, then!"

Instantly Ariel grew to normal size. The golden swirl began to settle around the King.

"Oh no!" Ariel screamed. "No!"

Slowly King Triton shrank. His crown fell to the ground.

In seconds all that was left of him was a small quivering lump with big, sad eyes.

Sebastian looked at him in shock. "Your Majesty," he whispered sadly.

"Daddy!" Ariel cried out weakly.

Ursula snatched the crown and put it on. "At last it's mine!" She cackled with her newfound power.

Ariel looked up, away from her father. Her own soul now felt hardened. She had disobeyed her father's strictest rule and fallen in love with a human. She had even made a deal with her father's enemy. And after all that, he had still given his soul to save her.

Ariel felt her blood boil. Hate bubbled up within her. "You!" she snarled at Ursula. "You monster!"

Ursula grabbed the trident and pointed it at Ariel. "Don't fool with me, you little brat! Contract or no, I'll blast—"

Shhhhhunk!

A harpoon ripped through one of Ursula's arms. "Yeeeeooooow!" she cried out in pain.

Prince Eric swam above her. "Why, you little fool!" Ursula shouted up at him.

Eric felt as if his lungs were about to burst. He had to go back to his rowboat.

"After him!" Ursula ordered Flotsam and Jetsam.

Eric swam upward and burst through the surface. As he gulped and took in a huge breath of air, Flotsam and Jetsam pulled him back under.

"Come on!" Sebastian shouted to Flounder. They both darted toward Eric. Sebastian pinched Flotsam as hard as he could. Flounder gave Jetsam a whack in the face with his tail.

The eels let go of Eric. But Ursula was prepared. She picked up the trident and aimed it upward. "Say good-bye to your sweetheart!" she said to Ariel.

Ariel grabbed Ursula's hair and pulled. Screaming in pain, Ursula jerked backward. The trident's ray went off

course—and hit Flotsam and Jetsam. With a burst of light, the eels were destroyed.

"My babies!" Ursula cried. "My poor little poopsies!"

Ursula's sadness quickly turned to anger—glowing, steaming anger. Black smoke circled around her.

Ariel swam to the surface. "Eric," she yelled, "you've got to get away from here!"

"No, I won't leave you!" Eric replied.

The sea began to rumble. Eric and Ariel looked down. A gold object rose out of the water and came between them. Ariel felt something solid beneath her, and she and Eric were pushed upward.

Then, like an ancient volcano coming to life, Ursula— a thousand times her normal size—burst through the surface. Ariel and Eric were two mere specks clinging to her crown. Ursula's body cast a shadow that seemed to swallow the sea for miles around.

Ariel and Eric grabbed hands and jumped. "You pitiful fools!" cried the Sea Witch, her voice resounding like a bass drum. Her trident had grown with her, and she swung it high. "Now I am the ruler of all the ocean! The sea and all its spoils must bow to my power!"

The sky cracked with lightning. A wave rose between Eric and Ariel, forcing them apart. "Eric!" Ariel screamed.

Ursula's face was grotesque. Her deep, terrifying laughter boomed out as she swirled the trident in the water.

Eric was drawn into a whirlpool that twisted him violently around. The whirlpool was so powerful, it stirred up the wreckage of an ancient ship from the ocean floor.

Ariel clung to a rock at the bottom of the whirlpool. Above her, in the rapid rush of water, Eric swam toward the shipwreck, grabbed hold, and pulled himself aboard.

The ship's broken mast was jagged and sharp, but its steering wheel was intact. Eric closed his hands around it.

The Sea Witch loomed over the circling waters. She looked down at Ariel and—*CRACK!*—sent a ray toward her, shattering the rock. Ariel jumped away. She landed on the seafloor, in the dead center of the whirlpool.

"So much for true love!" Ursula thundered. Carefully she pointed her trident at Eric's ship.

Eric gritted his teeth. Ursula's face filled the sky. He swung the steering wheel sharply toward her.

The ship lurched, its mast swung wide—and pierced into Ursula's belly.

"*RRRRRRRRAAAWWWWWRRGHH!*"

Ursula's cry of pain blotted out the sound of thunder. Giant lightning bolts tore through the sky. As they struck Ursula, she glowed and sizzled. Screaming, she began to sink. Her tentacles lashed out. One of them swiped against Eric's ship and pulled the ship and Eric underwater.

Then, slowly, like a sinking island, Ursula disappeared forever.

CHAPTER FOURTEEN

As King Triton's trident sank slowly to the ocean floor, the nest of souls was transformed back into merpeople. The sea was filled with their shouts of surprise and delight.

King Triton, too, was restored to his former self. He looked up to see his trident float into view. He grabbed it and smiled.

But there was no time to rejoice. He had to find Ariel. With a powerful thrust, he shot toward the surface.

There he spotted Sebastian and Flounder, who led him to a nearby shore where Ariel was sitting on a rock, staring sadly downward.

At the edge of the sand, Prince Eric lay unconscious.

"She really does love him, doesn't she, Sebastian?" King Triton said.

"Mmm," Sebastian agreed. "Well, it's like I always say: Children have got to be free to lead their own lives!"

King Triton raised an eyebrow. "*You* always say that?"

Sebastian gave the King a nervous glance. Then the two of them broke into laughter. "Well, then, I guess there's only one problem left," the King said.

"What's that, Your Majesty?" Sebastian asked.

King Triton sighed. "How much I'm going to miss her."

Sebastian's jaw fell open in surprise. King Triton raised his trident and sent a beam of light toward Ariel.

Ariel looked up. At the sight of her father, she was filled with happiness. And then her tail was transformed into two legs, and suddenly she was wearing a gorgeous blue dress.

Ariel was human again—this time for good.

Eric began to stir. He sat up, held his head, and looked around. Then he saw Ariel coming toward him out of the ocean.

A smile lit up Eric's face. He ran to Ariel and swept her up in an embrace.

They were free. They belonged to each other.

And finally, they shared a long, long kiss.

To this day, the merpeople still talk of Ariel and Eric's wedding. They tell of the glorious cake and the grandness of the wedding ship. And no one will ever forget King Triton's wedding present.

After Ariel and her father shared a tight embrace, King Triton waved his trident in a great arc, and a dazzling rainbow appeared in the sky. It expressed Triton's hope that the young couple would have a brilliant, colorful future. And they did.

Disney's Aladdin

Adapted from the film
by A. L. Singer

Disney's Aladdin

In a faraway land, where the sun scorches the fiery desert, there lies an ancient secret.

It is a lamp, long forgotten and buried deep beneath the shifting sands. It is small and simple. It bears no fancy design and contains no precious jewels. To all but the wisest among us, it would appear dull and worthless.

But this lamp is not what it seems. Long ago, it held the greatest power in all the lands of Arabia. Its magic changed forever the course of a young man's life. A young man who, like the lamp, was more than what he seemed.

The tale begins on a dark night, where a dark man waits with a dark purpose. . . .

The man's name was Jafar, and he was prepared to wait. His beady eyes and pointed turban gave him the look of a cobra about to strike. Perched on his shoulder, a parrot cocked its head impatiently. Beneath him, his horse shifted and gave a restless snort.

The treasure was buried out there somewhere. Only one person would be able to find it—the person who possessed two halves of an ancient scarab. Jafar had one half, and soon he would have the other. Then the treasure would be his. And with it, he would become the most powerful man in Agrabah.

In the stillness, Jafar heard the clopping of hooves as a rider approached.

The man was a common thief named Gazeem, and he had agreed to bring Jafar the other half of the scarab—in return for a part of the treasure. Jafar had promised.

Jafar had lied.

"You are late," he said.

Gazeem dismounted and bowed his head. Jafar was the royal vizier, the chief adviser to the sultan. It was not wise to upset him. "My apologies, O Patient One," Gazeem said.

Jafar glared. "You have it, then!"

With a grin, the thief pulled half the scarab from his pocket.

Jafar reached for it, but the thief held it back. "What about the treasure! You promised me. . . ."

Screech! The parrot swooped down from Jafar's shoulder, grabbed the scarab, and dropped it into Jafar's bony hand.

"Trust me," Jafar said. "You'll get what's coming to you."

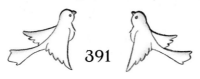

391

Quickly he took out his half of the scarab. He could feel his blood pounding as he fit the halves together. They glowed. Then . . .

BOOOOOM! A clap of thunder shook the desert. The scarab leapt from Jafar's hand as if it were alive. It streaked across the dunes in a blaze of light.

Jafar spurred on his horse. "Quickly, follow the trail!" he shouted.

Gazeem mounted his own horse and raced after Jafar. Bright as a comet, the scarab shot toward a small sandstone. It circled around it, then paused in the air.

Crack! The scarab suddenly split into halves again and plunged into the rock, each half wedging into a small hole.

Jafar stopped his horse and jumped off. The pulsing scarab stared out at him like a huge pair of eyes. An exhilarating chill bolted through him. There was no turning back now.

RRRRRRRROMMMMMMM! The earth began to tremble. The strange eyes flashed wildly. Gazeem cowered in fright.

Slowly the rock began to grow upward. It expanded in all directions, changing shape. The eyes remained, and now ears formed, then a nose. Last was a mouth, huge and gaping. A column of white light burst from within, almost blinding Jafar.

The rock was now a tiger face, frozen in a furious, silent roar. Jafar stared in awe. His frightened parrot clung to his shoulder, digging in its claws.

"By Allah!" Gazeem murmured. "A tiger-god!"

"At last, Iago!" Jafar said to his parrot. "After all my years of searching—the Cave of Wonders!"

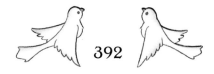

"*Awk!*" Iago screeched. "Cave of Wonders!"

Jafar pulled Gazeem close to him. "Now, remember," he snarled. "Bring me the lamp. The rest of the treasure is yours, but the *lamp* is *mine!*"

Gazeem swallowed hard. He turned toward the mouth of the tiger-god and began walking slowly.

"*Awk!* The lamp!" Iago repeated, loud enough for Gazeem to hear. Then he leaned in close to Jafar's ear and whispered, "Geez, where'd you dig this bozo up?"

"Ssshh!" Jafar snapped. Iago allowed no one to know he could speak like a human—no one except his master, that is. But right now, Jafar was in no mood to listen. He was watching. Watching and waiting.

"*Who disturbs my slumber?*" boomed the tiger-god, its voice rumbling the ground once again.

"Er . . . it is I, Gazeem, a humble thief." His voice was a nervous squeak, and his knees felt weak and shaky.

"*Know this!*" the tiger-god said. "*Only one may enter here. One whose rags hide a heart that is pure—the Diamond in the Rough!*"

Gazeem cast a doubtful glance behind him. "Go on!" Jafar commanded.

Frightened, Gazeem turned back toward the cave's opening. A flight of stairs led downward into . . . what? He couldn't tell. Carefully he began walking down.

RRRRRAAAAUUUGGHHHHH! The tiger-god's thunderous roar was like nothing Jafar had ever heard. Gazeem's shriek could be heard only for a moment, and then the tiger-god's mouth slammed shut, silencing the thief forever.

393

"*Seek thee out the Diamond in the Rough!*" the tiger-god commanded.

Slowly the rock collapsed into a mound of sand. The scarab halves flickered, then went dark.

Jafar stared in silence as Iago dove into the mound and resurfaced, spitting out sand. He picked the scarab halves up and flew back to Jafar. "I can't believe this!" Iago said. "We're never going to get ahold of that stupid lamp!"

"Patience, Iago, patience. Gazeem was obviously less than worthy."

"Now *there's* a big surprise!" Iago said, rolling his eyes. "So what are we going to do? We've got a big problem here—"

But Jafar just reached out and squeezed Iago's beak shut. He needed quiet. "Only one may enter . . . ," he said. "I must find this one—this Diamond in the Rough."

The Diamond in the Rough—Jafar understood what that meant. A common person, poor and unwashed, who had shining qualities within.

There was only one way to seek this person out, and Jafar knew just how to do it.

An evil grin spread across his face. He hadn't gotten the treasure tonight, but no matter.

He was close—oh so close. And before long, his waiting would be over.

CHAPTER TWO

"Stop, thief!"

The guard shouted at the top of his lungs as he chased a raggedly dressed boy through the crowded marketplace of Agrabah.

The boy zigzagged skillfully around the outdoor stands—fruit sellers, clothing merchants, bakers, trinket sellers. In his right hand, he clutched a loaf of bread. Beside him ran a small monkey dressed in a vest and a hat.

"I'll get you, street rat!" the guard shouted.

Street rat. If there was one name Aladdin hated, that was it. The sultan's guards looked down on the poor people of Agrabah—people such as himself. Sure, he swiped food sometimes. He had no choice—he had to eat. But he was no street rat.

"Come on, Abu!" Aladdin called to his pet monkey. He ran to a nearby house and leapt onto its low, flat roof. Then he and Abu sprinted from rooftop to rooftop, landing on a pair of clotheslines and finally falling into a soft pile of clothes.

Instantly he was snatched up by a pair of thick, hairy hands.

It was Rasoul, the head of the sultan's guard. Rasoul was a man of few words, but if there was one thing he did well, it was catching young thieves.

"Gotcha!" Rasoul said, lifting Aladdin up.

Abu leapt onto Rasoul's shoulder and shoved the guard's turban over his eyes. Aladdin quickly wrenched himself free, and he and Abu bolted away. They wove through the marketplace, past a camel salesman, a rug merchant, a jewelry cart. . . .

Suddenly Abu stopped. The little monkey's eyes were fixed on the cart.

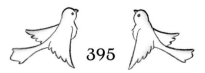

Abu had one big weakness—sparkling jewels. He crouched beside the cart, reaching up to steal a pendant.

"Stop him!" someone yelled. Dozens of faces turned toward Abu.

Aladdin spun around. He grabbed Abu by the back of his neck. To their right, the guards charged closer. To their left, angry townspeople closed in. Aladdin and Abu ran straight ahead toward a stairway that led to a tall tower. They raced up the stairs and in through a window. Aladdin grabbed a rug, and using it as a parachute, he and Abu leapt from another window to the other side of the building. They jumped again, this time landing safely in a quiet little alley, darkened by the shadow of the sultan's palace doors.

There the sounds of the marketplace were muffled. Aladdin exhaled and sat down. He was *starving.*

"All right, Abu, now we feast!" he said, breaking the loaf of bread in half.

But before he could eat, he saw a frail boy and girl in the shadows. They said nothing, but their wide, staring eyes spoke for them. Aladdin could tell they hadn't eaten in days.

He looked at the bread. He had risked his life to get it—and his mouth was watering like crazy. But he couldn't let them go hungry. With a sigh, he held his half out to the children. "Go on, take it," he said softly.

Abu scowled, but he handed over his piece, too.

The girl smiled. She took Abu's bread and gave his fur a gentle stroke.

Abu liked that. People didn't usually treat him so nicely. He tipped his hat and strutted away proudly—and smacked right into Aladdin's legs.

But Aladdin didn't even notice. His eyes were focused on something straight ahead. "Wow . . . ," Aladdin muttered.

The marketplace had fallen silent. Right through the middle rode a man on a horse. He wore robes of the finest silk, studded with jewels. As the people cleared the way and bowed, the man thrust his chin proudly in the air.

Aladdin wandered out of the alley and into the crowd. Everyone was murmuring about the rich-looking man.

"That's Prince Achmed," a woman said, "on his way to the palace."

"Just another suitor for the princess," an old man said, shaking his head. "He'll ask to marry her, and she'll throw him out—just like all the others."

Aladdin stared in awe. If the princess could reject someone like that, she must be a pretty amazing girl!

Aladdin felt a tug on his leg. Abu was pulling him toward the crowd. Aladdin could see a group of poor children clustering too close to Prince Achmed's horse. Suddenly the horse bucked, frightening the children, and the prince shouted, "Out of my way, you filthy brats!"

Angered, Aladdin broke through the crowd and strutted right up to Prince Achmed. "If I were as rich as you," he yelled, "I could afford some manners!"

"Out of my way, you flea-bitten street rat!" Prince Achmed kicked his horse and brushed past Aladdin, knocking him down into the mud.

Burning with anger, Aladdin leapt to his feet and started to run after the prince's horse. "I'm not worthless! I'm not a street rat!" he shouted. He ran all the way to the palace doors. With a loud clang, they slammed shut in his face. "And I don't have fleas!" he shouted at the closed doors.

Prince Achmed never even turned around. Aladdin bowed his head sadly and slumped back into town.

As a chilly darkness settled over Agrabah that night, Aladdin and Abu climbed to the roof of a crumbling old building. There were only a few mats and a couple of worn-out pillows, but to Aladdin and Abu, this was home.

Abu curled up on a pillow and closed his eyes. With a smile, Aladdin covered him with a soft mat. "Someday, Abu, things are going to be different," he said. "We'll be dressed in robes instead of rags. And we'll be inside a palace, looking out—instead of outside looking in."

In the distance, the sultan's palace loomed majestically. "That'd be the life, huh, Abu! To be rich, live in a palace, and never have any problems at all."

With a sigh, Aladdin lay down to sleep.

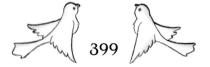

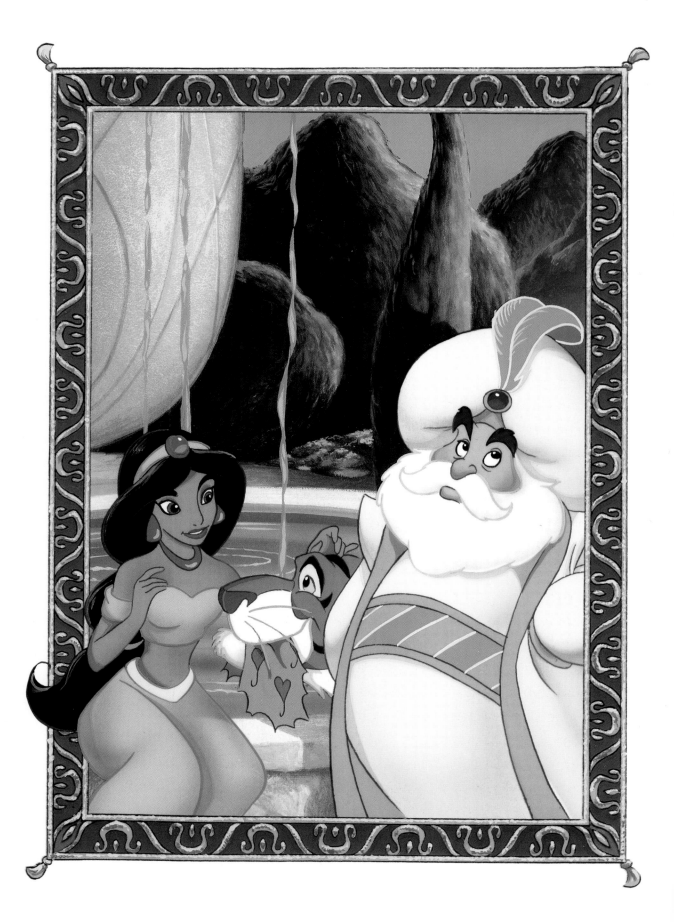

CHAPTER THREE

"Yeeeooow!"

The scream came from the palace menagerie. It echoed into the throne room, where the sultan covered his ears.

Whack! The door slammed against the throne room wall. In stomped an angry Prince Achmed. "I've never been so insulted!" he shouted. "Good luck marrying *her* off!"

"But . . . but . . . ," the sultan sputtered.

The prince marched right by him and out the other door—revealing a big hole in the seat of his pants.

"Jasmine!" the sultan bellowed. He was a roly-poly old man, happy and kind, and loved by his subjects. Only one person could get him upset— his daughter, Princess Jasmine. He loved her dearly, but she was so . . . stubborn. All he wanted her to do was marry a prince. Every princess did it. But Jasmine! *No.* No one was good enough for her!

He waddled into the palace menagerie. The sound of water was all around, flowing down marble waterways, spouting into pools from hand-carved fountains. It was the most beautiful place in all Agrabah. But the sultan noticed none of that now. "Jasmine!" he called again.

"Rrrrrr . . . ," came a soft growl.

There was a flash of orange and black. The sultan found himself face-to-face with a tiger, its teeth clamped on to the missing piece of Prince Achmed's pants.

"Confound it, Rajah!" the sultan said, grabbing the ripped material.

Rajah slinked away to the back of the garden, where the sultan's daughter sat at the edge of a fountain. "Oh, Father, Rajah was just playing," she said, gently stroking the tiger. "You were just playing with that overdressed, self-absorbed Prince Achmed, weren't you!" she said to Rajah.

Jasmine was more than beautiful. Princes from miles around risked their life

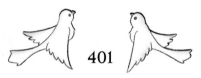

crossing the desert to see her. Each vowed to conquer the world for her love.

But as for Jasmine—well, she'd had enough of half-witted princes and bragging noblemen. If only one of them would show a little intelligence . . . some kindness and honesty and a sense of humor wouldn't hurt, either.

The sultan shook his head. "Dearest, you've got to stop rejecting every suitor. The law says you must be married to a prince by your next birthday. You have only three more days."

"The law is wrong!" Jasmine replied. "Father, I hate being forced to marry. If I do marry, I want it to be for love."

"It's not just the law," the sultan said gently. He hesitated for a minute before continuing. "I'm not going to be around forever, and I just want to make sure you're taken care of."

"But I've never done anything on my own! I've never had any real friends—except you, Rajah," Jasmine said, giving her tiger a pat on the head. "I've never even been outside the palace walls!"

"But Jasmine, you're a princess!" cried the sultan.

"Then maybe I don't *want* to be a princess anymore!"

"*Oooooo!*" The sultan threw up his hands and stomped back into the throne room.

A shadow appeared behind him. It was the tall, thin shadow of a man in a pointed turban, with a parrot on his shoulder. In his right hand was a long staff with a snake head carved at the top.

The sultan turned around. "Ah, Jafar, my most trusted adviser!" he said. "I am in desperate need of your wisdom."

"My life is but to serve you," said Jafar with a tight, thin-lipped smile.

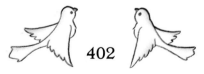

"Jasmine refuses to choose a husband," the sultan said. "I am at my wit's end!"

"*Awk!* Wit's end!" Iago squawked.

The sultan reached into a china bowl and took out a cracker. "Have a cracker, Pretty Polly!" he said.

If there was one thing Iago *hated,* it was eating crackers. Especially the dry, stale ones the sultan had. He practically gagged as the sultan stuffed the crackers into his beak.

"Your Majesty certainly has a way with dumb animals," Jafar remarked. "Now then, I may be able to find a solution to your problem, but it would require the use of the Blue Diamond."

The sultan backed away. He clutched at the ring on his finger.

"My ring has been in the family for years—" he protested.

Jafar held his staff in front of the sultan's eyes. The eyes of the snake head began to glow. "It's necessary to find the princess a suitor, isn't it!" Jafar said, moving closer. "Don't worry . . . everything will be fine."

The sultan could not stop staring at the snake head. His willpower was draining away. "Everything will be fine," he droned as he slipped the ring off his finger and gave it to Jafar.

Jafar smiled. "You are most gracious, my sire," Jafar said. "Now run along and play with your toys, hmmm!"

"Yes . . . ," the sultan said dreamily, waddling away.

Jafar turned and left the throne room. As he hurried down a marble corridor, Iago began spitting out the crackers. "I can't take it anymore! If I have to choke down one more of those moldy, disgusting crackers, I'll grab him by the neck and—"

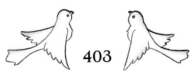

"Calm yourself, Iago," said Jafar. "This Blue Diamond will reveal to us the Diamond in the Rough—the one who can enter the cave and bring us the lamp."

At the end of the corridor, Jafar entered his private quarters. "Soon *I* will be sultan, not that jumbo portion of stupidity!"

"And then," Iago crowed, "I stuff crackers down *his* throat!"

At the other end of the dark room, Jafar pushed open a secret door, revealing a spiral staircase. He began climbing the stairs that led to his private laboratory. In every corner of the room, potions bubbled in glass beakers. There was a huge cauldron in the back and an enormous hourglass on an old table.

Jafar walked toward the hourglass, holding the Blue Diamond. "Now, Iago, we go to work."

Early the next morning, Jasmine crept to the palace wall. Rajah followed close by, his shoulders slumped in sadness.

"I'm sorry, Rajah," Jasmine said, "but I can't stay here and have my life lived for me."

Tears welled up inside her. It was hard enough running away from her father. But having to look into Rajah's eyes made it more painful than she could have imagined.

She had to make her move now, otherwise she might change her mind. Stepping onto Rajah's back, Jasmine quickly climbed the garden wall. Pausing at the top, she said, "I'll miss you, Rajah. Good-bye."

Then she disappeared over the side, into the land of her subjects—a land she had never visited before.

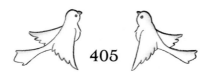

Breakfast is served, Abu!" said Aladdin as he cracked open a ripe, juicy melon. Perched on an awning, the two friends had a perfect view of the bustling marketplace below. All around them, merchants announced their wares. "Buy a pot—brass and silver!" called one.

"Sugared dates and figs!" shouted another as he strolled by a crowd of people watching a fire breather. "Pistachio nuts! Let the fire breather roast them for you!"

"Fresh fish!" cried a third vendor. Aladdin watched as the man waved a large fish high in the air, almost smacking it into the face of a young girl who was covered with a thin cloak. She staggered backward, bumping right into the fire breather. He belched a long plume of fire.

"Oh!" the startled girl cried out. "Excuse me. I'm sorry!"

Aladdin stopped eating. He couldn't help staring. Maybe it was her eyes, so deep and kind. Or her hair, like a waterfall made of the blackest silk. Or her perfect skin, or her . . .

Aladdin blushed. He *never* thought of girls that way. But this one— well, this one was different. Special somehow. Aladdin watched her as she made her way through the market.

Jasmine spotted a ragged little boy standing in a daze in front of a mound of ripe fruit. "You must be hungry," she said, taking an apple from the cart. "Here you go."

The child beamed. Clutching the apple, he ran away.

"You'd better pay for that!" the vendor said.

"Pay?" Jasmine looked puzzled. She had never paid for anything in her

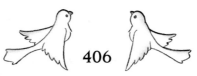

life. "I'm sorry, sir, I don't have any money, but I'm sure I can get some from the sultan—"

"Thief!" The seller grabbed her arm. With his other hand, he pulled out a shiny knife. "Do you know what the penalty is for stealing?"

Suddenly Aladdin darted between them and grabbed the vendor's arm. "Thank you, kind sir, I'm so glad you found my sister!" he said. Turning to Jasmine, he scolded, "I've been looking all over for you!" Jasmine was about to protest when Aladdin whispered, "Just play along. . . ."

The seller pulled Aladdin aside and said, "You know this girl? She said she knew the sultan!"

"She's my sister," Aladdin replied. Then, lowering his voice, he said, "Sadly, she's a little crazy. She thinks the monkey is the sultan."

Quickly Jasmine began bowing to Abu. "O Wise Sultan," she said. "How may I serve you?"

People in the crowd began to laugh. Aladdin helped Jasmine up and said, "Now come along, Sis. Time to see the doctor."

As the seller stared at Aladdin and Jasmine, Abu snatched apples off the cart and stuffed them into his vest.

Jasmine stopped in front of a camel and said, "Hello, Doctor, how are you?"

"No, no, not that one," Aladdin said. "Come on, Sis." He called over his shoulder, "Come on, Sultan!"

Abu followed after them. He puffed out his chest, imitating the sultan— and three apples tumbled out of his vest.

The seller turned red with fury. "Come back here, you little thieves!" he shrieked.

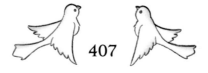

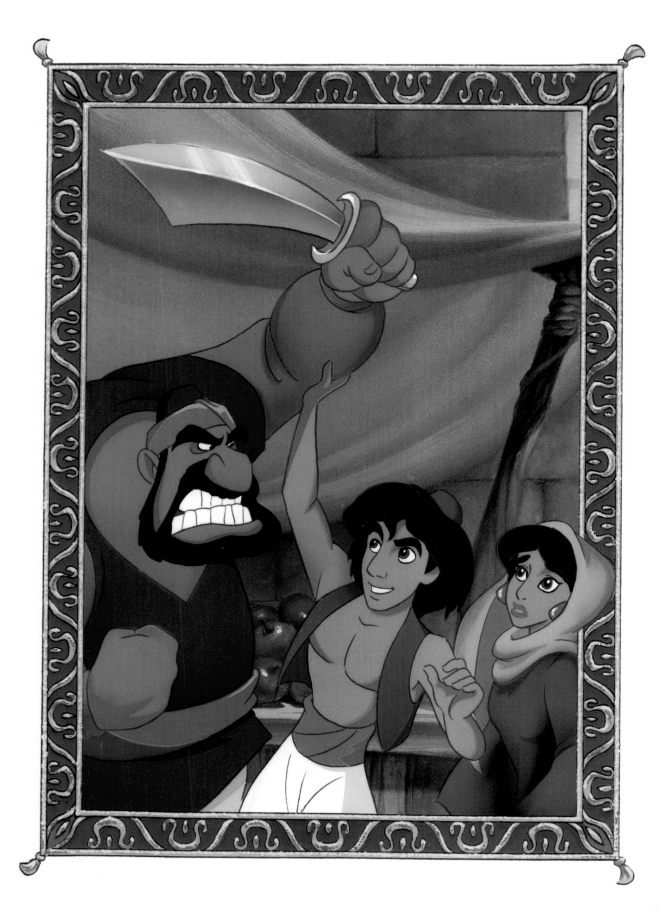

But it was too late. The three of them broke into a run and disappeared into the crowd.

At the palace, Jafar chuckled with evil glee. Iago was frantically turning a wheel that was attached to a generator. Electricity spurted from the generator into a bubbling cauldron. Slowly a shimmering blue cloud formed in the air.

The Blue Diamond was encased in a frame above an enormous hourglass. Jafar swept his arm in front of it, chanting, "Part, sands of time! Reveal to me the one who can enter the cave!"

He flipped the hourglass over. Then, with a loud *crrrack!* a bolt of lightning shot from the cloud. It struck the diamond, which exploded into a pulsing blue light.

The sand in the hourglass began to glow and swirl. Slowly an image began to form—an image of Aladdin running through the marketplace.

"That's the clown we've been waiting for!" Iago blurted out.

"Yes, a ragged little urchin. How perfect—he'll never be missed!" Jafar looked at Iago with a twisted grin. "Let's have the guards extend him an invitation to the palace, shall we?"

Aladdin, Abu, and Jasmine jumped from rooftop to rooftop in the market-place. Aladdin could tell Jasmine had never been to that part of Agrabah before. But he had to admit one thing—when it came to roof hopping, she was a fast learner.

When Aladdin and Abu finally reached their home, Jasmine looked around and said, "Is this where you live?"

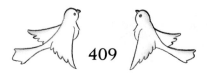

"Yep, just me and Abu," Aladdin replied. "It's not much, but it has a great view." He pointed toward the palace. "Amazing, huh? I wonder what it would be like to live there and have servants and valets—"

Jasmine sighed. "And people who tell you where to go and how to dress."

"That's better than here," Aladdin replied. "Always scraping for food and ducking guards—"

"Never being free to make your own choices," Jasmine said. "Always feeling—"

"*Trapped*," they said at the same time. Their eyes met, and they smiled. Aladdin blushed, then quickly took an apple from Abu and tossed it to Jasmine. "So where are you from?" he asked, changing the subject.

"What does it matter?" Jasmine answered. "I ran away, and I'm not going back. My father is forcing me to get married."

"That's awful!" Aladdin said.

Jasmine's eyes met his again. Suddenly Aladdin couldn't speak, couldn't even move. Strange feelings raced around inside him, feelings so strong they made him dizzy. Who *was* this mysterious girl?

Aladdin could hear Abu chattering wildly, but he didn't listen. All he could see, all he could hear, was Jasmine.

"Here you are!" a voice roared.

Aladdin snapped out of his trance. Below them stood a group of the sultan's guards, swords drawn.

"*They're after me!*" Aladdin and Jasmine said together. They stopped, looking at each other in confusion, then spoke again at the same time: "They're after *you?*"

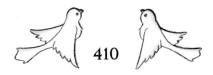

But there was no time to figure things out. Aladdin looked over the opposite side of the roof. There was a pile of hay below. "Do you trust me?" he asked Jasmine, pulling her close. Their eyes locked again.

"Well . . . yes," she replied.

"Then jump!"

Aladdin, Jasmine, and Abu leapt off the roof. They landed safely in the hay and quickly got to their feet. Aladdin spun around, ready to sprint for his life.

But it was too late. Rasoul loomed over him, smirking. "We just keep running into each other, eh, street rat? It's the dungeon for you, boy!"

Jasmine stepped in Rasoul's path. "Let him go!"

"Look, a street *mouse!*" Rasoul snarled. With a laugh, he pushed Jasmine to the ground.

Jasmine sprang to her feet. Anger flashed in her eyes. Regally drawing back her hood, she said in a firm, commanding voice, "Unhand him, by order of the princess!"

"The *princess?*" Aladdin repeated.

The guards froze in shock. "Princess Jasmine!" Rasoul said. "What— what are you doing outside the palace?"

"Just do as I command," Jasmine said. "Release him."

"I would, Princess," Rasoul replied, "except my orders come from Jafar. You'll have to take it up with him."

And with a sheepish shrug, he dragged Aladdin away.

"Believe me, I will!" Jasmine exclaimed.

Back at the palace, Jasmine stormed into Jafar's chamber.

411

There he was, looking as sneaky and sinister as always. "Princess," he said, "how may I be of service?"

Princess Jasmine looked him sharply in the eye. "Jafar, the guards just took a boy from the market—on your orders."

"Your father has charged me with keeping peace in Agrabah," Jafar said. "The boy was a criminal. He tried to kidnap you."

"He didn't *kidnap* me!" Jasmine replied. "I ran away!"

Jafar's brow creased with concern. "Oh dear, how frightfully upsetting. Had I but known . . ." His voice trailed off.

"What do you mean?" Jasmine asked.

"Sadly, the boy's sentence has already been carried out."

Jasmine shuddered. "What sentence?"

Jafar sighed. He put a hand on Jasmine's shoulder. "Death," Jafar said softly. "By beheading."

A gasp caught in Jasmine's throat. "How . . . how *could* you?"

She turned and ran out, not stopping until she reached the menagerie.

Rajah bounded happily toward her, but Jasmine ran right by him. She collapsed by a fountain, tears running down her cheek.

Do you trust me? the boy had asked her. Yes, she had. This boy was so different from the others—funny, kind, friendly. . . .

And now he was dead. Because of a stupid mistake.

"Oh, Rajah," she said. "This is all my fault. I didn't even know his name."

Jasmine buried her head in Rajah's fur and wept.

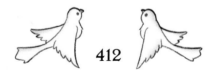

The palace dungeon was cold, dark, and dirty. Not even the sultan had ever entered it. All prisoners were brought there by Jafar—and not one had escaped.

Aladdin was determined to be the first. He grunted loudly, struggling at his chains, but they held fast to the stone wall.

Jafar had lied to Jasmine. Aladdin was alive—but not for long, if everything went according to Jafar's plan.

Aladdin collapsed to the floor with a sigh. "She was the *princess*," he said to himself. "I can't believe it!"

Just then a shadow appeared on the wall—the shadow of a small monkey poised between the bars of the prison window. "Abu!" Aladdin cried, spinning around. "Down here!"

Abu hopped down. He frowned at Aladdin and chattered angrily as he did an imitation of a pretty girl walking.

Aladdin knew he was being scolded for paying too much attention to Jasmine. "Hey, she was in trouble," he said. "I'll never see her again, anyway. I'm a street rat, remember? Besides, there's some law that says she's got to marry a prince." He exhaled with frustration. "She deserves a prince."

Abu pulled a small pick out of his vest pocket and unlocked Aladdin's cuffs. Grinning with triumph, he pulled Aladdin toward the window.

But Aladdin just slumped to the floor. He was still thinking of Jasmine. "I'm a fool," he said.

"You're only a fool if you give up," came a crackly voice.

Aladdin turned to see an old snaggletoothed man hobble out of the shadows. His white beard hung to the floor, and he had a hump on his

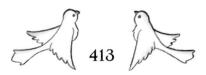

back. He looked as though he had been in the dungeon for years. "Who are you?" Aladdin asked.

"I am a lowly prisoner like yourself—but together, perhaps we can be more. I know of a cave filled with treasures beyond your wildest dreams." The man shuffled closer, smiling. "There's treasure enough to impress your princess, I'd wager."

Abu's eyes lit up at the mention of treasure. He tugged at Aladdin's vest.

Neither of them saw Iago peek out of the old man's hump and whisper, "Jafar, could you hurry up? I'm dying in here!"

Aladdin gave the prisoner a forlorn look. "But the law says she has to marry—"

Jafar cut Aladdin off. He raised a bony finger and spoke once again in an old man's voice. "You've heard of the Golden Rule? Whoever has the gold makes the rules!"

"Why would you share this treasure with me?" Aladdin asked.

"I need a young pair of legs and a strong back to go in after it." Jafar walked to the dungeon wall and pushed one of the stones. Slowly an entire section of wall opened, revealing a hidden stairway. "So, do we have a deal?"

Aladdin was hesitant, but he shook the old man's hand.

Jafar cackled with excitement. "We're off!"

It was dark by the time they reached the Cave of Wonders. Jafar took out the scarab pieces and fit them together once again.

Aladdin stared in awe as the pieces flew into the sandstone and the massive tiger-god arose.

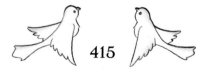

"Who disturbs my slumber!" the intimidating voice boomed. Jafar motioned for Aladdin to go closer.

Abu jumped into Aladdin's vest. Aladdin tried to keep from trembling. "Uh, it is I . . . Aladdin."

A tunnel of harsh light shot from the tiger-god's mouth. Aladdin had to turn away. *"Proceed,"* the voice continued. *"Touch nothing but the lamp."*

"Quickly, my boy," Jafar urged in his old man's voice. "Fetch the lamp, and then you shall have your reward!"

Cautiously Aladdin stepped inside the tiger-god's mouth. Through the blinding light, he saw a long stairway leading downward. At the bottom there were mountains of gold. *Cascades* of gold. Coins, jewels, plates, bowls, goblets, chests, all piled together as far as he could see.

Abu was practically hypnotized by the sight of all that gold and went straight for an enormous treasure chest.

"Abu!" Aladdin warned. "Don't touch *anything*! We have to find that lamp."

Abu grumbled, but turned from the chest and followed his master through the cave—until he sensed a strange movement behind him. He spun around to look.

Nothing—just a purple carpet with gold tassels, lying on the floor. Abu turned and ran toward Aladdin.

This time something tapped Abu on the shoulder, then snatched his hat. Abu spun around again.

It was the carpet, walking along behind him.

"Eeeeeeeeeee!" Abu shrieked, jumping on Aladdin for protection.

In fright, the carpet quickly ran behind a large pile of coins.

"Cut it out, Abu!" Aladdin said.

Abu jabbered away, pointing to the large mound. Aladdin turned and saw a tassel stick out, then quickly pull itself in.

Aladdin moved closer for a better look. He could see the carpet moving away from him. "A magic carpet!" he said. Then he called, "Come on out, we're not going to hurt you."

Using its two lower tassels as legs and its upper ones as hands, the carpet slowly emerged and handed Aladdin Abu's hat. Aladdin's mouth hung open in disbelief.

Abu snatched the hat and began scolding the carpet. The carpet slowly walked away, drooped over in shame. "Hey, wait a minute, don't go!" Aladdin said. "Maybe you can help us find this lamp. . . ."

The carpet whirled around and began pointing excitedly. Aladdin grinned. "I think he knows where it is!"

Rising off the ground, the carpet began to fly. Aladdin and Abu followed it into another cavern.

Aladdin stopped in his tracks. This cavern made the other one look like a waiting room. It stretched upward so high Aladdin couldn't see the ceiling. The walls were a cool blue, unlike any color he had ever seen in the desert. A lagoon of aqua blue water stretched from wall to wall.

In the center of the lake stood a tower of solid rock with only a series of stepping stones leading to it. On top, lit by a magical beam of light, was a small object.

It was too far away to see, but Aladdin knew that it must be the lamp. His heart began to race. It wouldn't be easy to get to the top. First he would

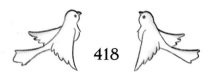

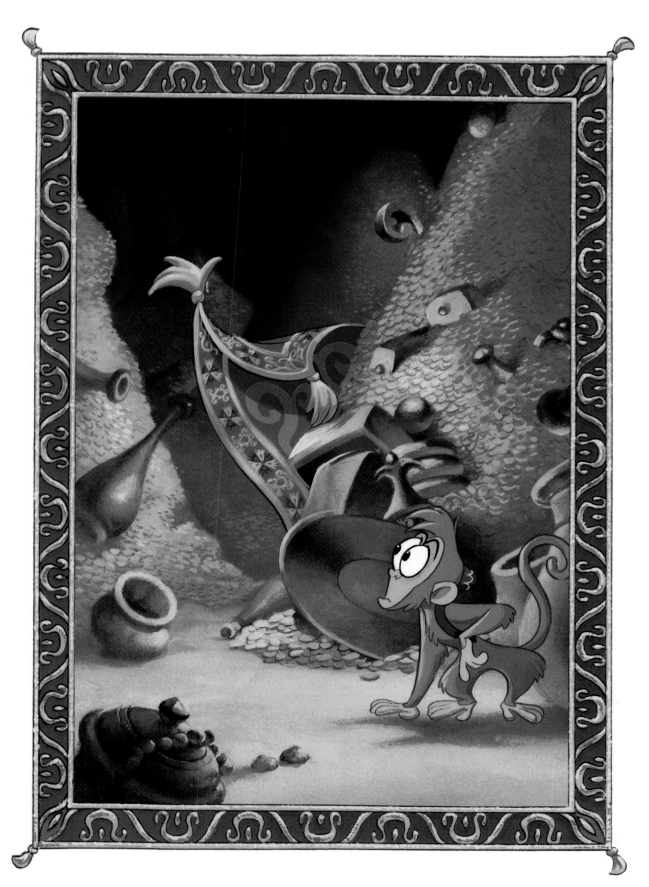

have to hopscotch across the rocks, then he would have to climb the steep, jagged tower of rock.

"Wait here," he said to Abu and the carpet. "And remember, don't touch *anything*."

Springing from stone to stone, Aladdin arrived at the base of the tower. With a sudden groan, the sloping rock transformed into a staircase.

Aladdin smiled. Someone—some*thing*—was on his side. He raced upward, two steps at a time.

At the top, the lamp came into clear view.

It was dusty and dented and cheaper looking than the worst used lamp he had ever seen in the marketplace.

Aladdin picked it up. "This is it!" he said to himself. "This is what we came all the way here for?"

Out of the corner of his eye, he spotted Abu and the carpet. They were in front of a large golden statue that looked like a giant monkey idol. Its arms were outstretched, and in its cupped palms it held an enormous red jewel.

And Abu was reaching right for it.

"Abu!" Aladdin shouted. "*No!*"

But it was too late. Abu had the jewel in his hands.

The ground began to rumble instantly. Rocks and dust fell from above. The voice of the tiger-god echoed like a cannon: "*Infidels! You have touched the forbidden treasures! Now you shall never again see the light of day!*"

The jewel began to melt in Abu's hand. Panicked, he put it back into the palms of the statue.

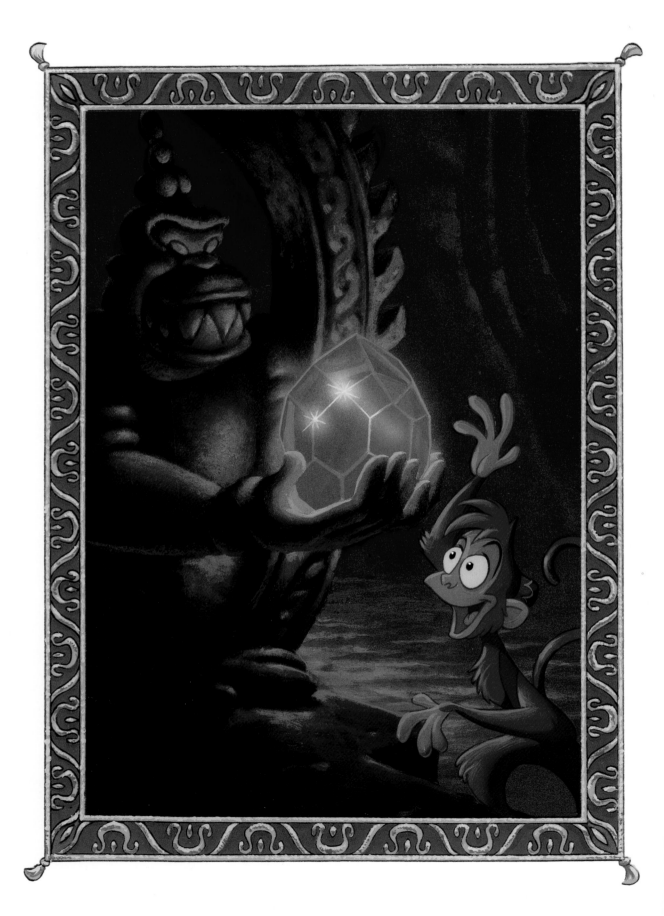

But the damage was already done. The stairway beneath Aladdin transformed into a long chute, and his feet gave way.

With a last-minute lunge, Aladdin grabbed the lamp. Tumbling down the chute, he saw the lagoon become a pool of boiling lava. He closed his eyes, bracing himself for the end.

Whoosh! He stopped in midair. Something was pushing him upward. His eyes sprang open.

The carpet had caught him, and it was whisking him away!

The cavern shook violently. Aladdin held tightly to the carpet. It dodged right and left as large rocks fell from the ceiling. Aladdin looked down, searching for Abu.

"Eeeeee!" came a cry from below. There he was, hopping across the stepping-stones and screeching. Over his head, a boulder hurtled toward him.

With a burst of speed, the carpet streaked down. Aladdin plucked Abu away from danger, then flew toward the cavern entrance. The ground below erupted as the piles of dazzling treasures burst into flames. Aladdin and Abu looked down in horror. The coins and jewels were melting!

The carpet raced to the stairway, charred by a wave of lava. They could see the starry night sky through the entrance above. Just a few more feet . . .

Thunk! A jagged piece of rock fell onto the carpet, pinning it to the ground.

Aladdin and Abu tumbled onto the stairs.

Aladdin looked down at the carpet in dismay. There was no way he could save it. It would be hard enough to save himself.

423

He looked up. He could see the opening at the top—freedom. Abu scaled the steps and hopped outside.

Aladdin followed as fast as he could, but the stairs began to shake. He lost his footing.

Springing to his feet, he lunged for the top step. His fingers clutched on to it—just as the entire stairway buckled beneath him.

Aladdin dangled over the collapsing cave. "Help me!" he cried. "I can't hold on!"

Still dressed as the beggar, Jafar peeked over the edge. "First give me the lamp!"

There was no time to argue. Aladdin held it out.

Jafar's eyes gleamed as he grabbed the lamp and stuffed it into his robe. "At last!" he shrieked in triumph. Leering at Aladdin, he pulled out a dagger.

"What are you doing!" Aladdin cried.

"Giving you your reward!" Jafar replied. "Your *eternal* reward!"

Abu leapt at Jafar, biting him hard on the arm.

"Yeeeeaggggh!" Jafar screamed. He fought hard, but Abu held tight.

Finally Jafar dropped the dagger. With a furious gesture, he flung Abu into the cave.

Aladdin's fingers could hold on no longer. He let go.

The walls of the cavern raced by him as he and Abu fell head over heels.

CHAPTER SIX

Aladdin awoke on the cave floor. The fire was out, the lava gone; only the steady drip of water echoed throughout the cave.

On top of him lay the carpet and Abu.

Aladdin groaned and sat up. The carpet fell off, and Abu began to stir. Above him, Aladdin could see no opening, only the solid ceiling of the cavern.

"We're trapped," he said. "That two-faced son of a jackal! He's long gone with that lamp."

Abu jumped up. Something bulged in his vest—a jewel, Aladdin figured. Like a magician, Abu waved his arms, reached into his vest, and pulled out the hidden object.

Aladdin blinked and shook his head. It was the lamp!

"Why, you little thief," Aladdin said with a smile. He took the beat-up lamp and studied it carefully. "There's something written on it, but it's hard to make out."

Aladdin rubbed the faded words with his sleeve. It was almost impossible to get the grime off. He rubbed harder and harder—then suddenly stopped.

The lamp was glowing!

Aladdin gasped. Abu and the carpet backed away.

Then . . . *Poooof!* Colorful smoke erupted from the lamp's spout. It whirled crazily, growing into a blue cloud, slowly forming into a shape— an enormous flowing shape with arms, a chest, a head, and a wild-eyed face with a long, black, curling beard.

"Ten thousand years will give you *such* a crick in the neck!" the blue creature said.

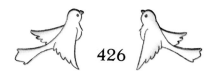

426

Aladdin and Abu watched as he then grabbed his own head and twisted it all the way around. "Wow, does that feel good!" he said. "Nice to be back, ladies and gentlemen. Hi! What's your name?"

"Uh . . . Aladdin."

"Hello, Aladdin! Can I call you Al? Or maybe just Din? Or how about Laddie? 'Here, boy! Come on, Laddie!'" He whistled and pretended to call a dog. Then, in another puff of blue smoke, he *became* a giant dog.

His eyes wide, Aladdin turned to the carpet. "I must have hit my head harder than I thought."

The creature changed back to his original form. "Say, you're a lot smaller than my last master!" he said.

"Wait a minute," Aladdin said. "I'm your *master?*"

"That's right! And I am your genie, direct from the lamp! Right here for your wish fulfillment! Three wishes, to be exact—and *ixnay* on the wishing for more wishes! *Three,* that's it! No substitutions, exchanges, or refunds!"

"Three wishes?" Aladdin said. "Any three I want?"

"Uh, almost," the genie replied. "There are a few limitations. Rule number one—I can't kill anybody, so don't ask. Rule number two—I can't make anybody fall in love with anybody else. Rule number three—I can't bring people back from the dead. Other than that, you got it!"

Aladdin liked this genie. He decided to tease him a little. "Limitations!" He sighed. "Some all-powerful genie. I don't know, Abu, he probably can't even get us out of this cave."

The genie put his hands on his hips. "Excuse me! You don't believe me!" Jumping onto the carpet, he scooped up Aladdin and Abu in his mammoth hands. "You're getting your wishes, so sit down, and we are out of here!"

427

He put them down, then swung his arm overhead. A thunderous boom resounded above them, and a crack opened in the cavern's ceiling. Rocks and sand fell aside, and early morning light poured in.

The carpet began to rise. It spiraled upward, picking up speed. Aladdin held tight as the genie reared back and let loose a laugh that shook the walls.

Aladdin couldn't keep from laughing himself. The desert air never smelled so good.

He was free.

And he still had his three wishes left.

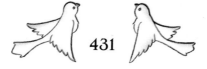

Jafar, this is an outrage!" the sultan yelled, pacing the throne room. "From now on, you're to discuss sentencing of prisoners with me—*before* they are beheaded!"

Princess Jasmine scowled at Jafar as he bowed his head. On his shoulder, even Iago looked sorry. "My humblest apologies to both of you," Jafar said.

"At least *some* good will come of my being forced to marry," Jasmine said. "When I am queen, I will have the power to get rid of *you,* Jafar!" With that, she stalked out to the menagerie.

"Jasmine!" the sultan called, running after her.

Jafar watched them leave. His sad, sorrowful look began to disappear. All his rage and frustration bubbled up. "If only I had gotten that lamp," he muttered through clenched teeth.

"To think we've got to keep kissing up to that chump and his chump daughter the rest of our lives," Iago said.

"Until she finds a chump *husband,*" Jafar remarked. "Then she'll have us banished—or beheaded!"

"Wait a minute, Jafar!" Iago said. "What if *you* marry the princess? Then you become the sultan, right!"

Jafar walked slowly to the throne and sat down. It felt *wonderful!* "Hmmmm," he said. "The idea has merit. . . ."

"Yeah!" Iago squawked. "And then we drop papa-in-law and the little woman off a cliff—ker-*splat!*"

Jafar burst out laughing. "I love the way your foul little mind works!"

In a desert oasis just outside Agrabah, the carpet swooped down to the sand.

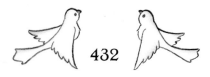

The genie turned to Aladdin with a proud grin. "Well, how about that, huh! Do you doubt me now?"

"Nope," Aladdin said. "Now, about my three wishes . . ."

"Three?" the genie said. "You are down by one, boy!"

Aladdin smiled mischievously. "I never actually *wished* to get out of the cave. You did that on your own!"

The genie thought for a moment. "All right," he said with a laugh. "You win. But no more freebies!"

Aladdin hopped off the carpet and began pacing around. "Hmm . . . three wishes . . . What would *you* wish for?"

"Me? No one's ever asked me that before." The genie thought it over for a moment. "Well, in my case . . . freedom."

"You mean, you're a prisoner?" Aladdin asked.

"That's what being a genie's all about." The genie shrugged. "Phenomenal cosmic powers, itty-bitty living space."

The carpet, Abu, and Aladdin peered inside the small lamp. "Genie, that's terrible," Aladdin said.

"To be free, to be my own master—that would be greater than all the magic and all the treasures in the world." The genie sighed. "But the only way I can get out is for my master to wish me out, so you can guess how often that's happened."

Aladdin thought about this for a moment. "I'll do it," he finally said. "I'll set you free."

"Yeah, right," the genie said, rolling his eyes.

"No, I'm not lying," Aladdin said. "I promise—after my first two wishes, I'll use my third wish to set you free."

"Okay, here's hoping!" said the genie. "Now, what is it *you* want?"

"Well," Aladdin said, "there's this girl—"

"Wrong! I can't make anyone fall in love, remember?"

"But Genie, she's smart and fun and beautiful. . . ." Aladdin shrugged and looked at the ground. "But she's the princess. To even have a chance, I'd have to be—"

That was it! The answer was right in front of him! "Hey!" Aladdin said. "Can you make me . . . a prince?"

The genie raised an eyebrow. "Is that an official wish? Say the magic words. . . ."

"Genie, I wish for you to make me a prince!" Aladdin blurted.

"*All right!*" The genie began circling around Aladdin. "Now, first we have to get rid of the fez-and-vest combo." With a sweeping gesture, he conjured up a robe of fine silk and a turban with a dazzling jewel and shining gold trim. "Ooh, I like it!"

"Wow!" Aladdin could hardly believe how . . . *princely* he looked. No one would dare call him "street rat" now. He picked up the lamp and hid it under his turban. No decent prince would dare be seen with such a piece of junk.

"Hmmm, you'll need some transportation. . . ." The genie looked at Abu. "Uh, excuse me! Monkey boy!"

Abu shot away, trying to hide. But it was no use. With a snap of his fingers, the genie turned him into a camel. "Hmmm . . . not good enough," the genie said, snapping his fingers again. This time Abu appeared as a magnificent stallion. "Still not enough. . . ." With a decisive snap, Abu was transformed again, this time into an elephant. "What better way to

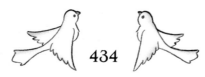

make your entrance down the streets of Agrabah than riding your very own elephant! Talk about trunk space!"

Aladdin could do nothing but stare, dumbfounded. The genie was on a roll. He gestured wildly, laughing at the top of his lungs. "Hang on to your turban, kid!" he shouted. "We're going to make you a star!"

afar rushed into the throne room, holding a large scroll. "Sire," he called to the sultan, "I have found a solution to the problem with your daughter!"

"*Awk!*" squawked Iago. "Problem with your daughter!"

"It's right here." Jafar unfurled the scroll and began reading: " 'If a princess has not chosen a husband by her sixteenth birthday, then the sultan shall choose for her'!"

The sultan nodded. "But Jasmine hated all those suitors. How can I choose someone she might hate?"

"Not to worry, there is more," Jafar said, unrolling the scroll further. " 'In the event a suitable prince cannot be found, a princess may be wed to—' Hmmm, interesting . . ."

"What?" the sultan demanded. "Who?"

" 'The royal vizier.' " Jafar looked up. "Why, that's *me!*"

"But I thought the law says only a prince can marry a princess," the sultan said, reaching for the scroll.

Jafar quickly set it on a table and picked up his staff. "Desperate times call for desperate measures, my lord."

The snake head began to glow with hypnotic light. "Yes," the sultan said, his eyes glazing over. "Desperate times . . ."

"You will order the princess to marry me," Jafar said confidently.

"I will order the princess to—"

Ra-ta-ta-taaaaaah! The sound of trumpets blared in through the window. The sultan blinked and turned toward the noise. "Wha—what? I heard something!"

Instantly the spell was broken. The sultan rushed to the window and looked out. Muttering, Jafar followed.

A huge band was marching down the main street. A giant peacock float moved slowly behind; lions and bears in colorful painted cages rolled by. People filled the streets to see the grand procession approaching.

"Make way for Prince Ali Ababwa!" the bandleader sang. Behind him strode a majestic elephant, its trunk held proudly in the air. On its back, a canopy bounced up and down.

From the canopy, Aladdin grinned and waved. The crowd roared with admiration. Dancers whirled around him, swordsmen marched in perfect step, and dozens of attendants walked alongside. Abu lumbered on proudly, and the carpet made a perfect cushion for Aladdin on Abu's bumpy back.

The genie floated among the crowd, changing himself every few minutes into a drum major, a harem girl, an old man, a child. In each disguise, he told everyone what a splendid prince was approaching.

By the time Aladdin got to the palace gates, he was the talk of Agrabah. His entire entourage—Abu, swordsmen, brass band, dancers, and all— marched right into the throne room.

As the sultan and Jafar stared, Aladdin slid off Abu's back and onto the carpet. "Your Majesty," Aladdin said, bowing in front of the sultan, "I have journeyed from afar to seek your daughter's hand."

"Prince Ali Ababwa!" the sultan said with a bright smile. "I'm delighted to meet you. This is my royal vizier, Jafar."

Jafar did not look delighted at all. "I'm afraid, Prince Abooboo—"

"Ababwa," Aladdin corrected him.

"Whatever," Jafar said. "You cannot just parade in here uninvited and—"

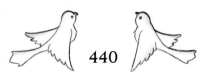

440

"What a remarkable device!" the sultan exclaimed, looking at the carpet. "May I try!"

"Why, certainly, Your Majesty!" Aladdin said. He helped the sultan onto the carpet. It took off, flying the sultan around the room.

As the old man hooted with delight, Jafar eyed Aladdin suspiciously. "Just where did you say you were from!"

Before Aladdin could answer, the carpet swooped down and let the sultan off. "Well, this is a very impressive youth, and a prince, besides!" Lowering his voice, the sultan said to Jafar, "If we're lucky, you won't have to marry Jasmine after all!"

"I don't trust him—" Jafar said.

The sultan ignored him. "Yes, Jasmine will like this one."

"And I'm sure I'll like Princess Jasmine," Aladdin said.

"Your Highness!" Jafar blurted. "On Jasmine's behalf, I must say—"

"Just let her meet me," Aladdin interrupted. "*I* will win your daughter."

None of them had seen Jasmine enter from the menagerie, with Rajah behind her. "How dare you!" she said. "Standing around, deciding my future. I am not a prize to be won!" With that, she turned and stormed out.

Aladdin's heart sank. He was sure she'd like him as a prince. He never thought *this* would happen.

"Don't worry, Prince Ali," the sultan said. "Just give her time to cool down. She'll warm to you."

Aladdin and the sultan walked into the menagerie. Jafar watched them silently, then turned to Iago. "I think it's time to say bye-bye to Prince Abooboo. . . ."

CHAPTER NINE

For the rest of the day, Aladdin waited in the menagerie. Jasmine's room was overhead, but she refused to come to her balcony.

As night fell, Aladdin began to give up hope. "What am I going to do?" he moaned. "I should have known I couldn't pull off this stupid prince act."

Abu looked at his master and swung his trunk in sympathy.

"All right," the genie said, looking up from a game of chess with the carpet. "Here's the deal. If you want to court her, you have to tell her the truth. Just be yourself!"

"No way!" Aladdin said. "If Jasmine found out I was really some crummy street rat, she'd laugh at me." He looked up at Jasmine's balcony and drew himself up straight. "I'm going to go see her," he said. "I've got to be smooth. Cool. Confident."

The genie sighed. He knew Aladdin was in for trouble.

The carpet slid beneath Aladdin, lifting him up to Jasmine's balcony. Through her window, Aladdin could see her playing with Rajah. "Princess Jasmine!" he called out.

Jasmine turned and walked to the window. "Who's there!"

"It's me," said Aladdin. Then, remembering his Prince Ali voice, he added, "Prince Ali Ababwa."

"I do not want to see you!" Jasmine snapped.

As she turned back into the room, Aladdin stepped off the carpet and onto the balcony. "Please, Princess, give me a chance!"

Rajah leapt into his path. Aladdin jerked away, almost losing his turban.

443

Jasmine narrowed her eyes. "Wait. Do I know you? You remind me of someone I met in the marketplace."

Aladdin backed into the shadows. "The marketplace? Why, I have *servants* who go to the marketplace for me! So it couldn't have been me you met."

"No, I guess not," Jasmine said, looking disappointed.

A bee buzzed by Aladdin's ear. He moved to swat it until he heard it speak—in the genie's voice! "Enough about you," he said. "Talk about *her!*"

"Princess Jasmine, you're—uh, beautiful," Aladdin said.

"Rich, too," she said. "And the daughter of the sultan."

Aladdin smiled. "I know."

"A fine prize for any prince to marry," she said, playing along.

"Right! A prince like me!"

"Right! A prince like you!" Jasmine repeated. "And every other swaggering peacock I've met. Go jump off a balcony!"

Jasmine turned and strode into her chamber.

"Mayday! Mayday!" the genie said, still disguised as a bee. "Stop her! Want me to sting her?"

"Buzz off!" Aladdin replied.

"Okay," the genie said. "But remember—*bee* yourself!"

"Yeah, right," Aladdin muttered as the genie flew under his turban and into the lamp.

Jasmine looked over her shoulder. "What?"

"Uh . . . I said, you're *right!*" Aladdin sighed. "You . . . aren't just some prize to be won. You should be free to make your own choice."

444

Dejected, Aladdin turned away. He climbed over the railing and stepped off the balcony into space.

"No!" Jasmine cried. But Aladdin didn't fall—he was hovering in midair.

"How are you doing that!" Jasmine said, stunned.

"It's, uh, a magic carpet," Aladdin said.

Jasmine looked over the railing and touched the carpet. "It's lovely."

"You don't want to go for a ride . . . do you!" Aladdin gave her a hopeful look. "We could fly away and see the world. . . ."

"Is it safe!" Jasmine asked.

"Sure." Aladdin held out his hand and smiled. "Do you trust me!"

Do you trust me! Jasmine had heard those exact words before, said in the same way. "Yes," she said softly, taking his hand.

She stepped onto the carpet, and it took off. Losing her balance, she fell into Aladdin's arms. He blushed, but he liked the feeling—and he could tell Jasmine did, too.

The carpet soared over the palace. Agrabah stretched out below them, a cluster of twinkling lights. And above them, the stars of the desert sky winked a thousand times as they glided over the sands. In the distance, the sea seemed to be made of the blackest ink.

Swooping among the pyramids, Aladdin and Jasmine whooped with joy. When the carpet flew through an apple orchard, Aladdin reached way out and grabbed an apple for the princess.

He flipped it to her with a lopsided smile. The casual flip; the smile; *Do you trust me!*—all of it was exactly like the boy in the marketplace. Was it possible!

She decided to find out. The carpet finally set them down on the roof of

a tall pagoda, and they watched a fireworks display in the distance. "It's all so . . . magical," Jasmine said. "It's a shame Abu had to miss this."

"Nah," Aladdin said. "He hates fireworks. He doesn't really like to fly—"

Aladdin caught himself in midsentence.

"It *is* you!" Jasmine blurted. "Why did you lie to me? Did you think I wouldn't figure it out?"

"No! I mean, I *hoped* you wouldn't—that's not what I meant—" Aladdin groped for words. His stomach churned. He *couldn't* let Jasmine know the truth. "Um . . . the truth is, I sometimes dress as a commoner, to escape the pressures of palace life. Yeah. But I really am Prince Ali Ababwa!"

Jasmine looked unsure. "Why didn't you just tell me?"

"Well, you know . . . royalty going into the city in disguise . . . sounds a little strange, don't you think?"

Perfect! He knew he had her now. After all, *she* had been in disguise when he met her.

"Not that strange," she said, resting her chin on Aladdin's shoulder.

Together they watched the fireworks until they were too tired to keep their eyes open. The carpet then flew them back to the palace, hovering outside Jasmine's window.

Jasmine stepped onto the balcony, then turned toward Aladdin. They smiled at each other over the railing—until the carpet gave Aladdin a gentle nudge forward.

His lips suddenly met hers. She didn't move a bit. In the soft light of the stars, they shared a long kiss.

447

"Good night, my handsome prince," she said, backing into her chamber.

"Sleep well, Princess," Aladdin replied.

As she disappeared behind a curtain, Aladdin grinned. "For the first time in my life," he murmured dreamily as the carpet floated down to the garden, "things are starting to go right."

He snapped back to reality when he felt the hard grip of rough hands on his shoulder. Turning around, Aladdin came face-to-face with Rasoul.

Before Aladdin could move, another guard slapped manacles on his wrists and ankles. Rasoul stuffed a gag in his throat.

"Abu!" Aladdin tried to yell through the gag. "Abu, help!"

He looked around wildly until he spotted Abu—hanging from a tree, tied up with thick rope. The carpet tried to fly away, but another guard threw it into a cage.

Jafar emerged from the shadows. On his shoulder, Iago was grinning. "I'm afraid you've worn out your welcome, Prince Abooboo," Jafar hissed.

Aladdin whirled around. He struggled with his chains. If only he could reach his turban. The lamp was underneath—and the genie was inside the lamp.

Jafar looked calmly at the guards. "Make sure he is never found."

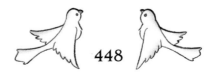

CHAPTER TEN

*I*n the chill of the desert night, the guards rushed Aladdin to the sea by camel. And without a word, they pushed him over a cliff.

Aladdin plunged into the water with a loud splash. In the dim moonlight, he could see his turban floating away. The lamp slowly emerged, then dropped to the seafloor.

He kicked his legs, desperate to reach the lamp. He groped with his hands. . . . There—he had it. But his strength was leaving him. He tried to rub the lamp, but he was weak . . . so weak . . .

Sploosh! The genie materialized, wearing a shower cap and holding a scrub brush. "Never fails," he said. "You get in the bath, and there's a rub at the lamp. Hello?"

Instantly his smile disappeared. Aladdin was limp.

"Al! Kid! Snap out of it!" the genie pleaded, grabbing Aladdin. "I can't help you unless you make a wish. You have to say, 'Genie, I want you to save my life!' Got it?"

Aladdin's head bobbed ever so slightly.

"I'll take that as a yes!" The genie let go of Aladdin and swam in a circle. A whirlpool formed, spinning Aladdin upward.

He burst through the surface, coughing and flailing. Before he could fall, the genie scooped him up and flew away. "Don't scare me like that!" the genie scolded.

Aladdin looked around with excitement. He was alive—wet and humiliated, but alive. As they flew back toward Agrabah, Aladdin looked into the smiling face of his rescuer.

"Genie, I . . . Thanks" was all he could say.

449

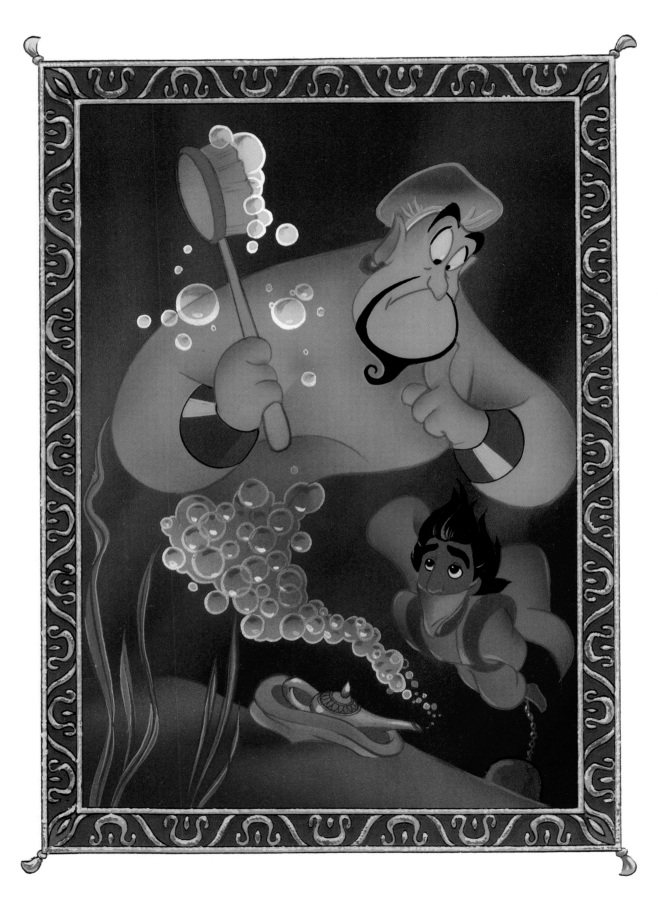

Jasmine had never been happier. She couldn't stop humming, and she couldn't stop thinking about Aladdin.

As she unbraided her hair in the bedroom mirror, she didn't notice her father walk in, with Jafar behind him. "Jasmine . . . ," the sultan began.

She turned around. "Oh, Father! I just had the most wonderful time. I'm so happy!"

The sultan stared straight ahead. "You should be, Jasmine," he said in a dull voice. "I have chosen a husband for you. You will marry Jafar."

Jasmine gasped.

Jafar stepped forward. The snake head of his staff glowed brightly, working its hypnotic spell on the sultan.

"Never!" Jasmine said. "Father, I choose Prince Ali!"

Jafar laughed. "Prince Ali left, like all the others. But don't worry. Wherever he went, I'm sure he made quite a splash."

"Better check your crystal ball, Jafar!" came a voice from the window.

Jafar turned. Iago squawked in surprise. It was Aladdin!

Jasmine ran to him. "Prince Ali!" she cried. "Are you all right?"

"Yes," Aladdin said, "but no thanks to Jafar. He tried to have me killed!"

"Your Highness," Jafar said, "he's obviously lying."

"Obviously . . . lying . . . ," the sultan repeated mechanically.

"Papa, what's wrong with you?" Jasmine said with dismay.

Aladdin leapt across the room toward Jafar. "I know what's wrong!" He pried the staff loose from Jafar and smashed the snake head on the floor.

"Oh! Oh my . . . ," the sultan said, shaking his head. "I feel so strange."

"Your Highness," Aladdin said, holding the broken staff in the air. "Jafar's been controlling you with this!"

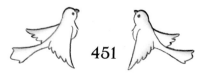

451

The sultan's eyes narrowed. "Jafar! You—you traitor! Guards! Arrest Jafar at once!"

But Jafar had caught sight of something he hadn't noticed before—peeking out of Aladdin's turban was the magic lamp! He lunged for it, but the sultan's guards seized him.

"This is not done yet, boy!" Jafar said. Reaching into his robe, he pulled out a magic pellet and threw it on the floor. In a puff of smoke, he and Iago were gone.

"Find him!" the sultan yelled to his guards. "I can't believe it—Jafar, my trusted counselor, plotting against me!"

His shocked expression changed to a smile when he turned back to Jasmine and Aladdin. "Can it be! My daughter has finally chosen a suitor?"

Jasmine nodded, and the sultan threw his arms around Aladdin. "Oh, you brilliant boy! You two will be wed at once! You'll be happy, prosperous—and then you, my boy, will become sultan!"

Sultan! Aladdin swallowed nervously. This was supposed to be the happiest moment of his life, but he was suddenly very worried.

Iago flew around Jafar's lab in a blind panic. "We've got to get out of here!" he said. "I've got to pack!"

But Jafar was deep in thought. He burst out with a sudden laugh and gripped Iago by the throat. "Prince Ali is nothing more than that ragged urchin Aladdin!" he said. "He has the *lamp*, Iago!"

Iago's eyes narrowed. "Why, that little, cheating—"

"But *you* are going to relieve him of it!" Jafar said with a sinister grin. "Listen closely." Iago leaned in as Jafar whispered his master plan.

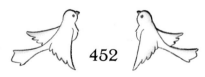

452

CHAPTER ELEVEN

Aladdin was given the most comfortable suite in the palace, but he barely slept that night.

By dawn he was pacing back and forth, holding his turban, the lamp inside. Abu and the carpet sat outside by the window, watching him with concern.

"Huzzah!" the genie cried, popping out of the lamp. "Aladdin, you've just won the heart of the princess! What are you going to do next?" He lowered his voice to a whisper. "Psst. Your next line is, 'I'm going to free the genie'!"

"Genie," Aladdin said sadly, "I'm sorry, but I can't. They want to make me sultan—no, they want to make *Prince Ali* sultan. The only reason anyone thinks I'm worth anything is because of you! What if they find out the truth? What if Jasmine finds out? She'll hate me." Aladdin looked into the genie's pale, disappointed face. "Genie, I need you. Without you, I'm just Aladdin."

The genie tried to control his anger. "I understand. After all, you've lied to everyone else. Hey, I was beginning to feel left out. Now, if you'll excuse me. . . ."

With that, he disappeared into the lamp.

"Genie," Aladdin called out, "I'm really sorry."

The genie's lips stuck out of the spout and razzed him.

"Fine!" Aladdin snapped, throwing a pillow over the lamp. "Then just stay in there!" As he stomped away, he could see Abu and the carpet watching him from the window. "What are you guys looking at?"

As Abu and the carpet turned away, Jasmine's voice came from the menagerie. "Ali! Will you please come here? Hurry!"

"Coming, Jasmine!" Aladdin called out the window.

He rushed outside. As he ran to the menagerie in the direction of Jasmine's voice, he passed a group of flamingos in a pond.

At least they all *looked* like flamingos.

Iago snickered to himself. His imitation of Jasmine had worked—and his flamingo disguise was perfect, thanks to Jafar's magic. When Aladdin was gone, he hurried into the empty room and quickly stole the lamp. Hooking it with his beak, he flew outside and straight back to Jafar's lab.

"Ali! There you are," said Jasmine. "I've been looking all over for you!"

Aladdin turned around, puzzled. Abu and the carpet scampered to his side. Jasmine was running toward him. But how could she have been "looking all over" when she had just—

"Hurry," she said, taking him by the hand. "Father's about to make the wedding announcement."

They climbed the stairs of a tower that overlooked the courtyard. Townspeople clogged every square inch trying desperately to see the royal couple. Jasmine stepped onto the platform and took her place next to her father. Smiling, the sultan announced to the crowd: "Ladies and gentlemen, my daughter has chosen a suitor—Prince Ali Ababwa!"

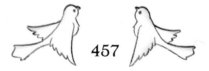

CHAPTER TWELVE

igh in another tower that overlooked the courtyard, Jafar and Iago watched as Aladdin was about to step before the roaring crowd.

"Look at them cheering that little pip-squeak," cried Iago.

"Let them cheer," Jafar said as he held the lamp tightly and began to rub it. "At last," he said. "The power is mine!"

In a puff of smoke, the genie appeared. "Al, if you're going to apologize, I—" The genie's jaw dropped when he saw Jafar.

"*I* am your master now!" Jafar said.

"I was afraid of that—"

"Keep quiet!" snapped Jafar. "And now, slave, grant me my first wish. I wish to be sultan!"

As Aladdin stared down from the platform, the crowd suddenly became hazy. Clouds swirled over the palace, and with a loud tearing sound, the canopy over the platform was ripped off. Jasmine and Aladdin looked around in confusion as a strange magical light engulfed the sultan. And when it stopped, the sultan was on the floor—in his underwear! The crowd gasped.

There was someone else on the stand now—someone tall, dark, and dressed in the sultan's robes. He held a snake staff in his right hand.

"Jafar!" Aladdin exclaimed.

Jafar turned with a sneer. "*Sultan* Jafar to you!"

"What manner of trickery is this?" the sultan demanded.

"Finders keepers," Jafar said. "I have the ultimate power now!"

A shadow fell over the courtyard. Everyone looked up.

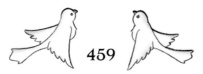

Aladdin's breath caught in his throat. Abu and the carpet clutched each other in terror. Looming over them like an evil giant was the genie. He placed his hands on the palace as if he were about to crush it.

"Genie, stop!" Aladdin shouted. "What are you doing?"

The genie's eyes were full of sadness. "Sorry, kid," he said. "I've got a new master now."

With a mighty heave, he lifted the entire palace off the ground. The people of Agrabah scattered, screaming as debris fell around them. The genie then flew to a mountain high above the city and set the palace down there.

Jafar let out a deep, triumphant laugh. "Now, you miserable wretches—bow to me!"

"We will *never* bow to you!" Jasmine replied. Aladdin and the sultan stood by her.

"Then you will cower!" Jafar said. He whirled around to face the genie. "My second wish is to be the most powerful sorcerer in the world!"

His snake staff began to glow, and green lightning crackled around it. Rajah let out a roar and lunged at Jafar. Jafar waved his staff, and in midair, Rajah was transformed into a kitten. As Rajah landed softly on his paws, Jafar glared at Jasmine and Aladdin. "Take a look at your precious Prince Ali—or should we say, *Aladdin!*"

A bolt of light shot from the staff. It surrounded Aladdin and Abu. Instantly Abu became a monkey again. Aladdin's robe, slippers, and turban disappeared. He fell to the floor, dressed in his old rags. "He's nothing more than a worthless lying street rat!"

Jasmine looked at him, confused and hurt. "Ali?"

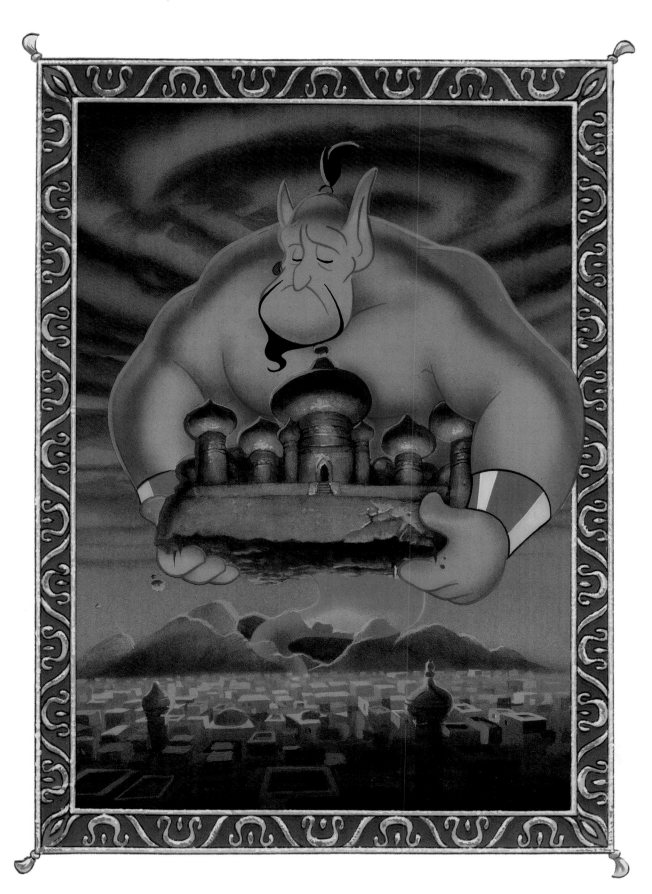

"Jasmine . . . I'm sorry," Aladdin said.

"Face it, boy, you don't belong here," Jafar said.

"Uh, where does he belong? Could it be . . . the ends of the earth?" Iago taunted.

"Works for me!" Jafar cried as he waved his staff again.

Aladdin and Abu suddenly levitated off the ground and into the open window of a narrow tower. In an instant, the tower rocketed over the horizon. The carpet sped after it.

Jasmine watched in horror as the tower vanished over the horizon. The genie sadly turned away.

With a devious laugh, Jafar shouted, "At last! Agrabah is mine!"

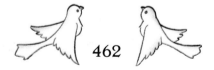

CHAPTER THIRTEEN

When Aladdin awoke, he was cold—freezing cold. As he made his way out of a snowbank, an icy wind whipped snow into his face.

Where was he? Through the raging blizzard, he could see the tower lying in pieces, half-covered with snow. Just beyond it, a cliff plunged downward into darkness.

A crash . . . that was all he remembered. He must have been thrown out of the tower, unconscious.

A brown lump caught his attention. "Abu!" he called through chattering teeth. He raced over and dug his pet out of the snow. "Are you all right?"

Shivering, Abu nodded weakly.

Aladdin tucked Abu into his vest. "Oh, Abu, this is all my fault. I should have freed the genie when I had the chance. Somehow, I've got to go back and set things straight."

He felt a tickling sensation on his leg. Spinning around, he saw the carpet reaching toward him. It was caught beneath a huge chunk of the tower.

Aladdin tried to pull the carpet free, but it was stuck tight. He and Abu started digging a trench around it, but the tower began to teeter.

"Look out!" Aladdin shouted. The tower began rolling toward them.

Calculating quickly, Aladdin ducked, curling Abu into his arms. The tower rolled over them, right where there was a window opening. Unharmed, they watched as the tower plunged over the cliff.

Freed from the tower, the carpet scooped up Aladdin and Abu and flew above the clouds.

"All right," cried Aladdin. "Now, back to Agrabah!"

Jafar loved the view from his new throne room. The palace was where it *belonged* now—on a mountaintop, not in the midst of the rabble. He happily sipped from his wine glass while the genie massaged his feet. The *former* sultan was now suspended from the ceiling like a marionette. He was dressed in a jester's outfit, and Jafar and Iago snickered at the ridiculous sight. Rajah, still a kitten, paced anxiously in a cage.

Jasmine sat at the window, her wrists in shackles, her eyes filled with sadness.

Jafar reached out with his staff. He hooked her shackles and pulled her close. "It pains me to see you reduced to this, Jasmine. You should be on the arm of the most powerful man in the world." With a wave of his staff, he made her chains vanish. A crown appeared on her head. "Why, with you as my queen—"

Jasmine took his glass and threw the wine in his face. "Never!"

Jafar bolted up from the throne. "Temper, temper, Jasmine," scolded Jafar. "You know what happens when you misbehave. . . . I'll teach you some respect!" He glared at the genie. "Genie, I have decided to make my final wish—I wish for Princess Jasmine to fall desperately in love with me!"

"No!" Jasmine said, backing away.

"Uh, Master," the genie said, "I can't do that—"

"You will do what I order you to do, slave!" Jafar roared as he grabbed the genie's beard.

Nobody noticed Aladdin and Abu peeking into the throne room window behind them—nobody except Jasmine.

She was about to scream when Aladdin shushed her with a finger over his mouth. He, Abu, and the carpet climbed silently into the room.

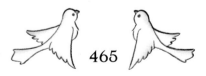

Jasmine thought fast. "Jafar," she said with a seductive smile, "I never realized how incredibly handsome you are!"

Jafar spun around. His jaw hung open in disbelief—and so did the genie's.

"That's better," Jafar said. He slinked toward Jasmine, a cocky smile on his face. "Now, tell me more about . . . *myself.*"

"You're tall, dark . . ." Jasmine could see Aladdin, Abu, and the carpet sneaking toward the lamp. Now the genie saw them, too. He was trying to stifle an excited giggle.

"Go on . . . ," Jafar said.

Abu was inches from Iago now—and Iago was turning around. Jasmine quickly put her arms around Jafar, locking him in place. "You're well dressed," she continued. "You've stolen my heart. . . ."

With a quick leap, Abu grabbed Iago off his perch and put a hand over his mouth. They both tumbled to the ground.

"And the street rat?" Jafar said, drawing closer to Jasmine.

"*What* street rat?" Jasmine asked.

Crassssshhh! Abu and Iago knocked into a table, sending a pot to the ground.

Jafar started to turn. Jasmine had no choice but to pull him close and kiss him—passionately and on the lips.

Now was Aladdin's chance for action. But he couldn't move. All he could do was stare. There she was, the girl for whom he had risked his life, kissing . . . *him.*

Jafar pulled back. He was dazed with joy—until he saw the reflection of Aladdin in Jasmine's crown.

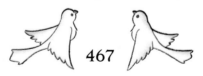

"You!" he said, whirling around in blind rage. His arm snapped forward, pointing his staff at Aladdin.

Zzzzzzap! A flash of light struck Aladdin in the chest. He flew backward, crashing into a pile of jewels.

"How many times do I have to kill you, boy?" Jafar said, drawing his arm back for a second shot.

Jasmine leapt at him, pushing his arm aside.

"You deceiving shrew!" Jafar snarled. "Your time is up!"

He turned his staff on Jasmine. Instantly she was trapped inside a giant hourglass. The upper chamber was full of sand, and it slowly spilled through the opening onto her. There was more than enough to bury her alive.

Zzzzzap! With a stroke of the staff, Jafar turned Abu into a cymbal-clanking toy monkey.

Zzzzzap! The carpet began to unravel. Aladdin ran to stop it. Jafar called out, "Things are unraveling fast, boy."

"This is all your fault, street rat! You never should have come back!" *Zzzzzzap!* Aladdin jumped back. A sword clattered to the ground beside him, then another. He looked up. Dozens of razor-sharp swords fell from the ceiling.

Jafar gestured again, and a wall of fire burst from the floor.

Aladdin grabbed one of the fallen swords. "Are you afraid to fight me yourself, you cowardly snake?" Aladdin said, batting away the swords as they fell.

Jafar made his way toward Aladdin, forcing him closer to the fire.

"A snake, am I? Perhaps you'd like to see how snakelike I can be!"

Jafar held out his snake staff with both hands. It began to grow, coming

468

to hideous life, wrapping Jafar himself into its skin. Swelling, hissing, Jafar became a monstrous cobra, his head rising toward the ceiling. The flames rose with him, becoming a ring of deadly coils surrounding Aladdin.

With an unearthly roar, Jafar lunged. Aladdin swung his sword.

Shink! He struck two of Jafar's fangs, which clattered onto the floor.

"Rickum-rackum, stick that sword into that snake," the genie shouted.

"You stay out of this!" Jafar hissed. He lunged again, knocking Aladdin to the floor. The sword flew out of his hand.

"Ali!" the sultan cried, watching helplessly from above. "*Jasmine!*"

Aladdin rolled away, catching a glimpse of the hourglass. The sand had risen swiftly, covering all but Jasmine's head.

Without his sword, there was only one chance. Aladdin ran for the window and leapt onto the balcony. Jafar slithered after him. Quickly Aladdin ran back in, then ducked out another window.

Jafar followed from window to window, tangling his long body into a knot. He shrieked with pain.

Aladdin picked up his sword and ran toward the hourglass. Jasmine's nose was barely above the sand, her eyes wide with fear. Aladdin drew back the sword, ready to smash the glass.

With a resounding boom, Jafar pulled down the wall. He was free— and he threw his coils around Aladdin.

Aladdin's sword was caught in midair. He struggled to get loose. "You thought you could outwit the most powerful being on earth!" Jafar bellowed.

Aladdin wrenched left and right. In a corner of the room, the genie watched helplessly.

The genie!

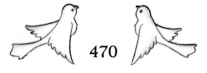

Thinking fast, Aladdin said, "You're not so powerful. The genie has more power than you'll ever have! He gave you your power, and he can take it away!"

The genie ducked behind a pillar. "Al, what are you doing? Why are you bringing me into this?"

"Face it, Jafar, you're still just second," Aladdin continued.

Jafar loosened his coils. He turned his slimy face to the genie. "You're right. His power does exceed my own—but not for long!"

Aladdin fell to the floor as Jafar slithered across the room. "Slave!" Jafar called to the genie. "I'm ready to make my third wish. I wish to be—an all-powerful genie!"

The genie looked at Aladdin, his blue face now chalk white. "Your wish," he said in a small, wavering voice, "is my command!"

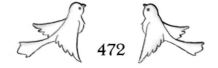

CHAPTER FOURTEEN

The genie gestured. A swirling current of energy encircled Jafar, and he began to change shape. The fire disappeared. His cobra body became wider and wider until he took on the roundness of a genie. "Yes!" Jafar shrieked. "The power! The absolute power!"

Quickly Aladdin picked up his sword and smashed the hourglass. Jasmine slid forward with the cascading sand. "What have you done!" she asked as Aladdin pulled her free.

Aladdin smiled. "Trust me."

"The universe is an open book before me!" Jafar yelled. "Mine to command, to control!" The dome of the palace exploded as Jafar rose to the sky.

Before he could say another word, gold shackles clamped around his wrists—just like the ones the genie wore. A lamp began to materialize beneath him, new and shiny.

"*Whaaat!* What is happening!" Jafar demanded.

"You wanted to be a genie!" Aladdin picked up the new lamp and held it out to Jafar. "You got it—and everything that goes with it!"

Jafar's legs were now a trail of vapor, a trail that disappeared into the lamp's spout. "No!" he said, his eyes bugging out in terror. "*Nooooooo!*"

Screaming with anguish, Jafar reached his hand upward. His fingers clasped Iago's feet. "Wha—hey! Let go!" Iago screamed.

With a dull *thoomp*, Jafar and Iago were sucked into the lamp.

Everyone in the throne room fell into an awed silence. Jasmine, the sultan, and the genie stared at Aladdin.

"Phenomenal cosmic powers," Aladdin said with a shrug. "Itty-bitty living space!"

The genie let out a loud cackle. "Al, you little genius!"

Instantly the room began to return to normal. Back on his feet, the sultan sighed with pleasure as his robes materialized on him. Abu became a live monkey again. Rajah grew back into a tiger, breaking free of his small cage. And the carpet looked brand new.

The genie grabbed the lamp and went to the balcony. "Shall we? Ten thousand years in the Cave of Wonders ought to chill him out!" He wound up and hurled the lamp, sending it end over end toward the desert.

Smiling proudly, the genie flew outside. He grew to a gigantic shape, picked up the entire palace, and began carrying it back to its rightful place.

CHAPTER FIFTEEN

*L*ater that day, when Agrabah had returned to normal, Jasmine and Aladdin stood on the throne room balcony.

"Jasmine," Aladdin said softly, "I'm sorry I lied to you . . . about being a prince."

Jasmine nodded. "I know why you did."

"I guess . . . this is good-bye?"

Jasmine turned away. "That stupid law! It isn't fair!" Slowly, tearfully, she faced Aladdin again. "I love you."

Suddenly the genie popped through the window. "Al, no problem—you've got one wish left. Just say the word, and you're a prince again!"

"But Genie," Aladdin said. "What about your freedom?"

"Al, you're in love. You're not going to find another girl like this in a million years. Believe me, I've looked."

Aladdin looked from the genie to Jasmine. He knew how much freedom meant now. Not only to the genie but to Jasmine—and to himself. Just as she needed to be free of the sultan's laws, Aladdin needed to be free, too. Free to be himself.

"Jasmine . . . I do love you," he finally said. "But I can't pretend to be something I'm not."

Jasmine bowed her head. "I understand."

"Genie," Aladdin said, "I wish for your freedom. It's about time I started keeping my promises."

In a flash, the genie's gold cuffs vanished. He was stunned. "Quick! Wish for something—anything! Say, 'I want the Nile!'"

"Er—I wish for the Nile," Aladdin said.

"NO WAY!" said the genie, with a laugh. "I'm free!" he shouted, his face lighting up. "I'm free! I'm off to see the world!"

"Congratulations!" the sultan said, peeking out behind him.

"Genie, I'm going to miss you," Aladdin said.

"Me, too, Al," the genie replied with a fond smile. "No matter what anybody says, you'll always be a prince to me!"

"That's right!" the sultan agreed. "You've certainly proved your worth as far as I'm concerned. If it's the law that's the problem, then what we need is a new law!"

Jasmine looked at him, stunned. "Father?"

"From this day forth, the princess shall marry whomever she deems worthy!"

"I choose you, Aladdin!" Jasmine cried instantly.

Aladdin was ecstatic. "Call me Al," he said.

He and Jasmine burst out laughing. Aladdin took her in his arms, and the two of them began twirling around the balcony.

"Well!" the genie said with a huge smile. "I can't do any more damage around here. And now I am out of here! Bye-bye, you crazy lovebirds!"

Like a rocket, the genie launched himself into the sky. The sultan followed him with his eyes until the genie disappeared over the horizon.

Aladdin and Jasmine didn't even notice him leave. As they shared a long, dreamy kiss, they didn't notice much of anything—except each other.

478

DISNEY'S
Beauty
and the
Beast

Adapted from the film
by A. L. Singer

Once upon a time in a faraway land, there was a magical kingdom where just about everything was perfect. The land was green, the people were happy, the castle was majestic.

The young Prince, however, was another story.

He had grown up with everything he desired, yet his heart remained cold. He was selfish, spoiled, and unkind. Yet because he was the Prince, no one dared say no to him. No one dared try to teach him a lesson.

Until one bitterly cold, raw, winter night.

On that night, an old beggar woman came to the castle, shivering and weak. The servants led her to the Prince. She bowed to him, taking a red rose from her basket.

"Kind sir," she said, "would you grant me shelter from the cold? I regret I have no money, but I can offer you this small, perfect rose as a token of my gratitude."

The servants had taken pity on the poor woman, but the Prince saw only her filth and ugliness. "Be gone, you foul beggar," he said. "And look not at my mirrors on the way out, lest they crack in horror!"

"My lord," the woman said, "do not be fooled by my outward appearance. For beauty is found within all things."

"I see," replied the Prince. "Then find beauty within someone else's house!" He turned to his servants. "Take this old bag of bones away, I say!"

But before the servants could touch her, she began to glow with a powerful light. As they looked on in awe, the old woman was transformed into a beautiful enchantress.

The Prince shook with fright. In the eyes of this enchantress, he could see an anger that was terrifying. "Please forgive me," he cried, dropping to his knees. "I . . . I didn't know—"

But she wouldn't let him finish. "I have seen that there is no love in your heart," she said. "That makes you no better than a beast—and so you shall *become* a beast!"

"No!" the Prince protested. "Please . . ."

The enchantress raised her hands high. Slowly the boy changed. Dark hair sprouted on his face and hands. Claws grew from his fingertips. He screamed with pain as his teeth became long and sharp.

"I hereby cast a spell on the entire castle," the enchantress declared. "You shall remain a prisoner here—and you shall have no human company."

Instantly, everyone else in the castle changed too. The head of the household, Cogsworth, became a mantel clock. The maître d', Lumiere, became a candelabra. The cook, Mrs. Potts, became a teapot. Others became furniture, china, even silverware—until not one human being was left.

The enchantress then held up the rose. "This rose will bloom until your twenty-first birthday, and then it will wither and die. You have until then to break the spell. If you don't, you will be doomed to remain a beast forever."

"But how can I break the spell?" said the frightened boy-beast. His voice was now a raspy snarl.

The enchantress leaned closer to him. "The only way to break it is to love another person and earn that person's love in return."

She placed the rose in a bell jar on a table, then pulled a small silver mirror out of her basket. "I also leave you with a gift. This enchanted mirror will show you any part of the world you wish to see. Look well, for it is a world you can no longer be part of!"

Then, in a flash of light, the enchantress disappeared.

The Beast stomped out of the room and ran up the stairs of the castle tower. Up, up, up he climbed, tripping over his new, clumsy, hairy feet. When he finally reached the top, he looked out the tower window.

He was shocked by what he saw. There was not one person on the castle grounds, not one house, not one road, not one grassy field. The sunny countryside had been swallowed up by a thick, gray mist.

He had to earn another person's love. That was what the enchantress had said.

"But who on Earth could learn to love a beast?" the boy thought in despair.

He reared his head back and howled. It was the howl of a caged animal. It was the howl of a boy who had lost everything.

ar away from where the castle now lay hidden was a charming little village. And in that village was a girl more beautiful than any other girl in the land. Her name was Belle.

She was so lovely that when she walked through her tiny village, everyone noticed. The baker, the blacksmith, the fruit seller, the milkmaid—even the children would stop what they were doing to watch her pass.

But Belle was unaware of their glances. She was always too busy reading. She even read while she walked.

"All that beauty," the villagers would say, shaking their heads. "It's a shame she's not normal. She always has her head buried in a book. She's just as strange as her father."

To Belle, there was nothing strange about reading. In books there was adventure, romance, excitement. There were dangers and Prince Charmings and happy endings. Books were more interesting than her dull, humdrum village, where every day was the same as the day before.

As for her father, Maurice, well, Belle was very proud of him. To her, he was the most clever inventor in the whole world.

True, he was a bit forgetful. True, his inventions never seemed to work exactly the way they were supposed to. But Belle knew he would prove himself to the world someday.

And when he did, maybe he would take her away from this small town. Maybe he would take her somewhere glamorous and exciting where she could meet her own Prince Charming.

But till then, she would have to wait—and read—and fight off the foolish men who tried to win her love.

Like Gaston.

Gaston was a fine, handsome hunter, admired by many of the young women in town. He was also a braggart, a coward, and a cheat.

One fall day, as Belle walked through the town square, reading, Gaston said to his constant companion, Lefou, "There she is, Lefou. She's the lucky girl I'm going to marry."

"The inventor's daughter?" said Lefou. "The one with her nose in a book? She's odd. She's . . ."

"She's the most beautiful girl in town," Gaston added. "And don't I deserve the best?"

"Of course. . . . I mean, yes, but . . . ," Lefou stuttered.

Gaston ran after Belle with Lefou following close behind. When Gaston caught up with her, just outside the marketplace, he slowed down. "Hello Belle," he announced with a cocky smile.

Belle barely glanced up from her book. "Hello Gaston," she answered.

Gaston grabbed Belle's book out of her hand. "My dear, it's not right for a girl to read. It's time you got your head out of these books and paid attention to more important things—like me."

"Gaston, may I have my book please?" Belle said, trying to control her anger.

Gaston grinned and threw her book into a mud puddle. "What do you say we walk over to the tavern and look at my trophies?"

He gripped her arm but Belle shook it loose. "Please, Gaston," she said, furious that he had ruined her book. "I have to get home to help my father. Good-bye!" She picked up her book and began walking away.

As Lefou approached, he muttered with a sneer, "Your father? That crazy old loon. He needs all the help he can get."

Belle spun around. "Don't talk about my father that way! He's a genius!"

But before she could say anything else—BOOOOOOM!—an explosion shook the ground.

A plume of smoke rose from a small house just up the road. Belle's house!

"Papa!" Belle screamed. She ran home as fast as she could.

When she yanked open the door of her father's workshop, thick smoke billowed out. In the midst of it, sitting beside a broken hulk of wooden slats and metal gears, was her father, Maurice.

She ran to his side. "Are you all right, Papa?"

Coughing and muttering, Maurice stood up and kicked his invention. "How on Earth did that happen? I'll never get this boneheaded contraption to work!"

Belle smiled, relieved that he wasn't hurt. "Oh, yes you will," she said. "And you'll win first prize at the fair tomorrow—*and* become a world-famous inventor."

"You really believe that?" Maurice said, a small smile flickering across his face.

"I always have," Belle said confidently.

"Well, then, what are we waiting for?" Maurice said, grabbing a tool. "I'll have this thing fixed in no time!"

As Belle watched him work, she began thinking. Gaston's mocking words came back to her: *"It's not right for a girl to read."*

"Papa," she said, "do you think I'm odd?"

Maurice popped out from behind his invention, his glasses crooked, his hair standing on end. "My daughter? Odd? Now where would you get that idea?"

"I don't know, I'm just not sure I fit in here," Belle said. She looked at her father sadly. "Oh, Papa, I want excitement and adventure in my life . . . and I want someone to share it with."

Belle's voice had grown soft with that last comment. Her father nodded knowingly. "Well, how about that Gaston? He's a handsome fellow."

"He's not for me, Papa," Belle said. "He's crude and conceited."

"Well, don't worry. This invention's going to be the start of a new life for us." Maurice gave his daughter a warm smile. "Then we'll get out of this place and you can have a chance at those dreams."

Before long, Maurice had the contraption working again, with plenty of time left to take it to the fair. Belle helped him load it into a wooden wagon, then they hitched the wagon to their horse, Philippe. Slinging a cape around his shoulders, Maurice mounted the horse and started off.

"Good-bye!" Belle shouted, waving after him. "Good luck!"

As Philippe trotted down the road, Maurice held a map tightly, making sure to follow the correct route. It wasn't until three hours later that he realized something awful.

The map was upside down.

Maurice groaned. Nothing around him looked familiar. "Now we'll never make it to the fair," he said. "Belle will be so disappointed."

Philippe slowly approached a fork in the road. There was a sign there, but the words on it had faded.

To the left, the road continued along a river. To the right, it disappeared into a thick, misty forest. Maurice peered up both roads, then pulled Philippe to the right.

Philippe reared back and shook his head.

But Maurice just pulled harder. "Come on, Philippe. It's a shortcut. We'll be there in no time."

Philippe went to the right, into the forest. The road grew narrower and trees made black shadows on the ground. Slowly, a thick, gray fog settled over them. The drip, drip, drip of water from a tree echoed in the dead silence.

A sharp wind whistled through the gnarled branches, causing them to twitch like sharp, bony fingers. Maurice held his jacket closed against the sudden cold.

Then a long shadow skittered among the trees, rustling the leaves. Philippe stopped. He looked around fearfully.

"Uh, we'd better turn around . . ." Maurice began.

But it was too late. A pair of pale yellow eyes appeared in the brush. Philippe whinnied, rearing up on his hind legs.

"Whoa, Philippe!" Maurice yelled, but he couldn't hold on. He tumbled to the ground as Philippe galloped away.

"Philippe?" Maurice whispered into the darkness. He got up quickly and looked around frantically. Again, he saw the yellow eyes, and hoped against hope that they belonged to something friendly.

But there was nothing friendly about the animal's angry growl, or its long, sharp, glistening teeth.

It was a wolf!

Rrrrrrrrr . . .

Maurice backed away from the wolf's growl. "N-n-no," he muttered. "No!"

The wolf sprang toward him. Maurice turned and ran. He crashed through the underbrush, ignoring the branches that lashed his face.

Then he saw another shadow, and another. It was a whole pack of wolves! Maurice ran left, then right. The wolves were panting, snarling. He looked back to see many pairs of yellow eyes gaining on him.

And that was when a dim, far-off light caught his eye. He raced toward it. But the trees became thicker. Thorns ripped his pants, branches seemed to push him back like arms.

Then he smacked against something hard. Metallic. A gate! "Help!" he cried out. "Is someone there? Help!"

The gate creaked open.

Maurice raced through, then slammed it shut after him. Seconds later, with a loud crash, the wolves hurled themselves against the gate and fell away.

Maurice heaved a sigh of relief. His heart was beating

furiously. He turned around, hoping to find that light.

What he saw took his breath away.

He had found the light, all right. It was coming from an enormous castle. A dark, old, crumbling castle surrounded by mist.

It looked as though no one had taken care of the castle for ages. Yet the light meant someone was inside, so Maurice walked toward it.

He crossed over a bridge. Below him was a dried-up moat. On the other side of the bridge were the castle grounds. Weeds and vines crept up garden walls and tangled around broken marble statues.

Just then a thunderbolt split the sky, casting a harsh white light over the castle, and instantly rain began to fall in torrents.

Light still flickered through the castle's open door, so Maurice stepped cautiously inside.

On a table just inside the door there was a beautiful, lighted candelabra and a mantel clock. Beyond them was the largest room Maurice had ever seen. Rich-looking but tattered tapestries hung from the walls. Tarnished and chipped statues stood in corners. The floors were covered with thick, dusty carpets. Dark archways led to dark, faraway rooms.

Staring with wonder, Maurice managed to call out, "Hello?"

His voice echoed in the dim parlor.

Then he heard voices. The first said, "Poor fellow must have lost his way, Cogsworth."

The second snapped, "Keep quiet, Lumiere. Maybe he'll go away."

"Oh, have a heart," came the first voice. Then, louder, it said, "You are welcome here, monsieur!"

"Who said that?" Maurice asked. "Where are you?"

Maurice felt something tugging at his cloak. He whirled around but saw no one.

"Down here!" said the second voice.

When Maurice looked down, his eyes grew wide. The *mantel clock* was tugging at him! It had arms and legs—and a face!

"I am Monsieur Cogsworth," the clock said, in a manner that was not very friendly.

Then the candelabra spoke with a welcoming voice. "And I am Monsieur Lumiere, at your service."

"You're . . . you're alive!" Maurice said, picking up Cogsworth and poking him. "How can that be?"

"Please put me down, sir," Cogsworth said, "or I shall give you a sound thrashing!"

Maurice obeyed, saying, "I beg your pardon, it's just that—AAAAAAH-CHOO!" The sneeze exploded out of him.

"You are soaked to the bone, monsieur," Lumiere said. "Come warm yourself by the fire."

"No!" Cogsworth retorted. "I forbid it! The master will be furious if he finds him here!"

But Lumiere ignored him, pulling Maurice into a spacious drawing room where a roaring fire gave off a warm, amber glow. Maurice settled himself in a comfortable leather armchair. A footstool, yapping happily like a dog, scooted under Maurice's feet.

"Well, hello there boy!" Maurice said.

"Oh, no, no, no, no, no!" Cogsworth cried, putting his hands over his eyes. "I am not seeing this!"

A tea cart rolled into the room. On it was a round teapot with a plump, friendly face, and a small, chipped teacup.

"I'm Mrs. Potts and this is my son Chip," she said. "Would you like a spot of hot tea, sir?"

"No!" Cogsworth shouted. "No tea!"

"Yes, please," said Maurice gratefully.

As Mrs. Potts poured tea, Cogsworth grabbed Lumiere. "We've got to get him out of here! You know what the master will do if . . ."

"Calm yourself," Lumiere said. "The master will never have to know. Now hush, our guest is falling asleep."

Cogsworth sputtered with frustration. But Maurice was indeed falling into a deep, blissful sleep. . . .

WHAMMMM!

The door flew open and Maurice jumped in his chair. The footstool yelped and scrambled under a table. The tea cart quickly rolled away, and Cogsworth dashed under a carpet.

Maurice spun around. There was someone—some*thing*—standing in the doorway. It towered on thick, hairy legs, and its head and arms were covered with matted fur. As it stepped toward Maurice, its foot pounded the floor like mallets. Under thick, tangled brows, its eyes glared angrily and its nostrils flared. "There's a stranger here," he growled.

Maurice wanted to run, but he couldn't. Fear had him frozen.

Lumiere stepped forward quickly. "Master," he said, "you see, the gentleman was lost in the woods, so . . ."

"RRRRRAAAAGGGGGHHH!" The force of the Beast's roar blew out Lumiere's candles.

Cogsworth peered out from under the carpet. "I was against it from the start," he said. "I tried to . . ."

The Beast sneered at Maurice. "What are you doing here?"

"I was lost in the woods," Maurice answered, his eyes wide with fright, "and I . . ."

"What are you staring at?" the Beast demanded.

"N-n-nothing," Maurice stammered.

"You come into my home and stare at me!" the Beast accused.

Maurice bolted for the door, but the Beast blocked his way. "I meant no harm," Maurice said. "I just needed a place to stay."

The Beast grabbed Maurice by the shirt with his claws. In a sinister voice that made Maurice's blood run cold, he said, "I'll give you a place to stay!"

Right then, the only thing Maurice could think of was Belle. He had a strange feeling that he would never see her again.

Gaston and Lefou walked briskly down the road from town. They wore their finest formal clothing. Behind them was a priest, a brass band, and just about every person who lived there.

When they reached Belle's house, Gaston turned. He held up his hands and everyone stopped. "Ladies and gentlemen, I'd like to thank you all for coming to my wedding! But first," he said, chuckling, "I'd better go in there and propose to the girl!"

The crowd laughed. Gaston marched to Belle's door and knocked hard.

Inside, Belle was reading. She put down her book, went to the door, and opened it a crack. "Gaston, what a pleasant surprise," she said, trying to hide her disappointment.

Gaston pushed the door open and barged in. "You know, Belle," he announced, "there's not a girl in town who wouldn't love to be in your shoes. This is the day your dreams come true!"

"What do *you* know about my dreams?" Belle said.

Gaston plopped down on Belle's chair and plunked his muddy boots on the table—right on her book. "Picture this," he said. "A rustic hunting lodge. My latest kill roasting on the fire. And my

little wife massaging my feet while her little ones play on the floor—six or seven of them. And do you know who that little wife will be? You, Belle!"

Belle's jaw fell open in shock. He was proposing to her—and he had invited the whole town to watch! The nerve!

He stood up and tried to throw his arms around Belle. But she backed away toward the door, thinking frantically. "Gaston, I'm . . . I'm . . . speechless! I don't know what to say!"

Gaston followed her in a circle around the room, finally pinning her to the door. "Say you'll marry me!"

"Well, I'm really sorry, Gaston," Belle said, groping behind her for the doorknob, "but . . . um, I . . . I just don't deserve you. But thanks for asking!"

She found the doorknob and pushed. As the door opened, she ducked out of the way. Gaston lost his balance and tumbled out.

She slammed the door shut just as Gaston landed in a mud puddle.

The crowd fell silent. Lefou walked slowly up to Gaston. "She turned you down, huh?" he said.

Gaston got up, furious. His fists were clenched, his eyes were burning. Nervously, people began to back away.

Then, suddenly, Gaston burst into laughter. "Turn *me* down? Nonsense! She's just playing hard to get!"

Smiling, with his head held high, he strode back to town.

The crowd stood silently, watching him. Many of them admired his dignity. Many of them wanted to laugh.

But none of them could see the expression on his face change. None of them could see the smile quickly turn into a fierce, angry grimace.

And none of them could hear his solemn vow: "I'll have Belle for my wife. One way or another."

Belle stayed in her house until every last person had left. "Imagine me, the wife of that brainless fool," she said to herself. As she opened the door to take a walk, she heard a familiar noise— Philippe's whinny.

"Papa?" she thought. "Back so soon?"

But when she looked up the road, she saw Philippe was alone. She ran toward him, crying out, "Philippe! What's the matter? Where's Papa?"

Philippe snorted and whinnied anxiously.

Belle was terrified. "We have to find him! Take me to him!"

She leapt on Philippe, and he galloped down the road. Carefully he retraced his steps until they came to the forest, which was as dark and creepy as before. But this time Philippe was determined to make it through. The wind howled and whistled, pushing branches in his path, but he trudged onward.

Belle felt her skin crawl. In her worst nightmares she had never imagined a place so horrible.

Suddenly, at the sight of the rusted gate, Philippe began to buck anxiously. "Steady, Philippe," Belle said. She hopped off and pulled him toward the gate. Pushing it open, she spotted a hat lying on the ground.

It was her father's hat.

"Papa!" she cried. "Come on Philippe!" She dragged her horse onto the castle grounds, barely noticing the surroundings. Tying Philippe to a post, she ran into the castle.

"Papa?" she called out as she entered the grand hall. She ran through it and up a curved marble staircase. "Papa, are you here? It's Belle!"

When she reached the top of the stairs, Belle ran down a corridor—right past Cogsworth and Lumiere.

Cogsworth was frozen with surprise. Lumiere burst into tears. "A girl!" he cried. "A beautiful girl! After all these years, she's come to fall in love with the master and break the spell. Soon we will be human again!"

"Nonsense!" Cogsworth snapped. "She's here because of that fellow locked in the tower. He must be her father."

"Then we must help her!" Lumiere said. He ran through the castle, taking a shortcut to get ahead of Belle. He stopped in the corridor that led to the tower stairs.

Belle reached the stairs. When she saw Lumiere's flickering light, she called out, "Hello? Is someone there? I'm looking for . . ."

Lumiere moved up the stairs, then sat on a small shelf. Belle quickly followed him. When she got to the top she looked around, puzzled. There was a candelabra and a row of doors with small slots at the bottom. "That's funny," she said. "I'm sure there was someone . . ."

"Belle?"

The voice that called her was hoarse, but she knew exactly who it was. "Papa!" she screamed. "Where are you?"

Maurice's face peered out from the slot in one of the doors.

"Here." He reached his hand through the bars.

Belle ran to the door and grasped his hand. "Oh, Papa, your poor hands are like ice," she said. "We have to get you out of there!"

Shivering, Maurice said, "I don't know how you found me, Belle, but I want you to leave at once."

"Who's done this to you?" Belle demanded.

"No time to explain!" Maurice said. "You must go. Now!"

"No, Papa, I won't leave you!" Belle vowed.

Suddenly Belle felt darkness settle over her. She thought the candelabra had flickered out.

But when she turned around, she realized the darkness was a shadow. The shadow of someone enormous, someone she couldn't see.

"Who's there?" she said.

But the Beast didn't answer, not at first. He couldn't. The words wouldn't come. He felt ashamed of his ugliness as he stared

at the most beautiful human being he had ever seen.

"Who are you?" Belle asked, as she peered into the darkness.

Softly, the Beast said, "The master of this castle."

"I've come for my father," Belle pleaded. "There must be some misunderstanding. Please let him out. He's sick!"

"He shouldn't have trespassed!" the Beast replied.

Belle struggled to see the face of her father's captor. "Please, I'll do anything to save his life," she said. "Take me instead!"

Silence hung in the air. The Beast looked at Belle carefully. Her hair, her eyes, her lovely face, made him feel warm inside. It was the first time in years he had felt that way. "You would take his place?" he asked.

"Belle, no!" Maurice shouted. "You don't know what you're doing!"

"If I did take his place," Belle continued, "would you let him go?"

"Yes," the Beast answered, "but you must promise to remain here forever."

The corridor froze with silence again. Belle thought for a moment. Who was this man? Before she could give an answer, she needed desperately to know. "Come into the light," she said.

The Beast stood still. He was ashamed to show his face in the presence of such perfect beauty.

But a desperate hope glimmered inside the Beast. Maybe, just maybe, she wouldn't mind what she saw. Maybe she would like him.

Slowly, he moved into the light.

Belle's eyes widened. She gasped with horror and turned away.

"No, Belle!" Maurice said. "I won't let you!"

But Belle was gathering her strength. She knew there was only one thing to do, as dreadful as it seemed.

She turned to face the Beast. "You have my word."

"Done!" the Beast said. And he quickly unlocked the door and began dragging Maurice out of the castle. Belle screamed and Maurice struggled, but he couldn't break the Beast's iron grip. "Please spare my daughter," he pleaded. "She had no part in this!"

But the Beast didn't even hear him. As he forced Maurice off the castle grounds, there was only one thought on the Beast's mind.

He had the girl all to himself now. Forever.

*N*ow that Belle was locked in the tower, the Beast had no idea what to do with her. He mumbled to himself, pacing back and forth beneath the tower stairs. "After all these years . . . after I'd given up . . . what do I say to her?"

Lumiere watched him for a long time. He wanted so much for the Beast to do the right thing. Maybe, just maybe, the Beast could make Belle fall in love with him. And if he did, the spell would finally be broken.

It was the only hope for Lumiere, and for all the other servants, to become human again.

Gathering up his courage, Lumiere said, "Uh, master, since the girl is going to be with us for quite some time, perhaps you should offer her a more comfortable room."

The Beast growled, and Lumiere backed away in fright.

Then, muttering again, the Beast began to climb the tower stairs. He shuffled down the corridor to Belle's door and paused.

Now it was *his* turn to gather up courage.

When he opened the door, Belle was on the ground, her head in her hands. She looked up at him with tearful eyes. "I'll never see him again—and you didn't even let me say good-bye!"

The Beast frowned. He hadn't seen this kind of behavior before. He didn't know people could care so much for one another. "I'll show you to your room," he growled. He walked back into the corridor, snatching up Lumiere in his thick hand.

"My room?" Belle was confused. She thought the Beast wanted to keep her in the tower. She followed him down the stairs and through a long maze of corridors. They both remained silent, until Lumiere could stand it no longer. "*Say* something to her," he whispered to the Beast.

The Beast felt butterflies in his stomach. "I . . . uh, hope you'll like it here," he finally said to Belle. Quickly, he looked back at Lumiere for approval.

Lumiere smiled. "Go on," he urged.

"The castle's your home now, so you can go anywhere you like," the Beast said. He thought a moment then added, "Except the West Wing."

"What's in . . . ," Belle began to ask.

Before she could finish, the Beast whirled around angrily. "It's forbidden!"

Lumiere groaned. The Beast wasn't exactly charming Belle.

They walked in silence again until they reached a large guest room. The Beast opened the door, and Belle walked in cautiously.

"If you need anything, my servants will attend you," the Beast said.

"Invite her to dinner!" Lumiere whispered to him.

"Oh." The Beast nodded, then turned back to Belle. "You'll . . . uh, join me for dinner."

But Belle wanted nothing to do with him. Silently, coldly, she pushed the door closed.

But the Beast stopped the door with his hand. There was fury in his eyes, the fury of a person who had never been disobeyed in his life. In a gruff, threatening voice, he said, "That's not a request!"

Belle slammed the door in his face. The Beast snarled and stomped away.

Lumiere sighed with frustration. This love affair was not getting off to a good start.

Back in the village, in a noisy tavern, Gaston was doing what he did best—bragging. He was bragging about his hunting, about his eating, and about his drinking.

He only stopped bragging once, when the tavern door swung open with a loud WHACK!

The tavern fell silent. Everyone watched as a filthy, wet man stumbled in from the snow. At first no one recognized him.

"Help!" he cried out, his face pale with terror. "He's got her! He's got Belle locked up in his castle!"

Laughter filled the tavern. "It's crazy old Maurice!" one of Gaston's friends yelled.

"Slow down, Maurice," Gaston said. "Who's got Belle locked up?"

"A horrible, monstrous beast!" Maurice replied. "You've got to help me!"

"All right, old man," Gaston said. "We'll help you." With a wink at his friends, he pointed to the door.

Two of the men lifted Maurice by his arms, walked him to the door, and tossed him outside. As they slammed the door behind him, the tavern crowd hooted and cheered.

But Gaston grew serious. He pulled Lefou aside and said, softly, "Crazy as he is, that old man may be of use to us, Lefou. I have just thought of a plan, a plan that will make Belle my bride!"

With a sinister grin, he whispered his plan to Lefou.

Maurice ran frantically through the village streets. "Please help me!" he shouted to everyone he saw. "My daughter has been captured by a beast!"

Everyone ignored him. "Old Maurice has finally lost his marbles," they all thought as they walked away.

As the snow continued, Maurice sank to his knees in the street. He raised his head upward and gave one last, desperate cry: "Will no one help me?"

But the only answer was a harsh, whistling wind. Maurice was all alone.

And he knew poor Belle was doomed.

Belle threw herself on her bed and sobbed. The mattress was soft, with a beautiful silk bed cover that matched the curtains. Everything in the room was the finest she'd ever seen, from the carved wooden night table, to the handwoven rug, to the large wardrobe near the bed.

But to Belle, none of that mattered. The room was a prison. No matter how beautiful it was, she could never consider it home. If the Beast was going to forever keep her from her father and the things she loved, then she would hate him and his castle forever.

"And I will never have dinner with him!" she vowed to herself. "Even if he is the only other living thing in the castle."

A sudden knock on the door interrupted her thoughts. "Who is it?" she asked.

"Mrs. Potts, dear," a voice said. "I thought you might like some tea."

So there *were* some other people in the castle, Belle thought. The voice sounded friendly enough, so she opened the door.

But there was no one there—no person, that is. Just a teapot, who happily walked right in. Behind her skipped a little chipped teacup.

Belle gasped. She backed away, right into the wardrobe. "Careful!" the wardrobe said.

Belle spun around, and gasped again. The wardrobe had a face, just as the teapot and cup did. They were alive—all of them! "This . . . this is impossible!" Belle said, sitting on the bed.

"I know it is," Wardrobe said, "but here we are!"

The teacup looked up at the teapot and said, "I told you she was pretty, Mama. Didn't I?"

"All right, Chip," Mrs. Potts answered. "Now hold still." Chip stood next to her obediently, and she carefully poured some tea into him.

Smiling with excitement, Chip hopped over to Belle. "Slowly now," Mrs. Potts called out. "Don't spill!"

Belle smiled. Chip was cute. "Thank you," she said, picking him up and taking a sip.

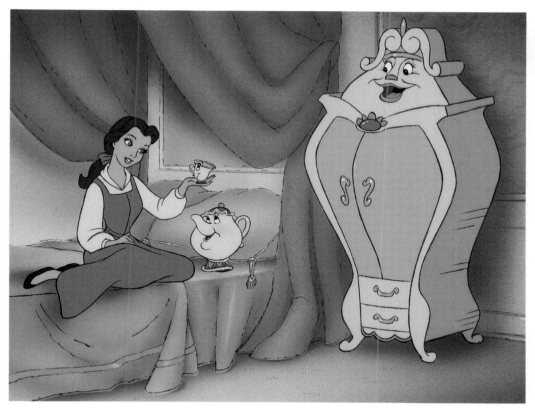

"That tickles!" Chip said with a giggle.

"You know, my dear," Mrs. Potts said, "changing places with your father was a very brave thing to do."

"We all think so," Wardrobe agreed, sitting next to Belle on the bed.

Belle cast her eyes downward. "But now I've lost my father, my dreams—everything!"

"It'll turn out all right in the end, you'll see," Mrs. Potts said gently. Then, turning to Chip, she added, "Come now! I almost forgot there's a supper to get on the table!"

As Mrs. Potts and Chip scurried out the door, Wardrobe pulled a long, silky gown from one of her drawers. "Ah, you'll look ravishing in this at dinner," she said.

"That's very kind of you, but I'm not going to dinner," Belle answered.

"Oh, but you must!" Wardrobe insisted.

Just then, Cogsworth appeared in the bedroom doorway. "Ahem!" he said, clearing his throat. "Dinner is served!"

But Belle was not going to budge from that room, even if every object in the castle came and begged. Her answer was no!

Snow fell outside the dining room windows. The table was set with the finest china. Mrs. Potts had come out of the kitchen to reassure the Beast, and she sat with Lumiere on the mantel over a roaring fire. They watched the Beast pace back and forth.

"What's taking her so long?" the Beast growled.

"Try to be patient, sir," Mrs. Potts said.

"Master," Lumiere added, "have you thought that perhaps this girl could be the one to break the spell?"

"Of course I have!" the Beast roared. "I'm not a fool! But it's no use. She's so beautiful and I'm . . . well, look at me!"

"You must help her see past all that," Mrs. Potts said.

"I don't know how," the Beast replied sadly. "And the worst thing is that the rose has already started to wilt."

"Well, you can start by making yourself more presentable," Mrs. Potts said. "Straighten up. Try to act like a gentleman."

"Give her a dashing smile," Lumiere suggested.

"But don't let your fangs scare her," Mrs. Potts added.

"Impress her with your delightful wit!" Lumiere said with excitement. "Shower her with compliments."

"But be gentle," Mrs. Potts said, "and sincere."

"And above all," they said together, "you must control your temper!"

KNOCK! KNOCK! KNOCK!

Someone was at the door. "Here she is!" cried Lumiere. The Beast ran a paw through his hair and tried to smile. The door flew open.

But it was only Cogsworth.

"Well, where is she?" the Beast demanded.

"Uh . . . who?" Cogsworth said nervously. "Oh, ha ha! The girl, you mean! Well, she's in the process of . . . uh, circumstances being what they are . . ."

The Beast glared at him impatiently. There was no way out for Cogsworth. He had to tell the truth. "She's not coming," he said, his voice a frightened squeak.

"RRRRRRRRAAAGGGGHHHH!" the Beast roared, bolting out of the room. He bounded up the stairs to Belle's room with Lumiere, Cogsworth, and Mrs. Potts running behind.

"You come out or I'll break the door down!" he bellowed, banging at her door.

"I'm not hungry!" Belle shouted from inside.

"Master," Cogsworth said carefully, "please attempt to be a gentleman."

The Beast's nostrils flared with anger, but he knew Cogsworth

was right. He took a deep breath. "It would give me great pleasure if you would join me for dinner," he said through gritted teeth.

"No, thank you," Belle's voice shot back.

That was all the Beast could take. "Fine!" he yelled. "Then go ahead and starve!" He whirled around to face Cogsworth and Lumiere. "If she doesn't eat with me, then she doesn't eat at all!" he roared.

As he stormed away, Mrs. Potts remarked, "Oh, dear. That didn't go very well, did it?"

Cogsworth threw up his hands and sighed. "We might as well go downstairs and start cleaning up. Lumiere, stand watch here and inform me if there's the slightest change."

"My eyes will never leave the door," Lumiere replied.

The Beast didn't stop until he'd gotten to his lair in the West Wing. He threw his door open and clomped into the room, mut-

tering to himself, "I ask nicely but she refuses! What does she want me to do, beg?"

He grabbed the magic mirror off his dressing table, the mirror that allowed him to see anywhere he desired. "Show me the girl!" he demanded.

Slowly a vision of Belle's room appeared. Belle was sitting on her bed, arms crossed in anger. Wardrobe walked over to her and said, "The master's really not so bad once you get to know him. Why don't you give him a chance?"

"He's ruined my life!" Belle replied. "I don't want to have anything to do with him!"

The Beast didn't want to hear any more. As he put the mirror down, his eyes filled with sadness. "She'll never see me as anything but a monster," he said to himself. "It's hopeless."

Before his last word was finished, another petal fell from the rose. The Beast shuddered as it fluttered to the tabletop.

ater that night, Belle sneaked out of her room. There was no one standing guard, but she could hear giggles down the hall. Glancing to her left, she saw Lumiere flirting with a pretty feather duster.

She tiptoed down the hall. Her stomach was pained with hunger. She hadn't wanted to eat dinner with the Beast, but that didn't mean she wanted to starve!

She walked quietly down the stairs. It wasn't hard finding the kitchen. Down a long hallway she could hear the clanking of pots and pans behind a door.

Slowly she pushed the door open. For a moment, everyone in the kitchen froze. Cogsworth was there, along with Mrs. Potts, and a very angry-looking stove.

Cogsworth was the first to speak. "Splendid to see you, mademoiselle," he said, with a deep bow. "I am Cogsworth, head of the household."

Immediately, Lumiere ran in, out of breath and looking guilty. Cogsworth gave him a sharp glare and said, "And this is Lumiere."

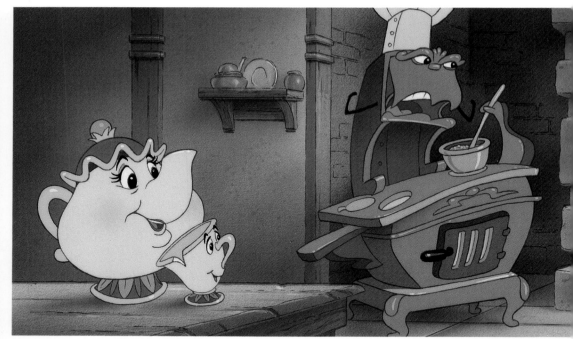

Lumiere reached for Belle's hand and tried to kiss it, but Cogsworth slapped him away. "If there's anything we can do to make your stay more comfortable . . ." Cogsworth said in an unconvincing tone.

"I *am* a little hungry," Belle replied.

Mrs. Potts's eyes lit up. "You are?" she said. Turning to the others, she called out, "Hear that? Stoke the fire! Take out the silverware! Wake the china!"

"No!" Cogsworth shouted. "Remember what the master said. If she doesn't eat with him, she doesn't eat at all!"

But no one listened to Cogsworth. Instead, all the objects flew into action. The stove began cooking on all burners. Platters full of good food leapt into the oven.

Smiling, Lumiere gracefully escorted Belle into the dining room. "Mademoiselle, it is with deep pride and great pleasure that we welcome you," he said grandly. "And now we invite you to relax and pull up a chair as the dining room proudly presents—your dinner!"

He acted like the master of ceremonies at a show, and that's exactly what Belle saw: a show. She watched in wonder as the plates, platters, and silverware all danced and sang on the table. Then a chair slid underneath Belle, and pushed her toward the table. The first course was served.

The kitchen door swung open time and again. Each time, Belle's mouth watered. And each time, a platter of food came out, more delicious than the last.

The name of each dish was announced in song and dance. There were hot hors d'oeuvres, beef ragout, cheese soufflé, and a dessert of pie and flaming pudding. It was a lot of food, but Belle managed to clean every plate. She'd never had a dinner so delicious, nor seen a show so unusual!

When it was all over, she burst into applause. Even Cogsworth had gotten into the spirit of things, dancing his heart out. He and Lumiere and the rest of the objects all bowed deeply to her, grinning with pleasure.

"Bravo!" Belle exclaimed. "That was wonderful! I've never

been in an enchanted castle before. I'd like to look around now, if that's all right."

Cogsworth snapped out of his good mood. "Wait a second! I'm not sure that's a good idea. The master . . ."

"Perhaps you'd like to take me," Belle said to Cogsworth. "I'm sure *you* know everything there is to know about the castle."

"Well, actually," Cogsworth said, his chest puffing with pride, "I do!"

Strutting proudly, he led her on a tour of the castle. He talked and talked, explaining every single detail in every single room. Lumiere followed behind, but he quickly became bored. He looked around, humming and singing to himself.

As they neared the West Wing, Cogsworth and Lumiere

realized something terrible. Belle had disappeared.

"Mademoiselle?" Cogsworth called out.

Out of the corner of his eye, he spotted Belle moving up a dark set of stairs.

Instantly, Cogsworth and Lumiere raced ahead of Belle and blocked the way.

"What's up there?" Belle asked.

"Nothing!" Cogsworth replied. "Absolutely nothing of interest in the West Wing. Dusty, dull, very boring."

"Ah, so this is the West Wing," Belle said, remembering the Beast's warning. "I wonder what he's hiding up there?"

She started to take a step up, but Cogsworth didn't budge. "Perhaps mademoiselle would like to see something else," he said

desperately. "We have tapestries, gardens, a library . . ."

"You have a library?" Belle asked.

"Oh, yes, indeed!" Cogsworth said. "With more books than you'll ever be able to read in a lifetime!"

He and Lumiere led her back downstairs. She followed, as Cogsworth went on and on, "We have books on every subject, by every author who ever set pen to paper. . . ."

The truth was that Belle did want to see the library, but her curiosity about the West Wing was getting the better of her. She lagged farther and farther behind her two hosts, then stopped.

They were so involved in describing the library that they didn't notice. Belle spun around and ran back to the West Wing stairs.

She raced up the stairs, taking them two at a time. But when she got to the top, she stopped. Before her, a long, gloomy corridor stretched into darkness. Its walls were lined with mirrors, each one broken. Slowly she walked past them into the deep shadows.

At the end of the corridor was an enormous wooden door. Above it, two hideous carved faces sneered at her. They seemed to be saying, "Stay away! Stay away!"

Belle took a deep breath. She pushed the door, and it creaked open.

Belle's eyes widened. A gasp caught in her throat. The room was like nothing she'd ever seen before. Every corner, every surface was covered with filth. Vines grew into the room from an open window and twisted around broken furniture, cracked mirrors, and ripped paintings. Closet doors hung crookedly from torn hinges, and bed coverings lay in a dirty pile against one wall. In a corner was a stack of bones that looked as though they had been chewed on.

Belle's stomach began to churn. As she walked into the room, she shivered. "Is this where he lives?" she thought.

A painting on the wall caught her attention. It was a portrait of a young boy. Belle thought there was something familiar about his eyes, but she couldn't be sure. The painting had five deep slashes across it, as if the Beast had ripped it with his claws.

But then Belle noticed the rose. Although it was drooping and most of its petals had fallen off, it seemed to shimmer. She went closer, reaching out her hand toward it. The petals were so delicate, so beautiful.

Belle was so enchanted by the rose, she didn't notice the hulking shadow of the Beast in the open window.

"AAARGGGGHHH!" the Beast roared as he leapt in front of Belle.

Belle screamed and backed away. Her fingers never touched the rose.

The Beast stomped toward her, smashing everything in his way. "I warned you never to come here!" he shouted, hurling a heavy chair as if it were made of paper. "Do you realize what you could have done?"

"I didn't mean any harm," Belle pleaded.

The Beast answered by throwing a table against a wall. "Get out!" he bellowed. "Get out!"

Belle wasted no time. She got out, all right—out of the castle. Promise or no promise, she was *not* going to stay there!

Philippe was waiting outside, exactly where she'd left him. She hopped on and shouted, "Take me home!"

Philippe's hooves thundered against the frozen earth. In seconds they were out of the castle grounds and into the woods. Belle felt a rush of happiness.

But as soon as they plunged into the woods, that feeling

ended. The forest was every bit as dark and thick as she remembered it. Philippe had to slow to a walk, dodging branches that hung down like long claws. In the mist, he couldn't see more than a few feet in front of them.

But there was no mistaking the eyes.

The yellow, fierce eyes of the wolf pack.

With angry growls, the wolves attacked Philippe's heels. Philippe whinnied and reared onto his hind legs.

With a crash, Belle tumbled onto the forest floor. One wolf

spotted her. Then another.

The wolves lunged at her. She scrambled away, grabbing a thick branch. Her heart raced with fear as she swung the branch at them.

They danced around the branch, stalking closer. Belle tried to back away, but as she did, she tripped on a tangled root. A jolt of pain shot through her ankle, and Belle fell to the ground.

The wolves pounced. Belle felt their claws on her neck. There was nothing she could do now but scream.

Then, suddenly, someone pulled the wolves off Belle.

She could still hear them snarling behind her, only now they were attacking her rescuer! She turned and was startled when she saw who it was. It was the Beast!

She pulled herself to her feet and ran to Philippe's side. Together they watched helplessly as the Beast fought the furious animals. The wolves slashed him with their teeth and claws, and the Beast howled in pain.

But he was more than a match for them. One by one, he grabbed each wolf and hurled it away. The smarter ones slunk away when they realized it was a losing battle.

Soon the Beast stood alone. His face was twisted in agony. He tried to walk toward Belle, but after a few steps, he fell to the ground with a groan.

Belle looked to her left. The road to escape was narrow, but she and Philippe were free to take it. They were free to gallop back to her house, free to leave the Beast and his horrible world behind.

The Beast moaned. He glanced up at Belle with a look of shock and pain.

And Belle realized at that moment that she couldn't leave. Not while the Beast lay wounded in the snow.

"Help me take him back, Philippe," she said softly.

She led her faithful horse to the Beast and helped him to his feet. Together they trudged back to the castle. The Beast limped along, leaning against Philippe.

In the castle's grand hall, Belle nursed the Beast's wounds. He squirmed in pain. "If you hadn't run away, this wouldn't have happened!" he said angrily.

"If you hadn't frightened me, I wouldn't have run away!" Belle replied, cleaning one of his cuts with a wet cloth.

"Well, you shouldn't have been in the West Wing!" the Beast snapped.

"And you should learn to control your temper!" Belle said. They glared at each other for a long moment. Then their eyes dropped. Belle pulled her scarf off and began wrapping it around

one of the wounds. "Now hold still. This may hurt a little."

The Beast gritted his teeth and didn't move. Finally, Belle said what she'd been meaning to say since they were in the woods. "By the way, thank you for saving my life."

"You're welcome," the Beast said with a smile.

Pain or no pain, he suddenly felt very good inside.

At that same moment, Gaston and Lefou were walking toward Belle's cottage with a strange man dressed entirely in brown. His name was Monsieur d'Arque, and he was tall and skinny with a sharp nose and small eyes. He was the head of an insane asylum called Maison des Loons, and was part of Gaston's evil plan.

For a bag of gold, he had agreed to throw Maurice into his asylum—unless Belle would agree to marry Gaston.

What they didn't know was that Maurice had left the cottage to find Belle. At that moment he was entering the woods on foot.

When Gaston found that the cottage was empty, he turned to his partners and said, "They have to come back sometime, and

when they do, we'll be ready for them. Lefou, stay here and keep watch."

Lefou waited by the stairway. Gaston and Monsieur d'Arque walked slowly back toward the village to find out where Maurice and Belle were. "*No one* will stop me from having Belle this time!" Gaston angrily proclaimed.

Snow had fallen during the night, covering the tangled vines and the broken statues. The blanket of white made the castle grounds look almost cheerful.

Since the evening of the wolf attack, the Beast was a lot more cheerful, too. And it was all because of Belle. Her recent kindness and attention had brought out the best in him.

From his bedroom window, he watched Belle walk Philippe, and he thought to himself, "I want to do something for her."

He decided to give her a special gift, and with the help of Cogsworth and Lumiere, he thought of a good one. But it would take a lot of planning—and a lot of cleaning.

After hours of preparation, the gift was ready. The Beast led Belle down a hallway and stopped in front of a set of double doors. "I want to show you something," he said, "but first you have to close your eyes. It's a surprise."

Belle did as she was told. The Beast opened the door, then took her hand. He led her inside a dark room with a high ceiling. "Can I open my eyes now?" she asked.

"Not yet," he said. Letting go of her hand, he went to a window and pulled back a curtain. Sunlight poured into the room.

"Now," the Beast said.

Belle opened her eyes, and they sparkled with delight. It was a beautiful library, stacked with shelves and shelves of books. At one end, there was a roaring fire with a stuffed leather armchair in front of it.

"I can't believe it!" Belle said in awe. "I've never seen so many books in my life!"

The Beast smiled. "You like it? It's all yours," he said.

"Oh, thank you so much!" Belle exclaimed.

Hiding around a corner, Cogsworth and Lumiere smiled at each other. Maybe the spell could be broken after all.

Over the next few days, things began to change between Belle and the Beast. They were becoming friends! Belle learned a lot about the Beast, too. He didn't know how to eat with a fork and knife, so she taught him. He didn't know how to read, so she read to him. She taught him how to feed birds and how to play in the snow.

"She doesn't shudder when she touches my paw anymore," noticed the Beast.

"There's something about him I didn't see before," thought Belle. "I thought he was ugly and cruel, but now he seems sweet and gentle."

The Beast was actually learning how to have fun for the first time in his life. He was discovering feelings inside himself, tender feelings he didn't know he could have. Feelings for Belle.

It wasn't long before the Beast realized something shocking: He was in love with Belle, and he knew he had to do something about it.

He had to tell her.

But how? Not just any old way. He had to create a magical moment, sweep her off her feet. He would invite Belle for a night of dancing in the ballroom!

He was delighted when she agreed. On the night of the dance, the Beast did some things he had never done before. He bathed himself, dressed up, and even combed his mane.

As he walked to the ballroom stairs to wait for Belle, the

Beast looked completely different. His mane shone in the light; his outfit was elegant. Lumiere provided romantic candlelight, and Mrs. Potts sang a love song.

When Belle appeared at the top of the ballroom stairs in a shimmering gold gown, the Beast felt himself freeze. He was stunned by her beauty, and he was also very nervous.

He walked up the stairs, took her hand, and with a gallant smile, he escorted her down. Then he whirled her into dance position. He lifted his huge, hairy foot and took the first step—and practically mashed her toes.

The Beast was horrified. He'd gone to all this trouble to create a perfect evening, but it wasn't going to work. He was so clumsy!

Belle didn't even frown. She gave him a warm smile and did what she had been doing for the last few days—she taught him.

The Beast slowly picked up the steps, and before long they were sweeping gracefully across the dance floor.

Soon, laughing and out of breath, they decided to go out on the balcony. As the Beast opened the glass door, cool air rushed in. The night was still, and the ground glimmered with snow in

the moonlight. Above, the stars winked at them by the thousands.

As she looked up, Belle sighed and smiled.

And the Beast knew that this was the moment of truth. "Uh, Belle," he said softly. "Are you . . . happy here with me?"

Belle thought a moment. She had to admit that she was happier than she had expected to be. "Yes," she answered.

But the Beast could sense sadness in her eyes. "What is it?" he asked.

Belle looked at the Beast. She was close to tears. "If only I could see my father again. Just for a moment," she said. "I miss him so much."

The Beast returned her gaze for a long time. He had the power to let her see her father. And he realized now that he would do anything for her. "There is a way," he said.

Without another word, he led her into the West Wing and up to his room. There, he took the magic mirror from his table and handed it to her. "The mirror will show you anything," he said. "Anything you wish to see."

Belle held it up. "I'd like to see my father, please," she whispered.

The mirror began to glow. An image appeared, dark and blurry. As it became clearer, Belle could see trees and bushes. It was the forest, and there was something moving through it. Something slow and hunched, like a wounded animal.

When the being looked up to the sky, Belle recognized her father. "Belle," he called out, his voice cracked and hoarse. Maurice fell to his knees, shaking and coughing.

"Papa!" Belle screamed. She turned to the Beast with panic in her eyes. "He's sick! He may be dying! And he's all alone!"

The Beast swallowed hard. As he looked at Belle's tear-streaked face and saw the pain that was ripping her apart, his heart skipped a beat. He could feel her pain as if it were his very own. "Her father needs her now, but so do I," thought the Beast.

He glanced toward his table and saw two shriveled petals clinging to the dying rose. Soon they would fall off. If he let Belle go now, he would never know if she loved him and the spell would never be broken. He would remain a hideous Beast forever.

But as he turned and looked into Belle's eyes again, he knew there was only one thing to do.

"You must go to him," he said, slowly speaking the words he knew would seal his doom forever.

Belle stared at him in disbelief. "You mean, I'm free?"

The Beast tried hard to keep his voice steady, without emotion. "I release you. You're no longer my prisoner."

Belle gripped his hand joyfully. "Oh, thank you!" She began to run out the door, but turned back when she realized she was still holding the mirror.

The Beast shook his head. "Take it with you," he said, "so you'll always have a way to look back . . . and remember me."

Belle clutched the mirror to her chest. "Thank you for understanding how much he needs me," she said.

"I need you just as much!" was what the Beast wanted to say. The words welled up inside his heart and went racing right up to his mouth.

But he never said them. Instead, he just nodded.

Belle touched his hand briefly and ran out, her gown flowing behind her.

The Beast stood on his balcony. He watched Belle emerge from the castle's front door, mount Philippe, and gallop away, the moonlight glinting in her silken hair.

When they were gone, the Beast did something he hadn't done since he was a boy.

He threw back his head and howled, with a pain that cut to the bottom of his heart.

"Thank goodness he's still alive!" was all Belle could think when she found her father in the snow. He was soaked, he had a fever, and he didn't even recognize her. But he was alive.

She managed to get him onto Philippe, and together they galloped at top speed through the snow-covered forest. All the way home, Maurice kept repeating things. "It should have been me!" he muttered, and "I'm not a thief!" and "Run, Belle! Run!"

When they got to their cottage, Belle instantly put Maurice to bed and he fell into a long, deep sleep. For hours, she mopped his brow and held his hand. Belle worried that he would never recover, never recognize her again.

Finally he awoke with a moan. "It should have been me . . . me!" His eyes flickered. He gave Belle a blank stare. Then, slowly, he smiled. "Belle?"

Belle was filled with relief. He knew who she was! "It's all right, Papa," she said. "I'm home."

Joyous tears filled Maurice's eyes. He sat up and threw his arms around his daughter. They hugged and laughed and cried.

"I missed you so much!" Belle said.

"But how did you escape the Beast?" Maurice asked.

"He let me go," Belle said softly.

Maurice was shocked. "That horrible Beast?"

"He's different now, Papa," Belle said with a sigh. "He's changed somehow."

Just then Belle noticed a small movement out of the corner of her eye. There was something moving in her saddlebag. She flipped open a flap, and there was Chip, Mrs. Potts's teacup son! He gave her a guilty smile.

Belle smiled back. "Oh . . . a stowaway."

RAP! RAP! RAP! RAP!

Belle and Maurice were both startled by the loud knocking on the door. With a shrug, Belle covered Chip again, went to the door, and opened it.

There stood a tall, skinny man dressed in brown. Behind him was a wooden wagon with the words Maison des Loons on the side. A crowd, led by Lefou, was gathering next to the wagon.

"May I . . . help you?" Belle asked.

"I am Monsieur d'Arque," the man said. "I've come to collect your father."

"He was raving like a lunatic outside the tavern!" Lefou added. "We all heard him, didn't we?"

Most of the crowd mumbled in agreement. A few men, dressed in the white uniforms of the Maison des Loons, stepped toward the house.

"My father's not crazy!" Belle said, standing firmly in the doorway. "I won't let you take him!"

Maurice walked up behind Belle to see what was going on. As soon as Lefou saw him he shouted, "Maurice, tell us again. How big *was* that beast?"

"Well, I'd say eight—no, more like ten feet tall!" Maurice answered seriously.

The crowd hooted with laughter. "You don't get much crazier than that!" Lefou shouted.

Forcing their way past Belle, Monsieur d'Arque's men grabbed Maurice and pulled him outside.

"No!" Belle screamed, running after them. "You can't do this!"

Suddenly Gaston stepped out of the shadows and right into Belle's path. With a calm smile, he said, "Poor Belle. It's a shame about your father."

"You know he's not crazy!" Belle snapped, eyeing Gaston with suspicion.

"Hmmm . . ." Gaston pretended to think hard. "I might be able to clear up this little misunderstanding, *if* . . ." His voice trailed off.

"If what?" Belle asked.

"If you marry me," Gaston answered.

Belle stepped back in shock. He was grinning at her, certain that his plan had worked.

"Never!" she said.

Gaston shrugged. "Have it your way." He waved at Monsieur d'Arque's men. "Take him away."

Belle raced back into the house and brought out the enchanted mirror. Standing on the front steps, she shouted, "My father's not crazy and I can prove it!"

The crowd stared at her. Monsieur d'Arque's men stopped. Gaston looked up, worried.

"Show me the Beast!" Belle said to the mirror.

The mirror glowed. The crowd gasped. Slowly the Beast's image appeared. He paced the balcony in torment. Then, raising his head, he let out a bloodcurdling howl.

People in the crowd screamed and ran away. Monsieur d'Arque's men dropped Maurice and quickly rode off in their wagon. "Is he dangerous?" someone yelled out.

Belle looked tenderly at the Beast's image. She knew he was howling from a broken heart. "Oh, no. I know he looks vicious, but he's really kind and gentle. He's . . . my friend."

Gaston was furious that his plan had failed. He was also very jealous. "If I didn't know better," he said to Belle, "I'd think you had feelings for that monster."

"He's no monster, Gaston!" Belle snapped. "*You* are!"

Gaston grabbed the mirror. He whirled around to the crowd, red with fury. "She's as crazy as the old man!" he announced. "The Beast will come after your children in the night! He'll wreck our village!"

The crowd began to panic, shouting angrily.

"No!" Belle protested.

But Gaston kept right on. "We're not safe until his head is mounted on my wall! I say we kill the Beast!"

Belle tried to stop Gaston, but he signaled to his friends. "Lock them in the cellar!" he ordered.

"Get your hands off me!" Belle screamed.

"We can't have them running off to warn the creature!" Gaston yelled to the frightened crowd. So Gaston's men forced Belle and Maurice down the cellar steps.

The door slammed shut over their heads. The last thing Belle saw was Gaston leading the crowd toward the forest. They were yelling over and over, "Kill the Beast! Kill the Beast!"

*L*umiere, Cogsworth, and Mrs. Potts were moping in the castle foyer when they heard voices outside.

"Is it she?" Mrs. Potts asked excitedly.

They all ran to the window, hoping to see Belle. But their happy expressions turned to shock. It wasn't Belle at all. It was Gaston and his angry mob!

"Invaders!" Lumiere cried out.

The castle objects began running into the room from all directions. "Barricade the door!" Cogsworth ordered. "Mrs. Potts, warn the master!"

BOOOOOOOM! The castle shook as the mob attacked the door with a battering ram. Cogsworth and the other objects piled themselves against the door.

Mrs. Potts sprinted to the Beast's lair, where he was sitting silently. His head was bowed, his body slumped.

"Master, the castle is under attack," Mrs. Potts said.

The Beast looked up. His eyes were lined with red, as if he'd been crying. "It doesn't matter now," he said. "Just let them come."

"But Master . . . ," Mrs. Potts began.

BOOOOOOOM! The sound of another battering-ram attack cut her off. "Kill the Beast!" came the chant from the crowd. "Kill the Beast!"

With a deafening crash, the door fell in and the objects scattered.

But when Gaston's mob barged in, they stopped short. They knew someone had to have been holding back the door, but now the room was empty. All they could see was a candelabra, a mantel clock, and a few other objects.

"Something fishy's going on around here," Lefou said. He cautiously crept closer and closer to Lumiere.

With a sudden jab, Lumiere poked him in the eyes.

"YEOUCHHH!" Lefou screamed.

"CHAAAAARGE!" Lumiere bellowed.

The battle was on! Gaston's men couldn't believe what they were seeing. Candelbras, clocks, dishes, fireplace tongs, footstools,

and brushes—all fighting!

As his men fought, Gaston slipped farther into the castle. He would find the Beast himself.

Meanwhile, outside the cottage, Maurice's invention stood on top of a gentle hill. It was a large contraption, a maze of ropes, levers, pulleys, wheels, bells, and whistles. Only Maurice knew what it was supposed to do. Only Maurice knew how to work it.

But there was someone else walking around it at that moment. Someone very small, and very smart. Someone who could sneak out of the house unnoticed.

It was Chip!

He looked the contraption over once, twice. He turned a few knobs, pulled a few levers, gave it a little nudge. . . .

WHIIIRRRR . . . BONK . . . BLEEP . . .

The invention coughed to life! It began to roll forward. Chip jumped up and down with glee. It rolled to the left, then to the

right, then directly toward the cellar door.

Maurice and Belle both heard a loud rumble. Maurice peeked through the window in the cellar door and saw the contraption barreling toward them. "Belle, look out!" he shouted.

They both ducked away just as the contraption came bursting through the cellar door. On it, hanging from a small lever, was Chip.

"You did it, little teacup!" Belle shouted happily.

"Let's go!" Maurice said.

They ran outside. Philippe saw them and whinnied joyfully.

"Philippe, my old friend," Maurice called out. "Take us to the castle!"

In the castle, the battle raged on. Gaston's men stormed the kitchen and the dining room. Everywhere the objects rose up to defend their home.

But Gaston was in a quieter place, upstairs, just outside of the Beast's lair. He inched closer to the closed door and pulled an arrow out of his quiver. Lashing out with his foot, he kicked the door down.

The Beast slowly turned from his place at the window. When he saw Gaston, he didn't react at all. Nothing mattered to him now.

Gaston fired an arrow. It sliced through the air and landed firmly in the Beast's shoulder.

"RRRAAAAAHHHHHRRRRGGGHHH!" The Beast shrieked in agony and fell to the floor.

He crawled slowly across the floor and out onto the balcony. Gaston ran to him and gave him a sharp kick. With another howl of pain, the Beast tumbled over the balcony railing. He landed on the smooth, sloping slates of the castle roof.

"Get up!" Gaston shouted, as he grabbed a club that hung on the wall.

The Beast tried, but only got as far as his knees. Rain had begun to fall, making the roof wet and slick.

Gaston climbed out on the roof and held the club high. With a mighty blow, he brought it down on the Beast's back.

The Beast howled again and collapsed. As he slid down the side of the roof, Gaston repeated, "Get up!"

He hit the Beast again and again. The Beast tried to rise, but he was too weak. He was now dangerously close to the edge of the roof. A few more inches and he would fall off. A few more inches and it all would be over. He would never again have to think of Belle, his lost love.

As Gaston raised his club for the final blow, the Beast caught one last glimpse through his window. He saw the rose, with one petal left.

"NOOOOOOO!" a scream rang out from below.

With his last ounce of strength, the Beast turned his head. The voice was familiar. It made his heart pump wildly. It made his every sense quicken. Could it be?

Yes. It was Belle. She was racing toward the castle on her horse, along with her father. The Beast felt himself come alive again, as if waking from a nightmare.

Gaston glared at the back of the Beast's head. "YEEEAAAHH!" he shrieked at the top of his lungs, and brought the club down as hard as he could.

*T*he Beast spun around. Gaston's club was coming toward him at lightning speed. There was no time to think. The Beast's hand darted out. His palm smacked into the side of the club, and stopped it in midair.

Gaston was stunned. He backed away as the Beast slowly rose to his feet. The Beast's shadow seemed to swallow Gaston. He flailed wildly with his club again and again, but the Beast blocked it each time.

Roaring with fury, the Beast stalked after him. With a swipe of his long arm, he whacked the club out of Gaston's hand.

Below them, there was a clatter of hooves on the castle stairs. Philippe had galloped right into the castle!

But the Beast hardly heard it. He was burning with outrage. He wanted revenge!

The Beast lunged forward and grabbed Gaston by the neck. With a furious roar, he hoisted Gaston into the air.

"Let me go!" Gaston pleaded. "Please . . . I'll do anything!"

"Kill him!" The words raced through the Beast's mind. He

grabbed Gaston with his other arm, twisted Gaston's body, and prepared to break his neck.

Then he stopped.

Maybe it was the terror in Gaston's eyes. Maybe it was Gaston's helplessness. Maybe the time spent with Belle had made the Beast softhearted.

But whatever the reason, he let Gaston down and said simply, "Get out."

Then he saw Belle. She stood in his room, looking out the window. Her face was pale, her hair wet and messy from her wild ride. She was out of breath and looked exhausted.

But she was the most beautiful sight the Beast could ever imagine.

He began to limp toward her. She smiled warmly and held

out her arms. But suddenly her body went tense. A look of panic shot through her face. "Beast!" she screamed, as she pointed over his shoulder.

It was too late. Gaston was in midair, lunging toward him with a knife. By the time the Beast could react, the knife was squarely between his shoulders.

His agonized roar echoed into the night. He staggered around and faced Gaston with a look of horror and anger.

Gaston went white with fear. He took a step back without looking and his foot landed in a rain gutter. He tried to pull it out, but he couldn't take his eyes off the Beast.

The Beast stumbled forward. Gaston yanked his foot out and lost his balance. Whirling his arms like a windmill, he fell and slid to the edge of the roof.

And then, in a flash, he was gone. Only his scream remained as he plunged over the side.

The Beast turned back to face Belle. He climbed slowly onto the balcony, tried to plant his feet, and fell.

Belle ran to him and cradled him in her arms.

In spite of the pain, he managed a weak smile. "You . . . came back," he said, gasping with pain. "At least . . . I got to see you one last time. . . ."

Belle fought back tears. "Don't talk like that," she said. "You'll be all right."

Suddenly there was a sound of clattering footsteps in the

Beast's room. Cogsworth, Lumiere, and Mrs. Potts ran to the balcony window. They stopped, frozen with shock at the sight of their fallen master.

Behind them, the rose's last petal wavered in the breeze.

"Maybe it's better this way," the Beast said. He was struggling to keep his eyes open.

"No! Please . . . please!" Belle cried out in anguish. Tears flowed down her cheeks and spilled onto the Beast's face. She leaned closer to his limp, wounded body. She planted a tender kiss on his cheek. "I love you!" she cried.

As she spoke, the rose's last petal fell to the table.

For a moment, all was quiet, except for the muffled sounds of Belle's weeping.

Then something remarkable happened. Suddenly the rain began to sparkle and shimmer with light. Then the air began to glow.

The Beast opened his eyes. He felt a healing warmth throughout his body. He looked at his hands. The hair was disappearing! Long, strong fingers remained where a mangled paw had just been. He gasped, then reached up to touch his face.

It was smooth! And his wounds were gone. He felt as healthy and strong as . . . as . . . He could barely bring himself to think the words: "As healthy and strong as a young prince."

Could it be, or was this some sort of dream?

One look at Belle's face was enough to give him an answer. She was staring at him as if she'd never seen him before.

And behind her, glowing magically, the rose was in full bloom!

The Prince rose to his feet. It all came back to him—how it felt to stand perfectly straight, how it felt to be *human*. He hadn't forgotten.

But he was different now. He was taller, older, stronger. And most important, he was looking at the whole world differently. Not with greed and anger and spite, but with kindness, understanding, strength—and love.

"Belle," he said gently. "It's me."

She looked at him, startled for a moment, not knowing what to believe. But there was something about his smile, about the look in his eyes. It *was* the same being with whom she had fallen in love.

With a radiant smile, Belle ran into his arms. And there on the balcony, as the sun peeked over the horizon, they shared a long kiss.

The kiss seemed to bring new magic to the castle. In a swirl of light and colors, Cogsworth turned into a robust man with a mustache. Lumiere became a tall, dashing maître d'. Mrs. Potts turned into a plump, sweet-faced woman.

"The spell is broken!" Cogsworth said, his voice choked with emotion.

The Prince grinned at his faithful servants. He turned briefly from Belle and embraced them. All over the castle, he could hear screams of joy. The objects, from the East Wing to the West Wing, were all becoming the people they once were.

Memories flooded back to the Prince. Memories of a beautiful, shining castle with flags flying and people running about, working, laughing, singing. A lush green meadow. A moat of deep blue water.

The night was lifting—and so were the years of gloom. As the sun rose, the countryside burst into bloom.

But none of it was as lovely as the vision the Prince held in his eyes right then—Belle's smile.

It was a smile that the Prince hoped to be looking at for the rest of his life.

In one last burst of magic, everyone in the castle was whisked into the ballroom. Musicians played, lights twinkled, and the floor shone like a mirror.

The Prince held out his hand, and Belle joined him for a dance. As they swirled around the room, Belle saw happiness in every corner. Mrs. Potts was hugging her little teacups, who were all real, live children, including one with a chipped tooth.

"Chip!" Belle called out, waving to him.

She swirled around again and saw her father, Maurice, looking at everything in awe. He glanced beside him. Wardrobe was now a lovely lady-in-waiting. She winked at him and he blushed.

The footstool, now a happy dog, raced between people's legs as they got up to dance.

Belle laughed. For years, she had thought fairy tales could only be read about in books. But as she looked into the adoring eyes of her Prince, she knew that what was happening to her was real. And she knew exactly what the ending to her real-life fairy tale would be.

She and her Prince would live happily ever after.

LIST OF ILLUSTRATORS

Snow White and the Seven Dwarfs
Illustrated by Fernando Guell and Fred Marvin

Sleeping Beauty
Illustrated by Ric Gonzalez and Dennis Durrell

Cinderella
Illustrated by Robbin Cuddy

The Little Mermaid
Illustrated by Ron Dias and Philo Barnhart

Aladdin
Illustrated by Kenny Thompkins and James Gallego

Beauty and the Beast
Illustrated by Ron Dias and Ric Gonzalez